Soaked and cold and exhausted, they sat huddled together on a ledge about seventy-five yards from the parking lot, leery about getting too close, but watching and waiting impatiently for the car to pick them up. She hadn't stopped checking her watch—and it was only eight minutes when the old but trusty green station wagon drove into the lot and pulled up. She sighed in relief, then stood up, gathering the children to her. "Let's go, my darlings."

They headed to the car, and Lauren thought about the cries of anguish back in the woods. She would have to send someone out there. And she would have to call the police ... and then of course she would have to tell them everything she knew....

A STRANGER
IN THE HOUSE

A STRANGER IN THE HOUSE

Gloria Murphy

A SIGNET BOOK

SIGNET
Published by the Penguin Group
Penguin Books USA Inc., 375 Hudson Street,
New York, New York 10014, U.S.A.
Penguin Books Ltd, 27 Wrights Lane,
London W8 5TZ, England
Penguin Books Australia Ltd, Ringwood,
Victoria, Australia
Penguin Books Canada Ltd, 10 Alcorn Avenue,
Toronto, Ontario, Canada M4V 3B2
Penguin Books (N.Z.) Ltd, 182–190 Wairau Road,
Auckland 10, New Zealand

Penguin Books Ltd, Registered Offices:
Harmondsworth, Middlesex, England

First published by Signet, an imprint of Dutton Signet,
a division of Penguin Books USA Inc.

First Printing, October, 1995
10 9 8 7 6 5 4 3 2 1

Ⓓ REGISTERED TRADEMARK—MARCA REGISTRADA

Printed in the United States of America

PUBLISHER'S NOTE
This is a work of fiction. Names, characters, places, and incidents either are
the product of the author's imagination or are used fictitiously, and any
resemblance to actual persons, living or dead, events, or locales is entirely
coincidental.

To our daughters

Thank you
Alice Martell,
Audrey LaFehr,
Laurie and Bill Gitelman,
and Joe

Prologue

It was as though a bird had slipped inside her head, mistook her brain for seed, and started nibbling. A state-of-the-art brainscoop designed by the police to shut her off and turn her on. Hard to do both at the same time, of course, like operating a yo-yo with a stick gear instead of a string. What the police wanted was for the young girl to come clean, tell them what she saw, what she did. Not to sit and stare at them blankly, not to flip out and swear like a trooper.

A trooper—she couldn't help but muse over the word in a mind that felt hot and gooey. It could use a chunk of ice to harden it up, she thought, and as her mind looped back to the word trooper, she felt something cold press her head. *Oh, yes, excuse me, sir, would that be a state trooper, a storm trooper, or just a local yokel trooper? Around the world in eighty days, the one who's caught is the one who pays ... Yuck, yuck, double yuck. So okay, I've wasted enough time already, where are you, Handsome Prince Fucking Charmer? Go quick and grab*

*your horse and get here before my brain is eaten
clean away.*

Today her long dark hair had none of its usual
sheen or her skin its rosy glow, but she looked
serene and lovely still, almost angelic in sleep.
Two male aides dressed in hospital green wheeled
her gurney through the swinging emergency-room
doors to the corridor where her father was
waiting.

He immediately rushed to her side: a clear
plastic bag hung from a pole, connecting a tube,
feeding liquid into her veins; an icebag sitting on
her forehead concealed a lump she had gotten
when she fell against the sink in the bathroom.
"Will she be okay?" he asked stupidly. He knew
they were only aides, but he was a man desperate
for reassurance. "Look, I need to talk to the
doctor."

"Just follow us to her room. The doctor will be
coming soon to answer any questions," one of the
men said. The girl was transferred to a bed, and
a nurse with a chart came in to take her pulse
and blood pressure, followed by the same doctor
the father had met earlier.

Before he could be bombarded with questions,
the doctor raised his hands to forestall them.
"She's going to be okay, Mr. Grant," he said. "At
least, physically. We had to pump her stomach, of
course. We figure she must have taken a dozen
sleeping pills, enough to put out a good-sized
horse. It was touch and go for a while . . . yes, I'd

say you didn't find her a moment too soon." The doctor rubbed his palm over the bald horseshoe of his crown, his expression a mixture of sympathy and disbelief. "Christ, ten years old. Why would a kid that age want to kill herself?"

Chapter One

Don't talk to strangers was one of those crucial messages mothers continually struggle to get across to their children, and Lauren Sandler, a young, single mother, was no exception. Lauren, who lived with her daughter in a small loft at the top of a defunct office building in New York City, did her best to follow her own advice. But occasionally even sound rules were meant to be broken.

Perhaps the lovely spring day was responsible. Lauren and five-year-old Chelsea were enjoying it at the Orange County fairgrounds in Elmwood Valley, only fifteen minutes from her sister Fern's house and eighty miles from the stress of the city. Or maybe it had to do with the stranger himself, not that he seemed eager to be friendly when she first saw him at the shooting concession picking off water-propelled wooden ducks with an electronically beamed rifle. He was doing a respectable job of it judging by the heap of junk prizes on the counter beside him. In fact, it was Lauren's daughter who had taken her by the hand and dragged her to the booth.

But Chelsea wasn't impressed by the stranger's pile of string dolls, rubber worms, plaster dinosaurs, or colorful paper parasols and fans. She pointed over the counter to the top of the display case to a black and white furry three-foot dalmatian—a twenty-five-coupon card propped up against its fat front paw. "Mommy, look at him," she said. "Doesn't he look almost real?"

She hadn't actually asked for it, and maybe that's why Lauren wanted to win it for her. But want was hardly enough in this case—she had never fired a gun before, and it wasn't easy to get the knack of it, so after wasting a dozen rounds of ammunition, she laid the gun down on the counter, admitting defeat. It was then that the stranger, who had been standing silently by, glanced their way, then got the concessionaire's attention. Nodding to his winnings, he said, "What do you say we have here, thirty-five coupons?"

The man seemed to do a quick computation in his head, then he nodded affirmation.

"Okay, I'm trading them in." Gesturing to the top of the display, he said, "Give the little girl the dog."

The concessionaire was handing it over to a wide-eyed Chelsea, even before her mother had the opportunity to react. But if she was upset over not having been consulted or had any notion of making Chelsea return the gift, it all disintegrated when the stranger spoke to her. "I guess I ought to apologize," he said. "I had no business not clearing it with you first, but she seemed . . . well, it was just that she wanted it so much."

He was tall, lean, good-looking. He wore brown chinos and a tan blazer and had the most wonderful dark eyes, sad eyes, and a strong chin with a cleft in it. He extended his hand—no ring. Although she judged he was in his early forties, their age difference did not bother her. Her sister, of course, would comment on it, but Lauren's only wish was that she had worn something nicer than jeans.

"How do you do? The name's Jonathan Grant," he said, and she must have looked somewhat apprehensive because he added, "Most folks around here know me. Grant Architect and Engineering. We do a little consulting for the town."

No longer hesitant, she took the hand he was offering. "I'm Lauren Sandler," she said, then turned toward her daughter, who would clearly need a review of the "stranger" warnings. "And this little dalmatian lover here, her name is Chelsea."

He looked at Chelsea who was now dancing around, not much bigger than her newfound friend. She was grinning from ear to ear, an unrestrained mop of golden curls encircling her full-cheeked face. "She is a sweetheart, all right."

She nodded. "Thank you. And for the gift as well, it was very generous."

Shrugging away her gesture of gratitude, he seemed to make no further attempt to engage her.

"The fair's great, lots of new exhibits this year,"

she said. "Your first time this season?" Taking up forty-five acres, the Orange County Fair was a yearly event that ran from May through Labor Day. The largest revenue bearer for the county, it featured science and history displays, crafts, exotic food vendors, farm animals, amusements, sporting competitions, entertainment, and about a half a mile away a lovely wooded area with a duck pond and picnic area.

"Contrary to what it seems," he said, smiling a slightly off-centered smile that she liked instantly. "I came on business, to inspect the staging for the amphitheater."

Lauren was already busy plotting—she would be staying the weekend at Fern's, so if he didn't live too far . . . but she could see in his body language that he was already considering making a getaway, and would unless she took matters in her own hands. "Jonathan, I was wondering—" she began. Then stopping, she began again, "Well, if you have no plans . . . would you like to go for a drink later?"

Okay, she had said it. But evidently not sure what to do with her forwardness, he stood there as if weighing the situation. It was the nineties, and at twenty-eight years old, a career woman, once married and divorced, it wasn't the first time she had asked a man out. Yet as she stood under his scrutiny, her confidence, usually at a respectable level, nose-dived as she waited to see if the stranger would be good enough to relieve, if not her thirst, her embarrassment. What a splendid example for Chelsea.

At last he did rescue her, insisting that instead of the drink she suggested, he take both her and Chelsea to a great little Italian place he knew on Route 95. Before she left the fairgrounds, Lauren stopped at a phone booth to call Fern's real estate office, to tell her they would be late coming home and why. And though her big sister instinctively started to question the wiseness of traipsing off with a stranger, the moment Lauren mentioned the name Jonathan Grant, Fern knew who he was.

When they returned later to her car still at the fairgrounds parking area, it was ten o'clock—the lot was nearly vacant. Chelsea was sleeping, and Jonathan lifted her out along with the stuffed dalmatian she was still grasping, and transferred her to the back seat of her mother's car. The adults, savoring each other's company, stood outside in the dark and continued to talk. Now on surer ground, the conversation took a more personal turn. "So, you were simply going to walk away from me this afternoon, weren't you?" Lauren teased.

"Maybe. Not that I wanted to . . ." He paused a few moments, as though he were deciding how much to say, and having made his decision went on. "It's been a while since I met a woman . . . one I'd consider dating. My marriage was a good one, so I guess I never expected to be going this route again, and I'm not even sure if I'm up on the new rules." She sensed his dark eyes on her now, probing her, and when she met his stare, she felt a slow current travel along her shoulders and knew he felt it, too. "I didn't feel ready, Lauren. Not until now."

Earlier he had mentioned that his wife had died, but she hadn't questioned him further, and he hadn't elaborated. Now like a clogged drain freeing, the story came out, and as it did, it explained the sadness Lauren had detected earlier. "My wife didn't simply die," he said. "Nancy was murdered. And to make it worse, if that's even conceivable, she was pregnant, about to begin her fourth month. We'd been trying for quite some time . . ."

He paused a moment, needing the time to get hold of himself. This couldn't be easy for him to tell, Lauren thought, wondering if this was the first time he had actually talked about it. "The baby . . . it would have been a boy," he said finally. "It happened a year ago. One of the first-floor windows had been tampered with—that's how the intruder got in. It appeared to be an attempted robbery, but all the person had time to take was the jewelry Nancy was wearing: an engagement ring, a wedding band, a jade necklace. The police figure she was in the basement sewing room, on her way upstairs to the kitchen. She was an excellent homemaker . . . a cook, seamstress . . . She was working on a layette for the baby."

Lauren nodded, having always admired women with domestic skills, but never having put much effort into developing any herself. "He must have heard her footsteps coming up the stairs, because the police think he jumped out, surprised her, then whacked her with a baseball bat. She fell backward . . . down the stairs."

"Oh, gosh," Lauren said, a chill rushing through her, horrified that such an awful thing could happen in a sleepy little town like Elmwood Valley. "I hope they caught—" she began, feeling her own outrage, but stopped short.

He put his hands in his pants pockets, leaned back against the car, and looked up, gazing at the stars. "Oh, they had a suspect all right, but there was nothing significant to link him to the crime other than his miserably violent background."

He lowered his eyes to meet hers. "The suspect was Jay Phillips, a guy from over in Monticello. At fifteen he killed his sister by smashing her head against a rock, but since he was convicted as a juvenile in New York State, he lucked out—he was shipped to an institution, then let go with a clean slate when he turned eighteen. How's that for justice? I'm not saying he killed Nancy . . . I don't actually know. It's just that I don't believe people like that get rehabilitated."

Lauren remembered reading that the percentage of homicides actually solved was frightfully low. "I suppose without a witness, there's not much hope," she said.

"Actually, there might have been a witness."

"But?"

"Well, it gets complicated. The witness, or so we believe, is my daughter."

Surprised to hear he had a daughter and naturally curious, Lauren waited for him to continue.

"Her name is Emily. She just turned eleven a couple of weeks ago. That's why ..." he said, pausing and peeking into the back seat where Chelsea—arms and legs tightly drawn in—was sleeping. Without a word, he slid out of his blazer, reached inside with it, and gently placed it over her before turning back to Lauren. "I try not to talk much about her. When I do it usually gets me incredibly sad or angry, neither of which I know how to handle. I have found myself at an occasional shooting range, trying to work out a little anger, even doing something as pointless as shooting wooden ducks at the county fair."

A cynical smile creased the corners of his lips. "Emily was in the fifth grade ... Nancy had picked her up at noon from school, the nurse had called reporting that she'd had a run-in with one of her classmates and had fallen on the pavement. Nothing serious, just a few scratches and bruises. Whoever it was who killed Nancy wasn't aware that Emily was home. Thank God. Otherwise she might not be alive today."

Lauren automatically switched Jonathan's daughter's face with her own daughter's face, feeling the horror of it. "But if she saw who it was?"

"All we really know is as soon as Emily was able to, she grabbed the phone in the kitchen, dialed 911, and screamed into the mouthpiece, 'It was a stranger!' The operator couldn't get her to say anything else, not her name or address, so she had her hang on to trace the call. When the police arrived, they found Emily crouched on the kitchen floor, her eyes closed, still holding the phone receiver ..."

He turned around, pressing his tight fists against the roof of the car, and went on. "She was traumatized; she blanked ... And they couldn't even reach me. I was way the hell in Syracuse. The only time I'd ever dealt with this company, but of all the days to be away, it had to be then." He paused before pulling himself together. "According to Dr. Strickler, Emily's psychiatrist, because she was unable to deal with whatever she saw, her defenses kicked in. Her reaction is not atypical or necessarily unhealthy—kids often dump memories they can't handle. It might not have been so bad had she not withdrawn the way she did." He turned around now, facing Lauren. "She's been at the Bateman Clinic ever since, working at finding her way back."

The Bateman Clinic, located west of Boston, was a psychiatric residence for emotionally disturbed children and adolescents and, according to everything Lauren had heard, one of the finest facilities of its kind in the country, and one of the most expensive. "I don't know what to say, Jonathan," she said, finally moving closer to him, placing her hand on his arm. "I'm sorry."

"She's doing better these days," he said, forcing lightness into his voice. "Really. There was a time when she wouldn't talk ... not to anyone, me included. But in the past couple months, I've seen progress. Even her doctor admitted it, and you know how conservative those guys tend to be. Naturally there're no guarantees, and I'm not asking for any. I just want a shot for her is all, one stinking shot. And though you might think I'm deluding myself, I feel it in my gut that one day soon my girl is going to come home."

Fern was waiting up for Lauren and Chelsea when they got to her house in nearby Middletown. While she put on a pot of tea, Lauren carried Chelsea to the cot in the spare room, undressed her, and got her to bed ... still thinking about Jonathan.

She felt emotionally wrung-out, as though she had just been deeply intimate with this man, but on an emotional level, unlike anything she'd ever experienced. He had no need to tell her how he felt about his daughter. The love was a part of him. She could feel his pain and sadness, and though the word guilt was never mentioned, it was clearly there. While he was at a business meeting with a colleague, his house was broken into, and though logic told him one thing, Jonathan Grant was tormented by the fantasy that there was something he could or should have done to save his family.

When he helped Lauren into the car, he'd closed the door quietly so as not to awaken Chelsea, then bent forward. She thought he would kiss her. She could never remember wanting a man as much as she wanted him. But he only pressed the lock button on Chelsea's door and then ran the back of his knuckle gently along her cheek. "Good night," he said.

"Your blazer," she said, beginning to turn. But he reached in and put his hand on her arm, stopping her.

"Next time," he said.

She swallowed hard—oh, yes, there would be a next time. Most definitely.

"Okay, go ahead," Fern said now as Lauren returned to the kitchen and sank into a chair. She placed a cup of sweetened tea in front of her. "Start talking."

She looked up at her sister—an older version of Lauren, people who knew them would say. They were both tall and blond, had good bone structure and skin and big, wide-set blue eyes that lightened and deepened in color coinciding with their emotions. Fern, fifteen years older than Lauren, was more of a mother to her than a sister, since their mother died when Lauren was sixteen. Fern had partially financed Lauren's college tuition, even encouraging her to study acting if that was what she wanted.

Although Lauren had tried acting, she soon realized she didn't have enough talent or dedication for it. Besides, she preferred the work behind the scenes. It wasn't until Fern left Manhattan to open a real estate business that Lauren, having just graduated from City University with a communication's degree, finally found the job she wanted and earned her much-desired independence.

But that didn't mean Fern wasn't always on the other end of the telephone line, asking questions, checking into Lauren's life, and giving advice—asked for or not. And it didn't mean Lauren didn't still manage to screw up with a short-lived marriage, which rated a zero in all but the production of one little girl named Chelsea. Though she often ignored Fern's advice, Lauren saw it as indicative of how much her sister cared, and if it were to stop, she'd no doubt miss it.

"Well, let me see now," Lauren said, as though she were weighing all that had gone on since that afternoon, "what would you like to hear? Okay, how about this? When he finally left Chelsea and me at the fairgrounds to go on back to his car, he locked our doors and waited until we left, then halfway here, I spotted his car in the rearview mirror. He had followed us back here and though he parked across the street, he didn't leave until Chelsea and I were safely inside."

She nodded. "You're right, I like it. What surprises me is that *you* do."

Lauren prided herself on her ability to take care of herself and her daughter, ever since the day she brought Chelsea home from the hospital. Deciding to discharge herself the day after giving birth, but unable to get through to her inattentive husband, she called a taxi. Only to walk into her bedroom with Chelsea to find him entertaining another woman. With the telephone off the hook.

Mark Brewer was history—though he pleaded for another chance, she had nothing left in her heart to give. She filed for divorce, taking back her maiden name. But that was the easy part—the hard part was juggling the responsibilities of a child, a career, and a home, and doing it alone. The truth was, for the first two years of Chelsea's life, Lauren was terrified. But no one suspected that—at least, no one but Fern. "Did I say I liked it?"

"You don't have to, I can see it on your face. How old is he?"

"Forty-one."

"Nearly my age. Gosh, Lauren, that's too old."

She smiled and shook her head. "Why did I know you would say that?"

"Which I suppose means you have no intention of listening."

The nice or not-nice part about such a close, open relationship was that the opposition was no secret. In fact, Lauren could have written Fern's script if she had a mind to: *He's wiser, set in his ways, has more experience, is surer of who he is; he'll be settling into old age just as she's hitting her stride; he's a substitute for the father she never had but wanted.* None of the above applied . . . besides which, they wouldn't have made a difference. "I've listened, Sis," Lauren said briskly. "I know what you think. In this case, I don't agree."

"I'm not saying he's not a nice person—" Fern began, but Lauren cut her off. Jonathan wasn't just nice and he wasn't just attractive, there was something compelling about him. Clearly a strong-minded individual, yet he was warm, caring, gentle, and attentive . . . no, nothing at all like Mark. For that matter, not many men she'd met could hold a candle to Jonathan. "So, are you going to tell me what you know about him or am I going to have to find out all on my own?"

Fern shook her head, then in a disgruntled tone asked, "Who says I know anything?"

Lauren reached over and slapped her sister's hand in jest. "Would you please stop giving me a hard time. You immediately recognized his name when I mentioned it so you clearly have heard some gossip about him."

Finally letting the conflict go, she said, "Well, I do know he grew up a few hundred miles upstate, in Rochester—came here with his wife after he graduated college. Apparently he inherited a lot of money when his parents died."

That made sense, Lauren decided, thinking of the Lincoln Continental he was driving, the expensive clothes he was wearing, and, of course, where his daughter was hospitalized.

"Also I imagine he makes a pretty decent living doing what he does. Not that having money has helped him much . . ."

Lauren nodded, indicating she knew about what happened to his family. "Yes, what a terrible story," she said.

"I understand his wife was a lovely person. A sweet, pretty, stay-at-home type," Fern said. "People around here usually feel relatively safe—

but they were anxious for months after, talking about nothing else, locking their doors, keeping a close watch on their kids, and warning them against strangers . . ."

"His little girl saw it happen. She's in a private psychiatric residence in Massachusetts. It's nearly a two-hour drive, but he goes to see her every week."

"Despite any silver spoons he might have grown up with, it's my understanding that he was a devoted husband and father, what people might call a straight arrow." Fern let out a deep sigh. "Now what is it they say about bad things happening to good people?"

Lauren's thoughts had already skipped beyond that—she was determined to bring good back into Jonathan's life. When she ended her first marriage, she thought it unlikely she'd marry again, but suddenly she found herself imagining a future with Jonathan, wondering what it would be like to wake up in his arms.

But the charming story she had related to Fern about him escorting them home was not all that simple. This time Fern was only partially right—though Lauren did find his protectiveness of her and Chelsea flattering, she also found it a little disturbing. Jonathan was clearly uneasy, fearful that if he wasn't on guard, something like what had happened to his family could happen again.

Jonathan's overprotectiveness proved to be one of the most difficult aspects of their relationship.

Though Lauren had a good position as an assistant producer for the CBS morning *Home Show* taped in Manhattan, Jonathan hated that she lived and worked in such a crime-ridden city and kept after her to give up her job and move to Elmwood Valley, a wish that Fern concurred with. But she couldn't just give up a job like that, particularly when there were so few opportunities in her field.

So Jonathan would worry, telephone, and issue warnings: "Don't take the subway after dark, don't go near the Port Authority, don't talk to strangers . . ."

"Fern, is that you?" Lauren would tease, trying to deflect his fears with humor. But in truth, his fears were not groundless—more and more, the city was being compared to a war zone. Jonathan would drive in once a week to see her, bringing with him a bagful of groceries and pretty clothes or trinkets for her and Chelsea.

While she would nearly tear apart the kitchen trying to put together the perfect meal, he'd install double locks on her doors, check her smoke alarms and windows, and tell funny, creative stories to Chelsea. And when Chelsea was finally tucked away for the night, he'd make all of Lauren's fantasies come true. He was a marvelous lover—tender, passionate, knowing where to touch her, how to touch her . . . No one ever knew her the way Jonathan knew her.

And every Friday at six o'clock she'd pick Chelsea up from her after-school day care to head as fast as she could to her sister's house for the weekend, though very little of the weekend was actually spent with Fern. Sunday was visiting day at the Bateman Clinic, and she and Chelsea would accompany Jonathan on his weekly trips—he'd usually drop them off at a children's movie matinee or a nearby playground or museum while he visited with Emily.

Four months later—having sufficiently dazzled Lauren with love and attention, Jonathan held forth a three-carat pear-shaped diamond, the most magnificent ring Lauren had ever seen, and asked her to marry him. Teary-eyed, she said yes. Despite Fern's concern about how few months Lauren had known him, Fern had grown to like and respect him and could not deny how pleased she was at the prospect of having her baby sister so close by.

Though Jonathan was known and admired by many people in the small community, his life consisted primarily of work and family, seldom taking time out to nurture friendships. With one exception—Jerry Reardon, a funny, big-hearted guy who owned and operated an industrial construction business sixty-five miles upstate. It was Jerry who had given Jonathan advice on bidding as well as sending several jobs his way when he first started up his business.

As it was, Lauren got to meet Jerry Reardon only once. Jonathan and she were guests for the weekend at his impressive bachelor pad, a twelve-room condominium just outside Albany, and to Jonathan's delight, she and Jerry hit it off immedi-

Gloria Murphy

ately. But only six weeks later, just when Jonathan
was about to announce their marriage plans and
ask Jerry to be his best man, he received a call
that Jerry was killed in a construction accident.
Jonathan didn't take the loss of his friend easily,
and in view of it, adding to the disappointment
that Emily would not be at the ceremony either,
they decided on a small house wedding in late
November, less than a year from when they had
met.

Jerry's death was a tragedy that would no doubt
stay with Jonathan for years to come, but they
would not dwell on Emily's absence at their wedding—she would soon be home again. Like Jonathan, Lauren had to believe it. But in dealing with
something as fragile as a child's emotions, there
seemed a hundred hurdles to overcome for each
move ahead: Emily had finally begun to accept
the fact that her mother was dead, yet she went
into a tailspin at the mere suggestion of leaving
the security of the psychiatric residence and re-
entering the world.

Though her doctor had finally given Jonathan
the go-ahead to tell her about his and Lauren's
upcoming marriage, the announcement hadn't
gone over as well as they had hoped: she had
pressed her hands over her ears and turned away
form him, not willing to consider a new family,
let alone meet her new stepmother and sister.

It wasn't until four months after the wedding
that Lauren and Chelsea finally got to meet
Emily—the day Emily came home.

Chapter Two

Lauren had been busy in the kitchen since Jonathan left to get Emily. Though still an amateur cook, she tried, and Jonathan was always receptive and encouraging. Before resigning her job in Manhattan when they married, she and Jonathan had discussed it at length and agreed it was to be her last job, at least for a while. Having been brought up by nannies and two elderly parents, both dead, Jonathan felt that kids, even those in school, needed a full-time mother.

And though Lauren had once viewed herself as a career person, like other working women she had experienced the inevitable guilt that went along with leaving her child to be attended to by others. Now with Chelsea seven years old and in the second grade, Lauren was a stay-at-home mom, and if she ever got restless or had doubts that she might have made a wrong choice, the delight on Chelsea's and Jonathan's faces was there to reassure her.

Lauren slid the pan of lasagna with homemade sauce onto the bottom refrigerator shelf, then removed the biscuits for strawberry shortcake from their tins, to let them cool. These were Emily's favorite foods, but the collaboration of smells along with her anxiousness was making Lauren queasy. She glanced at the clock, then leaving the mess, rushed up the back kitchen stairs to shower and dress. Jonathan had phoned from the clinic saying he expected to be back on the road with Emily by ten-thirty, which meant they ought to be home anytime now.

When they purchased the house, Jonathan surprised Lauren with a private bath and dressing room. It had oodles of closet space and built-in drawers and shelves, eliminating all need for dressers. Best of all, it had a huge round sunken tub where she could have the luxury of baths with luscious smelling salts and oils, which Lauren doubly appreciated, having had only a stall shower in her city apartment. Now she picked a skirt and matching top, the kind of print Jonathan liked, and wishing that her stomach would settle down.

She slipped into her underwear, then moved to the eight-foot Formica counter over which a full-length gold-edged mirror was mounted. Pulling out the stool, she sat down, opened her jewelry box, and finding a pair of sterling leaf earrings, she put them on. She lifted her birth control pill container, twisted it a notch, and emptied the Saturday pill into her hand. Though Jonathan would gladly have her pregnant now, it was the one thing she had been adamant about. No baby, at least not until the family they had already was intact—

Emily home, the girls adjusted to each other, Emily adjusted to her new stepmother . . .

Using a blow-dryer, Lauren brushed the thick honey-blond hair that fell to her back. It hadn't been so long and glowing since her high school days. Finally with an unsteady hand, she applied a touch of lipstick and blush. *Steady yourself, Lauren,* she admonished. *This isn't a Fortune 500 job interview, it's a child you're meeting.* An eleven- , soon to be twelve-year-old shouldn't be that intimidating.

She hurried downstairs, smiling as she glimpsed the living room and foyer: twirling crepe paper streamers and balloons and cut-out cardboard signs—painstakingly designed and crayon-printed with the words WELCOME HOME EMILY—were hanging everywhere. A pair of children's scissors, a roll of tape, and scraps of cardboard and colored paper were in a pile on the carpet. Though Lauren had bought Chelsea the art supplies, the idea and execution were strictly hers.

"Oh, darling, it looks great," she said.

"Do you think so?" Chelsea asked, not fully convinced. She pointed to the sign in the front foyer, pinching up her face in dissatisfaction. "I messed up the W."

"I bet she'll never notice. By the way, who told you how to spell Emily?"

"In Emily's bedroom, in her closet, I found a tin box. Lucky for me, the lock didn't work. Her name was marked with Magic Marker on the inside cover."

"Chelsea!"

"I was just looking."

"You had no business being in her bedroom, and certainly no business going through her personal things."

Chelsea folded her arms at her chest, apparently indignant at what she perceived as an unfair accusation. "All that was in there was a jackknife, stale chewing gum, rocks, a bag of marbles, fake jewelry, and a bird's claw," she said, listing them as though she had memorized every article, and Lauren flinched at the claw. "Besides, the only reason I opened it was because I wanted to see if her name—"

"Stop, right now," Lauren said, and Chelsea stopped. "Now, none of that is really important. The point is, you simply shouldn't have been looking in her room at all. Next time you have the urge to see something not yours, ask."

"Who?"

"Whoever it belongs to, of course."

"But she wasn't here."

"In that case, don't look." Lauren refused to be outmaneuvered by a seven-year-old's logic.

Chelsea paused a moment, then took her last shot. "What about you? I saw you in her room."

When they moved in, Lauren had the painters put a fresh coat of white paint on Emily's walls and woodwork. In the big double window she had hung cheery apple-green and white striped tiebacks that went with a new matching bedspread. Though she considered putting up posters and other fun paraphernalia, she decided to leave those decorating decisions to Emily.

The moment Lauren learned Emily was coming home, she and Beatrice, the part-time cleaning woman, got busy polishing Emily's furniture, going through her dresser, taking out old clothes, and boxing them for Goodwill. After nearly two years in the hospital, none of Emily's old clothes would fit her anymore. Not wanting to be intrusive, Lauren purposely hadn't gone through desk drawers or touched anything other than the clothes brought from the old house.

"I didn't look into what wasn't my business," she said in answer to Chelsea. "Everyone has a right to privacy, you know." Then seeing the sorry expression finally enter her daughter's face, Lauren's voice lightened. "Even big sister people."

"She really will be my sister, won't she?"

"She already is."

"How about the adopted part?"

Lauren smiled. Chelsea never tired of asking the question or hearing the response, though she already had a view of the legal process as being way too lengthy. Jonathan had wanted to adopt Chelsea from the beginning, but it wasn't until last month that they had given up on finding Mark Brewer to get him to sign away his rights to the daughter he hadn't chosen to see since her birth.

It made Lauren wish she had never bothered to put his name on the birth certificate, but she had, and there was little point in trying to wish it away. Jonathan had finally petitioned the New York courts to allow him to adopt Chelsea on grounds of Mark having deserted her, and by late summer if all went as expected, it would be official. "Just another couple months," she assured Chelsea again.

She nodded. "Will Emily like me, do you think?"

Lauren reached down and scooped her daughter into her arms, kissing her neck and tickling her. "How in the world could she not like this funny little face?" Chelsea went into a fit of laughter, and finally Lauren let her go, putting her down and pointing her in the direction of the mess on the carpet. "Go clean that up. And hurry."

Chelsea got down on her knees, quickly gathering the scraps. "I think when Daddy comes home I'm going to give him the biggest, best hug I can find."

"Oh, yeah? And how is it he rates so high with you today?"

"Because I've always wanted a big sister, and he's the one giving me one."

Hands and arms full, her pink cotton dress bouncing around her, Chelsea rushed out of the room. Lauren realized that the mail had probably been delivered and slipped on her parka—Jonathan liked when the mail and newspapers were waiting for him. She had just shut the front door after her when she saw a black car slow almost to a stop near the high front gates, and though at first her heart leapt, thinking it was Jonathan arriving with Emily, it wasn't.

Whoever it was moved slowly on past their two acres of wooded frontage, someone no doubt lost and looking to catch a street number. She looked inward from the road, surveying their grounds, noting the twisted tree branches and dirty snow with patches of bare dirt that typified mid-March.

The house, less than four miles from the one where Jonathan had lived with Nancy and Emily on Candlewood Terrace, was in a fairly isolated area of Elmwood Valley, and though Jonathan had no difficulty leaving decisions such as decorating to Lauren, there were certain things he insisted upon: he had the locks on the doors and windows upgraded, and a security system that connected to police headquarters installed. The security included a twelve-foot chain-link fence with an alarm system and an audio/visual remote that let them scrutinize visitors before electronically lifting the gate and giving access.

Fern laughingly called the new house on Mountain View Road, with eleven spacious rooms, three fireplaces, and two staircases going to the second floor, "The Castle," and the gate that raised only to those with proper car apparatus, coded card, or permission of the hosts "The Drawbridge" across the moat. At this point Lauren joined the laughter—she had come to the realization that Jonathan's peace of mind would not return overnight, and though the security might have been a bit intense for her liking, if it was necessary for him to feel confident of his family's safety, what was so terrible?

Removing the newspapers and mail from the steel box that clamped to the gate, she hurried back to the house, sifting through it: mostly advertisements and bills, three business items for Jonathan, including the familiar manila envelopes from Michael Perkins, Jonathan's long-time attorney.

Back in the living room she dropped *The New York Times* and *The Wall Street Journal* onto the coffee table for Jonathan. The letters and bills went into the incoming box on the mahogany desk in his study, and the advertisements were all hers. She slipped them in the mail organizer in the kitchen—when she got the opportunity, she would look through them. Now she headed back to the bay window in the living room to watch for Jonathan.

She took a deep breath—she had looked forward to this day for so long, and now she was happy, excited, and scared to death. She just wished she'd had the chance to meet Emily sooner, it would have made it that much easier now for both of them. But despite Jonathan's urging Emily to meet her new family, she had refused—that was, until several days ago when her doctor phoned to say she woke up in the middle of the night insisting she wanted to go home.

Lauren was still sitting at the window when Jonathan's new black Lexus pulled up to the entrance, and the gate, receiving its signal, lifted.

She rushed to the foyer to call Chelsea who came bounding out of her bedroom and down the stairs, stopping on the step that would offer the best and fullest view of her new sister as she came through the front entrance and was greeted by the decorations.

But it didn't work as planned—the only one to come through the doorway was Jonathan, smiling and happy and carrying two suitcases, and when Lauren looked at him as if to ask where she was, he pointed toward the back of the house. "She's perusing the property. She'll likely be coming in through the kitchen."

Lauren gestured to Chelsea's artwork. Jonathan's smile dimmed. "Oh, you should have warned me." Then to Chelsea, he winked. "It's dynamite, Angel."

But it didn't wipe away Chelsea's disappointment, and in view of the effort put into the surprise, Lauren understood. "Come on," Lauren said, reaching for Chelsea's hand, "what do you say, we go find her?" And all three headed for the kitchen.

But apparently Emily still wasn't that eager. They watched her from the window next to the kitchen table—she wore a red parka and red and white hat—bigger, older, of course, looking nothing at all like her pictures. She took her time walking around the yard, examining things. "It must seem strange to her ... coming home to a new family, a new house," Lauren said, finding herself making excuses for her stepdaughter and wondering if it wasn't simply a way to ease her own awkwardness as she stood there feeling foolish waiting to meet her.

But just as Jonathan went to open the door and call her inside, Emily turned and, with her hands stuffed in her pockets, headed up the stairs to the deck. She came inside, and Jonathan put his arm around her. Grinning, he said, "Princess, I want you to meet you new mother and little sister, Chelsea."

It was the wrong thing to say—Lauren could see by the narrowing of the girl's eyes, showing her confusion or anger, or both.

"Welcome home, darling!" Lauren said, realizing immediately she had made mistake number two—her words though well meaning had sounded way too familiar. "We've been waiting all day, we thought you'd never get here—"

"You'll have to register the complaints with him," she said, referring to her father.

"Oh, no, I didn't mean that as a complaint. I just meant that we were so—"

But by that time, Emily had lost interest, rudely turning way and looking around the room. And as hard as Lauren tried to recover, to put all of them at ease, only wrong words came out. She found herself stringing together inappropriate phrases, wondering why she hadn't been better prepared while Chelsea, suddenly shy, clung to her. Finally Emily took off her coat, then her woolen hat, revealing a short-cropped haircut, better suited for a boy. "Well, do you like it?" she asked her father. "I picked the style from a magazine just special for coming home."

"It's ... it's just fine," he said. Though Lauren thought he hid his shock relatively well, she detected his disappointment. He loved girls in long hair and several times had raved about Emily's lovely hair. But after all, it was *her* hair.

"What do you want me to do with this?" Emily asked, referring to her coat and hat, but her expression revealing none of the anxiety Lauren was feeling.

Looking at her up-close, though, she could now see a resemblance to the photographs—the real difference was in her eyes—great dark pools, like Jonathan's, but they seemed to have lost their sparkle and dance. Was she imagining the coldness in them? Maybe it was simply that she no longer looked like a little girl ... except for the too-snug corduroy jumper and wide lacy-collared blouse she was wearing. Clothes shopping—yes, that was clearly a must.

"Well, so tell us, how was the ride home?" Lauren said, after having directed Emily to the front hall closet and fished out a hanger.

Emily shrugged, then handed her coat and hat to Jonathan to hang, which he did cheerfully. In fact, he couldn't have looked happier. If their first meeting was something of a disaster, he was apparently far too overjoyed at having his family finally together to notice.

* * *

Jonathan returned to the car for the remainder of the luggage, and Emily followed Lauren and Chelsea upstairs to her bedroom. Though Emily couldn't help but notice the decorations as she passed through the living room and foyer, she chose to ignore them. When they reached her bedroom, she reacted with indifference. And once inside, she plopped down on her new bedspread and asked to be alone. Chelsea looked crushed— once they got downstairs, Lauren sat her down. "I know you're disappointed, darling. Me, too. But I think we have to have some compassion for what Emily is going through."

"What's compassion?"

"Understanding. And kindness. Remember, she's been away a long time. The last she remembers, her mother was alive and happy, living not too far from here and married to her daddy."

"I can't understand that."

"Why not?"

"Because her daddy's my daddy, and he's married to you. Not her dead mother."

Lauren sighed, what did she expect? She was barely able to comprehend it herself. Though they had been married only four months, it seemed forever—more than once she wondered how she could have ever been happy before Jonathan.

Granted, her dear sweet husband occasionally let his concern get out of hand, but to Jonathan, family was priority. He wasn't one of those men who drank or gambled or stayed out late with the guys. He was home every night by five-thirty if not earlier, often with a surprise for "his girls." He was sensitive and generous almost to a fault—there was nothing he wouldn't do to make Lauren or the children happy. "If you want something, Lauren, anything at all, you need only ask for it," he would say. He was a rare man, and she hated to think of him as ever having been anyone's but hers.

But if she was ever going to scale that wall Emily had put up, she'd better think about it. Momentarily she wondered if perhaps they shouldn't have stayed on at 35 Candlewood Terrace, which after being on the market for months without a bite, Jonathan had recently given to Fern to list as a rental. Would the familiar surroundings have made it easier for Emily, or would the memories only have caused a setback?

Chelsea went about taking down her unappreciated work while Lauren headed to the kitchen to tidy up. Once Jonathan delivered the trunk to Emily's room, he came looking for Lauren, and as she poured tea for him, she had to say something. "Did you notice her eyes?"

"Excuse me?"

She didn't want to say cold. So instead she found another word. "Angry," she said. "And of course if she is, it would logically be directed at me."

"Come on, Lauren. I know this isn't easy for you, but I didn't expect you to be so critical. You know how much she's been through in the last year . . . and sure, I have no doubt there's anger still there. But we expected as much, didn't we?"

"Oh, of course, and I don't mean to criticize. I just want to understand her so I can help."

"You can help. By giving her unconditional acceptance, not by trying to analyze her every move."

"I'm sorry, you're right," she said. And she was sorry—she hadn't meant to be critical, but the anger, the chill in Emily's eyes, whatever it was, frightened her and she wanted to understand the child better, the child who was suddenly her daughter. Maybe she did understand—too well, and that was part of the problem. To Emily, Lauren was the other woman, so why shouldn't she be angry with her? She promised herself to do better. She said, "By the way, were there any final instructions from her doctor?"

Jonathan looked relieved. He hated to argue, typically retreating if it got too heavy. Now he took her hand in his and gently kissed it. "The doctor said that Emily's having requested to come home was a major step. By making the decision, she'll feel as though she has some control over her life. Of course she'll need to continue with therapy." With his other hand he reached into his back pocket, removing his wallet, taking out a paper, and handing it to her. "These are a few names of therapists in the area. Dr. Strickler will want to consult with whomever we choose."

She unfolded the paper, read the list of doctors—assuming this was a task Jonathan wanted her to handle.

Though she was a member of the PTO and a monthly book group at the library, Jonathan warned her not to get coerced into a dozen committees, only to wonder later how it had happened. But Lauren wasn't the committee type. She chauffeured Chelsea once a week to Brownie troop and gymnastics, even a couple of birthday parties where the mothers sat in the background and discussed their kids' achievements. All sunny, healthy activities to fill her day. But nothing to really prepare her for Emily, and she suddenly felt inadequate.

"Do me a favor, sweetheart, check them out, their credentials, see what you think and let me know. Give some special attention to Dr. Greenly in Middletown. Strickler knows her personally and gave her pretty high marks."

"Of course," she said, folding the list and sliding it into the mail organizer under the telephone. "I just wish there were something more I could do."

He lifted his hand to her chin, caressing her face and neck with his fingers. "But you are doing it, my darling—can't you see that? You're here for her; you're ready to make a good home for her. Of course, I hear and see; I'm not stupid. She's pretending as if she could care less, but that's not real. It only tells me she's frightened. Once she gets to know you, she'll fall in love with you as I did. Trust me, it'll come together; give it a little time. Of course there is one thing . . ."

"What, darling?"

"That haircut of hers looks like it was done with a buzz saw. It's awful."

She chuckled, knowing he was working hard to make light of it. "It'll grow out. Like you said, darling, give it time."

Emily spent the better part of the afternoon in her bedroom with the door locked, and though Lauren knocked once to ask if she could use some help unpacking, Emily called out a curt "no," through a closed door. Twice that afternoon Jonathan looked up from his newspapers and smiled in her direction, indicating for her to relax.

Easier for him to say, of course, not being the one with the major communication problem. Lauren wouldn't describe Emily's dealings with Jonathan as affectionate, but she did speak with him on her several excursions downstairs to re-stock on snacks, while making it a point to ignore Lauren and Chelsea. Lauren had never let Chelsea snack in her bedroom, but she kept her mouth shut now, not wanting to make an issue of it with Emily.

Once Emily interrupted a checkers game going on between Chelsea and Jonathan to ask her father to move a box for her in her bedroom. It was something she could easily have done herself, but delighted with the long-awaited arrival of his oldest girl, Jonathan naturally responded, happily doing whatever she wanted of him ... cajoling and laughing as he chased her up the stairs, never quite catching the envious look on Chelsea's face.

Lauren couldn't help but wonder if her reason for asking him to move the box was to break up the game, to irritate Chelsea. But as soon as the idea came to her, she sent it flying off. Even if it was true, it arose from sibling rivalry, a perfectly normal phenomenon, particularly in a situation like this. Surely it would disappear once the girls felt more secure. The bottom line was, it wasn't important—what was important was that she and Emily build a relationship.

Near the end of the afternoon, Emily appeared, wearing her coat and hat. "Where are you going?" Lauren asked, looking out the window at the dismal weather.

She ignored Lauren and, addressing her father, said, "I'm going out to look around."

"Just stay on the grounds, Princess," he said and she hurried out.

Lauren looked at him. "It's getting dark out."

"Not for another half hour at least. Besides, she's safe within the fence."

It would have been funny if it weren't so maddening—suddenly Lauren was the one worried. Chelsea came by right after, wearing her coat and hat, and announcing that she, too, was going out. And though Lauren was about to protest, Jonathan put his hand up, stopping her. Ten minutes later Lauren stood up and went to the window to look out: she spotted the children standing way back where the fence ended, just before the secured gate that opened into their woods. She sighed. Everything was okay, in fact, better than okay—they were standing next to one another, and it seemed as though they were talking.

Chelsea had slowly made her way down the backyard to Emily, then stood there staring while Emily kept her attention on a small, furry black spider crawling up the chain-link fence. Chelsea didn't say anything because she couldn't think of what to say, but decided Emily didn't look at all like her pictures: she wasn't nearly as pretty; she didn't smile like she did then; and even worse, her short, straight hair made her look like a skinned rat.

"What was it like living all that time in that place?" Chelsea asked finally, wondering if that would be one of those things her mother would say was none of her business.

But Emily's voice sounded almost friendly when she glanced over at Chelsea and answered. "It was horrible and sickening, the people running the place were mean. You see, it's not the kind of hospital where you stay in bed. You get up every day, get dressed, and go to your doctor's appointment or meals or Central—that's the big room where everyone hangs out. Or school, of course.

"You went to school there?"

"Sure, even crazy people have to learn."

"Oh. Well, it doesn't sound so scary."

"Believe me, it was. If you'd keep quiet for just a minute, I'll tell you," she said, looking at Chelsea only occasionally as she spoke—the rest of the time she followed the spider's moves. "You see, the patients wear a metal collar with their name engraved on it. And it doesn't come off until the patient's discharged."

"Do you take a bath with it on?"

"Do you take a bath wearing your toes and tongue? The collar is part of your body while you're there."

"Really?"

Emily heaved one of those sighs, like bigger kids do to littler kids to make them feel dumb. "No, Goldilocks," she said. "Of course, really."

Chelsea guessed the name was to make fun of her blond curls, though it was a whole lot better than the boy's haircut Emily had. "Well, what was the collar for?"

"One reason was so the guards could tell who was who. But the major reason was to make us stay put or lead us around. The thing is you can't trust a crazy person to stay in bed or show up for a doctor's appointment on time or go to school, so this was their way to get us to do what they wanted without an argument."

"You mean, like a dog on a leash?"

"You've got the picture."

Chelsea looked at her expression carefully, searching for signs that Emily was only joking with her, but if there were signs, she couldn't see them. "Did it hurt?"

"Only when you'd try to get away and the chain pulled tighter, choking off your throat so that you couldn't swallow. So if you were smart, you didn't try."

It sounded evil and awful, and Chelsea couldn't imagine that her father, Emily's father, the strongest and smartest and best father in the world, would stand for his daughter being treated in such a disgusting way. "What about Daddy?" she asked. "Didn't he see you wearing the collar when he came to visit you?"

There was a long pause, then Emily said, "Sure, he could see it. And he didn't like it much either, but what was he supposed to do? When a person gets locked up in one of those crazy houses, there's certain rules that apply to every patient there. Parents are demoted right off the bat—they're no longer in charge of you. The doctors and nurses and secretaries and toothless janitors become the lords and masters, and parents take their orders from them."

No, she still didn't believe it—Daddy would never put up with such a thing. But she went along with the story just the same. "You must have hated it."

"That's an understatement. But it was the bloody curse that was really the worst."

Chelsea was a wimp when it came to needles and blood so when she heard that, the fear must have headed right to her face. She knew it because Emily suddenly looked very pleased with herself. "Any girl who acted crazy would get it—

and, of course, that was nearly every girl there since that's why we *were* there."

"What would they get?"

The spider had finally reached Emily's height on the fence, and she scooped it into her cupped hands, letting it crawl first in one hand, then the other. "The curse, of course. Once a month we'd all start to bleed, and not stop for days."

"I don't get it. Bleed from where?"

"Our private places. Where do you think?"

"You mean, between your legs?" Chelsea said, her voice coming out in a breathless whisper. Even if she'd had a hundred million guesses she never would have thought to say there. But now with Emily giving her the idea, she winced. "But how? Why did it happen?"

Emily continued to play with the spider in her hands, making Chelsea shiver. "Because one of the lords or masters was angry with us and wanted to punish us, so she zapped us with the curse. And if you cried or complained, you'd get an increase in dosage. Then the blood would pour out of you like from a hose, and never stop. At least, not until you bled out and died."

"No, sir! I don't believe you!"

"Fine, you don't want to believe me? Then don't. Who cares? But you tell me why while I was there two girls I knew bled to death at night in their sleep?" She raised her hand like she was taking an oath. "Honest to God, hope to die."

"Well, if it was as awful and scary as you say, and you hated it that much, then why'd it take so long for you to decide you wanted to come home?"

"Good question," the older girl said, as though she were really impressed, and pumping Chelsea's ego in the process. That's why she wasn't prepared for the letdown when Emily answered. "It was a choice I had to make. What looked better, the douche bags at the hospital or you and your mother?"

And as she said it, she clamped her hand shut, squashing the spider inside.

It was at that moment that Lauren called them to dinner, and Chelsea instantly spun around and started back. She supposed Emily was following, but she didn't look. In her head she kept seeing the spider die, kept thinking of Emily's horrible story. She'd even sworn, honest to God, hope to die, a pledge not many kids she knew took lightly. Was Emily crazy or just a liar?

Chapter Three

Dinner was quiet—too quiet, Lauren thought. Though it seemed that the girls had been getting along well outside, there was no indication of that now. Emily didn't say anything, and just picked at the lasagna.

As soon as dinner was finished, Jonathan excused himself, remembering a business call he had to make, and Lauren sent Chelsea upstairs to begin her bath. Emily began to get up, but Lauren reached out and put her hand on hers. "Come on, stay a few minutes longer and talk to me," she said. Emily quickly withdrew from the contact, but stayed in her chair.

"What's wrong?"

"Nothing. I just thought we could chat is all." When there was no response from Emily, Lauren said the first thing that came to mind. "I imagine you're looking forward to starting school," she said. "Seeing some of the friends you grew up with."

"I haven't thought about it."

"Oh. Well, I don't suppose you've had time to

think much about anything. I mean, with all of this happening so fast." Emily looked up as though she hadn't a clue as to what Lauren was talking about. "What I meant was your decision to come home was kind of sudden. Not that I'm complaining, of course. No, not in any way ... We were all so excited and thrilled when we heard the news. Your father loves you so. He's been waiting so long for you to come home. But then I don't need to tell you that ..."

She paused finally, feeling as though her mouth had gotten out of control and wishing she had a better script. But since none was available, she forged on. "I've been eager myself, Emily. I really want to get to know you."

"Why?"

"A fair question," Lauren said. "I guess initially the reason is because of your father. I love him so much, and since you're the most important person in his life, it would naturally stand to reason that you'd be important to me, too."

"Better not waste your time."

"What does that mean?"

"What it sounds like. I have a mother. She may not have been great, but she was mine. And her lasagna was better than that slop you passed off at dinner."

Lauren refused to be baited. "It wasn't my intention—" she began, but didn't get any further, because suddenly Emily's hand moved and the plate of food went falling to the floor, breaking into dozens of pieces. With that, Emily stood up and started to leave.

"Wait just a moment," Lauren called, but Emily kept walking and would have left the room if not for bumping into Jonathan at the doorway. Seeing the distress on his daughter's face, he put his hands on her shoulders. "Hey, what did I miss here?" But she didn't even lift her head to look at him, much less respond, so he turned his question to Lauren. "Okay, maybe you can fill me in?"

Lauren gestured to the broken china and cold tomato sauce on the tiles. "I'd simply like her to clean up the mess she made. It was deliberate."

Jonathan looked back to Emily, and with tenderness and calm asked, "Is that right, did you do it purposely?"

She shook her head—still not looking at him. "No. It was an accident."

He nodded, his face expressing relief, and said, "It seems what we have here is a misunderstanding. So why don't you go off wherever you're going, and let Daddy take care of this?"

Emily ran off and Lauren stood there, glaring at him. "She did it deliberately, Jonathan."

"She claims it was an accident, and you claim it was deliberate. Is there just a remote possibility that your perception was off? Maybe it seemed to you like she pushed it, but her hand in actuality slipped, pushing the plate off the table inadvertently?"

Lauren considered it—she was almost positive she had seen Emily's hand move, but could she be so certain that it hadn't been an accident as Jonathan suggested? "Besides which," he went on, "is it really worth getting this upset about? And I don't know about you, but damn it, Lauren, I don't like the idea of either of the girls cleaning up broken china." He went to the cabinet, opened it, and reached for the whisk broom and pan, but she took it from his hands.

"It's all right, I'll clean it up."

"Are you sure?"

She was, and Jonathan retreated to the living room to his newspapers while Lauren swept up the broken china, washed the floor, then loaded the dishwasher. That done, she sank down on the stool beneath the wall telephone and sighed—she hated to admit it, but Jonathan had made sense. She reached up and lifted the receiver off the hook, and dialed Fern's number.

"Help," Lauren said in a feeble attempt at humor when her sister picked up. Of course, she and Fern had discussed the difficulties she might encounter with Emily coming home, even before they knew she was actually being discharged. Now, she was the perfect one to commiserate with.

"What's the matter?"

"Nothing really, at least nothing I shouldn't have anticipated. She's ignoring me, making it clear she wants nothing to do with me. She had a mother, a fairly good one from all reports, and isn't in the market for any bad imitations. Particularly one that can't even make a respectable lasagna. And to further emphasize that point, she pushed her plate of food to the floor.''

"Just keep in mind she's a very hurt little girl and doesn't mean it.''

"That sounds like Jonathan's thinking to me," Lauren grumbled.

"Well, I've never been a mother, but I've been a big sister. And I remember how you drove Mother up the wall. You were not as easy to handle as Chelsea is. You had what Mother and I would nicely refer to as your temper tantrums—getting angry and shooting off your mouth whenever you felt it was justified.''

"Oh, come on now, I don't remember being all that bad.''

"Lauren, if you actually meant all the rotten things you said to Mom, you might have ended up on Riker's Island or some similar correctional facility. Remember when you snuck out of the house at age twelve, decked out in a black satin strapless that you borrowed from some friend's older sister from up the street, to go clubbing with a guy who had to be at least nineteen?''

Apparently she'd had a thing for older men even then, Lauren mused. "I did?" she asked.

"You forgot? My, how convenient.''

"Well, now that I'm being reminded and I'm thinking about it, the story does sound a little familiar. Gosh, the same age as Emily. I'm horrified.''

"So give the girl some slack.''

Though she was hearing things she already

knew, somehow coming from Fern it made absolute sense. Of course it would take time, and of course she would have no choice but to be patient. Relationships didn't just happen; they needed work. She even hid her disappointment when later that night upon passing Emily's room, she found the striped apple-green and white tiebacks and matching bedspread in a heap on the floor outside her door.

She stooped down, gathering up the yards of material into her arms, then took it to pack away. No, this was not going to be easy. And it dawned on her that she didn't know the first thing about her stepdaughter—lasagna and shortcake aside, what were her likes, her dislikes? What made her happy, sad, excited?

Or angry?

On Sunday it was cold and sleeting, keeping them indoors, and though Lauren had tried to interest Jonathan and the children in one of their many board games, nothing ever materialized. After lunch, Jonathan received a telephone call that he took in his study. Once he was finished, he stayed there, working on some road plans for the county, and the children, avoiding one another, went off to their separate quarters, leaving Lauren feeling uneasy and restless. Her mood didn't begin to lift until the intercom signaled company. Lauren hurried to the kitchen and switched on the computer monitor.

"It's me, I forgot my membership card," a voice called out cheerfully. "Lower the drawbridge."

Lauren smiled—Fern was always misplacing her key card, among other things. She released the gate, letting Fern through. She called into the study to Jonathan. "Darling, Fern just pulled in."

"Great. We could stand a little shake-up around here. I've got a couple of hours of work here, but do some arm-twisting and get her to stay for dinner."

There was no need to twist any arms—Fern had been showing properties all morning, but her solitary afternoon appointment had canceled, freeing her for the remainder of the day. "So on the way here," she said as she produced her usual big shopping bag, this one from the Lord & Taylor at the mall, "I just happened to pass by and see a couple of things for the kiddies . . ."

"Oh, goodie, a present for me," Lauren said, teasing. "Does this mean you sold a house?"

"You are incorrigible," Fern said, shaking her head. "I was referring to Chelsea and Emily, not you."

Lauren headed to the stairs, but remembering the communications system, she rerouted to the kitchen. Despite the teasing, Lauren knew that Fern was almost as bad as Jonathan, forever shopping for things for her and Chelsea. Now reaching the kitchen monitor, she switched to Chelsea's room, focusing in on the area covered by the camera. "Yoo, hoo, anyone there?" she called, then heard scrambling as Chelsea moved into the viewing area. "Hi, darling, Aunt Fern's here. Come on down, and bring Emily."

Without waiting for a response, Lauren switched off the controls, and within minutes Chelsea was rushing Fern with a bear hug. Emily hung back, looking as though she wanted to be anywhere but there. "Emily, I want you to meet my sister Fern," Lauren said.

"*Aunt* Fern," Emily qualified.

"Oh, don't you go worrying about those labels," Fern said. "You can call me whatever feels right to you." And with that, she opened the shopping bag and took out two fanny packs, each in a snazzy, colorful cotton print.

Chelsea quickly put hers on, admiring it, buckling the strap, then opening the purse and sliding her hand inside, pulling out a big black and psychedelic pink barrette. She stuck it in her hair, then stepped over to the mirror over the lowboy. "Oh, I love this, Auntie, thank you. A kid in my class wears these; only mine's even nicer. How'd you know I wanted one?"

"Oh, you know me—I look into children's minds while they're sleeping."

Chelsea turned to Emily, allowing her into her confidence. "She doesn't really."

"Gosh, thanks for the tip," Emily ridiculed, "and here I was believing her."

But it seemed Chelsea wasn't about to let Emily get to her. She gestured to the shocking green barrette Emily had taken out of her purse. "Why don't you put it on?"

"Why don't you mind your own business?"

"What's the matter? You too bald for a barrette?"

"Chelsea, stop that!" Lauren said, surprised at the dig.

But Fern jumped in to handle it—she went over, took the barrette from Emily, and secured it in front, through the longer hair on top. "Nonsense, this looks fine. Take a look in the mirror."

"I would if I wanted to, pig face. But I don't." With that, Emily yanked the barrette from her hair, and along with the fanny pack threw it down and started for the door.

It took Lauren a moment for the insult to register. "Get back here!" Lauren demanded, and Emily stopped. "I want you to apologize to my sister right now."

"Why should I? She's the one who said I should call her whatever feels right for me. Is it my fault that pig face feels right?" She took off upstairs, and Lauren stood there watching as she went, embarrassed and speechless.

"Boy, if I had ever said that, you would have killed me!" Chelsea said, angrily stomping off.

True, she would have punished Chelsea, perhaps spanked her bottom, but Emily was older and besides, Lauren hadn't the relationship with her that she had with Chelsea.

"Forget it, it's not important," Fern said later, making excuses for Emily ... like Lauren had done herself initially. "I guess my timing was off on those silly barrettes. Kids that age are super sensitive when it comes to their appearance."

That was true, but after all, Emily was the one who had chopped off her hair. In any event, her behavior was inexcusable. And though it occurred to Lauren to go to Jonathan, to get his backup in handling such rudeness, she hated to admit that she didn't know what to do.

It was during dinner that Fern brought up the house on Candlewood Terrace. "Oh, my, can you believe it, it nearly slipped my mind?" she said, laying down her fork and knife and turning to Jonathan. "I got a response to the advertisement on your house."

"Good," he said. "Tell me."

"A renter, not a buyer, but there seems to be serious interest. In fact, he insisted I promise not to rent it before he got the chance to see it tomorrow."

Jonathan nodded. From the onset, he was convinced that with the depressed economy, the house on Candlewood Terrace would be a difficult sell. Added to that was Fern's belief that buyers were superstitious when it came to a house with a violent history. "Well, I hope it works out," Jonathan said. "It would be good to get people in there, at least until the market picks up, and we can sell. Rent won't take care of taxes and upkeep, but it'll cover the mortgage. Can this guy afford it?"

"He claims to have a contracting business. But

not to worry, I'll verify his income. His name is Gordon Cummings. Ever hear of him?" Jonathan's eyes narrowed—he laid down his fork and seemed a little surprised until Fern asked, "What's wrong?"

He turned back to her and shook his head. "Nothing. Just rolling the name over a few times in my head is all. With him being in the contracting business and all my ties to construction, well, you would think I would know him, wouldn't you?" Then without waiting for her answer, he shrugged, took a roll from the bread basket, and ripped it in half. "But the name doesn't ring any bells."

"Well, the reason may be that he's not based locally. Though he did mention having some family in town, and doing a few jobs in the area, he's actually from Saugerties."

Saugerties was thirty-five minutes north on the New York Thruway. "I see. So what about his immediate family, how many people are we talking about?"

"He's unmarried. No kids."

Jonathan's lower lip jutted out. "Really? Does he know what a big place it is?"

"Well, the ad specified eight good-sized rooms, but that didn't seem to deter him. I had the same concern initially, but to each his own. To me, extra space only means extra cleaning. But look at you people—Lauren needs eleven rooms to clean like she needs a second head."

"I don't argue that with you, and I'm sure

you're aware that since we moved in here, I've pleaded with her to have Beatrice come full-time. But that sister of yours can be mighty stubborn. She insists she likes to do for herself."

"She always did," Fern said. "She's also not used to having a housekeeper."

With that, Jonathan and Fern looked at Lauren, who was paying only minimal attention to the conversation. Though Jonathan might not have realized it, Lauren's biggest fear was that with too much time on her hands, she would surely end up a daytime TV junkie.

Besides which, Beatrice Barr, a mild-mannered woman with long, thin, gray-streaked brown hair that she wore wound up in a bun at the back of her head, had cleaned for Jonathan in the past. And now in her late fifties, despite her strong, lean body, it made Lauren uncomfortable to lay back and let a woman nearly twice her age do her cleaning. "That's only because I doubt Beatrice could put up with you on a regular basis," she said, directing her teasing to Jonathan.

His hands went to his chest in mock surprise. "Who me? Why, what do I do?"

"Well, let me see, how can I put this delicately?"

"No need to be delicate—we're all family. Just haul off and hit me face on."

"Don't say you didn't ask for it," she said, wagging her finger. "My darling, you are incredibly fussy."

He shook his head, waving his hand through the air. "Sheer nonsense."

"Oh? Let me bring up a few examples," she said, realizing at once that she was about to confront him with some truths. "Let's go with clothes: your black dress socks cannot be in the same drawer as your white tube socks; all underwear has to be ironed and folded to specification; and if there's a crease in a shirt or pair of pants, back it goes to the laundry."

He shrugged. "Okay. I plead guilty on all counts. But are those such big deals?"

"One might call it obsessive."

"Wait, am I hearing this?" he said, turning to Fern, then back to Lauren. "Okay, fess up, tell your sister, right now ... God's honest truth, do I complain?"

"What is there to complain about?"

"Is that an answer?"

She paused a moment, then relented. "Well, let us not forget that I bust my buns to please you." And to his credit, Jonathan rarely complained. But being so in tune with her husband, Lauren was good at detecting when he was upset or frustrated, if only by a change in tone or stiffness of expression. And when he was, she responded right away. "I've seen how cranky and finicky you can get with Beatrice," she said. "I'm afraid too much contact with you would stress her out."

His smile broadened—he leaned over the table and kissed her. "Just so long as I don't have that same effect on you, my love." Then turning to

Fern, he said, "Speaking of which . . . please check out this Cummings fellow's references, will you? The last thing I need is to get stuck leasing to some unsavory character who grows pot in the window boxes and throws all-night parties."

"I know it's hard, Jonathan, but have faith," Fern teased. "Let someone else do the worrying."

They went back to the discussion of the house, and Lauren's thoughts retreated to where they had been earlier—on Emily and how she could pierce her defenses. She had observed her through most of dinner without Emily noticing. She seemed particularly interested in Fern and her father's discussion of the house on Candlewood Terrace.

"Maybe you ought to ask her if the prospect of a stranger moving in there bothers her," Lauren suggested to Jonathan that night in bed after describing her observation.

"And then what? If it does, should we simply leave the house vacant?"

"I didn't say that."

"Then what are you saying? Look, sweetheart, there's a lot of things that are likely to bother her, but she's got to work through them. That's what we're here for, that's what her doctor will be there for. I think you're creating issues that don't exist. Let's simply enjoy that she's finally home with us. Okay?"

"Okay—"

"Do I detect a but?"

"No, not really," she said. "It's just that I was thinking."

"Go on."

"Well, I keep thinking how she took off her hat and asked you if you liked her new haircut? And . . . well, she must have known you wouldn't like it. Right?"

"Not necessarily."

"I think she would."

"What is the bottom line here? That she wanted to upset me?"

"Well, that is possible, isn't it?"

"Why?"

"Because you married me, that's why."

A long sigh, then, "Will you please tell me what's going on here? First you're upset because she's angry at you, then you're upset because she's angry at me. What is this about, do you want to turn me against my own daughter, is that it? Or maybe what you're getting at is, she's angry at me for not being there to protect her and her mother."

"Of course not, I didn't mean that at all! I just meant—"

But his expression stopped her and she looked up as he did, as they heard the bump against the hallway wall: Emily was standing there. The door was partially open, though neither of them had heard it open—now Emily's elbow had hit the wall making her presence known. How long had she been standing out there listening? "Hi, there,

Princess, what is it?" Jonathan said, immediately getting out of bed and going to her.

"I couldn't sleep," she said.

He put his arm around her, hugging her to him. "I've got an idea. You come with me, let the old man put you to bed with one of those special Grant originals. Remember Emily in the looking glass?" Emily smiled an uncertain smile, but one of the first Lauren had seen on her, as though the memory of the story had indeed registered. "Now, you're not too old for that, are you?"

She shook her head, then while Jonathan took a moment to slip on his robe, Emily turned her face to Lauren, her smile twisting away. Indicating what, that she hated her, that she had overheard the conversation between her and Jonathan? And if Jonathan had misconstrued what Lauren was getting at, what would Emily think?

Five steps backward, no ten. Lauren had only wanted to talk about the anger, to see where it was directed and why, and talk about how they might better help Emily. But apparently it hadn't come across that way. Particularly distressing was Jonathan's remark that Lauren wanted to cause a rift between father and daughter. That and knowing that Jonathan continued to feel responsible over what happened to Nancy and his daughter.

Though her purpose was to help, instead she managed to dredge up the old pain. She did try to explain herself further when Jonathan got back to bed twenty minutes later, but it only became worse—he became silent, turned away from her, and went to sleep.

Lauren now realized just how sensitive Jonathan was when it came to Emily. But rather than argue it through and get it over with, which would have made life far easier, certainly it might have ended the conflict sooner, Jonathan reacted as he often did and withdrew. And though these silences made her want to scream, there was nothing she could do about it.

Still, as much as she hated to admit it and would never do so to Jonathan, the method did have some plusses. If nothing else, it gave them an opportunity to consider the other's point. And that's what Lauren did the next morning as she went around tidying the house. There was a time when Jonathan didn't know for certain if Emily would ever be home, would ever talk to anyone let alone him, and now that she was home, he wanted to concentrate his efforts on the positive things, not the negative.

So despite his going to bed angry and silent and leaving the house that way the next morning, Lauren was feeling better by the time she made those phone calls to the list of psychiatrists. After questioning their nurses and taking into account locations as well as her belief that at Emily's age, a female doctor would be a better choice, she made an appointment for the following evening with Dr. Penelope Greenly, the therapist Jonathan had asked that she give special attention to.

Fern had left her briefcase at the house the night before, and Lauren called to tell her. While Fern was on the line, she asked if she would watch Chelsea the following night while she and Jonathan and Emily saw Dr. Greenly. Fern agreed, and as soon as Lauren hung up, she headed to the den where Emily was watching cartoons on television. "Time to go get dressed, we're going shopping."

"I don't need anything."

"Well, maybe you'll think of something," she said, not mentioning the sorry state of her clothes. "I can come up with two items offhand, curtains and a bedspread for your room. Your choice this time. Okay?"

She should have known better, but she was still in the learning stages when it came to Emily. Her favorite color, or so she claimed to Lauren and the salespeople at the bed and bath department at Macy's, was black—prints or checks or stripes would definitely not do. It was only when one of the saleswomen tempted her with a couple of white throw pillows, some black and white art deco, and a colorful cotton-looped rug that the choice became bearable.

After much wheedling, Lauren finally got Emily to pick out a few tops, though she wouldn't even look at skirts or dresses. So along with two pairs of baggy jeans, a jean jacket, a knapsack, and a slew of school supplies, Lauren picked out skirts, dresses, and underwear and had them sent. The big point of contention turned out to be shoes. Though they could agree immediately on Reebok sneakers, Emily refused every shoe put in front of her by the salesman, making clear she wouldn't wear any of them. She was determined to get a pair of men's tan, high-laced work boots.

"Your father will hate them," Lauren said.

"I don't care, I want them," she said, not budging an inch. According to the salesman, combat boots, hightops, and mountain boots were all the rage with young girls, and though Lauren found them hideous, she finally caved in. Once the purchase was made, they stopped for lunch at Friendly's, and if anyone would have asked Lauren how their day was going, she would have bubbled enthusiastically. But it seemed she had been deluding herself. They had put in their food order and Lauren was spreading her napkin over her lap when out of the blue, Emily announced, "You'll never be my mother, you know."

She was caught off guard once again, but this time she had thought enough about it that she likely could have come up with a response in her sleep. "As I wanted to explain to you the other day, Emily," she began, "I'm not trying to take your mother's place. But I am your stepmother. Now, I'm not quite sure what that entails, I've never been one before, so I guess I'm on just as shaky ground as you." She lifted her water glass, took a sip, then set it down.

"I imagine though it has to do with the people involved—what they want to put into the relationship, what they want to get out of it. I see no reason why we can't feel it out, you know, try to build a new friendship, something that's our own."

"There is a reason."

"Really? What is it?"

"I don't want to."

Lauren bit her lip, trying not to let Emily's negativity pull her down. "Why?"

"I don't like you."

"You don't even know me, it's not fair to make a judgment so quickly."

"I know you as well as I need to. And you're totally wrong for my father."

"Could you be more specific?"

Emily waited a moment as the waitress put their plates in front of them—tuna sandwiches for both, with a side of fries for Emily. "You let my father run you."

"That's not true."

"It's true, you're just too dumb to see it. You're going to end up hurting him."

"That's really not a fair assumption," she said, naturally upset but also touched by her need to protect her father. "Emily, I would never hurt your father. I love and respect him too much for that. I want only to make him happy."

"Sounds good, but I don't think so. You're not nearly strong enough to do the job."

"What does that mean?"

"Look, I'm just trying to warn you, Lauren. If you're smart you'll pack your bags, take your bitchy daughter, and get lost. And if you don't, you'll be sorry."

Lauren could feel her heart beat rapidly, as much for the gravity of the tone as the nastiness of the message itself. "If I didn't know better, I'd say that was a threat."

But the words went ignored—apparently Emily had said her piece. And as though nothing offensive had passed between them, she picked up her tuna sandwich and began to eat.

Chapter Four

After registering Emily in the middle school, they drove home in silence, arriving at the house at two-thirty. Emily immediately took her packages from the car and disappeared up to her room, and under the circumstances, Lauren was relieved to be rid of her. Not much later, Fern drove up, coming by to retrieve her briefcase. "I'll put on tea," Lauren said, but Fern shook her head. "Sorry, wish I could, hon, but I have an appointment."

But seeing Lauren's expression sink, she looked at her watch and qualified. "I can give you about three minutes and still make it. What's up?"

"She wants to break us up."

"Who, what are we talking about?"

"Emily. She wants to come between Jonathan and me. She came out and told me."

"That's ridiculous. She's only a kid."

"Ridiculous that she wants to or that she could carry through such a threat?"

Fern followed Lauren to the living room, her eyes darkening as she studied her sister's face.

"What's going on with you? Since when are you so insecure?"

"She couldn't have made it any clearer," Lauren said, unable to shake the unsettled feeling in her stomach since their talk. "She's not happy her father married me, but that's not something I was totally unprepared for. What I wasn't prepared for is the anger she feels and the intensity of it. Fern, she actually said she wants me out of Jonathan's life. And if I don't comply, I'll be sorry."

"Fine, an eleven-year-old kid who's been under psychiatric care for emotional problems shoots off her mouth. She even threatens you ... Now assuming for a moment that she means what she's saying, that she'd actually try to break up your marriage or somehow punish you, both of which are a bit farfetched ... Still, do you believe that Jonathan could be so easily manipulated?"

"I don't, not really. It's just that he's so susceptible when it comes to Emily."

"So? Jonathan is a sensitive man, a bit of a pushover when it comes to the women he loves. He's also a strong, intelligent man with a mind of his own. Now, do I really need to tell you this?"

"No, of course not. It's just that he seems so intent on protecting her from the enemy, so to speak. Which is wholly natural considering what she's been through, but—"

"If you're saying he's overprotective, Lauren, this, too, is no news flash."

"No, of course not, but all that is fine, I have

no trouble dealing with it. I guess, the difference here is, I'm not the enemy yet he's treating me as though I am."

Lauren had every intention of telling Jonathan about her conversation with Emily, that is, until her talk with Fern and a little rethinking of the issue. That's when she realized it would only place him in an impossible situation. Providing he even took the matter seriously, what recourse would he have? Go to his daughter and scold her for saying such things to his new wife? Of course, he could do that, but it would only force him to take sides and make Emily even angrier. So it came down to one thing: Lauren was an adult, Emily was a child. An adult was expected to master her emotions, a child was not.

She had always been strong and self-sufficient, she would handle it herself.

Jonathan had come home that night arms laden with gifts: a delicate Chinese geisha doll for Chelsea's growing collection of dolls from foreign lands, and for Emily a huge box labeled Tumbling Gems, which was filled with stones, a mechanical wheel to polish them, and enough paraphernalia to make the resulting gems into rings and pins and necklaces and bracelets. "So, did I do okay?" he asked the girls as they unwrapped their gifts. It was Chelsea who got to Jonathan first to jump into his arms and thank him with hugs and squeals. Deliberate one-upsmanship, but Emily seemed not to care.

Lauren stood off on the sidelines, watching Jonathan with the children. Oh, she hadn't forgotten Emily's tough stance with her that afternoon, but going over the words in her mind since, it had lost a lot of its punch. She wondered if perhaps her stepdaughter hadn't something in common with the girl she once was. Hot-tempered, brash, meaning only a portion of what she said.

Certainly Jonathan was wonderful with them, she thought as he engaged them next in some sleight-of-hand trick. Though neither girl addressed the other, they had briefly and temporarily joined forces in play. Lauren headed back to the kitchen to check dinner, feeling left out. But not long after, Jonathan came in and, smiling coyly, handed her a small, slim box. She stood there, looking at it. "What is this?"

"Do you think I'd leave out my best girl?"

"In case you haven't noticed, Jonathan, I'm not one of the children." He was no longer upset, and this was his way to apologize, but instead of letting it go like she really wanted to, she stood there like a petulant child—the very thing she claimed she wasn't. To his credit, he let it go. But whatever point she was trying to make, he dispelled when he kissed her.

"You're exactly who I want you to be, Lauren," he said, his lips moving lightly on hers, then drawing away when what she wanted was more. He placed the box in her hand. "Open it."

Inside was a wide gold chain necklace. She lifted it out, drawing in her breath. "Oh, Jonathan, it's lovely." She looked up at him. "But it wasn't necessary—"

He put his fingers to her mouth, stopping her, then took the necklace from her and, moving to her back, slipped it around her neck. He leaned forward, kissing the nape of her neck as he secured it, then ran his hands down her body, holding her close to him. "I love you, Lauren. I hate to fight with you."

There was an ache in her groin, tears in her eyes. She absolutely adored this man, and he was forever showing how much he loved her. Fern was right, of course, how could she have thought for a moment she would lose him?

Fern showed up after dinner, pleased with herself. She took a document out of her briefcase and held it out to Jonathan. "Well, how does a one-year lease sound?"

"Ah, my sister-in-law, you are a genius," Jonathan said, smiling and getting up to take the prepared lease. He looked it over. "No problem with the rent?"

"Not at all, I think it was fair. I did pause a moment though when I first saw your new tenant."

"Uh-oh, now the bad news comes. So what's the hitch, what's wrong with him?"

"Nothing really, I was just expecting something different, I guess. He's young, only twenty-two, but he seems responsible. He's a big guy, sort of lumbering, but a nice fellow. Polite, not your typical young party animal. He's had his own carpentry business since he quit high school at about seventeen. In fact, he wants to make some repairs and changes to the house providing you have no problems with it. No cost to you, of course."

Jonathan shrugged. "No, I have no problem with it. As long as it upgrades the property, and he understands that whatever he does stays when he leaves."

"I wonder why he'd want to," Lauren said. "I mean it's not like it's his property."

"Why not?" Fern said. "After all, when you can do it yourself, make something exactly the way you want it. And he can't yet afford to buy his own."

"But why there?"

"That's an odd remark," Jonathan said. "It is a nice house."

"Oh, yes, of course. I didn't mean that it wasn't." Then directing her next question to Fern, "Did you say anything about what happened there?"

"Actually I wasn't going to, I had no obligation to . . . but then I figured he'd find out soon enough from neighbors. So if he was going to be turned off, better it be now rather than have you stuck with a tenant who wants out."

"And obviously it made no difference," Jonathan said.

"Not at all. In fact, he knew about it."

"How?" Lauren asked.

"I mentioned earlier he had relatives in town.

A sister and her family, I believe. Well, apparently they knew which house it was—" Her mouth dropped. "Lauren Sandler Grant, I can't believe you stood there all this time not saying a word about it ... where did you get that stunning necklace?"

They all burst out laughing and the new tenant was forgotten.

Later that night, out of the blue, Jonathan said, "If the police come around asking to question Emily, you're to refuse. And let me know about it immediately."

She sat up in bed, looked at him. "I don't understand, why would they?"

He sighed. "I got a call from Detective Kneeland, he's been on the case since the beginning. Remember when I took that call in the study yesterday?" She nodded. "Well, I didn't say anything then, I needed time to absorb it, make sure I wasn't reacting emotionally. Christ, Lauren, they barely gave the kid twenty-four hours home before they started to descend on her."

"Even after all this time?"

"Well, the case wasn't solved, it's his job to try to solve it. And as much as I'd like to see that happen, the bottom line is, Dr. Strickler says she still has patches of memory missing, memories she wants no part of. Besides, my primary concern here is my daughter and I'm not willing to risk any setbacks."

"And you think if they talked to her that would happen?"

"I think it's highly possible. Don't you?"

She thought about it a moment and she had to agree. Besides, if Emily had something important to say, something she did suddenly remember about her mother's murder, wouldn't she offer up the information herself?

Emily dressed in her new jeans and combat boots to go to the psychologist's office, and though Jonathan couldn't hide his disdain, he said nothing.

For the first twenty minutes, the doctor, who spoke in a hushed monotone and had a distracting way of gaping with eyes magnified by thick-lensed glasses, talked to Lauren and Jonathan while Emily sat outside in the waiting room, looking distressed. According to Penelope Greenly, she had gone over Emily's records and spoken to Dr. Strickler. Then as though reading a prepared script, she gave a rundown of her background and method of treatment. Lauren, having earlier decided to deal with her problems with Emily's behavior herself, only listened—it was Jonathan who brought up Emily's negativity.

"Oh, my, I would think it peculiar had she given you unearned acceptance. Wouldn't you?" The woman posed her question to Lauren as her nose pinched, lifting the bridge of her glasses and creating a look of confusion at so moronic an expectation.

"Why, yes, of course, and I didn't really expect ..." Lauren said, stumbling over her words.

"You've taken a difficult road, Mrs. Grant ... not impossible, of course, I surely don't mean to say that. But with time and work and patience, you will earn her trust."

Jonathan turned to Lauren, smiling. "See, what did I tell you, my darling?"

Lauren felt patronized, both by the therapist and Jonathan, but sat there, nodding. She actually identified with Emily who looked none too pleased with the goings-on once she was allowed to enter the inner sanctum. She sat stiffly in a chair, looking past the woman, not saying a word the entire fifteen minutes they were there.

"Maybe we ought to interview other therapists," Lauren said to Jonathan once they got home, said good-bye to Fern, and the children had gone up to their bedrooms.

"Why, what's wrong with this woman?"

"I don't know, it's hard to put my finger on. Maybe someone younger would be better."

"What are you talking about? She couldn't be more than thirty-five."

"Well, someone who is more energetic, someone not so dreary and lifeless. I just have difficulty seeing her as a person able to talk the same language as a kid. I'm sure we can do better."

"You're the one who chose her, Lauren."

"I know, but based on a five-minute conversation with her secretary. Now that we've had the opportunity to meet her, well, maybe it was simply a wrong choice."

"Please, Lauren, give me a break. I thought she was fine. She's treated other youngsters, she went to Harvard for her post-graduate work, certainly she has the credentials."

"Emily didn't like her."

"At this point, I doubt there's a therapist alive Emily would welcome—I imagine she's sick of all of them, including her Dr. Strickler. And understandably so. Dr. Greenly will need to gain her trust. *She* understands that."

"And I don't?"

"I didn't say that, did I?"

"You implied it though."

He sighed, then nodded his head as though counting out a patience medication. He looked up finally. "Dr. Greenly is a professional, sure I would expect her to be intuitive about such things. If I meant anything, I guess it was that." When Lauren didn't respond, he said, "Look, Lauren, I understand this is no picnic for you, and it's not nearly over. What about having Beatrice in more often? She's always gotten along fine with Emily, she could be a help with the kids after school. You know, ease the load a little."

"What load? We have only two children, both of whom are in school."

"Okay, it was only a suggestion. Just that before you know it, summer will be here, and with the two kids ... I don't want them off in camp or anything."

"I wasn't considering camp. I'm fine.'

"By the way, if you don't mind me asking, what's with those awful boots?"

"It's the style, Jonathan . . . she wanted them."

He didn't push further, and neither did she. And Dr. Greenly would have to do. Maybe she wasn't as bad as she seemed.

"I never saw a room all in black," Chelsea said to Emily the next day passing her room and finding the door for once not closed. She stopped at the threshold to take a better look around. The jewelry maker Daddy had given Emily had been tossed on a shelf, the cellophane wrap not even off of the box. Chelsea wished she could play with it, but didn't want to ask.

"I guess you haven't seen much," Emily said. "Lots of movie stars do their houses in all black."

"How do you know that?"

"I just know."

"My room is in pink and white checks—it looks like an old-fashioned ice-cream parlor. Want to see?"

"Why would I?"

Chelsea shrugged, then she asked the questions she'd wanted to ask Emily her first day home. "Why don't you want a sister?"

Emily looked up from a comic book she was reading. "Did I say I didn't want one?" Chelsea's spirits lifted briefly, only to be smashed. "What I don't want is you."

She meant to make Chelsea cry or run and tattle on her, but she didn't. Instead she said in her best I-don't-care voice, "Well, you don't have a choice because I am."

"Not. You're just an interloper."

"What's that?"

"Someone who sticks her nose in someone else's life but doesn't belong."

"I do too belong. Daddy's already asked the court if he can adopt me legal."

"Liar."

"It's true."

By the look on her face, Chelsea could see she'd caught her big sister by surprise. But it didn't show in her voice when she said, "Who really cares? It may not matter anyway, because the fact is, you might be dead before that happens."

"You're not funny."

"Does it sound like I'm trying to be? It's easy to kill a kid, no harder than killing a frog. Ever kill a frog, Goldilocks?" Chelsea shook her head. "Well I did once, I cut its head off with a jack-knife . . . it was sure a lot of green slime. And the real kick was, his eyes stayed wide open through the whole thing, watching his own execution."

Chelsea could feel a shiver roll along her neck. "You are so disgusting."

"I'm just telling you things you ought to know. Isn't that what big sisters do?" When Chelsea didn't answer, she went on. "For instance, I'm really worried about you and your mother. You don't belong in this house."

"You're just a lot of talk. You don't scare me."

"No? Did anyone ever tell you how my mother was murdered?" When there was no answer, she said, "She got whacked a few times with a base-ball bat."

Chelsea drew in her breath. "I thought you couldn't remember any of that."

Her brow wrinkled, and she held up a finger for effect. "Wait a second here, I do think you're right about that. What do you think, Chelsea, did someone sneak into my room in the middle of the night while I was asleep to tell me?"

"I really don't care," Chelsea said, walking away. She didn't really know what Emily was getting at, only that she was making light of her own mother's murder. Of all the sisters she might have gotten, why did she have to get stuck with her?

By the next week, the highly charged tension in the household began to feel almost normal. Beatrice seemed genuinely pleased when she greeted Emily, but Emily reciprocated with bare politeness. Emily regularly strong-armed Chelsea or thumbed her nose at Lauren, except when Jonathan was nearby, at which time she'd water down her routine. Jonathan always backed Emily, and though Lauren might not have been good at the game at one time, turning the other cheek was getting to be habit.

"Why do you suppose I was such a brat?" Lauren asked Fern one day, trying to play amateur therapist and perhaps get a handle on Emily's behavior.

It took Fern a few moments before she answered. "I always believed you wanted a father. Being tough and bold and outspoken was a way to fight the pain, maybe the fear, too. Mother didn't much like my analysis. She said it was a bunch of psychobabble. Who knows, maybe she was right. Of course, if she agreed, she would have been admitting she was human, that despite her mothering skills, there was a hole the size of San Francisco in your life." After a pause, she added, "Why do you ask?"

"Just wondering is all," Lauren said. Was there a correlation? Lauren had apparently wanted the father who died in a car accident even more desperately than she remembered. And despite all the love Chelsea got from Lauren and Fern, didn't she practically jump right into Jonathan's pocket when he came along? Emily was different, of course. She was longing for her mother.

The day Lauren couldn't find the gold necklace Jonathan had given her, she could no longer turn the other cheek. She specifically recalled laying it on the counter in her dressing room the night before, but when she looked for it, it wasn't there. She pulled the place apart—looking through the drawers, the closet, along the floor, even in the adjoining bedroom. She asked Chelsea, but she hadn't seen it.

Finally, though dreading a confrontation with Emily, she knocked on her bedroom door. Not having been in her room since she'd hung the new black curtains, Lauren was taken aback when the door opened and she saw the apple cores, banana skins, empty juice bottles, half-eaten bags of food, papers, and books littering the bed and floor. Still, she stayed with her mission.

"I can't seem to find my gold chain necklace," she said. "The one your dad gave me."

"So?"

"I was wondering . . . have you seen it?"

"Uh-uh." Emily shrugged her shoulders dismissively, and Lauren stood there, looking into her dark, cold eyes, knowing in her heart that her stepdaughter had the necklace. "Well, if that's all?" the girl said, starting to close the door.

But Lauren's arm reached out to stop it. "Emily, if you have it, I want it."

"Look, I said I haven't seen it." Emily swung around toward her pigsty of a room and said, "But feel free to search. Maybe you want to look in the bag of pretzels."

"Why can't we get through to one another, Emily? Tell me what I'm doing wrong?"

Emily looked away. "Is that all?" she asked again.

Lauren shook her head, sighing. "Actually, no. I want you to clean this room."

"I like it the way it is, but if it bothers you that much, why don't *you* clean it?"

"Uh-uh, not a chance," Lauren said.

"Too bad. Then I guess you'll have no other choice but to go and squeal to my father."

Emily not only didn't care if Lauren complained to Jonathan, she seemed to encourage it—maybe to highlight the fact that Lauren couldn't handle her alone. But all the more reason she wouldn't give her the satisfaction. "And cause him to be ill?" she said. "No, I think I'll spare him."

"In that case, don't complain," she said. "Now I'll ask one more time, is that all?"

Lauren simply turned and walked out—there was nothing more to say. Emily had to have taken the necklace—where else could it have gone? The next morning after the children left for school, Lauren went upstairs and stood at the threshold of Emily's bedroom, prepared to search it. But after a few false starts, she gave up.

She wasn't really sure why—was it the funky smell of the room that made her squeamish or the repugnance she felt over the idea of invading someone else's space? Or maybe it was the fear of finding out something so bad about her stepdaughter that she'd be forced to go to Jonathan? But with respect to the room, Beatrice would be coming in a couple of days. Lauren would speak to her about getting Emily to help clean it up.

Chapter Five

Now added to Lauren's to-do list was to pick up
Emily from school once a week and drive her to
her ninety-minute appointment with her therapist,
at which time, Lauren would go to the Foodtown
across the way to do her weekly grocery shopping.
Coincidentally, this was also Chelsea's gymnastics
day, and Lauren arranged with the coach for
Chelsea to stay an additional hour to practice
until she could get back to pick her up. Though
Lauren initially looked at the driving time to and
from Dr. Greenly's office as an opportunity for
them to get dialogue going, she soon became
less optimistic.

It was stressful just trying to find a safe and
appropriate subject to talk about, something that
wouldn't put them immediately at odds. She hesitated to ask much about therapy, having already
been warned by Dr. Greenly that theirs was to be
a private relationship between doctor and patient,
and for her or Jonathan to attempt to intrude
would only compromise it.

But that particular Wednesday when Lauren

picked Emily up at school, she saw her leaning forward, ducking, apparently giving directions to the driver of a black car. The driver who she could see only from the back was wearing a blue baseball cap. She tooted the horn for Emily, unintentionally startling the driver, and he moved along.

"What was that about?" Lauren asked as Emily got inside.

Though she had a whole slew of pretty skirts, Lauren saw that Emily was once again wearing her jeans and boots. "Just a guy wanting to know which way to the principal's office."

Lauren nodded, thinking of warning her about the dangers of talking to strangers but hesitated, knowing that such advice to a nearly twelve-year-old was not apt to be taken well, particularly coming from Lauren. Besides, Emily had stayed on the sidewalk, hadn't gone anywhere near the car. Did Lauren expect her to ignore the fellow? "I noticed how you kept back, keeping a good distance from the car," Lauren said. "I like how you handled that."

Emily sighed deeply. "Really? Well, if that's the case, next time I'll be sure to stick my head in the driver's window. Oh, wait," she said, her finger touching her chin, "maybe that's only supposed to be on Be Friendly to Strangers week?"

Okay, so her comment hadn't been exactly subtle. The important thing was that Emily was clearly aware of what not to do. That she wanted to torture Lauren was another issue. So ignoring the sarcasm, she moved on. "Well, how's it going with the kids in school?" she asked.

Emily shrugged. The week before she had come home from school looking disheveled. Though she admitted she'd been in a fight, she refused to discuss it and insisted that Jonathan—who wanted nothing more than to rush down to the principal to straighten it out—keep out of it. Jonathan backed off.

"Well, what about classes?" Lauren asked, getting nowhere still. "Because if you're behind at all, I mean with you being in Bateman so long . . . well, the schooling there is apt to have been inferior. In any event, I . . . or your father could help. Or even a tutor if you'd rather. The thing is, don't be afraid to say."

Emily sighed pitifully. "Tell me, Lauren, does your battery ever run dry?"

So Lauren stopped trying to find a neutral subject. Instead she turned on the radio to some light music, and ignored the sneer it produced from Emily. It wasn't until Lauren remembered the garage door key that she'd had tucked in an envelope in her purse for a few days that she decided to take another stab at it. "Your father asked me to deliver a key to Candlewood Terrace."

Emily's attention was direct and immediate. "You mean, to my house?"

"Yes," Lauren said, not missing the way Emily claimed it as her house. "You know, your father rented it out recently. The tenant has already moved in." Emily nodded as if she knew, which made Lauren aware that though she seemed to be uninvolved and disinterested in the goings-on of the household, she had been listening. "Well, it seems Daddy forgot to attach one of the keys to the set."

"Yeah, so?"

"So I thought since it's not far out of our way, we could stop by and deliver it on our way home, leave it in the mailbox. That is, if you don't mind."

"Why should I?"

"Well, I don't know. Just that you haven't been there in a couple of years. I thought perhaps it might stir up memories that you weren't ready for."

"No, I want to go," she said, and though her words sounded sure, Lauren spotted certain signs of apprehensiveness, like the way she was chewing on her lower lip. But she had said yes, even reminding Lauren as soon as she emerged from her appointment. So they picked up Chelsea at gymnastics and headed to Candlewood Terrace. They pulled up at the brown clapboard house and big yard and ranch fence and long, empty double driveway leading to a detached garage—apparently Gordon Cummings wasn't home. Where the street met the driveway there was a mailbox; Lauren took the envelope from her purse and held it out to her. "Do you want to do it?"

Emily opened the door of the car and stood up holding tight to the car, staring at the house ... she was anxious all right, but it was as though she had signed some kind of contract with herself and wasn't about to back out. "This isn't necessary, Emily," Lauren said, beginning to get frightened that she had done the wrong thing to bring her.

But Emily didn't answer or waver. She moved away from the car and stood looking at the grounds before finally walking to the box and dropping the envelope inside. When she raised her head again, she was facing the house directly across the street and her eyes suddenly widened as a smile came to her lips. Lauren sighed, relieved—the tension of the moment was over.

Turning to see what prompted the mood switch, Lauren spotted a woman running down her front lawn heading toward Emily. Following behind, while stuffing an arm through a sweater sleeve as the storm door banged behind her, was a girl with two long, copper-colored ponytails. The girl looked to be younger than Emily.

The woman was tiny, probably a size three. She had unruly red hair and freckles ... and a cigarette was dangling from her lips. She flung the cigarette to the ground as she got nearer and, grinning, shouted out, "Oh, good Lord, Emily, I can't believe it's you!" Reaching her finally, she threw her arms around her, and though Emily's response was somewhat stiff and inhibited, she was clearly pleased.

Lauren watched for a few moments, listening to the woman ooh and aah over how big Emily had gotten. "Bigger than me!" she exclaimed, laughing. "And will you look at that wild haircut? I guess we've got to be happy you didn't go off and dye it purple!"

Lauren opened the car door and got out, with Chelsea following right behind her. Once the little red-haired girl took over Emily's attention, Lauren came forward and extended her hand to the woman. "Hi, I'm Lauren Grant," she said.

It took a few moments for it to register, then the woman's hazel eyes grew large. "Oh, gosh, yeah." She stuck out a thin hand as she studied her. "I heard Jonathan had remarried—" Then after a pause, she said, "If I seem rude, honest I don't mean to be. My name is Carla Abbot. Nancy and I were friends . . ."

Lauren nodded. "That's okay, I understand." Then she turned to Emily and the girl Carla had called Francine, who were now in a huddle talking. "It looks like the girls were, too."

"You bet. Emily was like a big sister to that one," Carla said, smiling and shaking her head at them. Lauren glanced down at Chelsea, who was looking at the whole festive scene grimly. Lauren reached out and with a hand on her shoulder brought her beside her. "This is my daughter Chelsea."

"Now how'd you guess I love that name, Chelsea?" the woman asked, seeming to be one of those people who was a natural with kids. After talking with her for a minute, she looked up at Lauren. "I did hear that Emily had come home. You know how news gets around? And I did want to call or stop by, it's just that I felt funny doing it. You know, with Nancy not being around, and me not having contact with Emily in so long. And well, under the circumstances . . ."

She was referring to her, of course, the new stepmother in Emily's life, and Lauren said, "Oh, no, please, I want you to feel free to call or stop by to see Emily. I'm delighted to meet someone she's so happy to see. Since she's been home, well, there's really been no one—that is, aside from her father, of course."

"Well, no more happy that we are to see her. Just wait till Louie gets home—he's my husband. Emily was always one of his favorites." She gestured toward the house. "Will you just look at my manners? Listen, would you like something— coffee, maybe a glass of soda pop? You just name it."

Lauren glanced at her watch—it was nearly four-thirty. "Oh, I wish I could, really . . . but I can't. I have groceries in back. Besides which Jonathan has this bad habit—he tends to start growling if he doesn't get his dinner on time."

She nodded her head, making the kind of face one woman makes to another to register understanding, and Francine called out, "Mom, can Emily stay to dinner? Please."

Carla looked immediately to Lauren, her eyes wide and appealing. "Gee, we'd love to have her. I can even drop her off later—at about eight o'clock, that is, unless you want her earlier—"

And she was just about to say no, to suggest that maybe another time might be better, some day after school or on a weekend or Francine could even come to their house to visit, when Emily came up to her and asked, "Can I, Lauren?"

After all her refusals to acknowledge Lauren's existence, let alone that she had an ounce of authority, Emily was now asking her permission to do something. And with such an entreating tone, Lauren wondered if Emily had asked to let her get behind the steering wheel of the car, she mightn't consider it as well. Fortunately, what she was asking was nothing so dangerous, but it was her chance to make headway with her stepdaughter. "All right, you can stay."

As the two girls rushed off to be by themselves, Carla noticed Chelsea's unhappy face, and said to Lauren, "You know, the little one's perfectly welcome—"

"No. Thank you, but no. Another time."

And there would be a price to pay for that, which began as soon as she and Chelsea got back in the car and drove toward home. "Why not?" Chelsea demanded.

"Because Emily apparently was close to these neighbors, and she hasn't seen them in a long time. So it's a very special time for them, almost like a reunion. Do you understand, darling?"

If she did, she wasn't letting on.

More surprisingly, Lauren had to contend with Jonathan who was suddenly panicked at the idea of his daughter not being under the protective seclusion of her own backyard. "She's not a baby," Lauren argued as she got a bunch of salad fixings from the refrigerator and carried them to the counter. "Get used to it because before you know it, she'll be out gallivanting all over town."

"What does that mean?"

"Only that we can't keep a lock and chain on her. Jonathan, you should have seen how thrilled she was when she saw Francine and her mother, how eager she was to stay and visit. Now how could I have possibly said no?"

Which seemed to puncture his resolve some, since his end goal was always to make his girls happy. He sat down in a kitchen chair, leaning it back and shaking his head. "I don't like it, Lauren, I'd rather she bring her friends here."

In the two weeks Emily had been home, this was the first indication that she had a friend or even wanted one, which was all the more reason to encourage it. "Chelsea goes to her activities, I've never heard you object to it."

"That's different, it's supervised—it's not kids running around neighborhoods by themselves."

And of course that was true. There were no neighbors around where they lived—at least none in close proximity, and even then, no children Chelsea's age. So when Chelsea went to a play group, it was always with Lauren tagging along. But still, that wouldn't go on forever. "This area is safe, Jonathan," she said, knowing full well he was thinking of the one time it wasn't safe. But she went on. "So we must trust them, we must ease up, at least, if we're not to smother them."

"I do trust them, implicitly. It's just the rest of the world I have trouble with."

"But you know the Abbots."

"Actually, I don't, at least not well. Carla was Nancy's friend, and then the kids played together. But Carla always struck me as kind of a careless mother."

Lauren thought about the light sweater Francine had put on to rush outside in the cold and Carla's smoking. So maybe Carla wasn't perfect, but it hardly qualified her as unfit, and she clearly liked Emily. Besides, Emily was nearly twelve, not a baby, and she was only visiting, not going there to live. Lauren took a chair next to Jonathan and took his hand in hers. "Darling, listen to me. Please. Among the many things I love about you is your total devotion to your family. But you must fight this urge to overprotect."

Emily, Emily, Emily. Chelsea rolled the name over her tongue after standing at the doorway listening for a few minutes to the talk going on between Mommy and Daddy. Everyone was always talking or worrying or fighting about Emily. Ugly, bald, douche-bag Emily who never once did the dishes since she'd been home, who answered Chelsea's mother back regularly, who never did what she was told, who never acted nice, and who never got in trouble over any of it.

*   *   *

Carla drove Emily home, and as soon as she saw the electronic gates go up to enter, she got spooked, refusing to go farther, even though Lauren assured her it was safe to drive through and Emily and Francine prodded her from the back seat. "Uh-uh, no, I can't do it," she said. "Don't ask me to."

Finally Lauren ran outside, down the driveway to the open gate, arriving there breathless. She went up to the driver's window. "What's wrong?"

"I guess just the idea of those huge gates slamming down after me freaks me."

With teasing in her voice Lauren said, "They do open both ways, you know."

"Oh, I know. So do prison gates. Oh, gosh, now you're going to think I'm trying to put down your house—or worse, that I've been to jail. Neither is true, honest—"

"It's okay, Carla," Lauren said. "What would you say if I fixed it so the gate wouldn't close?"

"Could you?"

Lauren pressed in some numbers, then closing the box, looked at Carla. "Voilà!"

Carla, still looking a little uncomfortable, drove Lauren and the kids down the long driveway to the house. When they got to the door, Lauren asked her inside for tea, but she begged off, issuing her own invitation. "Why don't you come to my house; in fact, what about tomorrow after school? You can bring Emily and that adorable little blondie of yours. We have a heated, walk-in bird coop out back—all the kids love it. We keep mostly pigeons, but there's probably a half-dozen other varieties if you look hard enough. You know, injured guys we take in to fix or those left behind in the rush south.''

Lauren didn't even pause—aside from the kids' activities and her occasional library or PTO meetings, or do-it-yourself project she was into, what else was there to do? She agreed. With Carla being so close to Emily, she might be able to help Lauren get through to her, get Emily to trust her. Besides which Carla was not at all like the other mothers she'd met since moving to Elmwood Valley, and she found the difference refreshing. Goodness, who else did she know who operated a bird sanctuary? It didn't dawn on her until later—the irony of it, that Carla, Nancy's friend, should become her friend, too.

"Just what am I getting into here, Angel? Don't I even get a clue before being taken to the gallows?" Jonathan asked, allowing Chelsea to lead him by the hand upstairs. She stopped right outside Emily's bedroom, and she could feel her heart beat with anticipation. She had never told on anyone before—in fact, she had always looked upon it as a chicken thing to do. But this time she didn't care one bit—in fact, she couldn't wait to get her big sister in trouble.

"I need to show you something," she said, turning the doorknob, then pushing the door open to Emily's gross, disgusting room. And by the way Daddy looked around, she could see he wasn't happy with what he was seeing. Still, she wasn't about to let him stop there. She led him over to the corner of the carpet—lying there was a potato chip swarming with ants. She pointed at it. "See that?"

Though he looked sort of disgusted, he said, "Thank you for showing me this, Chelsea. You did the right thing." Then he escorted her out of the room and downstairs, getting there in time to meet her mother coming in the front door, with Emily following. Right off, he said to Emily, "Please go to the den with your sister. Lauren and I need to talk." With that, he took hold of Lauren's elbow and steered her up the stairs.

"Looks like he's mad at her," Emily said, watching them go off.

"If I were you, I'd be more worried about myself," Chelsea said, and though her voice sounded snotty and sure, it was just a big lie. She felt an odd sinking in her chest, not at all sure she liked how this whole thing was turning out.

He had just about ambushed her when she walked in the house, but once she got to Emily's room and he pushed open the door, it was clear to Lauren what it was about. Apparently for some reason he had gone inside . . .

"What I want to know is, did you see this?" he asked, gesturing inside.

"I did. Last night."

"So?"

"Of course I told her to clean it."

"But as you can see, she didn't."

She sighed. She really hadn't wanted it to get to this, but of course that's where it was, and she had no other choice. "Jonathan, she refused. In fact, she suggested I tell you."

"Then why didn't you?"

"Because I don't like the idea of bothering you with this kind of thing. And it plays right into her hands to pit us against each other."

Jonathan walked into the room, stopped and pointed down. "Come, I want you to see this, Lauren." She came beside him and looked down at the swarm of ants . . .

"Oh, God," she said, jumping back, then beginning to stamp the ants with her foot. "I'm going to murder that—" she began, but as soon as the words were out, she knew how wrong they were. The horror on Jonathan's face confirmed that. "Darling, please," she began again, upset that she even needed to explain herself. "I obviously didn't mean it like that. But like you, I'm upset."

He sighed, then in a concerned voice said, "This is all too much for you, isn't it?"

"What does that mean?"

"Only that you need more help around here. I'm sure Beatrice would be glad to—"

She was appalled—not just by Emily's room but by her arrogance—and she was infuriated that Jonathan didn't see it the same way. "Damn it, I don't need Beatrice," she said. "And for pity's sake, Jonathan, this isn't really about keeping a clean house, is it? It's about Emily, her total disregard for our feelings. At the very least, why aren't you insisting she march up here and clean this up?"

"Because unlike you, Lauren, I don't see this as some kind of moral dilemma. I could care less who cleans the room, only that it gets clean. And if doing it is going to create a problem for our daughter, something she doesn't need more of at this juncture in her life, why not simply get it cleaned by a professional?"

Lauren could have argued about it being a lesson in hygiene, responsibility, civility, and a whole slew of other reasons why parents have always nagged their kids to do things that would have been far easier to do themselves, but she didn't. Perhaps she *was* nitpicking. When she was Emily's age, wasn't her room a disaster? And though she got better at those things with age, her apartment in the city was hardly a page out of *Good Housekeeping.* Jonathan's way of seeing it wasn't totally unreasonable—didn't Emily have enough pressures these days without making this into another? There was the adjustment at home, school, not getting along with classmates . . .

Besides, there were more serious issues to pounce upon if one wanted to pounce. She reached down to lift a couple of things off the floor to toss out, then gathered up the dirty dishes, holding back a strong urge to be sick as she was doing it. "Okay, Jonathan, maybe you're right about this one," she said.

"Does it mean we can end this ridiculous battle?"

"First let me tell you why I was here last night." He waited, and she stopped picking up and folded her arms at her chest. "I couldn't find the gold necklace you gave me. I'd looked everywhere. So I knocked on Emily's door to see what she knew about it."

"And had she seen it?"

"No. At least, that's what she told me."

"Are you saying you don't believe her?"

She took a deep breath, then let it go. "Yes, I guess that's what I am saying."

And though she thought it would be impossible for him to be reasonable following an accusation like that against his daughter, once again she was wrong. "In that case, let's find out," he said. Though she'd had ethical difficulties with searching Emily's space, if he had those same qualms, he was able to put them aside. He hunted around the room—under the bed, the mattress, on her dresser and desk, and nightstand, even going through her drawers and closet. Finally done and coming up empty, he said, "All right, Lauren, I didn't much enjoy that, but it had to be done, so I did it. Now does that satisfy you?"

She nodded—how could she possibly stand there and say it didn't? But she felt confused and exhausted, as though she'd been ground through a mill. He came over, took her in his arms, and she gratefully sank against his chest.

"Will you do me a favor, please?"

"What?" she asked.

"Share with me. If something bothers you, let me in on it—maybe I can get it to shrink back to size. That's why I'm here." He smiled, then pressed his lips to her forehead. "Now I'm going downstairs to see our girls. Are you coming?"

She shook her head, then releasing herself from his embrace, she headed to a heap of magazines and papers on the floor, kneeling to pick them up. "I'll just finish up here."

Chapter Six

The man standing in front of the school had dark-stained bags beneath his eyes and a thin gray brush of a mustache. And though he looked harmless enough, like a teacher or staff member, the way Emily was shifting her eyes as though looking for an escape made Lauren think otherwise. Lauren, arriving at the school and quickly appraising the situation, pulled her car into a no-parking zone, cut the engine, and got out. "Stay put," she said to Chelsea who was in the back seat.

"Excuse me," she called out as she got closer to them. Emily looked over and, seeing it was Lauren, appeared relieved; the man sighed annoyance as he muttered something to himself. "Hi, I'm Lauren Grant," she said. "Emily's stepmother." It was said both as a statement and question, clearly asking him to identify himself.

He reached into his rumpled gray overcoat pocket, withdrew a badge, and held it up for her. "Detective Kneeland. Elmwood Valley police."

Despite Jonathan's warning the week before, a

policeman was the last person she expected to see. "Oh," she said finally.

"Look, ma'am, no big deal. I got word that the little girl was back home, so I just thought I'd ask her a few questions. See if she remembered anything new."

Lauren put her hand on Emily's arm and told her to go to the car, which she did, then Lauren looked back at the detective. "It's my understanding that my husband asked that you not question Emily. You have no right to do this."

Now he tipped back on his heels and ran two fingers along his mustache. "Well, that's where you're wrong, Mrs. Grant. The police have every right."

"Oh, is that so? To question a minor, and without her parents' consent?"

"Sure enough. With an order from the court."

"Are you saying you have one?"

His wide jaw tightened. "I didn't want it to get to that, but if you force the issue, you'll see how quick I get one."

"Why?" she asked, deciding to appeal to his compassion. "Why are you doing this? I'm sure you're aware of what Emily's been through. Finally things are looking up for her and what do you do? You rush over to put on the pressure, despite that it might set her back. And for something long past."

"That something you refer to so easily was the taking of a life, Mrs. Grant. And it wasn't so long ago that Nancy's family has forgotten it. They live in New Hampshire, you know, farm people, decent people. And they miss and mourn her ... likely will for the rest of their lives. Nancy Grant was in her mid-thirties when she was killed, a young woman with a lot to live for."

Lauren had never really considered Nancy's family—other than her immediate family of Jonathan and Emily. Jonathan, of course, was now Lauren's husband, in a sense relinquishing his position in his ex-wife's family. With Emily, though, it was different—no matter who would play a significant part in her life, she would always and forever be Nancy's daughter.

It was a sobering thought, and Lauren had to make sure that in trying to help Emily to recover, she and Jonathan not ask that she give that up. "I'm sorry," she said finally. "That was incredibly insensitive of me. I guess what I meant to say is, we can't bring Nancy back. So why are we rehashing how it happened with a little girl who is having such a hard time dealing with it?"

"You seem to forget that there's someone still walking around out there, and he's free as a bird, which means that he might decide to do it again: to my wife, to my daughter, to the old lady or little kid living down the street, even to you or your kids, Mrs. Grant. Don't think for a New York minute that Mr. Grant isn't aware of that. I've seen that fortress he's built around his new family. Extreme measures maybe, but you sure in hell know why it's up there."

"We have to put Emily first," Lauren said.

"Her father and I don't want her hurt any more than she's been already. Besides, Detective, she can't help you. I'm sure my husband told the police, she hasn't regained any memories connected to the murder."

"Right, I understand. So it's a long shot. Maybe she can't remember a face or the confrontation itself, but with a little prodding she might be able to recall something that happened earlier that day, or the days leading up to it. Maybe while driving home from school with her mother, passing a car, seeing a stranger in the next yard as they were going into the house? Anything at all out of the ordinary, anything that might give me a new direction."

"Don't you think she's dwelled on it enough—" she began, but he talked right over her.

"If there's anyone who's dwelled on it, I guess it's me. You know, I've got facts about this case that could fill a computer disk ... but this is my computer, ma'am, right here," he said, his finger tapping his forehead. "I don't forget a thing, and nothing gets deleted until I say so ... and I'm not saying so. Not yet."

Realizing it was useless to argue, she started to go, but then he turned his tack. "You know, Mrs. Grant, in the long run the little girl will feel good about cooperating. After all, we're not talking about her witnessing some stranger murdered, we're talking about her mother, right in her own house. And yeah, sure, I agree, it's a stretch ... As you pointed out, significant time has passed between the murder and now, maybe the clues are too cold to lead anywhere. But till all avenues have been covered, I've got to pursue it."

He was relentless, but there was something to his argument ... What if Emily did have knowledge that she wasn't aware of, something that would lead the police to finding the killer? And what if she never got it out, would she someday blame Lauren and Jonathan for not encouraging her to cooperate? For letting her mother's murderer walk away scot-free? "Look, I'm not quite sure how I feel about this," she said, sighing. "In any event, I can't give my permission without first discussing it with her father. But I promise, I will talk to him."

He nodded, fingered his mustache. "Like I said, if we have to, we'll go to court. But I'll be frank with you, ma'am, your husband's a decent guy from what I see, respected in the community. I understand he's been through hell and back ... and the last thing I want is to bring the courts down on him."

Somehow it sounded more like a threat than a kindness.

She was still thinking about the detective when Carla placed the cup of tea in front of her—for herself, she poured a mug of black coffee. The kids stuffed a half-dozen peanut butter crackers in their jacket pockets and rushed outdoors to feed the birds, Chelsea being pulled along joylessly by Francine, who had been reminded twice by her mother that Chelsea was her guest. "Okay, you going to tell me what's wrong?" Carla said once the door slammed behind the kids.

"What makes you think something is?"

"Just that you seem preoccupied, like you left your mind out in the car."

She sighed, she supposed there was no reason she couldn't tell Carla—she as well as the entire town likely knew more about Nancy's murder than Lauren. "When I arrived at the school to pick up Emily, I found a detective with her, sort of an obnoxious guy, tries to give the impression he runs the police."

"Donald Kneeland. The description fits to a T. Dumb but hardworking and dedicated, an interesting mix. Elmwood Valley has a department made up of twelve cops, only three detectives— Kneeland is one of them. What did he want?"

"To talk to Emily, which he was trying to do when I arrived. She looked scared to death of him."

"Well, why wouldn't she be?" Carla shook her head angrily. "Jesus, why can't he leave that kid alone. Hasn't he already done enough damage to last a lifetime?"

Lauren's reaction was slow in coming, but finally she said, "What exactly does that mean?"

"Just how he wouldn't leave her alone after what had happened to Nancy. She must have told him a hundred times that she couldn't remember, but would he let it rest? It was when he actually came out and accused her of the crime that your husband went a little wild ... and put a stop to the whole thing."

"Accused her?"

"Emily." And Lauren still must have looked bewildered, because Carla qualified it. "Of Nancy's murder." Then, her voice lowering, "You didn't know?"

As the words penetrated, Lauren could feel herself grow cold and shaky. The surprise was twofold: Jonathan hadn't bothered to mention it, and why in the world would the police accuse a ten-year-old child of murder? She finally asked once she recovered her voice.

Carla lit a cigarette, putting out the match in an empty saucer on the table. "Because Elmwood Valley, as nice a town as it might seem, has a third-rate police force."

"But still, there must have been some reason that Detective Kneeland would have thought—"

"Oh, sure, he had his reasons. For one, whoever hit Nancy used Emily's baseball bat. So big deal, the bat was new—and according to Jonathan, it was right near the door in the kitchen when he left for work that morning, which would mean that anyone coming in could have seen and used it, then wiped off the fingerprints. Apparently it had been wiped clean. And then there was the drive home from school ... you see, that day Emily was let go early—"

"I know about that."

"Okay. Well as I understand it, Nancy stopped at the pharmacy to pick up some bandages and antiseptic for Emily's scratches, and one of the clerks at the pharmacy overheard them arguing. Okay, you're a mother. You tell me—is it so unusual for a kid to act up in a store and mouth off at her mother? Or a pregnant mother to get impatient with her kid?

"Being bawled out or even whacked once is hardly what I'd consider a motive for a kid to want to murder her mother. Would you? Also, Kneeland found no prints or other evidence around the house or property to indicate that anyone outside the family had been there. Which simply means that the killer was careful—after all, we already know he wiped off the bat ... But when an cop finds nothing, he tends to make what little he has into something it isn't."

As usual, Emily got away with it. It was her mother who had finally cleaned up the pigsty. And though nobody asked the question or mentioned it, somehow Emily figured out who told on her—Chelsea was sure of that by the way those dark mean eyes stared at her over the breakfast table.

Emily hadn't hit her yet, but she taunted her, and a couple of times when she thought Chelsea was about to run and squeal to her father, she'd grab her and hold her wrists and arms so tight, she once gave her a bruise on her arm. So that afternoon Chelsea was relieved that Francine was there with them. This way she got to hold the bluebird with the toothpick leg splinter and feed the pigeons, and even follow the older girls around, listening to what they said without fear of Emily's anger.

Not that their conversation was all that fascinating—at least, not until a green pickup truck pulled into the driveway of 35 Candlewood Terrace. Emily—looking like all her blood had rushed to her face—raced down to the edge of Francine's property to get a better look at the guy behind the wheel. Francine and Chelsea followed behind, then squatted next to her.

"There he is," Francine said, as though they had already talked about the new tenant across the street. While Emily looked him over, Francine went on. "His name's Gordon. He's got one of those queer haircuts with the ponytail that hangs over his shirt collar." Gordon got out of his truck, slammed the door, and began to walk toward the mailbox. Toward them.

He was big, with long arms and legs, and though he wasn't so bad to look at, he looked disjointed, like a pile of odd parts that didn't quite fit together. "He looks like a monster man," Chelsea said, wanting to add something to the older girl's conversation. "Don't you think he's kinda scary?"

Francine looked at her like she might agree. "Yeah, but my mom says he's nice."

Emily turned a stern face to Francine. "How does she know that?"

Francine shrugged. "I guess she knows him."

"You mean, she knew him before he moved in?"

"I don't know. She talked like she did, but I

never saw him before. She went over and said hello the day he moved in, but you know my mom, she's the friendly type." She rolled her eyes as if to put down her mother, then, her voice becoming concerned, asked, "Does it bother you he's living there?"

Emily's eyes went back to Gordon who was taking a magazine and a stack of envelopes out of the mailbox that was now his to use. "I guess some. At times I wish I still lived there, but then other times, I think maybe it's better I don't."

"I wish you did," Francine said.

"Maybe I'll move back someday."

"Could you?"

"Sure, that Gordon whatever-his-name-is only rents. But the house still belongs to me and my father."

Francine looked across the street, then in a whispered giggle said, "Wow, Emily, will you look at the way he's staring over here? Do you think he heard what we were saying?"

Gordon was looking all right, but there was someone else looking, too . . . though Chelsea was probably the only one who noticed him. A black car was parked about two houses down the street: the guy in the driver's seat was wearing a blue baseball cap.

Chelsea had made it a point to grab the front seat before Emily did. Now she turned to her mother and said, "Mommy, can Emily move back to her old house if she wants?"

"No. It's being rented."

"But I mean if that person moves out. Can she move back then?"

"By then Daddy and I hope to have found a buyer for it."

Chelsea turned to Emily in back and stuck out her tongue. "See? Told you."

Though Lauren was trying not to let the kids feel the brunt of her mood, all she could think about was the conversation she'd just had with Carla. And the more she thought about the business with the police, the more upset it got her. Why hadn't Jonathan told her, why did she have to hear it like this? What about that sharing he talked about, didn't it apply here?

The only reason Chelsea had been so brazen in the car was that her mother was there to save her—now, she sat in her room, thinking it wasn't such a good idea after all. As soon as they'd gotten upstairs away from Mom's earshot, Emily had chased her to her room, and while Chelsea stood in a corner, cowering, Emily took her dalmatian off the shelf and stomped on it with her big ugly boots.

"Next time, stay out of my room and out of my business!" Emily said, referring to what had happened the night before.

"I wasn't—"

"Don't lie, Goldilocks. It'll only get worse for you if you do."

After sitting in her room a while thinking about

it, Chelsea got the courage to go and knock on Emily's door. When the door opened, she just sort of held her breath and let the words come out. "I'm sorry I squealed," she said.

Emily looked at her. "Yeah, me, too."

"I won't do it again."

Emily nodded and her eyes seemed to soften, or was it just Chelsea's wishful thinking? Emily didn't say anything nasty, which Chelsea decided was a plus. Taking advantage of the moment, she gestured to the jewelry maker, still sitting in the same place on the shelf. "I bet that would be a fun thing to do ... I mean, if you ever decide to open it."

Emily's eyes chilled. She slammed the door in Chelsea's face, and stunned by the force of it, Chelsea fell to the floor.

Lauren had managed to keep it inside through dinner and until the children were finally in their rooms, at which time she blurted it out. "Carla told me Emily had been a suspect for Nancy's murder. Why didn't you tell me?"

It took Jonathan a moment to recover from what sounded even to her like an accusation, and when he did, he brought down the newspaper he was reading and looked at her. "Oh, so that's what you do these days, gallivant around town, gossip about Emily?"

"That's not fair," she said, and it wasn't—in one swoop, she suddenly found herself on the defensive. "Carla was not bad-mouthing Emily. In fact, she's one of her biggest fans. It only came up because I was so upset to find the detective—" His eyes narrowed and she sighed. "Detective Kneeland. When I got to the school, he was there trying to talk to her."

He sat forward, slapping the newspaper against the coffee table. "That bastard, he has no right!"

"Are you sure about that? According to him, he could easily ask the court for the right to question Emily."

"In his dreams. No, not this time. Not with Emily's history of mental illness. Dr. Strickler will write an affidavit, and Dr. Greenly will be happy to testify—"

"How do you know?" she asked, and Jonathan looked at her. "I mean, how do you know the doctor will testify? Maybe she doesn't view it as harmful to Emily."

"I've already spoken to her about this."

Again, she was surprised. "You spoke to her? When?"

Jonathan sighed. "Look, Strickler gave me those referrals when he first called to say Emily would be coming home. He stressed the importance of her having immediate follow-up. So naturally, the first thing I did was to call around—"

"Wait, stop! Do you mean to say that you had already spoken to the doctor?"

"Yes, but—"

"Then would you please tell me what was the purpose of giving me those names? Was it just a practice session designed to make me think I'm part of the decision-making around here?"

"Better watch yourself, darling, you're beginning to sound paranoid. So, yes, okay, I spoke to Dr. Greenly and was in total agreement with her philosophy, but is it so wrong that I wanted your input? The fact is, I told her both my wife and myself would be choosing Emily's doctor. If you had come up with another name, it would have been fine, we would have gone to see that therapist as well."

"But you suggested her—"

"Didn't I have a right to suggest?"

What was happening now was what always seemed to happen in disagreements between them. Somehow the details and interpretations got twisted and out of order once Jonathan got his hands on them. But she didn't let it go. "Jonathan, answer me. Why didn't you tell me that the police suspected Emily of Nancy's murder?"

He leaned his head back, his hand raised to his forehead, his eyes closed, as though his steam had suddenly ran out. "I couldn't, Lauren," he said, finally looking at her. "I couldn't bear to remember it, let alone talk about it. It was a nightmare. Try to imagine what it was like watching the terror on my daughter's face when she realized what that detective was implying.

"How do you think I felt knowing I hadn't protected her from that? First her mother is killed right before her eyes, then she's forced to listen to that crap! Okay, so it was a murder investigation, so maybe I should have expected that sort of thing. But I didn't. Not with a ten-year-old kid. And when he and the rest of the police turned on her, I just wanted to rip those bastards to pieces . . ."

Seeing the old pain twist through his features, it brought tears to Lauren's eyes—she moved closer, putting her hands up to his face. "Oh, don't, Jonathan, please don't torture yourself like this. It's not healthy, and it's not justified. As much as you would like to, you don't have control over the whole universe. I just wish I could understand why they would suspect Emily."

Calmer now, he took her hands from his face, then clasping them in his, he kissed them. Meeting her eyes, he said, "She was in the house at the time of the murder. For them, that was reason enough. They would have accused me just as easily if I hadn't had an alibi."

"What about the window? I thought one of the downstairs windows was tampered with?"

"It was, but they were willing to overlook that. If necessary, they were willing to say she was actually the one who tampered with it. To make it look good."

"A ten-year-old?" she asked, incredulous.

"Don't you get it, Lauren? Kneeland was fumbling around, trying to close the case. He's a joke. It was the first homicide he had ever dealt with, the first the town had in twenty-two years."

"I'm sure he's quite inexperienced. But do you think it'd be so terrible if he asked Emily a few questions, to see if she knew anything that could be used? I'm sure we could arrange to be there, or for that matter, Dr. Greenly could even be present."

He shook his head, adamant. "He questioned her, Lauren—back when it all happened. He showed her pictures. She didn't remember then, or didn't want to remember—whichever. And because she couldn't help his goddamned case, he dumped it on her—the result being she spent almost two years in a psychiatric institution. No way, this cop is not going to screw with her mind again."

And though the detective's argument had sounded reasonable that afternoon, it no longer did. Not now that she knew the whole story.

"I'm going to go telephone Mike," he said, standing. "I want a restraining order issued, keeping Kneeland and the rest of the force away from Emily. And until it's accomplished, I don't think Emily should be allowed to take the school bus to and from school. Darling, will you please see that you get to her school before dismissal? I don't want her waiting unattended again."

She nodded. He had asked, not demanded or accused her of anything, so why did she feel as though she'd just been struck? She admired her husband's strength and intelligence and self-confidence, but not for the first time a part of her wished he wouldn't be so damn sure of everything.

"What is it, honey," he said, apparently getting

some vibes from her. "Do you mind picking her up?"

"No, of course not," she assured him, and of course she didn't.

Lying in bed later after lovemaking, she felt marvelously at peace—her back against Jonathan's chest, he held her close, their bodies fitting as though they'd been poured into a mold. And she reflected on the little lies he had told . . . or, maybe better put, his personal spin on the truth. Though of course it bothered her—how could it not?—she did understand. She certainly understood his wish to shield his daughter from the police. But now, with Detective Kneeland determined to pursue the case, was the nightmare about to begin all over again?

She felt suddenly cold—she reached down and pulled the quilt to her chin. "Jonathan," she said.

Silence.

"Darling, are you awake?"

But there was still no answer. The question would have to keep until morning.

Chapter Seven

Jonathan was in the bathroom shaving when Lauren woke the next morning and got out of bed, remembering the question. She came up in back of him, wrapping her arms around him—he smiled, then winked at her in the mirror. "Darling," she said, rubbing her chin against his back, "how were you able to get the police to leave Emily alone? I mean, back when it happened."

He moved the razor to do his upper lip, then looked at her reflection . . . "That's an odd question."

"I suppose it is. But I was just wondering—did they simply accept your decision and back off or did you go to court? I mean, being a murder investigation, I know the police have a lot of leeway when it comes to such serious crimes."

"Yeah, well, as it happened I didn't need to do anything. Emily made it easy. She tried to kill herself."

Lauren's arms dropped away from him. She stood there for a moment staring at him. "Oh, my God, Jonathan! How awful. Why didn't you tell me?"

He lowered his eyes for a moment, as though trying to contain himself, then he found her reflection again in the mirror. "Why? Why would I tell you that?"

"Because I love you, Jonathan, that's why. Because I'm your wife, Emily is my stepdaughter, we should share things, particularly important things—"

"Damn it, Lauren, what is it you want to share? You want me to share with you how I broke down the bathroom door to get to her, how she was laid out on the floor with at lump the size of a fist on her forehead, how I put her in the back seat of the car and drove at breakneck speed to try to get her to the hospital before she died? Or how she had to have her stomach pumped to get the pills out of her system? Better yet, would you like me to draw some pictures so you can show it around to the local mothers? What is it you want from me?"

She backed up toward the door, fighting tears getting ready to spill, but he turned, grabbing her hand, stopping her. He pulled a towel off the sink and wiped the shaving cream from his face, then gathered her in his arms, burying his face in her hair. "I'm sorry, Lauren, forgive me for laying that on you. I'm just so damned tired of this. All I want is for my family to be safe and happy and for the rest of the world to butt out. Is that asking too much?"

*   *   *

Emily had tried to take her own life. Shouldn't Lauren have known that? Why, because she would be doing something more to reach Emily? Wasn't she doing all she knew how to do now? Surely she would have been more apprehensive had she known, more leery of taking on the responsibility of a child who hurt so much she wanted to die. But then, what had Lauren thought, that Emily got shipped off to live in a psychiatric residence without cause? No, that had never occurred to her—at least not before last night. But wasn't that what her question to Jonathan this morning was about?

And she was off base, but now suddenly Lauren saw Emily as being far more delicate than she had thought, giving still more credence to Jonathan's absolute refusal to push her too hard. But weren't there other factors to consider: what about how Emily felt toward her and Chelsea, how she wanted them out of her father's life? Should she worry that she might become desperate again?

She didn't even know what to look for, the telltale signs that the professionals say occur before a suicide. So many questions now coming into focus, things she should have asked the doctor initially had she been better informed. Questions that she dared not ask Jonathan, who was so defensive when it came to his daughter. The likelihood being he would deny there was even cause for worry.

At eleven o'clock that morning, after dropping off Emily at school and attending a lengthy and tedious PTO fund-raiser meeting, she found herself sitting directly across the desk from Dr. Penelope Greenly. "First off, If want to thank you for squeezing me into your schedule on such short notice," she said.

Dr. Greenly nodded. "I try to accommodate. And by your voice, I took it to be urgent."

"I'm sorry if I gave that impression. If it is urgent, it is only for me. It's just that I've learned a few things I didn't know before, things about Emily."

Dr. Greenly's eyes behind her glasses were wide and waiting.

"Well, for example, I was totally unaware that Emily had attempted suicide."

"This concerns you?"

"Well, yes, of course. Shouldn't it?"

"Well ... we are hoping that all her therapy has made a difference," she said, her voice low and without passion. "That was then, this is now, her mother had just been murdered, she had been a witness to it."

"Yes, but what about now? I think it was mentioned at our earlier meeting that Emily is not at all pleased about her father's marriage to me, and she's made her displeasure no secret. I'm concerned, if she tried to end her life once, isn't it conceivable she might again?"

"Of course, it's conceivable, I suppose anything is. But we are hoping that she's moved onward from that dark time when I first referred her to Bates."

Lauren sat up straighter. "Pardon me?"

"To Dr. Strickler, of course."

"Now I am confused. Are you saying you treated Emily prior to her going to Bates?"

"Oh, no, that's not what I'm saying." She looked a little flustered now. "Only that your husband called me initially, he had gotten a hold of my name, wanting me to refer a facility. I had studied Adam Strickler, in fact, I'm guided by his teachings."

"I see," she said, though she didn't really. Though it all seemed so simple, and likely it was, why had Jonathan not mentioned it, why had he led her to believe otherwise? Of course to be fair, she did remember Jonathan mentioning once that Adam Strickler knew Dr. Greenly personally, still why was there always something more to find out? But with the doctor gaping at her, waiting for her to go on, she brought her thoughts back to Emily. She cleared her throat . . . "With respect to Emily, should I be on the alert for anything in particular?"

"Well, often there are signs of morbidity, a need to talk about death, almost an obsession with it. Some people give away their possessions or become so lethargic they are unable to function. I have noticed none of that, have you?"

Lauren thought about it—she had seen hostility and spitefulness and belligerence, but nothing the doctor now described. She shook her head with relief—recognizing the absurdity that such offensive traits could actually offer relief.

"Well, we will continue to watch her, talk to her, take her emotional pulse as I like to say." The doctor sat forward, fixing her papers, her body language indicating Lauren's time had run out. "Much as we are doing now."

Lauren cleared her throat, wondering if she should ask, then finally plunging in. "Dr. Greenly, has Emily talked to you ... you know, confided in you?"

"Why yes, surely."

So she was batting low as usual these days— her assessment of the therapist being inaccurate, and along with needing to swallow that was the envy sitting heavy on her chest, wanting to choke her: this dreary lifeless woman was able to reach Emily where she wasn't. But that was her ego hurting—the feelings were childish and self-serving, she would have to get rid of them.

"My stepdaughter and I don't communicate," Lauren said, feeling as though she were announcing for the record her deficiency. "Look, Doctor, obviously the important thing is to insure that Emily never feels so desperate or despondent again. Maybe if you could tell me what she's feeling, then I'd be able—"

The doctor looked at the clock on her desk. "I'm sorry, but you do understand, I have other appointments. And I think that I explained earlier that what she confides in me about her feelings are confidential and must be kept so. After all, if I were to do otherwise, she would never feel free to say—"

"No, no, I understand," Lauren said, cutting her short and getting up clumsily, feeling as though she were some nosy neighbor fishing for information. By the time she got home, she had managed to get a grip on her emotions. She had also decided that Jonathan's failure to mention his brief dealing with Dr. Greenly was unimportant. It was nothing of any significance ... besides which, handling Emily's trauma and treatment alone as he was forced to do, she was only now beginning to understand what he went through.

Jonathan's lawyer had begun to draw up the papers and get the necessary affidavits to obtain the restraining order against the police. Meanwhile when Detective Kneeland phoned the house, Lauren told him their decision. "You weren't honest with me," she said. "I wasn't aware of your Gestapo tactics with Emily, the idea of accusing a ten-year-old of her mother's murder."

"Look, Mrs. Grant, I have a job to do here. Okay, so maybe I wasn't as sensitive as I should have been, but you've got to understand, it had to be proposed."

"Perhaps. But from what I understand it was way more than proposed."

"Look, I assure you this time—"

"No, you don't understand, there won't be a 'this' time. If there's anything further, please talk to Michael Perkins, he's our lawyer." With that she hung up.

*   *   *

A couple of days later Francine called Emily, asking her to visit the next day after school. "Why not ask her if she wants to come here?" Lauren said to Emily when she told her, knowing it would make Jonathan more comfortable.

"I want to go there."

"I'm sure she'd like—"

"I want to go there," she repeated. "Besides, if we're here, Goldilocks will follow us around."

Again, she ignored the use of the sarcastic nickname. "Well, younger sisters sometimes do those things. Though it might be annoying to a big sister, it's actually complimentary—it's a way of them saying that they want to be like her."

"I suppose that wouldn't be too repulsive if she were my sister. But she's not."

"I see," Lauren said, determined to keep calm though Emily would surely have liked to see her lose it. "Well, I suppose if you girls want privacy, I could arrange it."

"Don't bother," she said. "Watch my lips, Lauren, I want to go over there."

"I don't appreciate your rudeness."

"Maybe I wouldn't be so rude if I didn't have to say things a dozen times over."

"Okay, fine. Then maybe it would be better all around if you stayed home."

Still, by the next morning Lauren had thought about it, how happy Emily seemed around Francine, how good it was that she had a friend ... So as usual, she gave in, agreeing to drive Emily to Francine's after school. When she got there, she stayed a few minutes to chat with Carla. "I tried to get Emily to invite Francine to our place, but she insists she wants to come here. I'm afraid our magnificent yard with iron gates and locks doesn't hold the same intrigue as your yard." Then not able to resist a little teasing, she said, "But of course you and my yard aren't exactly on the best of terms either."

Carla pretended to wince, then with more seriousness said, "I wouldn't take it personally, Lauren, you know how kids are, you can't second-guess them. I think they like it here because it brings back so many good memories. Emily and Francine were a real twosome, together morning till night."

"I wonder about the bad memories, though. There were those for Emily, at least at the end. In fact, when I first drove out here to drop off the key to our tenant, I was apprehensive—I thought it might be too much for her to handle."

"I don't know, Emily's a tough kid, she always was. Strong and athletic—she could fight and out-run most of the boys. A curious kid, too, smart and good-natured and stubborn, seldom willing to let a thing go until she figured out what it was about. And though I have to admit she does seem quieter and more moody these days, she was never afraid to speak her mind."

Listening to Carla describe Emily, Lauren could catch glimpses of that girl. But only glimpses. There were darker sides to Emily, too, parts not so nice or pleasant, parts Lauren had seen that apparently Carla hadn't. But she didn't say that, she simply sighed. "Well, sadly, she wasn't tough enough," Lauren said.

Carla looked at her curiously. "Are you saying you blame her for not doing something for Nancy—"

"Oh, no, of course not. I'm just referring to her emotional breakdown. Not that I'm making light of the horror she went through, it would have been hard on anyone. But I keep thinking, if only she had been stronger, she might not have ended up at Bates . . ."

"Well, there's a couple of ways of looking at that. Maybe if Jonathan hadn't been so quick to put her there."

"My gosh, Carla, what would you have had the man do?" Lauren asked, thinking it was an odd criticism to make considering the circumstances.

"Who knows, Emily might have made it through given a little more breathing space. And as for Detective Kneeland, so he was a real asswipe, but wouldn't he have given up on her eventually? It's not as if he had anything on her . . ."

And as she said that, Lauren finally realized. "Carla, Jonathan didn't have a choice in the matter. Emily was in terrible shape. She overdosed on pills."

Carla took in a breath, stunned, her hazel eyes widening. "Oh . . . dear Christ. Why didn't anyone tell me?"

"Jonathan was naturally devastated, he wanted to keep it as quiet as possible," Lauren said, choosing not to confess that even she had not been told.

"Of course," Carla said. "Why wouldn't he? I won't breathe a word of it, Lauren, you tell Jonathan that for me. That poor little girl, to think she wanted to die."

Emily had taken the wide gold chain necklace out of the zipper compartment of her worn shoulder bag where she had put it and was now showing it off to Francine.

"Wow, it's beautiful," her friend said, taking it and putting it up to her neck. "Where'd you get it?"

"My father, of course," Emily said, lying—she couldn't just say she took it. Then taking on a contrived voice with sweeping facial and hand motions to go along, she said, "Oh, yes, my dear Francine, but you have no idea . . . The poor man loves me so desperately he simply knows not what to buy me next."

Francine chuckled. "You are such a weirdo, Emily. I almost forgot how weird, but you're fast reminding me." Then going back to the necklace, she said, "It must have cost a mint."

"Well, it wasn't a Kmart blue-light special." And it surely wasn't—no, there was nothing chintzy about the wonderful, perfect, handsome, to-die-for Jonathan Grant—Emily thought about all the fine gifts Daddy used to buy her and her mother, then abruptly came back to the present and said, "Lauren and Chelsea must not know a thing about this. They're sure to be envious—and that's all I need is an uprising from the two smiling darlings from Manhattan."

"Not to worry, I won't say—" Francine began when Emily suddenly tore the necklace from Francine's hands, dropped it back in the purse's compartment, and zipped it. Then she nudged her friend to look across the street.

Emily wasn't sure if Gordon was crooking his finger to invite them over at first, but the more she watched, the clearer it became. Francine had warned her that they oughtn't to stand so close to the road, especially with the bushes still so bare from winter, it would be too easy to get spotted. So Francine was right, he had spotted them, and Emily wondered if maybe that's what she had secretly wanted. She wasn't sure why though, maybe simple curiosity.

"I don't think we should," Francine said. "He's kind of spooky-looking."

"So what? What's there to be afraid of? Remember, I'm his landlord."

"It's not like he knows that."

"If he starts acting psycho, I'll tell him."

"Oh, yeah, great, that'll help a lot—" But Emily had already taken her friend's hand and was pulling her along. Francine gave one backward glance to her house, probably to check to see if Carla was watching from the window, but, of course, she wasn't. More likely she was sitting in front of the television watching *Oprah*. Besides, why would she mind if she saw them going over there, wasn't she the one who told Francine that the new neighbor was nice?

He was in the garage, sawing a plank of wood with a power saw when they finally came up to him. He turned the saw off and looked at them. What she hadn't noticed from a distance but noticed now were his brown eyes—big and warm, like milk chocolate. "Hi," he said, "so what're your names?"

Emily introduced them, first names only. He told them his was Gordon, which, of course, they knew, then it was silent for a few minutes, until Emily decided to start the ball rolling with, "So how do you like the house?"

"Hey, yeah, I really do like it," he said. "I just moved in a couple of weeks back." No news flash either, but they didn't say so. "Want to come inside and see?"

"Naw, no big deal, we've been, lots of times." Francine was quick to say and Emily didn't contradict her.

"Yeah? Well, I've been fixing it up some."

Emily got immediately interested, and though she thought maybe it wouldn't be such a hot idea going inside again, she had to see what it looked like. She squeezed Francine's arm. "Come on, let's go see," she whispered to her.

"No way."

"Don't be such a jerk. It's only my house."

"I don't think we should," Francine said, and though they were trying to whisper, unless Gordon was hard of hearing, he could hear every word. But he looked away, pretending he couldn't, which Emily supposed was the Miss Mannerly thing to do. Finally—like Emily knew she would—Francine agreed.

Now that it was all decided, she suddenly wasn't so sure about it herself. Her stomach suddenly felt like someone had dumped cold steel inside, and though it was weighing her down, making her uncomfortable, she was determined to follow through. So biting down hard on her bottom lip, she followed the fellow named Gordon inside her own house, then stood there looking around, as though waiting for something to happen. But nothing did. Emily looked up then and saw the new skylight in the kitchen ceiling . . .

She studied it for a few minutes, then followed Gordon into the living room where he pointed out the bookshelves he was in the process of building. Bookshelves—of course, a perfect idea, Emily thought, but for some weird reason it seemed as though the bookshelves had always been there when of course they hadn't.

Maybe she was looking pale or something because he asked, "Want a cold drink? Soda? Milk?"

She refused, but she did sit down and so did Francine. Gordon sat across from them, and though he seemed embarrassed at doing it, he kept looking over at Emily. "I like your haircut," he said to Emily finally.

"Yeah? Most people think I look like a freak."

"No way that could happen. You could shave your head and you'd still be pretty."

Emily sat forward, getting closer to him, as though if she got up-close enough, she might actually know who he was. "So you like this house, huh?" she asked.

He nodded, looking around, smiling proudly as though it were his. "Yeah, I do."

Emily gestured into the kitchen toward the skylight where thick beams of sunlight were rolling in, casting warm shadows over the appliances and floor tiles. "It's funny," she said.

"What's that?"

"Well, my mother always used to say the kitchen was too dark and dreary."

And he said nothing, just sat there looking at Emily and smiling.

Lauren, who hadn't spoken to Fern in days, brought her up-to-date later that afternoon on the phone, getting some of the same reactions from her that she'd had herself, being annoyed that Jonathan had kept so much from Lauren. "It seems to be getting more complicated rather than less," Fern said.

"Well, with respect to the police, Jonathan's attorney is sure he can get a restraining order. With Emily's psychiatric history, he believes it should be easy."

"Good—one thing out of the way."

"Then what? How do I reach her?"

"Personally I think you ought to be firmer. I mean, start to exert your authority."

"How, by beating her?"

"Don't be funny. What about punishing her?"

"How do you suppose I enforce a punishment? That only works if she'll listen."

"What about not letting her go to her friends?"

"I almost tried that."

"Almost?"

"Well, I did threaten but gave in ultimately. She's so vulnerable, Fern. She's already had one fight in school we know about ... according to what Francine told Carla, she's not getting along at all with her classmates. So the only real friend she has is Francine, and, of course, she adores Carla. She's not at all happy at home, the closest she comes is when she's at the Abbots. So how can I pull her away?"

"You say she's delicate, but she sounds tough to me. And let us not forget how she threatened you when she first got home. It certainly threw you."

"But that was before I knew ... How tough can a kid who tries to take her own life be?"

"So you're going to continue to let her beat you up?"

"Is that what I'm doing?"

"I think so. And what I'd like to know is why."

"Meaning?"

"I think you're still a little frightened of her, Lauren. I see you running in circles trying to get her to like you, and it's not working. You don't even look right these days—you look tired and harried. I think you ought to get your act together."

"Promise me you won't tell anyone we went there," Emily said once they were outside and back in Francine's yard.

"Why?"

"Because I said."

"Don't you think it was a little weird him saying how pretty you are?"

"Why, you think I'm a dog?"

"That's not what I meant. That guy is so old ... he's got to be in his twenties. I mean, he was looking at you as though you were some kind of princess or something." When Emily didn't say anything, she said, "Do you know him?"

"Why would you think that?"

She shrugged. "I don't know, just a thought."

"Well if I did, don't you think I would have told you?"

"Okay. No need to get pissed."

Emily didn't say anything, not until a few moments had gone by. "Francine, you heard what I said about the skylight, how my mother wanted the kitchen brighter?" Francine nodded. "Want to hear something even stranger?"

"What?"

"The bookshelves he's building in the living room? It seemed at first like they'd been there before, but, of course, they weren't. The thing is, she used to talk about getting them built."

Chapter Eight

That evening Jonathan told Lauren that the hearing was scheduled for the following week. "Mike wants you to testify," he said, coming in, kissing her, then plucking a celery stalk she was about to cut for the salad. "How was your day?"

She immediately broke off another stalk and rinsed it off for him. "So what did you tell him?"

"No problem, of course." He came around, looking at her. "I wasn't wrong to say that, was I?"

She shook her head. "No, of course not. But what could I possibly testify to?"

"Just the fact that you're the mother in Emily's life now, a court is going to want to have your input. And you can testify as to how she's doing."

"I can't say all is wonderful."

"No one is expecting that. Simply tell the truth. The fact that she's still having problems is more reason why we don't need her hassled by the police." He glanced through the kitchen window, then to Lauren, "Where're the girls?"

"Chelsea's upstairs playing with her dolls, Emily's having dinner at the Abbots."

With the last bit of information, he looked up, annoyed. "I thought we decided against that."

Though Lauren obviously hadn't forgotten his objections the first time Emily stayed to dinner, she thought they had gone beyond that. "What we decided is I'd transport her to and from school until this court injunction came through."

"I don't want her hanging around that house without proper supervision."

"She has—"

"I told you, I don't think highly of Carla."

She sighed, not at all in agreement with his objections to Carla. But still said, "Okay. Will it make you feel any better if in the future Chelsea and I went along, too?"

"What would really make me feel better is if both you and the girls stayed the hell home where you belong! Where I can feel relatively sure that you're safe."

She was about to object, to go after him, but changed her mind as he headed to the living room to get his newspapers. He was all on edge over the business with the police and Emily ... and then of course, he still wasn't without the old fears. But she just wasn't up to dealing with it right then—Fern was right about one thing, Lauren *was* feeling particularly out of sorts these days. She was also apprehensive at the prospect of testifying in a court of law—partially, she supposed, because she had never before done so, and partially because she didn't see how anything she could say would be relevant.

    *   *   *

"Be sure to set aside May ninth for Francine," Lauren said to Carla on the telephone the next day.

"As we speak I am marking it down on her social calendar. Now, are you going to tell me why? Oh, wait, let me guess," Carla said. "Now correct me if I'm wrong, but isn't Emily's birthday around that time—the seventh of May?"

"Bull's-eye. However, I didn't want to make the party for a weekday, I thought Sunday would be good. So what do you think of the idea, will she like it?"

"I say what kid doesn't like a party? What did she say when you told her?"

"That's just it, I haven't told her a thing, it's to be a surprise. One of the reasons I'm calling you is I need names of friends, youngsters she hung out with before . . . What I'm trying to do is get the kids over that hump . . . you know, the discomfort factor, none of them knowing what to say to each other in view of all the awful things that have happened. What they need is a minor distraction. I should have had a party to welcome her home, but it didn't occur to me. Now with her birthday coming, well, I get another chance."

"Gee, Lauren, it sounds great, but I don't know that I can help you that much. I mean she was only ten at the time, and she pretty much stayed around the house, playing with Francine."

"No kids came to visit or vice versa? What about friends from school?"

"Oh, I'm not saying there weren't any. In fact, now that you mention it, she must have had friends. I remember one year she was her classroom representative, and that's definitely one of those popularity contests. But still, that was in school."

So that's when Lauren got the idea of going to Emily's school. Karen Daniels, Emily's seventh-grade teacher, agreed to see Lauren during a free period the next morning. She was young—only her second year out of teachers' college—but marvelously enthusiastic, showing not just in her animated style but with her glowing smile.

Lauren started off with some brief background, then they discussed Emily's classwork, which to Lauren's relief was not the disaster she had imagined. "I'm not saying she puts a whole lot of effort into her work," the teacher who insisted Lauren call her Karen said, "but the bottom line is, she's keeping right up there with the rest of the class. Naturally I've seen her achievement test scores and know she's capable of more, but I didn't think it was wise to push her."

Lauren agreed, and told her so, then made the transition, "How about socially?" But before Karen could respond, Lauren said, "I prefer Emily not know I've talked to you about this."

"Sure, not a problem."

"Well . . . I assume you're aware that she's had some fights with classmates." Karen nodded, and Lauren continued. "She's doesn't want her father or me interfering, she's asked to handle it herself.

And as long as it doesn't get too out of hand, my husband and I have pretty much agreed to let her."

Karen smiled. "I think it's wise of you. Sure, when we see it get physical, we tend to get nervous—naturally if any of the staff or faculty see it get to that, we immediately break it up. But honestly I think the situation has peaked—kids typically tease and torture until they get bored with the subject or it blows up so to speak. We've had the blowup, the truce usually follows, and before you know it, the players will forget what it was they were even angry about and end up friends. Right now, I think we're around the truce stage."

"Have you any idea why? I mean, what they were teasing Emily about? I know how it is with the new kid in school, but Emily does not exactly fit that category. The kids all knew her, she grew up here, attended Rawson Elementary."

"Yes, I'm aware of that. And I really don't know what the teasing was about. But one of the teachers who knew Emily pretty well from Rawson said she is different now, not nearly as friendly or easygoing. Of course that's understandable, considering what she's been through. But kids are quick to pick up on attitudes and put up their own defenses."

"Karen, what would you say if I told you I was intending to do a little meddling in this situation. Nothing too obvious."

"I'm not sure I understand?"

"Well, Emily's birthday is coming up in a couple weeks. I want to have a surprise party for her—at our home, of course. And it dawned on me, since she knows these kids, and from what I understand, she was quite popular at one time, well, why not simply send out invitations to all her classmates? It might help smooth things over—after all, kids like parties, so what better way to renew friendships than to throw a party? Does that make sense to you?"

"Perfect sense, I think it's a great idea."

"Then you don't think the animosity is so severe ... I mean, I don't want Emily angry about this."

"I don't see why she would be? Like I said, if anything, it's been quiet on the home front, which to my mind means both sides are ready to negotiate peace. Wait here a minute, Mrs. Grant, I'll go photocopy a list of names and addresses for you."

Francine hadn't expected Emily that afternoon and was about to head over to the shopping plaza where a couple of kids from school hung out when Emily came over and busted the plans. Though the shopping center was only about six blocks from the house, Lauren wouldn't hear of Emily going, making her feel like a ditz. Francine had to quick act like she didn't want to go to the plaza to try to make her feel better, but it only made Emily that much more furious with Lauren. Of course it was because of Daddy's influence over her, she'd be dumb not to know that, but still that didn't excuse Lauren.

Probably even dumber was that here she was mad because of something she didn't want to do in the first place. "So where's the littlest smiling darling from Manhattan?" Francine said as she got her out of hearing distance, trying to get her out of her funk.

And it did help some, it almost made her smile. "She's at Brownie troop," Emily said. "Actually I didn't want to go to the shopping center," she said.

"Yeah, why not?"

"Because we've got better things to do."

"We do?"

Emily now took the lead, beckoning her to come along. "Come on, follow me," she said.

And she did—down the street and across, then, with Lauren and Carla inside, doubling back to the house directly across the street—Emily's house. "He's not even home yet," Francine said. "Didn't you see his truck's not here?"

"Of course, I saw. You think I'm blind?" That's when she took out the key ring.

"What're you doing?"

Emily put the key in the lock—the same key that had opened the door when she'd lived there—she had been carrying it around for days now, thinking about it and waiting until she had the opportunity to use it. "What does it look like?"

"Uh-uh, no way I'm going to be in on this," Francine said, starting to back away from the house. "If we get caught, Carla will break my hands and feet."

But Emily grabbed a hold of Francine's short jacket and held on to her so she couldn't leave. "Would you stay here, wimp! Remember, it's my house."

"Not now it isn't."

"Did you see my father sell it?"

"Well, there must be some law that says you can't just walk into a house that someone else is renting."

"Oh, I'm sure there is, but the problem is, we don't know about it. So that'll be our excuse if we get caught, we were just too dumb to know any better. People who cheat on their income taxes regularly use that one, and it works."

"Okay, I'll go," Francine said, and Emily released her jacket. "But what if Gordon catches us?"

She turned the key and opened the door, then held it while Francine came forward and hesitantly stepped inside the kitchen. "Will you quit being so nervous?"

Which, though Emily said it, she couldn't quite manage herself. But she took a deep breath, bit her lower lip, and led the way—walking slowly, silently, examining each room of the house, even going down to the sewing room in the basement where the police said her mother had been only minutes before being pushed down the stairs and clubbed to death with Emily's brand-new baseball bat.

*   *   *

Lauren had dropped Chelsea off at the church hall for Brownies, then come to Carla's with Emily while the meeting was in progress. While the two girls were outdoors, Lauren told Carla about her talk with Emily's teacher. "By the way, if I forgot to mention it, I expect you at the party, too. At my side. With the possibility of twenty-eight kids, I'll need the moral support." And before Carla could object, she said, "Don't sweat it, the gates will remain open in your honor."

"Thank you for putting up with me."

"Have I a choice?"

"So tell me about the party. Have you planned it yet?"

"Games, prizes. Live music, decorations, and lots of food, all to take place on the patio and back grounds."

"My gosh, it really sounds like an extravaganza."

"Do you think it's too much?"

"Maybe for us, but certainly not for the kids. What does Jonathan think?"

"Well, he wasn't for it exactly, you know how men are about the combination of a lot of strange kids and noise and games? But he caved in ... which he has been known to do once in a while," she said, smiling. "As long as it's on the grounds, of course." Carla began to say something, but Lauren looked at the kitchen clock and jumped up. "Oh, my gosh, it's nearly four o'clock, and

I've got to pick up Chelsea. But first I need to round up Emily."

"Why don't you go and come back for her . . .?"

She slipped on her jacket. "I can't, Carla."

"Why?"

"I need Emily with me."

"Why?

"You don't want to know."

It took Carla a moment before she heaved a sigh, indicating she understood. "Jonathan, am I right? He doesn't want Emily out of your sight."

"It's mainly this thing going on with the police. It's only until we have an order—"

"I wouldn't bet on it."

Lauren looked at her. "What does that mean?"

Carla got up and carried the cups to the sink. "Forget it, that was just my big mouth flapping. Louie's always telling me to mind my business. He's right."

But now despite her rush to leave, Lauren couldn't let it go. She went over to the sink and planted herself there. "Tell me. I'm not leaving until you do."

"Look, your hubby's a good guy and I don't like to be telling tales about him out of school—"

"But?

She sighed. "But, he about drove Nancy nuts with his hang-ups and rules. Francine and Emily would usually play over in their yard because Jonathan felt more comfortable with that, and though I took it personally at first, I got past it. As I said, Emily hadn't many friends or activities outside of school, and though I don't know for certain, I believe that was Jonathan's doing. I do know that Emily wanted to be on Little League, but he wouldn't let the kid wear jeans, let alone a baseball uniform. Okay, so maybe it wasn't the end of the world, but—" She stopped and shrugged. "Hey, look, what do I know?"

Well, maybe that's how it was back then. Though it was true Jonathan was overprotective with Emily now, sometimes where she herself got annoyed with it, he did have ample reason. The fact was, Chelsea had outside activities, and so long as they were organized and properly supervised, he did not object. And other than his irrational remark the other day, he never tried to curb Lauren's activities, not that there was much to curb, of course. If anything, hadn't he always pushed her to get more help around the house, give her more leisure time? Just so long as she was home by the time he got there. Not really such an unusual request ... didn't a lot of men want that?

In any event, by the time she managed to get some of that across to Carla and make it outside to the car, she was forced to do just what Carla had suggested in the first place—go and pick up Chelsea and come back after for Emily: the kids were nowhere in sight, and Lauren and Carla calling them elicited no response. Lauren had worked herself into such a state by the time she and Chelsea got back to Candlewood Terrace, Lauren came within inches of sideswiping a black sedan that was nearly at a standstill in the middle of the road.

She gave the driver a dirty look as he started to speed away, getting a fairly good look at him: he was in his mid-twenties, had a full face with prominent teeth, and was wearing a blue Yankees cap. She didn't recognize his face, but the baseball cap and car seemed oddly familiar: and then she thought back to that fellow who had asked Emily directions at her school ... But that was silly, wasn't it?

She pulled up into Carla's driveway, stopping the car. She had been gone almost ten minutes, but according to Carla, the girls were still among the missing, which was about when she bolted out of the car and began to go up and down the street shouting for them.

"Lauren, I'm sure they're okay," Carla said, following her. "Maybe they decided to walk down to the shopping center. All the kids go down to the dairy cream place—"

"But I specifically said— Oh, God, Jonathan will have a fit!" she said, feeling warm and light-headed as she climbed back into the car about to head to the center. And what about that black car? she thought. What about it? There was no one in it but that one guy ... wouldn't she have seen if there was someone in there?

One of Carla's hands suddenly clasped over her arm, and with her other hand she pointed across the street. "There they are, Lauren. It's okay."

Then she began to shout at the girls herself, likely for Lauren's benefit. "Where the hell have you been? We've been hollering all over the neighborhood! Didn't you girls hear? Now, both of you, get your rear ends over here!"

"What do we tell them?" Francine said quietly to Emily as they walked toward the street.

"That we didn't hear them. And we didn't, at least, not until the Manhattan darling dropped her calm and classy bit and started in with her shrieking."

"Where do we say we were?" Francine asked.

"On Saddle Hill Road." Which was the street that butted Emily's back property.

There was a long pause as they approached the street and the two mothers waiting across the street: the driveway welcoming committee—Carla and Lauren and the pesky kid. "Okay, so tell me now, what did you think you'd find there?" Francine asked, suddenly switching the conversation.

"I don't know," Emily said, and she really didn't. But there was definitely something odd about Gordon. And Francine picked that up right out of her thoughts.

"About Gordon, right?"

"Maybe."

"To do with your mother's murder?"

Lauren didn't mention the incident on the way home—the reason being, she was far more humiliated by her own inappropriate behavior than upset at Emily. The girl would be twelve next week, and here Lauren was behaving as though her toddler had wandered off alone at a carnival. Carla put on a good show, scolding the girls, but it was done so Lauren could save face.

Okay, so the police wanted to question Emily—something unlikely to happen now since the department had already been served the appropriate papers. Besides which, Jonathan told Emily that if the police were to approach her, she should refuse to talk. But aside from that, there was nothing to fear.

Yet here was Lauren, like some neurotic over-blown character Jonathan had created, in a panic over nothing. And with all the embarrassment, one thing from Carla's exaggerated and inaccurate sketch of Jonathan stood out in her mind, explaining Emily's inordinate attachment to her two pairs of jeans—apparently they were the first she'd ever owned.

"That was some time ago," Jonathan said later when Lauren brought up that he had not let Emily join in organized baseball. He followed Lauren to the cabinet where she removed a vase for the bouquet of red roses he had just come in with. "I suppose my objections had to do with her getting banged up. I didn't want her hurt."

Lauren filled the vase with water, then carefully arranged the flowers. Finally she set it on the kitchen table. "This was baseball, Jonathan, not football."

"But on Little League, which is a boys' thing."

"Not anymore it isn't."

"So the females wormed their way in," he said, shrugging. "Fine, but it's still primarily a boys' activity."

"Aren't you just a little embarrassed taking such a chauvinistic position?"

He smiled. "I never claimed to be a champion of women's rights, but then again, that's no secret to you." Standing behind her, he reached over, broke a rose off one of the stems, and slipped it behind her ear, kissing her as he did.

No, though she might not like to admit it, it was no secret—the man she loved and committed to spend the rest of her life with was indeed a throwback, with all the pluses and minuses that went along with it. She knew she wasn't about to change him, but for the girls' sake, she had to see that he didn't stifle them. She wanted them to be confident and independent—strong.

"What was it ... Emily putting in complaints about me?" he asked, his hands slipping beneath Lauren's sweater, lifting away her bra for his hands to freely explore.

"No, not at all," she said, sighing deeply and shaking her head while allowing him to assume it was Emily who had even discussed the subject of playing ball.

"Actually, she did have a bat—" Jonathan began, then what had become of that bat occurring to him, he buried his lips in her hair, and with fingers locked on her breasts so tightly, she gasped, then arched her back against him. "I'll never let anyone hurt you, Lauren," he said, his voice filled with emotion. "I promise."

Though so much had been made of the court hearing, it was easier than expected. Jonathan's attorney offered an affidavit on behalf of Dr. Strickler and Dr. Penelope Greenly testified. In light of that, Lauren's testimony seemed unimportant—at least to her, but Mike Perkins wanted the added insurance. And it opened her to questions that made her uncomfortable.

"Have you ever asked Emily about the events that took place the day of her mother's murder?" the city's attorney asked.

"No, I haven't," she said.

"Why not?"

"Because I look at it that if she wants to tell me, she will. Understand, please, I've only known Emily—"

"Please limit your answer to the question before you," he said, stopping her midstream.

But the judge interfered there. "This is an informal hearing, and I'd like to hear what Mrs. Grant has to say."

So she went on. "I've only been in the picture a short time. Though I've been married to her father for five months, I just met Emily when she came home six weeks ago."

"And how is she doing?" the judge asked, now taking the questioning into his hands.

"Well, things take time," Lauren said. "A lot

has happened, a lot of things for her to adjust to. I mean, I believe she will adjust in time, given love and patience." Was that what she really thought, or was she just too scared to consider the alternative?

"Mrs. Grant, has Emily any memories of what happened the day of her mother's murder?"

"According to her doctors, she hasn't."

"But what do you think?"

"I really think not," she said. Which was based on the assumption that any child in such a situation would ultimately say something to someone if their memory suddenly returned: to their doctor, to parents, to someone.

As it turned out, Detective Kneeland's threat was idle—a citizen, any citizen, had a right to refuse to answer questions put to them by the police, and in the case of a child who was apt to be intimidated, the child's parents had the right to intervene.

And though the police could argue that Emily was a key witness to a murder and that in the interest of justice the court ought to order their right to question her, Emily's emotional fragility was sufficient cause for the judge to issue the restraining order. So it was in less than forty-five minutes they were out of the courthouse with the order signed and secure in Jonathan's inside jacket pocket.

It was a lovely spring day—Lauren felt as though she were renewed with energy, and she headed right out to the mall to pick up some spring clothes for all of them and decorations for Emily's party, which was only ten days away. The jazzy invitations had already been sent—RSVPs to Carla's home phone—Lauren didn't want to take a chance that Emily might catch on. So far eight classmates had called saying they would come—so all was looking good. She kissed Jonathan good-bye, feeling more positive than she had in weeks.

It was after one o'clock when, bogged down with bundles, she heard her sister calling her name. She had not spoken to Fern in several days, not since she had suggested Lauren's perseverance and patience with Emily was motivated out of fear. "Look, I'm sorry I said that, I didn't mean to hurt you," Fern said, catching up to her and standing there, looking truly repentant.

"I know," Lauren said, then not able to keep herself from smiling . . . "Oh, Sis, it's so good to see you. I would even go so far as to hug you if I had a couple of free hands."

"Here let me help you with some of those," Fern said, pulling two bundles from under her arm, then kissing her. "Come on, you, lunch is on me."

As soon as they were seated in the darkened Chinese restaurant, Lauren told Fern about the restraining order. "It's a relief, one less thing to worry about. And then with Emily's party coming along so nicely, well, I'm hopeful . . . If she makes more friends, is happy with her peers, well, all things naturally follow. And I know what you're thinking, that I'll win acceptance by default or—"

"Now, now, don't go putting words in my mouth. Maybe you've got the right idea—when you're happy in one area of your life, it's certainly hard put not to spill off into other areas. And who really cares how or why it occurs."

Lauren picked up the menu, opened it. "So, tell me, why aren't you at work?"

"I had a free afternoon so I thought I'd browse a bit, look for a birthday present for Emily."

Lauren looked at her watch. "Speaking of which . . . Oh, gosh, Fern, I don't think I'm going to have time for this."

"Wait, let me guess this," Fern said, sighing, placing a finger to her chin, "Brownies, gymnastics, Dr. Greenly? Nope, none of the above. I give up."

"I'm supposed to pick up Emily at school at two-thirty. If I don't leave now, I'll never make it."

"I was under the impression that this daily pickup business was only temporary."

"It is . . . it was. But since I wasn't certain what the outcome would be this morning, I didn't tell Emily not to wait."

Fern, who had already been digging in her change purse, came up with a fistful of change. She held it out to Lauren while pointing to a phone down back near the rest rooms. "Call the school, tell the clerk to tell Emily to take the bus home."

"But—"

"But nothing. Go."

Lauren slid out of the booth—if Emily took the bus, she would be home just about the same time as Chelsea. Surely even this seven- and twelve-year-old could manage at home by themselves for forty-five minutes without a referee. "Okay, you've convinced me," she said. "Order me the chicken and broccoli."

Alice, the office clerk, had given the slip of paper with the message for Emily Grant saying, "Take the bus home after school, I'll be there in about an hour. Please don't fight with Chelsea, love Lauren," to Irene Olansky, this week's student messenger. Along with the message to be delivered to Karen Daniels's homeroom were two batches of handouts, three textbooks, a teacher's manual, and a bulletin board memorandum from the vice principal.

On the way to Miss Daniels's classroom, Harvey Quarterman snuck up in back of Irene and placed his hand full on her rear end. She whirled around to see whose hand it was, then seeing his ugly smirk, she slammed the pile of books at him catching him neatly on the side of his head. She had been too angry to notice the two handouts along with Emily Grant's message sail to the corridor floor. Who did that fuck-face Quarterman think she was anyway . . . one of those losers who hung around back of the boys lockers to give out freebies?

That's why when school was over, Emily didn't head over to the school buses, she waited for Lauren. For a while there was a lot of activity, and she busied herself watching people, trying to read their faces, wondering what kind of lies were hidden behind them. Buses closed their doors, pulled out of the school yard, teachers and staff headed to their cars in the parking lot ... She waited ten minutes, fifteen, twenty minutes ... and it was just about a half hour by the time she decided to walk the couple of miles home.

She had just crossed the street and walked the few hundred feet that took her up to the open fields when the black car pulled up beside her and stopped.

Chapter Nine

Over lunch, Fern showed Lauren the black-and-white-striped designer telephone she had bought for Emily's birthday: at the top of it stood a big white sheep dog on its hind legs, its open mouth serving as the cradle for the receiver.

"This is great," Lauren said, examining it. "I think she's really going to like it." She looked at Fern. "You know, this is quite nice of you—I mean, about now I would imagine the only gift you'd want to give Emily is a black eye."

"Well, I wouldn't go that far. But I can't say that I feel kindly toward her. I must have been in her company a dozen times since she's been home, and I haven't gotten a smile, let alone a friendly word. When she answers the telephone, she's downright rude. But mostly, I hate the way she treats you and Chelsea. I see you chauffeur her around, cater to her demands, bend over backward—"

"Wait, before we get too deep here. Are you going to suggest she intimidates me?"

"No, No, I promise I won't. I'm just amazed at your level of tolerance."

"So, I'm trying extra hard. That isn't bad, is it?"

"No, no, of course it isn't."

"Who knows, maybe I'm finally growing up." Then giving a sideward glance to her sister, "You don't suppose it's Jonathan I have to blame for this grim, but generous metamorphoses, do you?" But before Fern could comment, Lauren pointed at the telephone in its box on the table in front of them. "Of course, Fern, that's just the perfect thing—a dog. Jonathan and I have been wracking our brains for a week trying to come up with a birthday gift."

The elementary school bus stop was only about two hundred feet from the house and Chelsea as always was the only one to ever use it. Today when she ran home, she was surprised not to see her mother's car parked in the driveway, which meant she'd beaten both her and Emily home. And it felt kind of neat being home alone for the first time, needing to take out her magic plastic card from the small zipper compartment in her backpack and use it to open the gate, then the house. Once in the house, she headed for the kitchen.

She hung her coat and backpack over one of the chairs, then climbed the counter to search the cupboards for something to snack on. Finally with a stack of graham crackers and a box of raisins she headed to the den to watch TV, but after only a few minutes of searching the channels, she heard a creaking sound. She turned the television volume down and looked around—it seemed to be coming from upstairs. Or maybe downstairs . . . it was hard to tell.

Not feeling quite so grown-up now, she headed to the living room to the big bay window and looked out toward the street, there were no cars going by. Her mother had to drive Emily back and forth to school so the mean, ugly princess wouldn't get upset by the police. But they always got home before Chelsea, who except for gymnastics and Brownie days chose to go with the kids on the bus.

Now she heard another noise and spun around to confront it, but there was nothing to see. She looked out the window again—still no sign of the car. Where were they?

Emily recognized something familiar about the car, then the blue baseball cap: it was that same guy who had asked directions once in front of the school. He was smiling at her now, and with hand motions signaling her to the car.

But she stayed put, in fact moved a step backward. "What do you want?"

"Just wanted to talk to you about something. Come on board, I'll give you a ride home."

"No," she said, going on walking, acting as though nothing were wrong, but she was lying to herself—she knew something was wrong, but she didn't know what she was going to do about it. His car continued to follow slowly alongside her.

"You know who I am?" he asked.

She didn't answer—in fact, she looked away. Of course she knew who he was, but getting directions didn't exactly qualify them as friends.

"Hey, I'm not going to hurt you, kid. I just want to ask you a couple of questions."

"Leave me alone!"

"Shit!" he said, suddenly going from friendly to angry—that's when he braked the car and pushed open his door. And that's when her legs and head started to race. *Through the fields, and into the woods, to Grandmother's house I go . . .*

She called her aunt first—she hadn't wanted to bother her father at work, but didn't have a choice when she learned that Aunt Fern was out of the office for the afternoon. They paged Daddy from a job site, and he called back a few minutes later. The moment she heard his voice, she started to cry, and knew she was acting like a baby but didn't care . . . it took a few seconds before he could get her to tell him what was wrong.

"It's going to be all right, Angel," he said, his voice a little muffled and funny-sounding. "Take a look at that tall fence outside, if anyone tries to get over it, an alarm goes off. Why do you think Daddy had it put there?" When she didn't answer he went on, "Still, I don't like you being alone nor do I like not knowing where your mother and sister are. I'm on my way home. Figure it'll take me at the most fifteen minutes. Can you be brave until then?"

The moment she heard him say he was coming,

she began to feel better. "Uh-huh," she said, thinking how lucky she was to have gotten a father who told her stories and bought her presents and made her laugh and always took charge of everything. He instructed her to put on her jacket and go sit out on the front step until he came, so that's what she did.

After the Chinese food, Fern had gone with Lauren to the pet shop—not to buy, just to look to get some ideas on breeds to suggest to Jonathan. But the dogs were all so adorable, Lauren couldn't possibly decide which breed would be best. She took leaflets to go over later, slipping them in her purse, then looked at her watch. "I'd better get a move on, the kids are going to think I got lost."

"Why don't you give them a call? Just to tell them you're on your way."

"Good idea," she said, already leading the way toward the mall telephones. Once they got there, she deposited change in one of the phones and tried her number. It was busy. She waited a little, tried again—it was still busy.

"Go," Fern said. "I'll hang around until I get through. I'll let them know you're on your way."

Lauren hugged her sister tight, then when she finally let go, she smiled. "I feel so much better about things—really. Like suddenly there's a whole slew of positive energy beginning to generate. Maybe it all has to do with attitude. You think?" It was only a rhetorical question, and she was quickly on her way.

Fern leaned against one of the cement walls, wanting to give the line a chance to free before trying again. She felt relieved though, happy that she and her baby sister were once again on good terms, and that Lauren was feeling so positive about Emily. And she did seem to have more energy. Who knew, maybe it did have to do with attitude—one person reacting positively to another, and so on and so on. Maybe Lauren *was* getting closer to reaching Emily, and maybe this party would do all the things she wanted it to do.

She sighed, then moving to a phone, she picked up the receiver and punched in her sister's number, charging it to her credit card. It rang fifteen times—no answer. Strange. She called again to see if perhaps she had misdialed, but still there was no answer. Then it occurred to her—the kids must have gone outdoors.

It was then that her beeper went off . . .

Her father had more than kept his word; he was home within twelve minutes. As soon as he pulled up, he gestured Chelsea to get in the car. And it must have showed how awful she felt about getting him out of work like she did because right away he began to make her feel better. "Don't ever be afraid to call me like you did, Angel," he said. "You did the right thing. Don't be like your mom, refusing to admit when she needs a little help."

She nodded. "Where're we going?"

"To find your mother and sister," he said, already pressing in 411 on his car phone and asking for the number of Louis Abbot, Francine's father's name. Did her father think they would go visiting there and leave her at home? But what he said in his strong voice was, "Carla, Jonathan Grant here. Have you any clue as to where Lauren or Emily are?" Then he went on to explain it to her. There was a pause where Chelsea could just about hear Carla's voice, then he said, "No, forget that, I've already called the school, everyone's gone for the day. I even called her sister's business, I had them put a page out for her . . ."

And as soon as he hung up with Carla, the phone rang. Daddy picked up quick—by then, he was about to turn into the Grand Bell Shopping Center, where there was a Shop Rite, a cleaners, and a CVS, stores Mommy shopped at.

"Fern. Listen, I'm looking for Lauren," he said. "Have you seen her?"

Chelsea heard him sigh, then he was silent . . . finally he said, "I don't get it, what about Chels—" Then shaking his head, he said, "Forget it, I'll go into it with her when she arrives home. At what time did she and Emily leave?"

That's when the color in Daddy's face seemed to run out. "Are you saying, she never picked up Emily? Then where the hell is she?" The car now in the shopping center made a U-turn and, picking up speed, headed toward the back exit that was in the direction of Emily's school.

Chelsea was thinking that Emily might have gone to a friend's house, but aside from Francine, she had none. And though usually she wished her stepsister would fall off the earth, this whole thing was now getting to be scary.

When Lauren arrived home, no one was there, but Chelsea's backpack was dumped over the back of the kitchen chair. She was determined to keep cool, there was no reason to panic ... She went out back, looking around calling both girls' names. There were no shopping areas close by to walk to, no neighbors ...

Finally Lauren raced back inside and called Jonathan's office, by now her resolve to stay calm had all but diminished. Jonathan had been called away earlier, his secretary had reported ... an emergency she thought, but she would try to reach him. As soon as Lauren put down the receiver, she remembered the car phone and began to dial, but her mind went suddenly blank.

Oh, dear God, what kind of emergency?

Combing the area from the car, actually it was Chelsea who spotted Emily's red backpack lying in the field. Jonathan stopped, got out, and Chelsea followed, scared to stay in the car alone. He lifted the backpack and looked around, then with his hands cupping his mouth began to call Emily's name.

Finally he turned to Chelsea. "Angel, I need you to be brave for Daddy. Okay?" She nodded yes, but wasn't sure she could be. "I want you to go back to the car, get inside, and lock the doors. Then I want you to call 911. Tell whoever answers that you're with your father in a car in front of the fields across from the junior high. Tell them to send the police, it's an emergency. Can you do that?"

Could she? She didn't know ... "Where will you be?" she asked, testing out her voice—it was still working, but it didn't sound anything like she remembered.

"In the woods looking for Emily. Now get going."

"But—" she started, then seeing the fierce look on his face, she knew she hadn't a choice.

Once he saw her climb into the car and lock the doors, he began to run toward the woods. And just as she was about to pick up the telephone and call the police, the phone rang. She gasped, her hands pulled back as though something had touched them. But she inched them toward the phone, forcing them to lift the receiver, then brought the receiver to her ear ... and heard her mother's voice.

"Mommy," she began to cry and scream at once. "Someone stole Emily! Where are you?"

As soon as Lauren understood what Chelsea was trying to tell her, she called the police and they arrived at the scene just about when she did, just as Jonathan was coming out of the woods, his arm around Emily. Relief surged through Lauren's insides, causing her legs to nearly give way—Detective Kneeland quickly stepped over, intercepting, insisting she sit for a moment in the squad car.

But Emily was okay ... And as the story came out, Lauren learned that she had never received the message she'd left. Emily had waited for her and when she hadn't arrived, Emily began to walk, and that's when the man driving a black car and wearing a baseball cap stopped and chased her into the woods. But she had run and been crafty enough to escape him, hiding in a ditch. She dared to come out only when she heard her father calling. And the irony was—with Jonathan at Emily's side, Detective Kneeland was there questioning her.

"Had you ever seen him before?" Kneeland asked.

She nodded. "Once. When he stopped to ask directions."

"When, where—" Jonathan began, but the detective put his hand on his arm, indicating for him to butt out.

"Mr. Grant, would you please? Look, you want this guy picked up or what?" he asked, finally convincing him to back off. Then going back to Emily. "Now you said once. When was this?"

She shrugged. "I don't know, a while ago."

"Did you go over and talk—" he began, but that's when Lauren took over.

"No, she didn't," she said. "And it happened just about six weeks ago."

The way both men looked at her, she felt as though she were being cornered—instinctively she backed up against the door of the squad car, and her words appealed to Jonathan. "I was there to pick her up from school. To take her to her doctor's appointment. I had just arrived and had pulled up in back of this guy's car—"

"I don't understand, why didn't you mention it?"

"Because it seemed okay. I mean, she pointed the way to the principal's office, she didn't go near the car. In fact, I commented on how well she handled it. The guy . . . he hadn't made any moves to get out of the car, and then I beeped the horn for Emily." She could feel the sweat on her forehead, at the back of her neck . . . She felt as though she was going to throw up. *Oh, great, just what everyone needed.*

Now Jonathan raised his hand, holding up the works to escort Emily to the car and sit her inside with Chelsea. It was the right thing to do, of course, she had answered all she could answer, and there was no need for her to be subjected to more. Particularly since Lauren was probably more aware of the stranger than Emily.

"Did you get a look at his face?" Kneeland asked her finally.

She winced. "Not that time."

"There was another time?" Jonathan asked on cue. And why shouldn't he be upset? If the tables were turned, wouldn't she be appalled that he'd been so remiss?

"Yesterday," she answered finally. "On Candlewood Terrace. Emily and I were visiting friends while our seven-year-old was attending Brownies. I was concerned when I was ready to go and couldn't locate Emily—" She turned to Jonathan now, "It was nothing really. She had walked over to the next street—what is it?—Saddle Hill, with Francine."

"Please, Mrs. Grant, it would help if you would try to focus—" Kneeland said.

"Yes, of course. Well, I had gone to pick up Chelsea from her meeting, and when I was returning, I nearly ran into this black car, almost standing still in the middle of the street. It struck me then that I'd seen the car before. And the blue baseball cap."

"Okay. And that was on Candlewood Terrace?"

She nodded. "Yes."

"Can you describe him further?"

She thought a moment. "A thin face, bad skin . . . in his mid-twenties I think." She shrugged.

"And the make of the car?"

"Black, a sedan. I don't know makes at all," she said, feeling even more stupid and helpless . . . "But it did strike me that it looked similar to Jonathan's car." And then Lauren remembered the car that drove past the house the day Emily was to come home . . . "Oh, dear," she said, then her explanation again to Jonathan. "The day you went to get Emily at the clinic? Earlier . . . before you arrived back, there was a black car that drove by the house. Slowly, as though looking for a street number. I didn't see the driver, I didn't think anything of it. But at first, I thought it was the Lexus."

"It looked like it, but not exactly?" Kneeland asked.

She nodded.

"What was different?"

She shrugged. "It was shorter, squarer, I think . . ." Oh, God, she didn't know a damn thing about cars, and to make it worse, she wasn't even sure of that much.

The man had been watching her three times— at least three times that they were now aware of. For some reason, he was stalking Emily. And Lauren could give only the barest of descriptions. The detective left it at that with Jonathan's assurance that Lauren and Emily would look at police photos the next morning to see if they could recognize the man.

They had two cars there, Jonathan took Lauren's elbow and helped her into her car. "I'll be right behind you," he said.

But once they got home, Jonathan all but ignored her, not that she could really blame him for feeling as he did. Emily was not home two months and here she was nearly abducted. All this despite Jonathan's repeated warnings about his daughter's safety—warnings Lauren hadn't taken as seriously as she should have.

He attended to the girls—Chelsea for one wouldn't let him leave her, insisting he read to her, tuck her into bed, and sit with her while she went to sleep. He spoke to Emily for a while, but she begged off talking as well as dinner, saying she was tired and wanted to sleep. Meanwhile Lauren sat in the living room, twisting and tearing apart tissues in her hands and waiting for Jonathan.

It wasn't until after nine that he came down-stairs and sank into the easy chair across from her, his shirt creased, his tie askew, his dark hair standing in peaks, looking as if he'd been through a war. For the first time since they'd gotten home, he actually looked at her, and once again, she could feel the guilt engulf her. And then he began to speak—softly, sternly, the words coming out slowly, which served to add emphasis. "Do you understand how frightened I was when Chelsea phoned me crying this afternoon?" he asked.

Surely it had to have been reminiscent of Emily calling the operator the day of Nancy's murder. Lauren hadn't even thought of that, there being so many other awful aspects of this to contend with. And rather than having him go on with what she already knew, Lauren said, "I'm sorry, dar-ling. Please forgive me. But still I can't help think that this might not have happened if Emily had gotten the message—" She stopped right there, the words sounding so foolish and futile in view of the circumstances.

"Was it too much trouble to pick her up?"

She shrugged. "I truly didn't think it was necessary."

"And you know what, Lauren, to me that's the most frightening part of this. All those times you spotted that stranger around Emily yet instead of reacting, you chose to simply ignore it. Your behavior is reckless. Somehow I can't seem to impress upon you that it's the nineties, and damn it, there's crime out there!"

"But this has to do with the murder, doesn't it? Nancy's murder."

"Perhaps. I'm not going to say it's not possible, maybe likely, but that doesn't mean we live in a crime-free world. You're a mother, not some single career woman trying to tough it out. Don't you think it's time you took these things seriously?"

Yes, he was right . . . wasn't that proven by what happened this afternoon? And though she wished she had a rational defense, she had none. If that man was stalking Emily as was surely indicated, he could have abducted her while she was walking home by herself from the school bus stop. And what would have happened if Emily had been unable to escape him? "Lauren?" Jonathan said, and her head lifted, seeing he was waiting for an answer.

She shook her head, and when she spoke her voice came out a whisper. "Yes, I do." And then finally Jonathan, seeing her guilt and pain, took her in his arms. "Why, Jonathan, I don't understand?" she sobbed. "Why is this happening?"

Perhaps it was connected to Nancy's murder, no one really knew, least of all the local police. Though Jonathan had second thoughts about putting Emily through the additional trauma of looking through police photographs, he wanted the man caught. So he kept his word, the next day accompanying both Lauren and Emily to police headquarters. Though Detective Kneeland was not there as planned, one of the office staff set up the computer terminal for them. After nearly an hour of looking at faces whose features seemed to blend into one another, Lauren got up to get a cup of water from the dispenser. As she came back to the table, the room began to spin, and Jonathan jumped up and grabbed her just as she was about to stumble. "What is it, Lauren?"

"Nothing," she said, a little frightened by the incident herself. "I didn't eat, I guess."

But that was the end of their cooperation with the police—Jonathan ushered Lauren and Emily out, saying, "If you haven't found anything yet, it's unlikely you will."

Emily was silent and unexpressive on the trip to Dr. Greenly's office for the emergency session Jonathan had scheduled and insisted she attend. Watching Emily disappear inside the doctor's office, Lauren felt despondent: they were backing up once again. Added to that was the knowledge that until this sick person who was stalking her was caught, it was particularly unsafe out there for Emily. But Jonathan wasn't willing to talk about any of that then—he was at that moment concerned about Lauren. He ushered her out of the waiting room, across the street to a diner.

"I feel better," she said, biting into a slice of dry toast, taking a sip of sweetened tea. "Really. I guess with this awful episode yesterday, and not being much in the mood to eat breakfast this morning, well it must have gotten to me." But her excuse wasn't cutting it with Jonathan—once Emily was done with her appointment and dropped off at school, Jonathan headed toward town.

"Where're we going?" Lauren asked.

"To see the doctor."

"But I'm feeling all right. I don't need—" she said, but he didn't listen. Within twenty minutes she was sitting beside Jonathan in Doc Stevens's office, a kindly gentleman close to retirement age who'd been Jonathan's general practitioner since he'd come to Elmwood Valley fifteen years before. Gentle hands and a calm and easy bedside manner made what was usually a stressful event for Lauren easier.

After which he asked Lauren a few run-of-the-mill questions and she did her best to answer accurately. No, thinking about it now, she hadn't been feeling up to par. Tired some, but mostly her stomach had been a bit unpredictable. Her period? Well, no, now that she thought of it, but being on the pill, she did occasionally miss a period. None of the items major, more than likely caused by the stress she'd been under— But as agreeable as Doc Stevens was, he came up with a different diagnosis: Lauren, it appeared, was nearly three months pregnant.

Chapter Ten

Though Jonathan had been eager to have a baby from the beginning—perhaps never quite getting over the loss of the baby boy who died with Nancy—it was she who wanted to wait, at least until they had gotten their lives more settled. So despite the delight she had seen immediately rush into Jonathan's eyes, her initial reaction was disbelief. Naturally she had heard of the standard "accident," a precaution not doing the job for which it was intended, but surely with birth control pills it was only a minute possibility.

Still in sort of a daze, Jonathan—making an effort to keep his enthusiasm to bare minimum—led her to the car. "I know it's not what we planned, but is it really such a tragedy?"

"No, not a tragedy, of course not, but ... I don't understand, I didn't miss a single day."

"You heard the doctor, it occurs. Rarely, but it does." He opened the door and helped her inside, then went around. But he didn't put the keys in the ignition, not right away. "Look, darling, I need you to be happy about this."

She swallowed hard, looked at him. "Just give me a little time to get used to the idea."

"Then you're not saying, you don't want this child? That you'd consider aborting?"

"Oh, God, no, Jonathan," she said, reaching for him. "How could you think that?"

He took her in his arms. "Tell me you want this baby, I need to hear you say it."

"I want this baby, Jonathan. I mean, how could I not want our child?" Though he had pulled the words from her, they weren't lies—she did want this child. She just wished that the timing were better, and she said as much to him. "Look at what almost happened to Emily. How are we supposed to pretend everything is fine?"

He put his arms around her . . . "It will be fine, trust me. For a change, let me take care of things."

"Who do you think the stalker is, Jonathan. And why?"

"From here on in, I don't want you to worry about it, about anything. Do you understand?"

"But how can I not—"

"Lauren, stop right now and listen to me," he said, clasping his hands on her shoulders, and she did. "Emily will be safe, as will you and Chelsea— I will see to it. Now whoever this lowlife is and for whatever reason he's doing what he's doing, he will be caught if he persists in hanging around Elmwood Valley. We know what he looks like, and it's not that big a town. In the meantime, he's not going to get near Emily or Chelsea or you. He will not invade our lives again."

And by his fiery eyes, she knew he would gladly die to keep that promise.

When they arrived home, he insisted she go change into one of those silky lounging gowns he was always buying her, but she had never worn. He then sent her to relax on the sofa while he made her lunch. Fifteen minutes later, he brought in a tray and set it on the coffee table: a magnificent chef salad, a glass of milk, and a single red rose Jonathan had obviously snatched from one of the filled vases.

"Gee, maybe I could grow to like this," she said, trying to get into the spirit of things, intent on sidestepping any worries, intent on pleasing Jonathan.

But apparently he had already been thinking seriously about it, making plans, because he started to relate some of his proposed safety measures. "There's just a few more weeks left of school . . . from here on, I'll do the chauffeuring."

"I can do that."

"Maybe, but I'd feel better doing it myself. Besides, I want you and that baby of ours healthy. You're tired, stressed, and with sufficient cause. If things are going to change around here, it's going to begin with that." When he said "that baby of ours," a shiver of excitement rushed through her. For the first time since the doctor announced she was pregnant, the child she was carrying seemed real, and she suddenly started to picture faces of babies. All kinds of babies, but particularly boy babies. Most particularly, a boy that looked like Jonathan.

"Won't running a pickup and delivery service run interference with your work?"

"I'll set my appointments around the family; in fact, I plan to do a lot more of the paperwork at home. I'm also going to see to it that Beatrice is here full-time."

"What if she's not available?"

"She will be."

Lauren sighed, knowing he was right about needing Beatrice's help, but wishing she could handle it herself. But already she had proven she couldn't. "Well, it seems to me that you and Beatrice are going to be mighty busy. What can I do, Jonathan?"

"Just relax and continue to look beautiful. Concentrate your energies on bringing a healthy, unstressed child into this world. Does that sound so difficult?"

For a moment she could only imagine a caricature of herself: lying on a sofa in front of a television fiddling with a remote ... But she was being far too unimaginative. Surely there were alternatives. People painted, sculpted, they wrote poetry, children's books, got involved with photography, gardening ... Gardening didn't sound unreasonable. And what about simply lying in the sun, catching up on her reading. Taking long walks might be nice, too. "Oh, by the way, darling, Chelsea would prefer to take the school bus—"

"Sorry. Not until we find this guy."

It took a moment for it to register, and when it did, she looked up. "Do you think Chelsea's in danger, too?"

"I don't know, Lauren. Maybe, maybe not. In any event, I'm not willing to chance it, are you?" No, of course, she wasn't. She felt dense and inept, just like she had felt last night, it not having even dawned on her that there was that possibility . . .

Though Fern had wanted to rush over yesterday when she'd heard what had happened to Emily, Lauren had put her off, wanting to first deal with Jonathan. But now she wasn't surprised to see her once Jonathan left to pick up the kids at school.

"How's Emily?" was the first thing she asked as she followed Lauren into the living room. Lauren got back onto the sofa and Fern sat across from her.

Lauren shrugged. "It's hard to say with Emily. To me, she seems primarily angry—at no one in particular, at everyone, like she's not quite got it down who she ought to blame for what. I wish there were something I could tell her. I wish someone could tell me why a perfect stranger would go after her."

"And you're sure he's a stranger?"

"I'm certain. I saw him talk to her that day at school, and it was obvious she didn't know him, or didn't remember him," she said, knowing there was always that possibility. "This morning Jonathan took Emily and me to police headquarters to look at pictures and bios of convicts." Lauren shook her head helplessly. "You know, Sis, I never realized how many creeps were out there."

"An interesting comment from someone who has lived most of her life in New York City. It's like those sociologists who say that the home territory, no matter how hazardous, instills a false sense of security." Lauren reflected on the statement and Fern asked, "Well, so did you recognize anyone?"

"No, unfortunately. We're just going to have to keep closer tabs on Emily," she said. Then, "Fern, Jonathan is afraid Chelsea is in danger as well."

Fern sat forward with renewed concern. "Why is it I just assumed the attack had some connection to Nancy's murder?"

"Well, it would certainly seem so—and of course that was all brought out with the police. But still in all, nothing is certain, and Jonathan isn't willing to take chances or assume anything. He insists we start being more cautious."

"Well, he's right, of course," Fern said.

Lauren thought about boosting the mood by telling her the news about the baby, but decided to wait until Jonathan arrived home. But Fern looked at her watch at that point and asked, "Won't you be picking up the girls from school?"

"Yes. Well, today . . . actually Jonathan will be handling that until school lets out."

Now Fern took notice of the lounging gown she was wearing and the lunch tray still on the coffee table. "Oh? Is there some reason why you can't do it?"

"No. Well, yes in a way. I mean, not really, it's just that Jonathan ..." But everything she was saying now only added to Fern's confusion and distress. Lauren sat up—shaking her head and finally smiling. She might as well forget about waiting, because there was no way she could. "Sis, Jonathan took me to the doctor's this morning. Wait, wait," she said, holding up her hand like a signal. "Before you get in a tizzy— Well, it seems you're about to become an aunt once again."

There was a pause as Fern stood up, mouth open and speechless, then she started laughing. "I keep wanting to say, are you kidding? Isn't that what people always say? Oh, gosh, that is just the most wonderful news!" She came over and sank next to Lauren on the sofa, wrapping her arms around her. When she backed up, her eyes were all teary. "Oh, my dear, I can just imagine Jonathan's reaction when he heard the news. He must be thrilled!"

Though Fern didn't come out and say it—she was far too sensitive to do that, but she was thinking it—Lauren knew because she was, too: this time around things would be different. This time Lauren's baby would have a father who wanted it.

Fern—who had still another client to show property to—stayed only so long as to congratulate Jonathan, being careful that the girls—who hadn't yet been told—were out of hearing. When she and Jonathan walked to the door, Lauren could hear Fern express her concern over Emily. "Is there anything I can do?" she asked.

"Just see that your sister takes care of herself. That means relaxation, and no stress. The summer's coming, there's no reason she can't enjoy herself right here on the grounds where she's safe, where the children are safe. I've already spoken to Beatrice, she's going to be here regularly. And I'm going to be around the house a lot more, which will hopefully take the edge off Emily's difficult behavior. What do you think about an in-ground pool?"

"I think it's a wonderful idea. It sounds to me like you have things under control. But then again, I would expect nothing less of you." Lauren heard the pause where she imagined Fern was reaching up, kissing Jonathan's cheek. Then the door closed behind them. Though Lauren knew they had her interests at heart, she was a bit annoyed, disliking being talked about as though she were a child. She stood up, lifting the tray from the coffee table.

"Hey, what's going on in here?" Jonathan said, coming back into the room.

"I am allowed to carry a tray, aren't I?"

A look of contrition was immediately on his face. He gently pried the tray from her hands and set it on the table. "Okay, out with it. What did I do?"

"I really don't appreciate you and my sister discussing me behind my back."

"I see. Were we talking so quietly you couldn't hear?"

"No. But—"

"Was I, or for that matter was Fern, trying to keep something from you?"

"Stop it. I hate when you do that."

"Do what?"

His even-tempered and logical approach could be infuriating, and he knew it. "I heard you tell Fern that you had already talked to Beatrice. Suppose you explain how that is possible. We spoke about it only an hour ago."

"True, I mentioned it then, but it wasn't the first I thought of it, and you know that. After the frightening episode yesterday with Emily, it was clear you had too much to deal with. So okay, I plead guilty, I called her last night—"

Lauren sighed deeply—always the last to know. "You think it's my fault, don't you, Jonathan?"

"Come again?"

"What happened to Emily. And I can't blame you for thinking it either. If only I had picked her up. If I had—"

He put his hand to her mouth, stopping her. "Don't. The one responsible here is me. For not insisting we bring in help to begin with. What business did I have laying this on you, expecting all to run smoothly while I hightailed it off to work? I know Emily isn't easy to handle, it's going to take a while for her to adjust ... Now, add to that some sick character stalking her ... Still, the bottom line, Lauren, is that what nearly happened

can't happen again. We were lucky this time—
Emily got away. Suppose she hadn't?"

She could feel his arms go around her, and she
sank her face against his chest. What was wrong
with her? Why did she always have to be so self-
centered? Here she was getting teed off because
he was arranging things without her knowledge,
while he was stressing over the burden of Emily's
safety. As always his biggest fault, the one that
got him into hot water most often, was loving his
family too well, too hard. She sighed—women the
world over would plead to have it so bad. "Okay,
go ahead, Jonathan," she said, "I'm ready. Tell
me you've already make arrangements for the in-
stallation of that in-ground swimming pool I heard
you mentioning to Fern."

"Uh-uh, not on your life. No way you're going
to snag me that easily." Then looking down at her
with a wincing smile, "Well, maybe if you promise
not to be angry?"

She began to laugh, then beat her fists against
his back in mock anger. "Jonathan!"

"Okay, so I have a few ins with a construction
crew. And we didn't want the girls in camp, right?
So I thought a pool would be the perfect solution.
What more could they want?"

"Friends?"

"Fine. I'm not unreasonable. Let them invite
friends over."

Which reminded her of Emily's birthday party
and the puppy which of course she had forgotten
about when she arrived home yesterday. She told

Jonathan about it now, and he was for it, instantly sure that they would get a German shepherd.

"But are they friendly?"

"Absolutely, at least they are to their masters. Smart, loyal, too. It's a good idea, Lauren."

As it turned out, Chelsea welcomed her father picking her up, and did not dispute it when she heard he'd be transporting both girls to school for the rest of the year. Yesterday's incident was still on her mind and would likely take a while to fade. Lauren learned that Jonathan's doting on her included doing the grocery shopping as well. After getting rid of the lunch tray in the kitchen, he had Lauren draw up a list of what they needed, and she complied, knowing this part of the regime would ultimately end once he saw what a hateful job it was.

Not gone five minutes, the phone rang—it was Carla. "Good God, I've been trying to reach you since yesterday afternoon. Jonathan had called looking for you and Emily, and I've been worried sick since. Last night every time I tried you it was busy, this morning, no one was home. I must have left half a dozen messages ... Don't you people ever listen to that machine of yours?" Finally she paused to take a breath, then said, "So what happened?"

Lauren went on to tell her what had happened, listening to all the disbelief, then worry. "Maybe this guy was the one who killed Nancy," Carla said.

"That's possible, of course. But why would he come back, for what purpose?"

"Well, if Emily saw him?"

But it was a useless discussion, it didn't lead anywhere, so she was grateful when she could finally get to the part about the baby ... "Okay, now for the good news," she said. "Guess. Of course I didn't necessarily feel it was so good at first ... but the more I think about it—"

"You're pregnant," Carla said.

"How did you know?"

Silence, then a chuckle. "I don't know, you asked me to guess. So it looks like I did."

"Okay. Well?"

"Well, it's wonderful. I mean, as long as you're happy about it."

"I am. I know it's not what Jonathan and I planned, and if left to my druthers, sure I would have waited a little longer. But, Carla, well it must be those tricky hormones already at work ... the more I'm with the idea, the more it seems amazing and marvelous."

And at dinner, both Jonathan and she broke the news to the children. Chelsea, though low-keyed, was pleased by the fact that she'd soon get to be a big sister herself. Emily, still operating with the aftershocks of the day before, showed no interest, not even for the benefit of her father. So they put aside talk of the baby and turned to the subject of safety. Jonathan addressed it—he talked about the summer coming and how they would plan their activities within the grounds.

"I'm not saying you're still in danger, Princess," he said to Emily. "It's just that we don't know who that guy is or what he wants with you. Maybe he was just some harmless nut who likes to scare pretty girls. But until I know for certain, I'm not willing to take any chances."

His attention went to Chelsea, then Lauren, "Not with any of my girls. Now with the unpleasant part of this over with," he said, smiling wickedly. "I don't want you getting the wrong impression here, don't go thinking this summer is going to be a downer. Not at all. In fact, I have a few fancy surprises wiggling from my sleeve." His arm began to jump around as though it were alive, while he pretended to pull a message from out of his shirtsleeve and relieve the arm's activity. Which managed to get him some chuckles from Chelsea, if not Emily. "Here we go, girls— this week a construction crew along with a couple of backhoes are going to dig a hole right in our backyard."

"What for?" Chelsea asked.

"Well, according to what this says," he said, referring to his invisible message, "we're getting a swimming pool. Diving board, a water slide, the works."

Chelsea, able to forget all else, jumped into Jonathan's arms—for her, a child from the city, the marvelous house and grounds when they first moved in were culture shock enough, but a swimming pool in one's own backyard went to the limit. Perhaps even more exciting than a baby . . .

Emily got up out of her chair and headed for the stairwell ... Lauren rushed after her, catching up at the landing.

The thing neither Lauren nor Jonathan had considered was the connection to the little brother Emily lost when she lost her mother. According to Jonathan she had been looking forward to the baby almost as much as he and Nancy. So it was likely to take time to get used to the idea ... to feel comfortable with it. Now Lauren chose to ignore the baby issue and go to the easier one.

"The pool will be lots of fun, Emily. I'm sure Francine and Carla will want to come over often. And who knows, maybe you'll want to invite other friends as well," she said, hoping once again that the party will facilitate that.

"Is that supposed to make me happy?"

"Well ... it's not so bad, is it?"

"I don't know. Are you happy?" she asked, her question catching Lauren off guard.

"Yes ... of course I am. I mean, I wish all this terrible business with you would get solved and out of the way. But your father isn't going to let anything happen to us if that's—"

"You want a baby?"

She was surprised at the directness of it. "Of course," she said, thinking there was no need to go into detail. But it appeared she didn't have to ...

"Then why were you taking birth control pills?"

Lauren's first thought was, how would she know that? But she wasn't in the dark long. "I used your bathroom one day, I figured you wouldn't mind."

"My birth control pills aren't in the bathroom area, they're in the dressing room."

Emily shrugged. "So I browsed around a little, too. What's the big deal?"

"They're in my jewelry box. As a matter of fact, right where I put my necklace.... You remember the necklace, Emily, the one I still haven't found?"

"You know, Lauren, it would be refreshing to hear you speak your mind one of these days. If you think I stole your ratty little necklace, why don't you just come out and say so? Though you might want to ask yourself why would I want to? My father used to buy my mother way better stuff than that."

She turned and went upstairs—the confrontation lasted only a couple of minutes, only a few words were exchanged, but she managed to transpose Lauren's mood. Purposely, as though she would prefer Lauren's anger than her understanding. And though she knew she should take what she said with a grain of salt, still Lauren couldn't help but be disturbed. First the necklace, now finding out she was nosing around her dressing room, and more disturbing, she'd been privy to knowing she was taking birth control pills . . .

Could Emily have messed around with those. . . ? But she stopped right there—she was nearly three months along, and Emily had been home less than that.

*   *   *

From the doorway the next morning she watched as Jonathan and the girls got into the car and headed to school. Her stomach as usual these days was feeling unsettled, but being so warm outdoors, Lauren decided to try to ignore it. She took her coffee to the deck along with a covered stationery box, holding pens, notepads, and index cards: the party plans had been worked and reworked a half-dozen times, it was only three days away. Lauren hoped that by then Emily's mood would lighten.

Beatrice arrived soon after, first congratulating her on being pregnant, then insisting on making Lauren a healthy breakfast. Since insisting wasn't something she had seen her do before, Lauren had to assume it was Jonathan's influence.

"Look, before we begin this new arrangement, maybe it would be a good idea to talk about it," Lauren said, trying to scale her voice so as not to offend the woman. "I'm sure my husband has you thinking I need around the clock care, but the truth is, I'm as healthy as a horse. I'd rather you just went about your work and let me be."

Beatrice nodded, and went off while Lauren picked up the phone on the porch and called Carla. "Okay, what's the grand total?"

"Hold," Carla said, then coming back a few moments later. "Fourteen will-bes, including Francine and Emily. Twelve cannots and five no-responses."

"Okay, not so bad, certainly workable with the games and contests and all."

"What about Chelsea?"

"We're going to have a cake for Emily that Friday. Just the family. I'd rather this one be for kids in her own age group. I don't want to give her any excuse not to enjoy it."

"You're something else, you know."

"Oh, yeah, I'm sure you're right. Just ask Emily."

"I'm not kidding, it's not every stepmother who'd continue to fall over her feet trying so hard for a stepkid who puts up stone walls everywhere she turns. I was thinking about that last night, you know me having been good friends with Nancy and all. Well, I think Nancy would be pleased knowing Emily had you."

Lauren's shoulders arched, feeling a chill go over them. "Thank you, Carla, that was a nice thing to say."

Beatrice followed Lauren's instructions, that is, until about noon when Lauren drank the last of the low-fat milk and decided to go and pick up another gallon. She had already gotten into the car and put the keys in the ignition when Beatrice came rushing out of the house. Lauren rolled down her window to ask what was wrong.

"Where're you going?" the woman asked.

"Excuse me?"

"I mean, shouldn't I know? If your husband should call or if you're needed?"

She wasn't used to this—she wondered if she ever would be. "Just to the local market, we're out of milk."

"Oh, dear, no, Mrs. Grant," she said, opening the driver's door. "You must not. I'll do the shopping. That's my job, in fact, I already drew up a list."

"You drew up a list without asking me?"

"I would have, of course. Before going. Now, please, there's really no need—"

"Okay, fine, I understand what you're saying. But I don't mind, in fact, I want to get out."

"I'm sorry, ma'am, I cannot stand by and allow you to do this. It's not safe out there—"

Lauren glared at the determined set of her face, a face that might have been prettier had it smiled more. Was this the same woman who always appeared so timid? If so, it was with Jonathan, not her. Beatrice was having no trouble carrying out what were obviously her husband's instructions. Rather than argue, Lauren yanked the door from her hands, slamming it, then turning the ignition key, said, "Beatrice, it is not up to you to allow me to do anything. And if Mr. Grant should want to know, tell him I'll be back shortly."

With that the woman ran out in front of the car. She backed up a couple of feet and stood there, like she were instantly fired to the spot in stone, her arms folded against her chest. "Move out of the way!" Lauren shouted.

But she didn't, not after tears of frustration began to rise to Lauren's eyes. Damn it, it was all she could do not to run the woman down. But she didn't and that was only because Jonathan showed up right then, pulling open the driver's door. "Would someone please tell me what the hell is going on?"

"Ask her," Lauren said, grabbing her purse and rushing toward the house. "Jonathan, I want her fired!"

Chapter Eleven

It wasn't long before Jonathan was inside, in the living room, standing over her and pleading the woman's case. "Look, do me a favor, Lauren, blame me—not her. She's aware of what's going down around here, and she knows how I worry about you. I told her I wanted you to get rest, and that she was here to see that you got it." He shrugged now. "Obviously, I didn't mean for it to go this far."

"Did you fire her, Jonathan?"

"Lauren, I'm asking you not to. She thought she was doing the right thing—"

Clearly he hadn't fired her—Beatrice appeared in the doorway at that moment, her eyes red and puffy. She was dabbing at them with a white lace handkerchief balled in her fist. "I'm so sorry, Mrs. Grant," she said. "I just wanted to help . . . I know how your husband worries about his girls, and now with the baby on the way . . . But no, instead of helping, what do I do? I upset and insult you and behave like a crazy old lady."

Lauren wasn't about to dispute her, and Beatrice went on. "I know you want me to leave, so if you'll allow me, I'll go gather my things." Head bowed, she started toward the kitchen. Lauren looked to Jonathan whose eyes were pleading with her to relent, which, of course, she did. "Stop, Beatrice," she said finally, and the woman turned to Lauren, her eyes eager. "It won't be necessary for you to pack your things. But I warn you, this must never happen again."

Beatrice went back upstairs to continue cleaning, and Jonathan took Lauren to a seafood and salad bar out on the highway, later stopping at a jewelry discount house. Jonathan chose for her a thick gold chain bracelet with three charms that hung from it: the heart with diamond chips he had engraved with his name, and the two flowers, each with one of the girls' birthstone engraved appropriately. Though they were lovely, Lauren felt uncomfortable wearing a charm for Emily, something her stepdaughter might have resented had she known. But she didn't mention her reservation to Jonathan.

From there they went to a dog kennel where they chose a nine-week-old German shepherd puppy that they would leave and return for Friday afternoon so they could give it to Emily after dinner in a quiet family celebration.

Before they finally came home, they stopped at the store to pick up that milk.

It wasn't until later on the telephone when describing the whole outrageous incident to Carla that Lauren could even begin to see the humor in it. "Can you believe that woman? Actually blocking the car with her body."

"I've never said two words to her, but Nancy used to say she gave her the creeps."

"How so?"

"I think it bothered her that she was so quiet and unfriendly. She said it always felt like she was creeping around the house, trying to catch her doing something wrong."

"But she kept her on?" It was more a question than a statement, and Carla took it that way.

"Well, she only came once or twice a week, and her work was satisfactory, so I guess Nancy put up with her. And then there was that whole tie-in with Jonathan."

"Tie-in?"

"Well, that she had worked for him before . . . I think something like that."

Of course Jonathan had mentioned that Beatrice had worked for him in the past, but Lauren had taken that to mean during his marriage to Nancy. Had it been even longer? That night she asked him how long he'd known Beatrice.

He thought about it a minute. "I guess most of my life. I was about six when my folks hired her."

"Really?"

"Why do you ask?"

"Just that Carla and I were talking, and it came up . . . Why is it you never told me?"

"I thought I had—"

"Only that she worked for you, not that she first worked for your parents."

"What difference does it make?"

Lauren knew so little about Jonathan as a boy; the childhood that was lacking in love and warmth was not a subject he chose to discuss much, though she had tried on a number of occasions to get him to share more with her. "I don't suppose it makes any," she said. "It's just that I wasn't aware of it . . . and it caught me by surprise. Rochester is quite a distance away, how did Beatrice end up here?"

"She has a spinster niece who lives not twenty miles north in Little Canyon. When the niece bought a house, she invited Beatrice to come live with her. As soon as Beatrice got settled in, she called and asked if I had work for her. It's not all that complicated."

And it didn't sound it, it was just that it seemed odd that he wouldn't have mentioned it. But then men tended to be odd when it came to talking about such things, unlike women who would quite naturally bring it up in conversation. In any event, now that she knew, it occurred to her that finally she might get to know something more about Jonathan's childhood . . . through Beatrice.

It was nearly noon the next day—Lauren was lying on the chaise longue on the deck after getting over an episode of morning sickness—when she overheard Beatrice speaking to someone on the intercom, insisting Lauren was resting. She got up and came inside. "It's okay, I'm up," she said to Beatrice and took over the controls. On the screen was Detective Kneeland.

"Lauren Grant," she said, focusing the screen so he could see her. "How can I help you?"

"Good morning, sorry to bother you. But I have a photograph I'd like you to look at—"

"I don't know if you're aware of it, but Emily and I came in the day after the assault as we promised. To look at pictures. We did expect to see you."

"Yes, I'm sorry about that. There was an emergency in my family. Listen, the thing is there's one picture in particular I don't think you were shown, and I'd like you to see it." When Lauren didn't answer, he said, "Look, Mrs. Grant, please, it'll take a couple minutes. Just one look and I'm out of here."

She pressed the button to let him in, noticing Beatrice watching quietly from the laundry room off the kitchen. But the detective was true to his word, the whole thing only took a couple of minutes. He slid a picture out of a yellow envelope and held it up in front of her. "Well, what do you think?"

Her heart began to race. "That's him," she said.

Jay Philips, the original suspect for Nancy's murder, the young man who had smashed his sister's head open with a rock was now twenty-six years old, and had a black Hyundai that was apparently light-years away from a Lexus. But he was definitely the stalker. Now a garage mechanic in nearby Monticello, he was seldom seen outdoors without his blue Yankee baseball cap.

Being a minor when he committed his heinous crime, his picture hadn't been part of the computer file, but by late afternoon Philips was sitting only twenty feet away from Jonathan and Lauren who were sequestered behind a mirrored wall, viewing Detective Donald Kneeland interrogate him.

And though he first denied being the one to chase Emily, he finally admitted it. "Yeah, okay, so it was me. But big deal, it's not like I went and hurt her or anything."

"The question is, what did you have planned if she hadn't gotten away?"

Silence.

"How long have you been following her around, Philips?"

His body slouched in his chair, his arms crossed his thick chest, and his face tilted up, expressing indifference. Kneeland grabbed him by the back of his shirt collar and yanked him back to a sitting position. "Now, why don't you start cooperating before I feel it necessary to sit you even straighter. How long have you been following Emily Grant?"

He shrugged. "I don't know, a few weeks, a month maybe. I never touched her though, not even a finger. If she said I did, she's a lying little bitch."

"It looks to me that you were waiting to catch her alone, waiting for the right opportunity to go after her. That's pretty much what happened the other day, right?"

"No, it's not like that."

"What *was* it like?"

"I just wanted to talk."

"What in the hell would a fellow such as yourself have to talk about with an eleven-year-old kid?" When there was no response, Kneeland said, "I'd say the prosecutor might be able to pull a conviction for attempted rape here."

"Hey, that's a goddamned lie!" Philips said angrily. "I didn't lay a hand on her. I just wanted to ask—"

"Ask her what?"

There was a pause, then a big sigh. "Okay, I was worried, I heard she was getting out of the nuthouse, and I was scared they might a screwed her head on wrong. I know all about them shrinks, they plant stuff in your head . . . before you know it, you begin to remember shit that never happened. So the last thing I figured I needed was her coming home and saying she'd remembered what wasn't."

"Oh? Like what?"

He twisted in his chair. "Like maybe I was the one who killed her mother."

"Why would she think that?"

"Who the hell knows? But you guys sure thought so. And don't go saying you didn't. Not after the way you followed me around last time, bugging my friends and guys I work with, pulling me in three or four times for questioning."

"So you figure, why not go shut up the only witness."

"No, that's not it; I told you. I just wanted to know where I stood ... if she was going to try and finger someone for the crime."

"And what if she was, what then?"

He shrugged ... "Maybe take off; I don't know. Look, if I wanted to hurt her, I could've done it anytime." His eyes brightened and a smile snuck loose without his knowing. "Listen, I got a hunting rifle, I could've picked her off easy."

Kneeland laid it out for Lauren and Jonathan before they left headquarters—sure, they could get a restraining order ordering Philips not to go near Emily, but other than that and a stern warning from the judge, that was it—there was no case. According to what Emily said following the frightening after-school episode and verified for all of them again, he hadn't actually laid a hand on her, and previous to him asking for directions that one time at the school, she never saw him.

At least to the best of her recollection ...

But the taunting about picking Emily off with a rifle had penetrated Lauren's bones, chilling her. And she had taken hold of Jonathan's hand, needing it as a source of comfort. He was always the one to worry about their safety, and she, more likely the one to tease him ... but with animals like Philips loose, it no longer seemed so funny.

Aunt Fern came over that Friday night to help celebrate Emily's birthday, not that with Emily's attitude, anything could seem like a celebration. Fern's gift was a telephone, which was nice enough, Chelsea thought, something she wouldn't mind owning herself, but not too useful a gift for someone with only one friend.

It was all a little crazy, Chelsea thought: one girlfriend and two birthday parties, the second, which was to be held Sunday afternoon, would be a big deal attended only by kids Emily's age, kids who would only be there because it *was* a party. Wasn't her mother smart enough to figure out that they weren't really Emily's friends?

Chelsea wasn't being invited to the second party, though she had far more right to be there than any of her stepsister's nonfriends. Aunt Fern would pick her up and take her to the movies and out to lunch instead, something she might have liked under different circumstances. But as it was, she thought the whole arrangement stunk. And to make it even worse, they went and gave her a real live dog of her own, and said it was from all of them.

"It's not from me," Chelsea spat, but the only one who heard her was Mommy and she gave her one of those warning looks. Though Emily's eyes seem to light up seeing that German shepherd, she was likely trying to figure out how best to torture it without the scars showing. She didn't say 'thank you,' but that was okay with everyone ... no one ever expected much from Emily.

Chelsea didn't say anything until a while later when Emily carried the puppy into the laundry room—and she followed behind. Newspapers were already spread over a part of the tile floor, a wicker basket with a red pillow in it and a water dish sat in the corner. This was where the shepherd would sleep and play when he wasn't outdoors, Daddy had said, at least until it was housebroken.

"What're you going to name it?" she asked finally.

Emily laid the puppy in the wicker basket, then looking up, said, "I was thinking of Goldilocks, but I didn't want to get her grossed out thinking she looked anything like you. So I decided on a nicer name—Stew. Ever try dog stew?"

A shiver made a line down Chelsea's back. She was sick—the truth was, Emily was too mean to have a live animal, something that had to depend on her to live.

It wasn't the cake or ice cream or even the surprise birthday celebration that had weeded the distress and anger temporarily out of Emily's features; it was the puppy. The dog was a good idea, Lauren was pleased she had come up with it, expressing as much to Fern once the girls went off and Jonathan retired to his study. "I'm just keeping my fingers crossed that Sunday goes as well."

Sunday came, and Lauren couldn't have hoped for better weather. The party invitations stated two-thirty, so Jonathan would take Emily out at eleven o'clock: they would go down to the fairgrounds and browse around until it was time to return home, which was not before three. As soon as they left, Carla showed up with Francine—as promised, Lauren left up the gate, though these days she wasn't quite as comfortable doing so.

With Chelsea already gone on her afternoon excursion with Fern, Lauren, Carla, Francine, and Beatrice got busy setting up the yard.

Emily had thought it was kind of peculiar going off with her father, but didn't mind—in fact, she thought it might be nice. She and her mother and father used to go to the county fair lots, but that seemed like centuries ago. But as they drove there, she began to remember: every summer, three or four times a season, Daddy would take Mom and her to look over the exhibits, go for rides on the amusements, play games ... And if his girls were real good girls, he'd buy them gifts, then take them in dinner at that little Italian restaurant ...

Daddy was always at the center of everything, that's why it seemed so strange now as they walked past the game pavilion toward the fenced area with the farm animals that Emily couldn't remember him being there that one time ...

But where was Daddy? It was only a simple question, but it was as though the words had been injected beneath her skin and went racing through her veins, leaving her out of breath. She stopped walking and took a deep breath, shaken and confused ... about two hundred feet in front of her were signs of construction ...

"They're renovating the animal facilities," Daddy said, thinking that was why she had stopped. "It's going to be great, they're making a feeding and petting area."

But what her eyes were drawn to was the construction trailer off to the back.

The girl accompanying her mother to the fair-grounds had dark shiny hair that was worn in two thick ponytails gathered above her ears and swept along her shoulders. Despite her mother being pregnant and never going off of the block without Daddy, that day they got in the car and drove to the county fair. Mommy said it was a secret expedition, and she was not to let on to anyone. She was searching for a special gift for Daddy, which was a good thing, the girl decided, because he was always the one buying gifts and doing nice things for them.

Mommy gave her a handful of change and left her at one of the creature-buster booths: the balloons were in shapes of creatures, ready for the kill. "When you're done playing, you wait right here for me," she said. "No wandering around alone or Daddy will have my head." She was going to the Arts and Crafts pavilion, where a lot of wood and leather handicrafts were on display for purchase, just the kind of things that would make a perfect gift for Daddy. And before she left she said, "I'll be back in fifteen minutes, thirty tops."

But it didn't work out that way: Emily had harpooned the blue-white shark, the one balloon in the entire bunch that if busted would win a choice of any prize in the booth. There were stuffed animals and beaded belts, and tons of gaudy jewelry, even a flash camera and case. But she picked a baseball bat, and in her excitement headed right to the crafts section to show her mother.

The thing was she raced through the whole area, searching but could find her nowhere. She started back, this time not rushing . . . this time noticing the construction. . . .

And the only reason she would have had to climb the steps of the construction trailer, push the door open, and peek inside was because in the side window where the plastic blinds were only partially drawn she spotted Mom's big brightly colored carryall, the one Daddy had bought her as a surprise. And at first she thought it was Daddy's back she was staring at . . . the man on the cot with Mommy, kissing her. But there was a little ponytail of hair . . .

She backed down the stairs and ran, her mind racing as fast as her feet, not stopping until she reached a vacant spot near a couple of shade trees. She fell to her knees, then taking a wide swing back, whacked her bat up hard against a tree trunk as her thoughts went to Willie Campbell, remembering those things he'd said to her . . . things she ignored because she was so sure they were lies.

Now she wanted to shake Mommy until her teeth fell out—because all those disgusting things Willie *had said must have been true, she was nothing but a slut.*

And the stranger ... the cheater, the bastard home wrecker, the one with the bare back and the funny little ponytail. Of course. That was Gordon Cummings!

Chapter Twelve

Though Lauren was exhausted—by the end of two hours, the backyard decorations were complete: balloons, streamers, signs with funny pictures and sayings posted on trees. The balloon-breaking and penny-pitching setups were ready to run. They would play charades, twister, and have a modified scavenger hunt: kids would be paired and given index cards and a basket, each card having a scrambled message that when decoded would direct them to an object hidden somewhere within the five fenced-in acres. The first pair to return to the starting point with their correct objects would win the hunt.

The festivities would then move on to the patio, which had sliders that led to the ground-floor recreation room, where the kids would enjoy pizza and soda pop and birthday cake, wiggle and bend to the limbo and otherwise play and dance to the music of Skin and Bones, a five-piece high school band that promised party success.

"Sit right here, ma'am," Beatrice said, having brought a chair up next to her.

But before Lauren could be put off by the woman's orders, Carla seconded the motion. "You've been running around these grounds for two hours, and the party hasn't even begun. Either let up or I'm going to tell your man."

"Oh, no, don't do that," Lauren said, knowing Carla was only teasing but thinking of the hassle an innocent remark such as that might create. "But you're right, I am tired. You know, I can't remember being so tired with Chelsea."

"Well, you have to keep in mind you were a lot younger in those days."

"Oh, gee, thanks a bunch," she said, smiling. She finally lowered herself to the chair, nodding her appreciation to Beatrice who she still didn't trust completely.

She looked at her watch, feeling a rush of excitement. *Oh, please let Emily like this*. She had to freshen up still, kids would be arriving before she knew it.

All the kids—nine out of the fourteen were boys—came on time, within minutes of one another; Lauren had Beatrice take them out back where they couldn't be spotted when Jonathan drove in with Emily. Meanwhile she and Carla stood out front, patiently awaiting Emily's arrival, which was already fifteen minutes behind schedule. When they did finally spot the car's approach, the plan went into action: Carla disappeared, rushing out back to quiet the kids.

But she noticed the rigid expression on Jonathan's face, the way he was walking as he got out of the car and started toward her. She rushed up, meeting him halfway. "What's wrong, why are you late?" she asked, but before he could answer any of those questions, she followed with another. "Where's Emily?"

"She'll be coming along . . . but I'm going to tell you now, this isn't going to work."

"You told her?"

"No, of course not. Something happened at the fairgrounds, though I'm not quite sure what it was. We were going along fine—everything went without a hitch—in fact, we were having a pleasant conversation when suddenly she had some kind of anxiety attack. She's feeling calmer now, but hardly in party spirits."

"Maybe that will change. When she sees Francine and Carla, and the kids from school—"

"Look, Lauren, I don't know. This whole thing is giving me bad vibes." As he was saying it, Emily got out of the car and headed for the front door.

"Jonathan, for heaven's sake, everything is prepared and ready to start, the kids are waiting out back. Let's go get her and see." So clearly against Jonathan's better judgment, they headed Emily off, insisting she come around to the back entrance, Jonathan stopping partway there, letting her and Lauren go on ahead. When they finally walked into view and the kids shouted surprise and the music began playing, Emily looked flabbergasted.

But not pleased. Lauren's heart sank, but it was

minor compared to what she felt when she saw Emily's attention focus in on one particular blond boy.

Like a trapped animal suddenly become aware that the cage door had been opened, she tore after him, and since Lauren was the one closest to the attack, it was she who got there first, trying to pull Emily off. But Emily's hand shot out, whacking Lauren in the face, coming with such force that Lauren stumbled backward, tripping over a boulder and falling to the ground.

And from her grounded position, Lauren watched the remainder of the show unfold: Emily, not missing a beat, continued after the boy—ferociously beating on him, and Jonathan—coming first to Lauren's aid, then instructing Beatrice to telephone the doctor and get him out there—ran over and pulled Emily off the boy.

The boys now seemed crazed as though the initial incident had been simply a warm-up exercise to get the fun moving along: they began whooping, running, shouting, shaking their Pepsi cans, squirting the cola at one another, popping balloons, pulling down streamers and pictures and signs . . . And with the exception of Francine, who looked about ready to vomit, the girls stood off to the side, watching and giggling. The boys in the band jumped right up, scurrying to get their instruments safely back into cases.

It was like a freak show that had blown in through the gates, circling the ground, refusing to leave. Lauren's cheek was throbbing . . . as was her right ankle, and she wished it would all disappear, but the best she could manage under the circumstances was to fall into some kind of semi-awareness: she was ultimately aware of being lifted by Jonathan and wincing as she heard him shout out, "Carla, you're on immediate warning, the gate is going down."

Blessedly according to Doc Stevens, the pregnancy was strong and intact, it would take a lot more than that to injure it. But Lauren's ankle was sprained, needing to be wrapped, and her lip and cheek were swollen and bruised.

She still couldn't believe that Emily had actually struck her, nor could she believe the power behind the blow. It was unintentional, she believed that, but Lauren had seen no sign of repentance. And as for Emily's classmates operating with mob mentality, cheerfully joining in to make what was bad, worse . . . it was frightening. Jonathan had finally managed to quiet them and get them out, Beatrice driving some of them home in her own station wagon.

And if Lauren was stunned and disappointed by the whole affair, Jonathan was furious, taking Emily to her room and ordering her not to set foot out.

Aunt Fern was horrified, and so was Chelsea when she saw what had happened to her mother. And though her mother tried to make out like it had been an accident, Chelsea doubted it. The only good part was her sister was finally in deep trouble with Daddy—and Chelsea couldn't resist the chance of throwing it in her face. "Well, it looks like the loony stepsister has finally done it now," she taunted as she boldly threw open the door to her bedroom. "And I can't think of anyone I'd rather see—" But she stopped midsentence, surprised to see Emily slam down the receiver of her new phone. "Who were you calling?"

"Get out of here!"

"Francine? No, it couldn't be Francine, she just left and according to her mother, they weren't going straight home. Besides, after the big fool you made of yourself today, I doubt she'd even want to be your friend, let alone talk—"

She stopped there . . . because Emily was now coming toward her, her dark eyes forbidding and her fists rolling at her sides, readying them for action. But after seeing what Emily had just done to her mother, Chelsea wasn't staying.

They had stopped at the drugstore on the drive home from school . . . it was the last thing she wanted, what she wanted these days was to get away from her mother, away from the possibility of a confrontation, away from the subject that made her seethe with anger when she thought about it. But standing there waiting at the drug counter, her mother eyeballing her, she knew it was about to come to a head. "What is it, Emily," Nancy said. "You've been so cold and distant the last few days. It's as if your mind has gone on a trip."

Right ... actually it was over a week if Nancy really wanted to know. Not that it made a difference. "Which means you oughtn't to bother looking for it," she said.

"Please don't be flip."

"What do you want from me?"

"I want to know what's wrong."

"Do you really?"

"Would I ask if I didn't?"

"Okay," Emily said, trying to be laid back. "It's all about you being a slut."

But her mother wasn't so laid back when she said it—her mouth dropped, then her hand shot out and caught Emily on her cheek! And while her mother stood there stunned at what she'd done, Emily turned and took off for the car shouting out a few choice words. When her mother finally got herself together enough to come out and get behind the wheel, Emily went on to clarify, "You see, I never believed it until the day at the fair when I actually saw you, even when one of the kids in school kept telling me ... boy, what a hopeless jerk I am. And did you ever once think of Daddy— what about him?"

And all the way home her mother tried to explain about the underaged trailer goon she'd been fucking for the past eight months ... but the more she explained, the more furious Emily got. While she wanted to hear that it was all some terrible blooper, that her mother had gone temporarily in-

*sane, that she wasn't really her mother but some
indecent, overexposed stand-in floozy, she didn't
say any of the above. All she could do was stam-
mer and blubber and say she loved him, and that
someday maybe Emily would understand.*

*As they walked in the house, Emily picked up
her new baseball bat from where it was leaning
against the kitchen wall and headed into the living
room, carrying it, swinging it as she went. Understand? Uh-uh, Mommy, not on your life. . . .*

"Get up and dressed," the words sliced loudly
through Emily's thoughts, and she shot up in bed,
gasping as her eyes shot over to the intercom and
camera area above her desk—Beatrice's voice was
at the controls. She sighed, then sank back to her
pillow, peering carefully around the room, wondering if there were other cameras she didn't
know about.

If so, they were well hidden. Though Emily
tried to go back to where she left off, her memories had short-circuited, leaving her brain feeling
as though it were packed with cotton—a feeling
she had grown accustomed to. She got up and
dressed for school. Except for shoes—though she
had worn her work boots the day before and took
them off in her bedroom, this morning one of
them was gone.

Instead she wore sneakers . . . and as she came
out of her room she ran into old Beatrice carrying
a dish with some kind of crispy baked stuff . . .
"What're those for?"

"To settle Lauren's stomach."

"What about her ankle?"

"Why? Do you care?"

"No ... my mistake for asking. It was dumb of her to make that party. When you see her, tell her."

She headed downstairs, leaving the woman gaping after her, wondering if maybe she wasn't the one who took her boot. One thing she knew, she wouldn't want to be the recipient of one of Beatrice's secret recipes. She never did trust Beatrice, Daddy's old housekeeper, nurse, or whatever she used to be. And neither did her mother, Emily at this very moment remembered.

But the baseball bat, she *had* picked up the stinking bat ...

It all seemed eerily calm when she woke to the loud, unfamiliar grinding emanating from out on the grounds. Lauren lifted her head and looked at the bedside clock: ten o'clock, she couldn't remember the last time she'd slept so late. She sat up, as usual feeling a little queasy, but on the bedside table were a couple of thin wafers in a dish waiting for her. Jonathan's doing, she thought, shaking her head. She picked one up and nibbled on it.

Apparently he had gotten the girls fed and off to school, there was less than a week of classes left before summer vacation, and Lauren wondered if maybe it wouldn't have been wiser to let Emily stay out of school, not open the way for another confrontation. In fact, unless the situation could get settled somehow, a private school might be a better choice for her in September.

Lauren stood up, feeling some discomfort in her ankle, and hobbled to the window to find out about the noise. She shook her head: the swimming pool. Two backhoes were already digging a hole, about twenty-five feet from the back patio, apparently where Jonathan had instructed them to dig. Her attention moved back to the patio, where she had so eagerly put up decorations less than twenty-four hours before. All signs of a party were now gone.

She sighed, then headed to the shower. When she stepped out of the stall, she was surprised to see Beatrice standing there holding a towel. To keep from getting upset at the invasion of privacy, Lauren reminded herself how helpful the woman had been the day before: preparing for, during, and following the whole wretched scenario. "Thank you," she said, taking the towel and wrapping it around herself. "But this really isn't necessary. I'm fine."

Beatrice stepped back to the door to leave. "What would you like for breakfast, Mrs. Grant?"

"Tea and juice will be fine. What time did you get—" she began, but the woman couldn't hear her, she was already heading toward the stairs to get breakfast.

By the time Lauren got to the kitchen, the table was set, and in addition to tea and orange juice, there were a couple of warm blueberry muffins snuggled in a white linen napkin in a wicker basket, and with the smell making her mouth water, she realized her stomach for a change felt good. She looked at Beatrice. "That was you who put those wafers on the nightstand, wasn't it?"

"Those are homemade, an old family recipe . . . wonderful for morning sickness."

Now Lauren lifted out one of the marvelous-looking muffins and took a bite. "Hmm . . . this is really delicious, Beatrice," she said. "Another old family recipe?"

While cleaning off the counter and doing the dishes, she nodded. "That's right. When the young Mr. Grant was a boy, those were his favorites."

"Oh?" Lauren looked up at her. "Beatrice, tell me about Mr. Grant when he was a boy."

The woman shrugged. "I don't know, what is there to tell? He was smart always, disciplined and respectful, always the student who won the awards for being number one. Whether it was for math or English or science."

Lauren smiled as she dropped her hand to her nearly flat stomach. The thought of a baby growing that was the result of Jonathan and her love, a part of each of them, got her excited in a way she had never felt with her first pregnancy. "His parents must have been very proud," she responded automatically.

"Yes, of course, they were . . . but they were not in the habit of doling out praise. They didn't feel it should be necessary. They had certain expectations that the young Mr. Grant was to meet, and he, being a good son, saw that they were never disappointed. His father was an entrepreneur, he built a business from nearly nothing, turning it into a multimillion-dollar corporation. And his wife—right through it all—worked up there beside him."

She nodded and Beatrice went on. "She was an unusual woman—a trendsetter. In fact, she dressed in tailored suits long before it became fashionable."

Likely explaining Jonathan's desire to see a woman dressed in more feminine fashions. She had a picture in her head of a small, lonely, dark-haired boy by the name of Jonathan. As wonderful as it might have been for the elder Grants to have worked side by side, it managed to further exclude their son. "What kind of business?" she asked, and though Beatrice didn't say so, Lauren could see that she thought it odd that as Jonathan's wife she knew so little.

Still she answered the question. "They designed and manufactured boxing."

Lauren nodded. "I see. Well, whatever did become of it?"

"The young Mr. Grant was in his second year of college when his father died and left him the larger share of the business. And though his mother was still sharp-minded, she was getting on in years and apparently there was some concern for her failing health. Mr. Grant wasn't interested in running the business himself, so when a serious buyer happened along, over the protests of his mother who was not about to relinquish her power easily, he sold."

Lauren could understand Jonathan's decision—certainly designing boxing didn't sound nearly as exciting as designing roads and bridges and buildings ... Though it didn't sound like it was an easy decision in view of his mother.

"The young Mr. Grant took over the finances—to budget and invest so the money would grow. And of course with him at the helm, his mother wanted for nothing."

That sounded like Jonathan, so reliable, so there for his loved ones. Though his folks' parenting left a lot to be desired, he didn't allow it to poison him. Which meant, though he never said so, he loved them despite their mistakes.

Lauren looked at Beatrice as she finished cleaning the kitchen, and smiled. "Thank you for telling me these things," she said. "I like to hear about Jonathan's childhood, but he refuses to talk much about those days. And when you really love someone, well, you know how it is—" She shrugged, leaving her sentence dangling and feeling strange that she had confided that ...

But Beatrice kept her distance, not responding, only squatting down, opening the bottom sink cabinet, and fishing out the container of furniture polish and a shammy. "You certainly are going like a house afire today, Beatrice," Lauren said. "Slow down a little, don't overdo ... there's no rush. What time did you arrive?"

She turned to Lauren now. "I would have thought that Mr. Grant told you."

"Told me what?"

"Well, he's very concerned about you as you well know, now even more so with the injured ankle. He asked me to stay on. So I'm taking the bedroom that separates yours and the children's, that is unless you'd rather I take another."

As soon as Jonathan arrived home, she questioned him about it, though at this point her feelings for the woman had eased up. But still, to have live-in help, well, she hated the idea of losing their privacy and she said as much.

"The walls in this place are solid, darling. One of the things I checked when we first looked at it."

"There's more than one way to lose privacy."

"Beatrice is the all-time expert at being unobtrusive."

"I have no doubt, but you could have at least discussed it with me first."

"When was there time?"

Along with the response, she caught a weariness in his voice, something new, and she realized how often she'd been critical of his decisions these days. Instantly she felt guilty; so much of the worry and aggravation of the household fell on his shoulders. She placed her hand on his arm . . . "I'm sorry, I'm sure Beatrice's living here temporarily will work out fine."

"By the way," he said, "just so I won't be accused of doing it behind your back, I want to tell you I spoke to Emily's therapist earlier. Just to let her know what happened at the party. Emily wouldn't open up to me, perhaps she will to her. Now that I've said that, I want to end the subject. Please, Lauren?"

They shared a quiet lunch on the patio, served by Beatrice, and right after Jonathan left for an appointment. Soon after, she phoned Carla and was surprised at how cool she sounded. "Look, first, let me apologize for my husband's abruptness about the open gate yesterday. He didn't mean it to sound rude. He was just upset."

"Weren't we all," Carla said. "By the look of it, including Emily. What happened to her?"

"I didn't see her this morning, Jonathan did, of course. According to him, she wouldn't say."

"So didn't he ask?"

"Of course he asked. But Emily isn't exactly free with her conversation, Carla."

"Then you or Jonathan have got to make her talk."

She sighed heavily. "And just how do you expect us to do that?" she asked, the words reminding her of a similarly defensive conversation she'd had a few weeks back with Fern. Of course, if Chelsea had refused to talk to Lauren about something as important as this, wouldn't she have camped out at her doorway until she did? But Chelsea was not Emily, in temperament or anything else. Intentional or not, Lauren now had a twisted ankle and a bruised face to show for it.

"So suddenly Jonathan is the weak-kneed, ineffectual father, right out of one of those TV sitcoms? Funny, but it sure seems to me he says what he wants to say."

"You *are* angry about what he said to you yesterday, aren't you?"

"Not about the gate, Lauren. When I left, which wasn't until the doctor came and I knew you were okay, he told me it would be better if I stayed away."

Lauren hesitated only a moment, then said, "I'm sorry, I don't believe you."

"Believe what you want, Lauren. I went through this once before, and I'm not up to going through it again." With that, the receiver clicked in her ear.

And though Lauren went to dial her right back, Beatrice walked in. "Why don't you do that later?" she suggested, gently prying the phone from her hands. "It's just about nap time for mother and baby." And Lauren let still another thing go—despite sleeping in, she was much too weary to deal with Carla's accusation. Beatrice clicked off the cellular phone and slipped it into her apron pocket—Lauren watched as she fluffed her pillow, then felt her sandals coming off, her feet being lifted to the sofa . . .

Carla misunderstood, there was no other explanation, Lauren thought, feeling the gentle breeze of the cotton quilt as it fell gently over her body. Beatrice walked to the window and pulled the blinds—and as the light dimmed, her eyes closed.

Yes, a misunderstanding. She would straighten it out with Jonathan later . . .

The last thing that went through her mind before falling off was a ruckus she recalled overhearing that morning: Emily had been fussing with Beatrice . . . and Jonathan had stepped in to quiet her. Apparently Emily had misplaced one of her high-backed boots.

When Jonathan brought the girls home from school and Lauren confronted him with Carla's accusation, Jonathan verified her thoughts exactly. "Look, I may not have the same appreciation or fondness for Carla as you," Jonathan said, "but give me a little more credit, will you, I wouldn't be so unfeeling as to have said that."

"It's just that everyone was in such a nervous state at the time . . . Well, it would certainly have been easy to misunderstand. What exactly was it you said?"

"Only that you and the girls will be spending a fabulous summer on the Grant estate," he said, trying to engage her, then dropping his teasing, "Look, I made it clear that she and Francine were welcome to come over anytime. With the gates secured, of course. You do understand, Lauren, I have no intention of forgoing my family's security to satisfy Carla's hang-ups?"

Lauren's thoughts went directly to Jay Philips from Monticello—who by his own admission had had a rifle and had bragged to the police how easily he could have picked off Emily. Granted, Jonathan's attorney with Detective Kneeland's help got a judge to sign a restraining order, keeping Jay Philips away from the Grant family, but who knew if he'd abide by it.

Besides, Lauren wasn't foolish enough to believe he was the only potential threat around these days . . . her thoughts moved to the rowdiness and coarseness of those young people the day before. For goodness sake, they had a sophisticated security system, wouldn't it be foolish of them not to use it?

She nodded, and he carried on. "What I specifically said was, I hoped she wouldn't stay away because of it." He sat down on the sofa, being particularly careful of her sore ankle that Beatrice had raised up on a few pillows. He leaned over to her. "Look, if it'll make you feel better, I'll call Carla and explain—"

She shook her head. "Forget it. I'll take care of Carla. Meanwhile I want to talk about you."

"Uh-oh, what'd I do now?"

"Oh, come on now, Jonathan. By that remark, one would think I badgered you."

"I admit, sometimes it seems that way." Though a thin smile accompanied his words, she could see by his expression, it was not all meant in jest.

Again she felt she was being too critical of him. Perhaps taking him for granted. Was she doing to him what his parents had done? Which immediately made her feel guilty. She took his hands in hers, kissing them, then looked up into his magical eyes. "You did nothing at all, darling. It's just that Beatrice was telling me how bright a child you were, not that it surprises me. She told me how in school you'd walk away with all the academic prizes."

The smile now widened, spreading over his face. "You mean I hadn't bragged about that already?"

"Actually, not once. You do know that in marriage, bragging is allowed."

"Hey, Gordon, what's doing?" was all she said when he finally answered the phone.

"Who is this?" he asked.

"Fancy Nance ... want to dance, get in my pants? Sorry, jerk-off, not a chance."

A deep breath, followed by a long silence, then he said finally, "This is her kid, right, the one who was over the house that day with that little neighbor girl. Are you the one who called my answering machine twice, then hung up?"

"Wow, you sure are a smart one. Hey, do you think it was that overgrown brain my mother liked? Or was it that tender young meat she couldn't resist?"

"I'd say you're a real young girl to have a foul mouth like that."

"I remember you good. You were the one fucking my mother in the trailer at the fair."

A long silence, then he moved on to another subject. "Hey, Emily, you like the way I fixed up your house?" But before she could answer he went on, "I did it for your mother, to make her happy. I never got the chance to make her happy, you know, at least not the way I wanted to. Not the way she deserved."

There was a noise on the phone line and Emily said, "Hey, are you there?"

"Yeah, I'm here."

"I don't know what you're thinking, asshole, because she was happy already ... and without help from you. You likely don't even know who you are so why don't I clue you in. You're the prick who came in and screwed it up."

A long silence, then he asked, "So if you think that, what did you call about?"

"I wanted to ask a question."

"Go on, ask."

"Did you kill her, too?"

"I think you know the answer to that one better than anyone. Maybe you and me together—"

Was there a click on the line then? She wasn't sure because the door burst open. Emily dropped the receiver, then quickly fumbling to retrieve it with shaking hands, she hung up. Who did Gordon think was the murderer? Did he think it was her, is that what he meant? Or was he just pushing her buttons to see what she'd say?

Sure, she had been furious with her mother, she could remember that now, but the police hadn't been able to come up with anything against her— or for that matter against anyone. Strickler, the shrink, told her it was a transient stranger who killed her mother, a person she'd most likely never see again. But it wasn't her . . . and he had said it enough times so that she would someday pull a file in her head labeled: designer memories by Strickler.

But wasn't it time she got a better grip on her own rat-infested brain—at least whatever was left of it? Strickler hadn't even been there, so how could he know?

Though the stairs were difficult to climb with her bad ankle, escaping Beatrice's watchful eyes that afternoon seemed even more of a problem. Jonathan had closed himself in his study to work, and while Beatrice was in the den cleaning, Lauren finally managed to make it up the back stairs to Emily's room. She hadn't thought out exactly what she would say to her or what she might hear in return, so when she opened the door, there were no expectations.

Emily had been sitting on the floor, apparently talking on the telephone, and when Lauren came in, she was so thrown, she dropped the receiver and fumbled with it to hang it up. About a quarter of the floor space was covered with old newspapers, most of them smelly and damp and yellowstained.

"Your father told you the dog was to stay in the laundry room until it's housebroken."

Silence, while Emily seemed to be concentrating on a whole other dialogue.

"Who were you talking to, Emily?" she asked, but got still more silence. Francine, she imagined, not able to think of anyone else. Of course there was always the possibility of the therapist, but despite what the woman told her, Lauren still had trouble believing Emily confided in her. When Emily refused to respond, Lauren looked at her and said, "Gee, Lauren, I'm sorry for whacking you in the face. I'm sorry for causing you to stumble and hurt your ankle."

But the sarcasm didn't bring on the apology she was fishing for or any sign of remorse or even a simple explanation, just an undaunted, disinterested stare. Lauren's attention was then drawn to Emily's bed, the bottom edge of the black quilted bedspread swinging slightly on the floor. Lauren went and stooped down, lifting the edge of the material and finding the stowaway.

She reached out for the puppy, and he began to whimper. Against his will, she lifted him into her arms. As she got to the doorway, she stopped and turned. "According to Francine, the boy you went after yesterday is named Willie Campbell," she said. "Why him, Emily? What did he do to you?"

Chapter Thirteen

Lauren tried to repair the hurt feelings with Carla, but though Carla professed that all was fine, there still remained a distinct coolness in her voice. When Fern dropped by later, Lauren brought it up. "The real problem is, she doesn't like Jonathan, and from her perspective, I suppose I can understand it, he's not been exactly friendly toward her. And then, too, I have a suspicion that Nancy did a lot of bad-mouthing about Jonathan to her. Which, if course, we all know is a terrible mistake for a spouse to make ... it inevitably turns out that the couple makes up and the other party holds a grudge."

"Complained about what?"

Lauren shrugged, threw up her hands. "Who knows, Fern, just things."

"I hope you're not including me in that formula. I never hold grudges."

"Well, okay. Just that he was possessive. And though she's never come out and actually said it, it's clear she thinks he's somewhat of a control freak."

"And you don't think so?"

Lauren looked up. "Excuse me? Why is it I thought you liked Jonathan?"

"Oh, I do, I think he's a good man who adores my sister. But I don't live with him, nor am I his wife. Would I find it hard to be married to the man? Yes, likely. But then everyone is different. What is it they say, different folks, different strokes? Oh, don't get me wrong, if I thought for an instant he was manipulating you, causing you or Chelsea harm, I'd be whistling another tune."

"You're making it sound quite grim."

"Not at all. I just mean, he's bright, quick, opinionated, and likes the world to go his way—not an easy act to keep up with. Perhaps he was just too overbearing for Nancy to handle."

"But not for me, right?"

Fern hesitated, giving her a sideward glance. "Are you trying to tell me something?"

"No, of course not," Lauren said. "My goodness, where did your sense of humor go?" She laughed it away—after all, she had said it in jest, hadn't she?

Emily didn't just jump into it, she had thought it over carefully before agreeing to meet Gordon that night. She would wait until dinner was finished, until the darkness came . . . then she'd climb out her bedroom window that was only a short drop to the roof of the garage. From there she'd shimmy down the drainpipe, far enough to jump to the lawn. Though she hadn't done a lot of climbing in the last year or so, it still ought to be easy enough. Next was the chain-link fence, which was not a problem—Daddy had given her one of those key cards.

She would take Chelsea's bike from the garage—her old bike had a bad tire. Candlewood Terrace was only a few miles, even in the dark, only a ten- or fifteen-minute ride.

Gordon was hinting at something to Emily earlier when Lauren barged in and ruined things, but now when she called him back, he refused to say more, using her curiosity as bait to get her to come out there and talk. She wasn't a fool though, she knew he might just be playing sick games with her . . .

It was hard to determine how screwed up he was. Hadn't he been messing around with a married woman practically old enough to be his mother? Now wasn't he renting out his dead lover's house and fixing it up in a way that might have made her happy when she was alive? If that wasn't obsessing, then what was? Emily went to her closet, took the tin box from the back, and opened it. Inside, among a bunch of old treasures, was her super-sixteen jackknife—something she had once gotten through a tradeoff with some kid. She took it out.

Maybe not one of those fancy switchblades the girls in Bateman would secretly slip in their sock or up their pants leg or keep at night under their pillow, but it would do.

And it was easy, all of it going right according

to plan. By eight-thirty she was standing outside Gordon's house ... her house. She parked Chelsea's bike alongside the back of the garage, took the jackknife from her pocket, and opened it, then slid it in her jeans's pocket where she could get at it easily if she needed it. Then finally, feeling strangely calm, she knocked at the back door. What a joke—she could have used her key if she wanted to, but there was no need for that. When there was no answer after knocking and waiting, she tried the knob. And when it turned, she opened it and tiptoed inside.

Suddenly without being sure what had happened, she was running out of the house, jumping back on her bike, pedaling out of there as fast as she could. And when an hour had passed and she realized what she was doing, she didn't know where she was or where she was going. But she continued to pedal, because she didn't know what else to do. Calm, cool, flip, and empty-headed— *that's the way, Emily, fool 'em all, nothing really to worry about.* She hadn't killed her mother and she hadn't killed him. Right, Doctor Shrink?

Whenever the picture of the guy's smashed head came into focus, she'd fight hard to sweep it away. Screw it, it was her mind, and she had charge of all callers and well-wishers. He was definitely not on her guest list, heck, she hardly knew him. He was just some dumb, pathetic sex goon soon to be a three-inch spread in a local obituary column. She had no obligation to let him enter her head or go to his funeral or even feel bad. Well, wasn't life a hoot? Some things just got settled in their own good time, didn't they? That guy would not be squealing on who killed Nancy because he no longer knew.

She felt like peeing, which in turn made her feel like laughing. Was it not strange that a person was required to pee and shit when his world was spinning at the speed of light? Were there no priorities, no decorum? Pretty fancy vocabulary, huh, Emily? She might not have known her own name if asked, but her mind suddenly focused in on the unlikely name of Gordon Cummings.

Gordon Cummings, who in the heck was Gordon Cummings? She let out a loud sigh then as she recognized where she was and because it was probably the wisest thing to do under the circumstances, she turned the bike in the direction of Mountainview Road. And as she did, it came to her—Gordon was the nice young chap who fucked her mother and lived in her house, and whose head was smashed in with a fireplace iron. *Geez, Emily, what is with that memory of yours?*

Lauren fell off to sleep at about seven-thirty on the den sofa while reading a paperback, missing Chelsea's bedtime, and waking only when Jonathan walked in from the study. Now for the past hour she watched as he paced around the living room, but insisting nothing in particular was wrong, she tried to calm him, engaging him in conversation.

Finally she broached the subject of a private school for Emily in the fall. And he went for it—in fact, he said he knew of a reputable day school a couple of towns over, the transportation back and forth would present no problem. And considering the behavior of the public school children as witnessed the night before, he thought it would be a good move for Chelsea as well.

And as though the decision had somehow relieved whatever stress he'd been feeling, he smiled, then decided he wanted ice cream. "There's a couple of flavors in the freezer, take your pick."

"What about the girls?"

She looked at her watch, then shrugged. "It's almost ten . . . Chelsea is surely sleeping."

"I bet not Emily," he said slyly. "Why don't I check." She shook her head—how like him? With all his gruff and anger at Emily following the disastrous party, here he was worried that she wouldn't get the flavor of her choice.

He started upstairs as she was left thinking of ice cream and weight and her pregnancy, which in turn reminded her that she ought to be looking to find a good obstetrician. Doc Stevens was fine for colds and flus and sprains, but for their baby she wanted a specialist, and she was sure Jonathan would want that, too.

But she didn't have the time or opportunity to bring it up that night—the next thing she heard was feet pounding down the back stairs and jingling of car keys. Then Jonathan was heading through the den, fear in his eyes. "What is it, Jonathan?"

"Emily's gone. I've got to find her."

She stood up, immediately heading for the phone. "Let me call Carla," she said.

"No!" Jonathan cried. "Don't call anyone! Do you understand, Lauren?"

She backed away from the phone, nodding, though she didn't understand at all. He was just worried and wasn't making sense. "Wait, let me tell Beatrice, let me come—" she started, but he had already run out of the house.

She ran upstairs, quickly told Beatrice who had been using the sewing machine in her bedroom, then grabbing a jacket, Lauren hurried outside just as the gate was opening to let Jonathan's car through. But before she could run after him or get in her car to follow after him, it was suddenly okay . . . or so it seemed: someone was riding a bicycle through the open gates . . . and it was Emily.

She had taken Chelsea's bicycle and gone off to who knows where, and now she looked as white as a ghost as she sat on the sofa between Jonathan and Lauren saying in a frighteningly calm voice, "Gordon Cummings is dead."

"What do you mean?" he asked, having trouble digesting the name and putting it together with the man on Candlebrook Terrace. He looked at Lauren for help. "The tenant?" And when she nodded, he turned back to Emily. "How do you know he's dead?"

"I was there, I saw him."

"There? You mean, at the house?"

She nodded.

"I don't understand, why ... why would you go there?"

She shrugged. "It's our house, isn't it?"

"You went there because it's our house?"

"And I know him from being over at Francine's. We talked a couple of times."

Lauren felt a weight sink onto her chest ... good God, where was she while this was going on? There was a long pause at which time she could feel Jonathan's eyes accusing her, then he asked, "Have you been there before."

"Twice. Both times with Francine. Once Gordon was there, once he wasn't."

Jonathan looked confused, as though he were having tremendous difficulty assimilating the story. "And this time?" he said finally. "Did he know you were coming this time?"

She nodded. "He knew, I called him on the phone."

Jonathan ran his tongue over his lips—he looked almost feverish. "Okay, I want to get this straight, he expected you. Was anyone else aware of that? Francine, Carla, anyone?"

"Uh-uh, I didn't tell anyone, and I know he wouldn't have told anyone."

"Was anyone there when you arrived?"

"Just him. He was lying on the floor, his brains all over the carpet."

Lauren took a deep breath, trying to discourage any impulse to vomit, this was not the time to be sick. Though Jonathan flinched at the unnecessary description, he moved on. "Did you see anyone on the way there or coming home? Now think, someone driving by in a car, walking a dog?"

"Uh-uh."

"What about once you got there?"

She shook her head.

Then he put his arm around her, and though she didn't pull away, she stiffened. "It's going to be all right, Princess. I want you to go upstairs, get into your nightclothes, and go to bed. And I want you to forget all about this, just as though it never happened. Do you hear me?" She nodded again. "Remember, you didn't leave the house tonight, you didn't see or do anything."

"But don't you think—" Emily started.

"Listen to me, it's important. Please." He placed his hands on her shoulders and peered into her eyes. "Would Daddy steer you wrong, tell you to do anything harmful?"

She shook her head, her voice coming out a whisper. "No."

"Do you want to end up at Bates again?" Lauren could see fear reach into her eyes. "Then let your father handle this, do exactly as I say." He drew his arm around her tighter, comforting her. "Everything is going to be all right."

*   *   *

Emily went upstairs, and though Lauren felt as though she would soon explode, she waited until she heard her stepdaughter's door close before she spoke up. "I don't believe what I've just heard, Jonathan. What are you doing?"

"What I have to do, I'm protecting my daughter."

"From what?"

He stood up and began to pace the room. "Do you understand what this would look like if the police were to know she was there at the scene of the murder? They would never understand."

"Well, to be blunt, neither do I. Do you? It makes no sense. Maybe we ought to talk to Francine about it, maybe she can fill us in on this friendship."

"You will call or confide in no one," he said, glaring at her.

"This is serious, darling, a man was murdered."

"Precisely. And the police are immediately going to jump to the conclusion that Emily did it."

"But what would her motive be?"

Jonathan shrugged. "He was living in her house and she didn't like it . . . or, I don't know, damnit! Maybe she was having an affair with the guy."

"Jonathan. Dear God, she's only twelve!"

"And he's twenty-two, as I recall Fern saying. It doesn't sound impossible. Not these days."

"I don't know," she said, already doubting her instincts as she said it. "I've seen no indication that Emily's even interested in the opposite sex. Have you?"

"I'm simply giving you an example of what the police might say. What could so easily be twisted into a motive."

Lauren's thoughts went to the tenant, Gordon Cummings. What would they do, just leave the poor man there, wait until someone finds him? It seemed so wrong, for everyone, including Emily. Should she be told to forget everything, was that healthy? "Maybe we should discuss this with her therapist," she said, grasping at straws.

"Absolutely not, and Emily must not either. And as much as I hate to say so, to withdraw her outlets, it's a matter of priorities—what's more important here, her peace of mind or her freedom? Her peace of mind will come back naturally, after all, she has done nothing wrong—her freedom is what's at stake."

It was then that Lauren started feeling the fear that Jonathan was feeling. Not just intellectualizing it, but feeling it as he was. This was the second murder that occurred in the same house in two years in a town that was relatively crime-free. And both of those times Emily was the only other person in the house. Did he think she did it? Oh, dear Lord, could he think that?

No, Lauren was jumping to conclusions, she mustn't do that. Jonathan's fear hadn't to do with Emily's guilt, rather to do with the past ... sure Emily would be made a suspect in a murder she had nothing to do with. But what if she did do it? Sneaking out of the house after dark and going to visit a grown man did not look good. Suppose they did have something going on? Something sexual ... suppose a hundred and one different ridiculous scenarios ...

Her speculations were insane, most of all, disloyal—to both her stepdaughter and her husband. But now that she dared think such things, they would not easily go away. Through the night, she awoke a half-dozen times, believing Emily guilty, only to find relief by arguing back her innocence. Her best argument being, would she have the strength to overpower a man who, as Lauren recalled Fern saying, was quite big? A contractor, a man who gets plenty of exercise, not apt to be a weak man. Uh-uh, no, never. And indeed she made the ultimate case for Jonathan's insistence that they keep Emily's being at the murder scene a secret: if Lauren could so easily jump to such wrong conclusions about her twelve-year-old stepdaughter, what would the police do?

So when Fern called at about eleven o'clock the next morning, Lauren was prepared to hear about Gordon Cummings being found murdered, and because of all the anxiety and doubt she was experiencing, it was not difficult to make her reaction sound sincere. According to Fern, when the tenant didn't show up for work that morning, one of the workers from the job, assuming Gordon was ill, stopped by to pick up a power drill off his truck. He had no intentions of going inside, but as it turned out he needed the key to the truck's toolbox.

"Do the police know who was responsible?" she asked, feeling a terrible sadness go through her as she perpetuated the first lie she'd ever told her sister.

"If they do, they haven't said. But I can't help thinking how bizarre it is, Lauren, I mean this being the second murder in the same house. I can't help but think it's related to Nancy."

With all thoughts being focused on Emily since the night before, Lauren found it amazing that this particular equation hadn't entered her mind. But now that it had, wouldn't it put a whole other spin on it? Perhaps the same person was responsible for both murders ... But why, what kind of madman were they dealing with? Surely a psychotic. Would Nancy's case be opened again? And what about Jay Philips, shouldn't they be thinking of him?

"Lauren, yoo-hoo, are you there, honey? Are you okay?" Fern called over the silence.

"Yes, of course, it's all such a jolt. I'll have to call Jonathan right away."

"Good idea. I imagine the police are already on their way."

"Here? Why would they—"

And she must have sounded panicky as well as stupid, because Fern jumped in to explain something relatively simple. "Honey, think about it a moment. The murder was on Jonathan's property. Even if his ex-wife hadn't been killed there, the police would naturally want to ask you people questions."

"Right, I do understand that. But it's not like we even knew the man."

"Of course not, and I made that clear to a Detective Donald Kneeland who questioned me. I told them all the dealings with the tenant had been through me."

"Then you don't think they'll badger us?"

Suddenly Fern's voice lowered an octave. "Lauren, you're scared. Why?"

"Well, don't I have cause to be? Tell me you didn't think of it. For a while there Jonathan and I were considering living at that house ourselves. Suppose we had?"

As soon as Lauren got off the phone, she called Beatrice through the intercom, and she came downstairs immediately. "Is there something wrong, Mrs. Grant?"

"There's really no need to be so formal. I would like it if you called me Lauren."

"If you'd like," she said in her no-nonsense manner. "Now, what may I do for you?"

Lauren wrung her hands, not quite sure how to approach the subject but feeling she must. "Beatrice, did Jonathan mention anything about last night."

"Pardon me?"

"You remember ... when I woke you to tell you that Emily was missing?"

"Oh, that, yes, of course. In fact, he told me about it last night." And Lauren must have looked confused, because Beatrice added, "I got up with Chelsea and was on the way to the kitchen to get her a glass of milk when I found Mr. Grant up and pacing the living room. I know he didn't want to wake—"

"Wait, please, back up. What was wrong with Chelsea?"

"Oh, nothing to fret about, she woke up crying. Just one of those bad dreams children regularly have. She forgot what it was about the moment she woke."

No, not regularly—Chelsea hadn't had a nightmare since she was about three. Which made Lauren realize that all the stress and bad feelings going on since Emily's homecoming was taking its toll on her. "But I didn't even hear—" she began.

"You were sleeping quite soundly . . . I peeked in your bedroom to check." Lauren's expression must have indicated how disturbed she was because the woman went on to explain. "My first thought was that you'd want to go to her yourself, but when I saw you . . . well, I hadn't the heart to disturb you. It happens often in pregnancy; it's your body's way of taking what it requires, what the baby demands."

No, not a sound sleep, more like an uneasy, troubled sleep, she thought, remembering the dozens of times she woke up thinking about Emily, about the murder. And she did notice at least once that Jonathan was not beside her. But she didn't bother to correct Beatrice—she nodded, still finding it surprising that she had slept through Chelsea's crying. She had never done that, she thought, pausing a second to qualify her rambling thoughts—well, at least not to her knowledge. In any event, thankfully Beatrice was there.

Jonathan was home within twenty minutes of her call, and Detective Kneeland who had phoned to give her notice was in the living room waiting to see them both. When Lauren met Jonathan in the foyer, he kissed her and asked, "Did you tell him you had already learned about the murder, that your sister had called you earlier?"

"Yes, when he called. Just as you said for me to do. Beatrice let him in, I waited for you."

"Good, there's no need to lie," he said, and Lauren marveled at his words. If they weren't lying, just what would withholding information from the police be? Jonathan, feeling her anxiety, put his arms around her. "Now, my darling, there's no need to be nervous, we've done nothing wrong, certainly nothing criminal. You just follow my lead."

They were just protecting Emily from the injustices of the system, Lauren told herself as she and Jonathan walked into the living room where the detective was waiting. So first were the amenities, including an inquiry from the detective about Lauren's bruised lip and slight limp that Jonathan jumped in to explain happened when she walked into a tree while decorating the yard for Emily's birthday party.

Next came the other questions that surprisingly weren't of the number or intensity of those she had already asked herself. He wanted to know if either of them had known the tenant before he moved in. And had Nancy known him? the fact was, neither she nor Jonathan had ever laid eyes on Gordon Cummings, even once he'd moved in. And to Jonathan's knowledge, Nancy had never met him. Next he asked if Lauren or Jonathan had gone out that night at all, and of course, they hadn't. Jonathan called Beatrice in the room to verify that.

Though Lauren suspected Beatrice would have verified that they had flown to the South Sea Islands if Jonathan so requested, and the detective likely knew it, too. In any event, both she and Jonathan were responsible members of the community, so the man had no reason to doubt them. According to the detective, the murder took place sometime after eight-thirty the night before. So when Kneeland said, "I assume the kiddies were at home," as though where else would they be after dark, she thought she would pass out. But she didn't, she assured him they were—telling a second lie.

Finally it was Jonathan's turn. "Tell me, Detective, do you think this murder is connected to Nancy?"

"It doesn't look like anything was taken, though with this Cummings guy living alone we can't be certain of that. It might be some kind of vendetta . . . we'll be exploring that possibility, of course. My own gut feeling is that it is connected to Mrs. Grant's murder, but gut feelings, outside of television movies, rarely get court convictions. We've already questioned Philips, what with his history and all, but he's got an alibi. According to one of his low-life buddies, they were at his house till midnight shooting pool. Not a great witness, but better than nothing. So unless we can find more evidence at the murder scene, which my men are working on right now, I'm afraid we've got nothing substantial."

Lauren shook her head, her sorrowful thoughts going to the young man who was murdered. "Tell me, has Mr. Cummings's family been notified yet?"

"Yes, ma'am, we took care of that right off. Most of his family's over in Saugerties, but there's a sister and her family lives right in town. A Kathy Campbell."

Lauren's head shot up when she heard him say the name Campbell, her thoughts moving immediately to Willie and wondering if Kathy and he were related. Kneeland, not missing her abrupt motion, asked, "Is something wrong, Mrs. Grant?"

Chapter Fourteen

After their last strained conversation Lauren
didn't really want to telephone Carla, but she
called anyway. And if Carla was still angry, all
attitude seemed temporarily put on hold to deal
with the more important issues. "Oh, Lauren,
have you heard about it?" she asked as soon as
she heard her voice.

"If you mean the murder, yes. The police were
here, they left not long ago."

"They were here, too," Carla said. "They
wanted to know if I had seen anything unusual
last night . . . which I didn't. Do they think it's
connected to Nancy?"

She wanted to tell her how both Francine and
Emily had made friends with Gordon Cummings,
but, of course, if she told her that, it would naturally lead to other things, things she couldn't discuss. "They don't know . . . it seems they're just
doing a lot of speculating. Carla, did you know
him, I mean Gordon Cummings?"

"Why would you ask that?" she asked, for some
reason put off by the question. Then, getting a

hold on her attitude, said, "Forget that, I guess I'm a little rattled ... and why shouldn't I be? Here I am in this nice safe town everyone's always applauding, and two murders occur. Both right across the street from me."

"I understand ... don't think I haven't had the same kind of thoughts myself. I simply asked the question because I figured maybe you could answer ... Well, you see, I knew the tenant had family in town, but I didn't know who—at least not until Detective Kneeland was here. He mentioned Gordon's sister lived over on Holyoke Avenue. Her name is Kathy Campbell."

Total silence from Carla's end. Lauren continued on to ask the question, though she knew Carla was very much aware of what she was getting at. "Well, is she or is she not related to Willie Campbell? The boy at the party?"

A hesitation, then, "Yeah, as a matter of fact, she is. Kathy is Willie's mother."

And wouldn't that mean a possible tie-in between Emily's anger at Willie, and her going to see the boy's uncle, Gordon Cummings? Which *would* imply a motive? Of course Carla didn't know about that, but she did know that Emily attacked a boy whose uncle leased Jonathan's house, and seemed eager herself to find out why. Surely it was something that would have come up when they discussed it following the party. "It seems odd to me you didn't mention it," she said.

"How so? Emily tries to beat up this fellow's nephew. So what's the big deal?"

Carla definitely had an attitude ... one that wasn't there when they started talking, not until Lauren unintentionally upset her by asking how well she knew her neighbor. So she started over again, this time intentionally. "Carla, did you know Gordon Cummings before he moved in?"

"What makes you think I knew him at all?"

"You're obviously holding something back. So will you please tell me what's going on."

"Nothing is going on. Listen, Lauren, I have to go. Francine just this minute walked in the door from school."

"Wait, don't—" she began, but not in time. Carla had hung up. Beatrice walked in with a cup of tea. Damn it, she wasn't wrong, Carla was keeping something.

Lauren groaned—the puppy was in Emily's bedroom again, she couldn't see him when she opened the door and came inside, but the funky smell of the room was evidence enough: Emily had somehow managed to keep Beatrice out of bounds. Jonathan would have to deal with the issue, she wasn't up to it. Actually being this tired, she wasn't sure why she had climbed the stairs to Emily's room; though it was no doubt hopeless, she still had to take another shot at talking to her.

Emily looked bad herself, there were circles beneath her eyes; clearly, she, too, had not been sleeping well. "Did your anger at Willie Campbell have to do with his uncle Gordon?"

She looked at her, but said nothing.

"What was the connection, Emily? If you could only tell me ... maybe I could help."

"Will you just stay out of my life?"

She sighed deeply. "I am a part of your life, haven't you figured that out yet? I'm your step-mother, and like it or not, look around, I'm the best you've got!"

She couldn't believe she had actually said some-thing so cruel to a twelve-year-old, but rather than put the stops to Emily, it seemed to energize her. "Well, will you look at that," she said, her hands poised at her hips. "Finally the smiling darling from Manhattan has gotten herself in a heat. Well then I suppose now's as good a time as any to ask if I killed Gordon Cummings. And my mother, too, of course." At that, Lauren stood there, speechless, but Emily continued to goad her. "I know you've been wondering from the very beginning—you were dying to ask me, but just couldn't work up enough courage. Come on, Lauren, be a woman for a change."

Maybe it was the last part that got to her, but of course she was right, at least partially. Lauren might not have had doubts about her stepdaugh-ter originally, but she certainly had them now, and yes, she did want to ask. "Okay, Emily," she said. "Let's assume you wouldn't lie through your teeth. What did you have to do with Gordon Cummings's murder? And what about your mother?"

But Emily didn't answer. She looked up toward

the doorway, and Lauren's glance followed: how long had Jonathan been standing there?

Jonathan had gone into silences before, but always in response to something minor, soon to be forgiven and over with—not as a result of anything so serious. Suddenly it was as though he had taken a knife and sliced her right out of his life.

During the next couple of days while there for Lauren in body, he had deserted her in spirit: he spoke to her only when it was absolutely necessary, and then with such pure steel in his voice, it stunned her. The eleven rooms seemed more like a hundred, he made himself that scarce to her, spending most of his time working in his study, eating many of his meals there as well ... if not outdoors talking with the girls or giving directions to the pool men. And though they continued to sleep in the same king-size bed they had slept in since their marriage, never did the bed seem so cold or so big.

Though his silence initially infuriated her, it also gave her time to cool her head and think about all that was happening. She kept coming back to her original conclusions with respect to Emily—a child of that size could never have overpowered such a large man, even with a weapon. And Detective Kneeland must have believed that, too, having not been overly concerned with Emily's whereabouts.

And with respect to Jonathan's attitude now, how would she have responded had the roles been reversed? If this had been Chelsea whose innocence *he* had doubted, would she have been so quick to understand and forgive? No, in that moment of doubt she had betrayed him, something she could never imagine him doing to her. If she could have taken the words back she would have, but of course she couldn't. All that was left was to plead with him to talk about it ... and to apologize, both of which she did over and over again.

But he refused to discuss it or forgive her. Oh, he would, she was certain of that ... when he was ready.

She tried to keep Fern from knowing what was going on between her and Jonathan: if she was to confide that they were barely speaking, it would only bring up her having been suspicious of Emily, something she couldn't even discuss rationally without acknowledging that Emily had been at Gordon Cummings's house the night of the murder. And then there were Lauren's lies to the police, something she didn't want to think about, let alone admit.

But what first caught Fern's attention when she stopped over unexpectedly the next afternoon was Chelsea's lack of enthusiasm, despite a new sandbox and jungle gym that Jonathan had brought in just a few days earlier. Fern had gone out back with Lauren to examine the pool that was now in its final stages, and Chelsea was sitting on a swing, barely moving her feet, staring at the ground.

"What's wrong with her?"

"I think she's just bored," Lauren said, though she knew it wasn't that simple. There was the nightmare, the listlessness, the refusal to communicate, certainly not the usual bubbling Chelsea. But Lauren went on with the explanation she started. "Last day of school was yesterday, Brownies and gymnastics are over for the summer. There're no kids in the neighborhood to play with ... and me, well, forget it. I'm so worn out these days, I'm hardly what anyone would consider fun company."

"I don't imagine big bad sister is any help."

"Don't say that, Fern."

"You're right. It's just that I'm looking for some redeeming quality about that girl. Has she said a word yet about the party you tried to give her or perhaps about the smack in the face you took in return? Accidentally, of course?"

The marks of which were just about gone, but of course, Fern didn't know the half of it. Since their last disastrous confrontation, Emily had been nearly as withdrawn and brooding as her father, eating very little, often walking back along the grounds with the dog for company as if she were looking for a way out. Of course she had gotten out once, that catastrophic night she bicycled to Candlewood Terrace. Lauren shook her head now in response to Fern's question. "It doesn't really matter," she said.

"I'm sorry, honey, I don't mean to take it out on you." She looked over at the pool now, examining it, oohing and aahing over it, particularly the one corner where there was a heated Jacuzzi whirlpool that Lauren hadn't even known was in the plans, learning of it only when it was installed. But that was typical, wasn't it; wasn't she kept in the dark regularly? "You may not be that excited about this pool, but I am. Is there to be a diving board?"

"Oh, but of course. A twelve-foot slide, too."

Fern chuckled. "That man you're married to is quite amazing, he misses nothing. By the way, I noticed his car out there when I came in. Where is he?"

"In his study. Working."

"Too busy for me to pay a quick visit."

"I'm sure not. Go ahead."

She accompanied her sister inside, but when Fern entered the study, she stayed back out of view, eavesdropping as they talked. Jonathan greeted Fern enthusiastically—like Lauren, having no desire that she be aware of their fighting. "Sit," he said to her.

"I don't mean to interrupt your work, my brother-in-law, but I thought we ought to talk about the house," she said. "According to the police they're through with it, getting any evidence they're going to get. So I thought I'd get a service in to clean up."

"That sounds fine," Jonathan said.

"Though I've got to tell you, I don't think we have a chance in hell of renting it. I'd say, right now, that house is poison—so unless we find a tenant who is oblivious to superstitions and other such things, we can forget it. To be frank, I'm wary about the house's safety myself. The moment I heard about that poor fellow, I got on my knees to thank the Lord it wasn't my sister's family living there."

"Most houses are not hard to enter, it's certainly not limited to that house ... and there're people out there just waiting for the right opportunity. It's what I've been trying to get through to Lauren for a long time—it's a dangerous world out there."

"What do you think about it being connected to Nancy?"

He shook his head. "I don't know, Nancy's murder began as a robbery. There was no indication of that here, so maybe someone was looking to get this guy, which also might have been the reason he wanted to change locations. Who knows, maybe he wasn't quite so nice and sanitary as your check showed."

"Are you implying I didn't do a thorough—"

"Hold it, don't go getting thin-skinned on me, not everything shows up on those reports. With the status of crime out there, we ought to have a law requiring criminal activities and traits be listed on a person's TRW. Personally, I think these murders taking place in the same house is sheer coincidence. But if I have to take the unrented house as a tax write-off, so be it. As long as my wife and children are safe, I could care less about the money."

"Speaking of which, I'm worried about Lauren."

"Really, why?"

"I don't know, she doesn't look good ... or sound it. This pregnancy seems to be taking a lot out of her. I mean, I don't remember her being so worn out with her first. And I don't suppose all this other business has helped matters either." The chair legs scraped the floor, and Lauren could hear Fern standing up. "Listen to me, will you, being tired is surely a normal and common symptom of pregnancy. I'm just what you need about now, right? An overprotective big sister around to give you a few more needless worries." She chuckled, then teased, "Which is hardly necessary with someone like you around."

But Jonathan didn't laugh it off. "No, no, if you think there's cause to be concerned, then by all means say so," he said, his voice deepening with emotion. "My first marriage might have been good, Fern, but I've never loved anyone the way I love your sister." A pause, then, "But I don't suppose that's a surprise to you."

Lauren—still standing by the door, unseen—now stepped back, her eyes already filling with tears. Not a surprise to Lauren either, but right about now, she guessed it was good to hear it. Still in all, and though it sounded ridiculous, she envied Fern being in there with him, talking to him, with no bad feelings separating them.

She walked onto the porch and laid down in one of the chaises ... a little while later Fern came out. "I've got some free time, so I thought I'd take Chelsea for the afternoon. "Maybe a walk around the fairgrounds will pick up her spirits."

"I think maybe I should check with Jonathan—you know, see if he thinks it's a good idea."

"No need to, honey, I happened to mention it, and he thought it was fine."

Fern hadn't said anything about taking Emily with them, maybe because she didn't want her along, not that Lauren could blame her, or maybe because she knew Emily wouldn't go.

And oddly enough it was the common bond between Lauren and Beatrice that permitted Lauren to talk more openly with her. She not only knew what was going on, Lauren didn't have to be worried that she'd be judgmental of Jonathan. It was on the third day of the silence—Lauren was sitting outdoors, trying to read but unable to concentrate, while Jonathan was with the construction crew, giving instructions. Lauren put the book down when Beatrice brought her a bunch of grapes and a glass of cold skim milk. "Have patience, my dear," she said. "Before you know it, he'll be back to his old self."

Lauren looked up, surprised that the woman had spoken her view on so personal a thing. But rather than be disturbed by her remark, Lauren realized she wanted to talk about it. "You've seen him act this way before, haven't you, Beatrice?"

"People are the sum of their experiences."

"Who did that to him?"

"His mother. Once she did not utter a word to him for three entire weeks."

Oh, dear Lord, she thought, bad enough to go through a few days of such torture ... but to inflict it on a child, who has no emotional artillery to handle such a thing. "What could he possibly have done to deserve her silence?"

Beatrice pressed her lips together, remembering. "Noreen Grant liked tropical fish, she kept big tanks, a few in every room of the house. Jonathan began to scoop a fish out every day from one of the tanks and flush it down the toilet. Noreen didn't even notice it until there were nearly two dozen missing."

Obviously nothing a child could do would warrant his mother's silence, though clearly it was a mean thing for him to have done. Still Lauren knew there had to be more to the story. "Why did he do it?" she asked, finally.

And she was right—a very simple reason, too simple and ugly for her even to have imagined. "Because Mrs. Grant paid so much attention to those fish, of course," Beatrice said. "Since he was old enough to sit up, Jonathan was jealous of them."

She was stunned by the story, the idea of a child being jealous of fish was inconceivable. Not too much later she had a call from Carla and learned something else that stunned her. It started out with Carla saying, "Lauren, I haven't been able to think of anything else since our conversation the other day."

"I miss you a lot, Carla," she said, suddenly realizing how much she did miss her.

"I find myself in a real dilemma. I mean trying to be your friend, and still remaining loyal to Nancy."

"What does Nancy have to do with us?"

"First, you've got to promise not to breathe a word of what I'm about to tell you. Particularly to Jonathan."

Here she was again, being forced to keep a secret, though this time the positions were reversed—this time she was to keep something from her husband. No, she couldn't promise such a thing, it went against everything she believed. But before she could protest, Carla went on, "Look, I know this shits royally, I hate to go putting conditions on things. But there's no other way I can in good conscience tell you. And I think it's something you ought to know."

And of course she did want to know—if this had anything to do with the confusion and suspicions, if this could clear it up any ... "Okay," she said finally. "I promise."

"Well, you wanted to know if I knew Gordon Cummings before he moved in, and I did. Not really well or anything. I met him through Nancy."

Lauren's left hand lifted, cupping the mouthpiece of the phone, as if to keep it steady—so there was a connection between Nancy and Gordon. Oh, dear, she could already feel her heart hammering against her chest. "How? I mean, why? Carla, I don't understand ... what is it you're trying to tell me?"

"Lauren ... Nancy and Gordon were having an affair."

She gasped, she could feel her pulse in her ears. *Get a hold of yourself, Lauren—numerous women have affairs these days.* Then why should it stun her that this woman had one, a woman she'd never even known? Because Nancy was all the good things ... isn't that what everyone said? Because Nancy was married to Jonathan, so how could she have possibly wanted another man? Because Jonathan believed firmly that he'd had a good marriage—so how could he have been so wrong? "Did Jonathan know?" she asked.

"No, and he mustn't. I swore to her, Lauren, I gave my word. It wasn't just a dirty affair, she loved Gordon, she really did, and I think she would have gone off to be with him if it weren't for her ties to Jonathan. At one point she had decided to leave him, but she kept putting off telling him ... she was afraid of hurting him. And then, of course, she got pregnant ..."

"But he was only a kid, wasn't he?" Lauren said, remembering Fern's telling about him.

"Right, twenty-one years old then. He was a gentle guy, an odd bird, he didn't have many friends, he had quit school early. I doubt he'd had many women before Nancy."

"What could Nancy have possibly seen in him?"

She started to say something, then went silent . . .

"Go ahead, Carla, say it."

"Listen . . . Nancy wasn't a big city girl like yourself—"

"Oh-oh. Why do I feel like I'm being set up for the kill?"

"No, not really, it's the truth. Nancy was timid and insecure when she met and married Jonathan. Pretty, sweet, and a crackerjack homemaker—but aside from her homemaking skills, she was at a loss. Not that she was stupid, but she hadn't been around so to speak. All her confidence, which was limited at best, was reliant on Jonathan. The fact was, for the first ten years of their marriage, he ran her: he told her what to do, what to wear, what to think, what to say. Gordon stopped over her house once to deliver something for his sister for the PTO. And the rest is history, they got to know each other; they fell in love.

"You see, suddenly Nancy felt like a woman, not a little girl. Like maybe she had a brain and maybe she might have an opinion that counted for something."

"You can't blame Jonathan—"

"Look, before you go and get your defenses up here, I'm not trying to lay blame on anyone—maybe they were just wrongly matched, I don't know. I'm just telling you what she saw in a young, moneyless, inexperienced oddball like

Gordon. To be honest, I think she still had some feelings for Jonathan, more than what she was willing to admit ... or else his hold on her was just too powerful. She sure would have jumped through burning hoops not to have had to hurt him. And that's why you can't tell anyone—particularly him."

"No, of course, I won't," she said, knowing that though it was long gone, it would still hurt him ... and unnecessarily so. then, "Carla, tell me, whose baby was it?"

A loud sigh. "Nancy wasn't sure. Of course she had no choice but to tell Jonathan it was his."

"Did it ever occur to you that Gordon might have been angry about that? After all, it might have been his baby she was carrying. Did it ever occur to you that Gordon might have been the one—"

"Stop, Lauren, it wasn't him. If I thought that I would have told the police ... no matter what."

"How can you be sure?"

"First off, he was a marshmallow, not the type to step on an ant. Plus at the time Nancy was murdered, Gordon was sitting in my kitchen, bawling like a baby. He'd been doing some construction at the fairgrounds the last few weeks, and a week or so before, Nancy, who'd rarely left the house without Jonathan, drove down to see him. To announce that they had to break it off. Since then he'd been trying to convince her otherwise, but she had been sticking to her resolve."

Now she asked the question that she had been

ready to ask from the very beginning. "Carla, did Emily know anything about Gordon and her mother?"

"No, of course not. Nancy was very careful about that, the only time Gordon was ever over the house was when Jonathan was at work and Emily was in school. In fact, summer vacation was coming up about then, Emily was going to be home full-time which either way would have put a crimp in things."

"But suppose someone told her."

"I never told anyone, Lauren. Not even Louie."

"I'm not suggesting you. Gordon was young, maybe he wasn't quite so discreet as Nancy. Maybe he discussed it with his sister, Kathy, and maybe they were overheard ... Carla, what about Willie Campbell?"

Which would absolutely explain why Emily hated Willie. And Gordon, too ... but Lauren wouldn't, couldn't think like that. Because if she did, it wouldn't end there—if Carla knew and Emily knew and Kathy and her son and perhaps a couple of other classmates or parents knew ... what about Jonathan?

Chapter Fifteen

And then finally the punishment for her disloyalty was over—Jonathan had come home that night with the ice having been melted from his features, and a narrow white jeweler's box sticking out of his shirt pocket, and though Lauren was inclined to refuse the gift on principle, she loved this man and hungered to have him hold her again. She wanted the feud done with, so instead of protesting the injustice of the silence like she knew she ought to be doing, she cried like a fool and put it off to the reeling hormones of pregnancy.

He gathered her in his arms and she sank in comfortably, as though she'd come home, which brought on a whole new rush of tears. Jonathan took a handkerchief from his pocket and dried her eyes. "You can never do this to me again, Lauren," he said, "I can't take it. This past week I've felt like you'd gone away and I had no way to reach you." Listening, Lauren had the eerie, almost comic reaction that he was stealing her lines.

He handed her the box, and with his eyes glowing, he watched her open it and smiled when she gasped at the sight of the exquisite diamond necklace.

Though it was not the close-knit, amicable group at the dinner table Lauren wished for, that night was an improvement. Jonathan had returned to his seat at the head of the table, charming the girls, working his magic to get them to smile. Should it really be such an effort to get them to smile though, Lauren wondered. Chelsea's trip to the fair the day before with Fern had affected only a short-lived change. She would have to give her more attention.

Once dinner was over and the girls went heading off to their own separate activity, Jonathan announced he'd made an appointment for Lauren to see Doc Stevens at eleven the next morning. "You've been looking so tired," he said. Then concerned that he might have gone over the line by scheduling the visit without clearing it first with her, he said, "I hope you don't mind?"

Concern for her and the children's health and safety ... and now the baby's, and going always the one step beyond to achieve that end, was something she had come to expect of her husband. So where it might have intimidated a woman not as sure as she, Lauren was okay with it. Her thoughts went to Nancy then as they had so often since her conversation with Carla. No, it wasn't hard to imagine a strong, vital man like Jonathan taking control of things, certainly he did it with

Lauren as well. But there were limits and it was up to the woman to set those limits.

Something Nancy hadn't been able to do.

She looked up at Jonathan now, and in response said, "No, I don't, but I did want to talk about that. Don't you think I ought to be finding myself an obstetrician?"

"Why, don't you like Doc Stevens?"

"Oh, I do. It's just that ... well I thought a specialist in this case would be better."

"He's probably delivered more kids than the whole bunch of those rookie doctors at Elmwood Valley Obstetrics. I for one don't like the idea of four doctors sharing the monitoring and responsibility of a patient, which is how these groups operate. I particularly don't like it when that patient is my wife." Then he took the napkin off his lap, placed it on the table, and shrugged. "Listen, I feel totally confident with Stevens, but if he makes you uncomfortable ..."

No, it wasn't that, it really wasn't. She liked him, she did. The few times she'd seen him since coming to Elmwood Valley, he seemed quite competent, and Jonathan did have a strong point—she remembered back to when she was pregnant with Chelsea: there was certainly something to say for that personal touch versus never knowing who in the group would be examining her at prenatal visits. Or who would ultimately deliver the baby.

Besides, if Jonathan felt confident with Doc Stevens, then so did she ... certainly no one was more particular and conscientious than her husband.

She could have gone to the appointment herself, of course, but unlike her first husband, Jonathan would have none of it, eager to be a participant in anything and everything having to do with their baby's birth. And she felt proud and happy walking into the doctor's office, holding her husband's hand. She felt relieved as well to see another pregnant woman waiting to be seen.

According to Doc Stevens, everything was fine—the drowsiness was just one of those symptoms that most pregnant women experience, some to a greater degree than others. There was nothing really to do about it other than listen to her body's message by getting plenty of rest—pretty much what Beatrice had said.

"Do you like to read, Lauren?" he asked, for the first time taking the familiarity of her first name, and she nodded, assuming he was about to recommend a book on pregnancy. But instead he said, "Good, then you'll have no difficulty remembering the following essentials to a healthy and successful pregnancy for both mother and baby: *R is for rest, E is for exercise*—walking by the way is excellent—*A is for attitude*—by that I mean avoid worry and stress at all costs, only pleasant, positive thoughts and conversation allowed—and *D is for diet*—a good diet, my nurse will give you a copy of one on the way out."

"Well, I certainly won't easily forget that," she

said, smiling, taking the infantile approach in good humor—after all, it could have been worse, it could have been a jingle.

She told the doctor she wanted natural child-birth, delighting Jonathan who it seemed had never felt the wonder and joy of going through the birthing experience—Emily had been born by cesarean. As they left, the nurse gave Lauren a date for her next appointment, a sample diet, and a prescription for vitamins. As they walked out, she chided, "I'm now really confused, Jonathan, I'd like to know where V for vitamins fits into the operative word?"

He pulled her closer to him, smiling, leading her to the car. "If you promise not to haul off and clobber me, can I suggest we change that word to Dear."

Lauren gave him a dirty look though of course it did work fine. "No need to go spoiling it for the doc," she said. They laughed together—at that moment she was able to wipe away all of the neg-atives: Carla's announcement of Nancy's cheating that somehow got twisted to stamp the onus on Jonathan, and her suspicions . . . At that moment, everything felt perfect.

"Oh, my. What is it that makes you look so sad, my little one?" Beatrice asked.

Chelsea had been sitting on the deck, looking out over the yard, watching Emily and the dog in the distance. She looked up at the woman who had come into her bedroom three nights in a row when she had woken with nightmares—times she had called for Mommy, but Mommy didn't come. And Beatrice had been nice to her, too, getting her juice or milk, even telling her a story to help her go back to sleep. Stories she said she had told Emily's daddy when he was a boy. She liked that, it made her feel closer to Daddy.

She shrugged now, not so dumb as to put down her cruel sister to another one of Emily's loyal subjects. Stinking rotten Emily was number one in the household, though Chelsea couldn't figure out what anyone saw in her ... Of course, now with the baby suddenly in the picture, matters had become even worse—Chelsea was demoted to a measly number three in importance.

The woman put her hard hands on the girl's shoulders and followed her eyes to where Chelsea was looking. "Ah, so that's it, she is giving you a bad time, huh?" And without Chelsea even answering, she went on, "Your sister, Emily, is not the easiest one to get along with. Oh, no, not by a long shot."

Chelsea turned her head, looking up at Beatrice, surprised not to hear excuses for Emily's gross behavior. "Everyone around here seems to thinks she's perfect."

Beatrice stood there a few moments, then turned Chelsea to face her. "If I reveal some things to you in strictest confidence, can I trust you not to say anything?"

Chelsea loved secrets, particularly this secret

that promised to be something bad about Emily. She held up her right hand. "Brownie's honor."

"Well, that surely sounds good enough for me." She sat down in a chair and pulled Chelsea onto her lap. "The thing is, Chelsea, though your father loves both you and your sister, he favors you. Now, mind you, he would never admit it."

Chelsea shook her head. 'But he doesn't. I've seen what he lets Emily get away with."

"That's very true, but there are reasons for that. He fears that if he pushes her too hard, she will go crazy again, and of course he doesn't want that. So instead he's easy on her, he does not require of her what he might normally. But when it comes to your father's heart, you must trust Beatrice, she knows him like no other. And deep down he wishes Emily were like you."

Why like her, Chelsea wondered, and Beatrice must have read her mind, because she said, "He likes his girls to be sweet and obedient and poised—"

"What's poised?"

"Well, it is certainly not one who shouts or talks fresh or uses foul language."

"Things Emily does."

"Exactly. Daddy likes his girls pretty, he wants them to take pride in their appearance. And to know how to cook and bake and sew and take care of a house and family."

"Mommy says she's not the greatest house-keeper, but Daddy loves her."

"That's true, she is not perfect—not yet. But

we will work hard to make her so, won't we? Beatrice is here to teach." Then her arms tightening around Chelsea's waist, drawing her closer and whispering in her ear, "Some people can be taught these things, some cannot . . . but I bet you are one of the people I could teach."

Chelsea smiled. "Why me?"

"For one, you have loyalty, I can see it in you even now. In fact, that's Emily's biggest gap, the one ingredient that makes it impossible for your father to feel as he once did toward her."

Chelsea took in a deep breath, stunned at what Beatrice was saying. "What did Emily do?"

"Well, it happened when your father was married to her mother. What happened was, Emily had discovered secrets her mother was keeping from your father, harmful secrets. But rather than go directly to your father so he could make things right, she kept it to herself."

Daddy surely must have been furious at her keeping things from him; for instance, he'd told Chelsea many times to come straight to him with every problem, just like she had when Mommy left her all alone in the house. And it was a good thing she called him, too. If not, where would Emily be now? Not that Emily even bothered to be thankful. "How did Daddy find out?"

"Because Emily is not true to your father, does not mean Beatrice is not. Fortunately, I, too, became aware of the bad goings-on within the household."

Chelsea wondered for a moment what the bad

things were, but they were secret so she would not dare ask. Instead she said, "Did he make things right again?"

Beatrice smiled—not something she did often, and Chelsea thought that maybe once long ago she might have been pretty. "Your big, strong, handsome father? What do you think?"

"I think yes."

"Tell me something, my precious little one, would you like to please your daddy, the way Emily cannot possibly do?" Chelsea nodded ... no question about it, of course she did. "Well, if that's the case," the woman said, "suppose I appoint you as my official helper?"

"What does that mean?"

She held two fingers up, tight together. "It means you and I will be a team. You will stick close to Beatrice and she will teach you all her little secrets; she will teach you how to become Daddy's perfect little girl. Would you like that?"

She nodded her head, yes, she would like it a lot. She wanted her father to be proud of her. And though he might love her already, she wanted him to love her even more. She wanted to be number one in importance on his list of kids.

Before the baby, and before Emily.

Going out to lunch together after leaving the doctor's office was perfect, too. Jonathan and Lauren stopped at a sidewalk café and sat at a side table, exchanging looks and touches, behaving like the newlyweds they actually were—since

Emily had come home, much of the romance had been put on hold, and it felt nice to suddenly get it back. It made her aware of all the reasons she had married Jonathan, and in many respects that and her eagerness to set the record straight with Carla were what caused what happened next.

Though Lauren had always defended her husband against Carla's attacks, she was feeling as though she had awarded Carla too many liberties with respect to her criticisms. It probably never should have gotten that far, Lauren should never have put herself in the position of needing to defend him to her . . . to tell the things he was not, when in fact it was the things he was that she loved him for. He certainly was head and shoulders above Carla's Louie, who, though a nice enough fellow, was a sports enthusiast who shut her out of his life most weekends to drink beer and watch sports on television.

As they pulled into the driveway, Lauren said, "Darling, will you tell Beatrice and the children I'm going out for a while. I'll be back in about an hour." He looked at her, questioning, and she went on. "I'm not going far, just to visit Carla."

He pulled to a stop in front of the house. "Lauren, I don't want you to go."

"I won't be long . . . really."

"You know it's not safe out there; it's particularly not safe in that neighborhood. Now, is there some reason Carla can't pick herself up and come here?"

Lauren sighed. "You know there is."

279

"Why, because of me? Because if that's so, I'm perfectly willing to stay out of the way—"

"No, Jonathan, it's really not about that," she said, sighing, looking out the window. "It's just that I'd rather go there." As she said the last part, she thought of Emily saying pretty much those same words several weeks earlier when she argued for Lauren to let her visit with Francine. She looked at him now, surprised to see a change come over his expression, as though his eyes were once again distancing from her ... "Are you suggesting I *can't* go?" she asked, annoyed and on the verge of tears.

"No, not at all, Lauren. It's your choice." And with that, he got out of the car and went into the house. Damn it, why did he have to be like that? She sighed, sitting in the car a few minutes without starting it up, just reflecting on what had just occurred. And then deciding that if it was really all that important to talk to Carla, she could just as easily telephone. It was Lauren's choice, she simply decided it wasn't worth Jonathan getting this upset.

He was already in the study when she came in the house. He came to the door and while his eyes stayed on Lauren, he called to Beatrice in the kitchen, "Beatrice, will you go draw a bath for my wife, lots of those fancy bath salts." His eyebrows lifted a bit, questioning her if it was all right, and she nodded—it was a cool brisk day and she felt a little out of sorts, a bath might be nice. "I love you," his lips said. He went back into the study, closing the door. But it was he who came into the bathroom later, holding out a towel for her.

The pool and surrounding tile patio was completed a few days later, and Jonathan invited Fern and Carla along with her family to an outdoor barbecue to formally initiate it. Carla refused, later calling Lauren and pleading with her to understand, and though Lauren said she did, she didn't really. Still in all they had a fine barbecue without them—Beatrice prepared fruit and vegetable salads and Jonathan was head chef on the new gas grill. Chelsea seemed to have come out of her funk and was enjoying the pool and other attractions, going down the slide, playing in the water with Jonathan, then when he came out to lay on the chaise, floating by herself on her rafts.

"Hey, honey, want to take a trip to the city?" Fern asked Lauren, of course referring to Manhattan.

She looked up, immediately interested. "When?"

"Next Thursday, I've got to go in to see our accountant. I thought we could do some shopping, then go the Village and treat ourselves to lunch at O'Henry's."

Although it sounded like bliss—she hadn't been to the city since she'd gotten married—but thinking about going now, she suddenly felt uneasy. She looked at Jonathan as if to see what he thought, but he was lying quietly on the chaise with his eyes closed, apparently satisfied to leave the decision to her. "I don't know, maybe I shouldn't," she said finally. "I get so darned tired these days."

"Oh, poo, so you'll do something different and sleep a double shift when you get home. In fact, maybe that's just what you need to pick yourself up."

"Manhattan is not exactly the safest place to be."

"Oh, my, aren't you beginning to sound like the nervous tourist? What's going on here, Haven't we got our roles switched? I thought I was the one who couldn't wait to get out of there? Come on, loosen up, we're just talking for the day, not to live there. Think of all these yummy cheeses O'Henry's is—"

She was stopped by Jonathan, who had lifted his head, then holding his hand like a visor, shielding the sun so he could see her, he said, "Lauren has already made her feelings known, and from where I'm sitting, they couldn't be clearer. Pardon my bluntness, sister-in-law, but you're being a pain in the butt."

Jonathan laid his head back down, and Fern looked at Lauren. When she made no attempt to correct her husband, Fern shrugged good-naturedly. "Okay, excuse me, folks, I'm going off to where I'm appreciated." With that, she stood up, picked up one of the rubber rafts, and headed to the pool steps to join Chelsea. Lauren reached for her iced tea that was on the table beside her. As she did, her eye caught Emily sitting on the ground with the dog, not far from her.

Watching her.

Though Lauren did all she could not to dwell on Nancy's affair or Emily's possible motives for the murders, it was an impossible task. In fact, one day sitting out on the porch with Jonathan playing Scrabble, she stopped and asked, "Darling, what about Nancy's family? I mean, her parents, her sister and brother."

He looked up, his eyes questioning. "Okay, I'll bite. What about them?"

"Did Nancy have a good relationship with them during your marriage?"

He nodded. "I suppose, they communicated fairly often, mostly through letters. They visited us once, and we went up to New Hampshire once as well. Why do you ask?"

"I was curious, why they weren't involved with Emily? I mean, there hasn't been a card or letter or telephone call from them since Emily's been home."

He shrugged. "Not everyone has the same strong sense of family we do."

"I guess not. Back a while ago Detective Kneeland mentioned how they missed Nancy, that they would always miss her, and I imagine he's right. Well, it just seems that they'd want to have more contact with her only daughter."

Jonathan didn't seem to know, or for that matter, was he even that curious. And it was true, many families didn't keep in touch, for whatever reason. Lauren wondered, could it be that they, too, had their suspicions of Emily's involvement in her mother's murder? Though Lauren wouldn't dare ask Jonathan that.

It was only a few days later, one Wednesday morning while Jonathan was driving Emily to see her therapist and Beatrice had gone off to do some errands with Chelsea, Lauren found herself standing alone inside Emily's bedroom, determined to do what she refused to do before—go through it. And the strangest part was, she really hadn't a clue as to what she hoped to find.

But when she saw the tin fishing box in the back of the closet, she remembered it was the box Chelsea had looked through the day Emily came home—she lifted the lid, and as Chelsea had said, Emily Grant was printed on a sticker on the cover. She looked through the box: rocks, acorns, plastic animals. She shrunk back from what looked like a bird's claw . . . a jackknife . . . jewelry. But not junk jewelry as Chelsea had thought—the real thing: a diamond engagement ring, a platinum wedding band, a jade necklace, the jewelry reportedly stolen from Nancy's body when she was murdered.

Chapter Sixteen

What if Emily did kill her mother? And Gordon. At minimum, Lauren knew that Emily lied to the police. Frightened and confused, Lauren went to Jonathan about the found jewelry, but he managed to hedge the real issue. And maybe because of the shock of the whole thing, she wasn't much better.

Jonathan's addressed the issue of ownership. "Okay, so I wish I knew about the jewelry," he said, "but it belonged to her Mother. Hasn't she a right to it?"

"But shouldn't the police be told about it?"

"I might have agreed had I found this out way back when Nancy was killed. But as this juncture, why? Unless of course we want to stir up things even more. You realize, bringing it out would raise Emily as a murder suspect. Is that what you want?"

No, of course, it wasn't what she wanted, but if Emily was guilty ... Couldn't Jonathan see ... but even if he could, it was too horrible a thing to believe about your own child. A ten-year-old angry at her mother for sleeping with a man other than her father? Sure angry, but enough so to kill? Or did it make more sense to think a psychotic broke in—one of those deranged people who kill for no apparent reason, at least none linked to the victim? And the tampered window, indicating a break-in—would a ten-year-old be that crafty?

Also impossible to believe was a ten-year-old in a state of shock, going up to her mother's dead body and taking her jewelry. But Emily had done that, hadn't she?

"Lauren—" With newspaper rolled, Jonathan smacked it against the table edge, startling her.

She suddenly realized he had been talking and trying to get her attention. "I'm sorry, I guess I was off somewhere. What is it you were saying?"

"Only that I don't like this."

"What?"

"For one, what were you doing in Emily's room?"

"I was in her closet, putting away clean clothes," she said, which was clearly a lie but still the first thing that had come to mind. How easy it seemed to lie these days, she thought, proving that practice certainly does make perfect.

"I want you to leave those kinds of things for Beatrice, that's what she's here for."

"I was hardly exerting myself," she said, thinking how foolish it was that she was standing here defending something not ever true. Or that Jonathan should even be concerned about such things in light of what she'd discovered.

He shook his head, his eyes now critically examining her. "Then maybe you can figure out what you're doing wrong. Will you take a look at yourself?"

Her hands went immediately to her face, then her fingers going through her hair. "What?"

"You're tired, you're stressed, you look like hell. Pregnant woman are typically glowing and serene, but not you. What is it, Lauren, is your life too difficult? Am I asking too much of you?"

"No, of course not. I don't know what you're talking about," she said, beginning to turn, to go look at what he was seeing, but he put his hand out, stopping her, prodding her into a chair. "No, you sit right here." Two minutes later he was back, holding a large hand mirror that he'd taken from the bathroom. He held it out in front of her. "Go ahead," he said. "Look for yourself."

What other choice was there but to look? And he was right, too—her skin looked pasty, there were circles under her eyes, circles that hadn't been there before, and her hair looked unbrushed. She swallowed hard, feeling ashamed and embarrassed. "Okay, you be the judge," he said. "Am I wrong?"

She shook her head helplessly as though she had no rational explanation for it. "I'm sorry," she said, thinking how inappropriate the words sounded even while she was saying them. And he must have thought so, too, because he suddenly crouched down beside her chair and took her hands in his, caressing them, pressing his lips to them. She looked into his eyes, dark pools that made her feel dizzy. "I love you, Lauren, I sit at your feet and worship you. Whatever you want, you need only ask. You know that, don't you?"

"Yes," she said, but her throat suddenly was so dry, it barely came out a whisper.

"And I ask only one single thing in return—that you take care of yourself and our unborn child. You tell me, Lauren, please, am I being unreasonable?"

No, he wasn't. Nor was he wrong about how the anxiety was affecting her. Never did she realize how paranoic she was becoming or how outlandish her suspicions were than when Detective Donald Kneeland showed up a couple of days later, looking quite pleased, eager to tell her and Jonathan that Jay Philips had been arrested for the murder of Gordon Cummings.

"Whoa," Jonathan said, naturally as surprised as she. "Slow down a minute there. How the hell did all that happen? What about the alibi of his?"

"Fortunately, we managed to prove it phony. It turns out this buddy who was shooting pool with Philips during the time of the murder was on his way to the city. And fortunately, getting snagged on the way for speeding."

"That's great, I mean, of course, if it's him. I do assume you have more."

"Oh, sure, we've got more. My men found a

blue cotton thread on the living-room carpet at your house, a thread that matches our fellow's baseball cap. We figure that the hat must have fallen on the carpet during a struggle. At the arraignment this morning, Judge Nestor set bail for five hundred grand, which is a pretty good bet that Philips won't be walking the streets before trial."

Relief. Finally for the first time in weeks relief peeked through the gloom. Surely Jonathan felt the same as she. She reached for his hand and held it tight, then directing herself to the detective, she asked, "Why did he do it?"

"Motives are neat and nice, but not much of a requirement these days, Mrs. Grant. Guys like him are known to kill for no reason at all, just for kicks."

In this case, though, Lauren didn't agree, there had to be some motive. Or else she would have to believe it was a simple coincidence that Nancy and Gordon were murdered in the same house two years apart, and that Philips at one time or another was suspected of both crimes. Of course, the police weren't aware of the connection between the victims, she was.

So it made sense—if this guy killed Gordon, wasn't it likely he killed Nancy as well?

Fern had called several times in the two weeks since the swimming pool incident, twice asking Lauren to go shopping with her or out to lunch, both times Lauren begging off. The last time, Fern seemed a bit put off, but said nothing, and hadn't talked or dropped over until the day after Detective Kneeland showed up. Beatrice sent her out back where Lauren was down on the ground with a spade planting petunias Jonathan had picked up for her at the local nursery. Lauren proceeded to tell her the news about Jay Philips.

"Why, that's wonderful," Fern said. "Why on earth didn't you call and tell me?"

Lauren looked up at her, shrugging. "Oh, I don't know, just busy I guess."

"How're you feeling?"

"Good. Beatrice of course sees that I get my home-baked crackers every morning; they do wonders for my morning sickness. And though I still need to nap often, I'm also getting plenty of exercise—between the gardening, swimming in the pool, and walking around the grounds a couple of times a day. Jonathan usually joins me for my walk after lunch and again in the evening, and it goes without saying that he and Beatrice pamper me wickedly."

A few moments of silence, what seemed to Lauren like disapproving silence, then Fern broke it finally by saying, "Tell me, what do I need to do around here to get some iced tea?"

"Simply ask is all," Lauren said, smiling and standing, brushing herself off as she got up. Lauren went to the deck and inside while Fern tagged along; taking a pitcher of tea from the refrigerator, Lauren looked out the window to check on Emily. She had just spotted Chelsea with Beatrice in the dining room, polishing silverware, and now she saw Emily and the puppy as usual walking around the grounds.

Fern followed her glance to Emily and said, "So how're the kids doing?"

"Actually not too bad." And it wasn't a lie, certainly there was a noticeable improvement. Things seemed to have calmed down, fallen into some kind of acceptable order. While there was no friendliness between the girls, there was no bickering or complaints either, they pretty much stayed away from each other. And while there was no actual breakthrough between Lauren and Emily, she'd occasionally catch the girl watching her as though she wanted to speak. Still, as soon as she realized Lauren saw her, she'd turn away.

"Ever hear of Barkhamsted?" Fern asked, going onto a new subject; she pulled out a chair and sat, Lauren shook her head, poured the tea into tall glasses, and set the glasses on the table. "Well, it's a reservation, a forest with a lovely lake. There's picnic tables and barbecue pits, and what have you. I thought I'd play hooky someday this week and we could go—you, the kids and I. What do you think?"

Lauren shrugged, then lifting her arms, spreading them to take in the grounds. "Why? I mean, it seems silly, I've got it all right here at my doorstep . . . plus some."

"I understand that, but that's not the point."

"Do you mind telling me what is?"

"How about a change of scenery? My gosh, Lauren, you never seem to leave this place anymore. Don't you have an urge to see what the rest of the world is doing?''

Lauren sighed. "What is this about, Sis. Why are you doing this?"

"What it's about is, I don't get what's happening here, is that clear enough for you?" But the question was only rhetorical, she moved on quickly. "The issue as I see it is why do you absolutely refuse to leave this place?"

"Well if you really must have concrete reasons, let me begin with Emily—she was attacked by a man who it turns out is a cold-blooded murderer."

"But you've just told me he's been caught. Isn't that right?"

"There are other dangerous elements out there, Fern."

"Are you telling me you want to live in hiding?"

"Of course not," Lauren said, annoyed at the twisting of her words, and surprised that her sister would engage in that. But she continued on, trying to explain. "Look, Fern, in addition to not wanting to lug fifty pounds of equipment to some public place to do something I can do far better and more comfortably in my own yard, Jonathan goes out of his way to take time out from his work to be with me. At lunch, as well as other times during the day."

"You know, I do believe that is the real reason." Fern threw up her arms hopelessly. "And so if you didn't see him for one lousy day, what would happen, would you fall apart? You're behaving like a lovestruck teenager." She stared at her now, her blue eyes darkening to navy. "Or maybe it would be more accurate to say you're behaving like a woman so desperate and dependent, I no longer know who you are. I'm appalled, Lauren!"

"Not anywhere as appalled as I am standing here listening to what you're saying." The voice was deep and strong and reassuring and it came from behind—Jonathan's voice, and it was directing itself to Fern. "I don't care who you are, no one will come into my house and talk to my wife like that. What is it with you anyway, Fern, do you actually think your pregnant sister needs to be subjected to this kind of poison?" Fern, still so stunned at his unexpected presence, didn't answer immediately, but he wasn't waiting to see if she would. "I think you'd better go before I say something I'll be sorry for."

Fern looked from Jonathan to Lauren, her stare challenging. "Is that what you want?"

"I don't know—" Lauren began, trying to think of something wise to say, something that would cut through and fix the situation, bring it back to where it was before it got out of hand, but she could come up with nothing. "Maybe, it wouldn't be such a bad idea," she said finally. "I mean just for now ... just until—" She got only that far because Fern was up, out of her seat, and on her way to the front door.

Lauren looked from her sister to Jonathan, feeling as though she might die from the ache inside.

Jonathan came up to her, took her in his arms, cradling her. "I'm sorry, darling. I just couldn't stand by and listen and say nothing."

But it wasn't his fault ... Hadn't Fern asked her, hadn't she told her to go?

Chelsea and Beatrice couldn't help but overhear Jonathan's sharp words coming from the kitchen, then Aunt Fern rushed past the dining room, through the living room and out of the house, not even saying a word to Chelsea as she left. Chelsea looked at Beatrice. "Daddy was sure mad."

"If he was, I'm sure he had good reason."

Chelsea nodded, rubbed the chamois harder on the copper teapot, then held it up for Beatrice's approval.

She smiled, took it from her, and placed it back into the hutch. "Like a new penny. I've a niece named Penny. Before I came here, I lived with her."

"Is she mad you left?"

"Oh, no, she understands the Grant family comes number one. When your daddy phoned to say you needed me here, I barely took the time to pack."

"Can you bring her here to play?"

"Who?"

"Your niece, Penny"

Beatrice chuckled. "Oh, my no, she's much too old for that ... why she's all grown up."

"Oh." A long silence while Chelsea thought

how lucky she was to have Beatrice as her friend, especially with Mommy being so different these days: so quiet, never wanting to do anything fun, like she had caught the Emily disease. Then she began imagining how nice it would be to have a friend her age to play with, too. Finally she looked out the front window, where the driveway circled past the doors. "Beatrice, do you think Aunt Fern will be back?"

"I don't know, my sweet. But suppose we concentrate on more important things. For instance, I was thinking just this morning how much your daddy likes blueberry pie. How about you and me go blueberry picking?"

Whenever Emily would get it into her head that she killed her mother, Shrink Strickler—or now with the wand having passed to Lady Greenly— would dutifully fill her in on the script, the same script she'd told the police after the murder, then went ahead and forgot. And the more she heard the story told, the more it seemed real. In fact, there was a time at Bates that she could actually see the stranger's face because he'd turn toward her before whacking Nancy with the baseball bat. And it wasn't until the stranger in her head suddenly refused to turn her way that Emily became suspicious of the script.

Of course certain parts seemed to stay the same no matter how many times her brain replayed them: for instance, the day they came in from the fight in the car, Emily remembered Mommy going to the sewing room in the basement, which was where she'd go to get away from aggravation—which in this case was Emily. And Emily went upstairs to her bedroom, taking the bat with her. And when she heard loud voices and bangs coming from downstairs, she stood up, came to the top of the stairs, and called, "Mommy ... Mommy, is that you?"

Then she heard voices coming from the basement ... but her mother was the only one down there.

Emily went back for the bat, then gripping it, she started down. By the time she reached the living room, she could hear her mother screaming. She rushed to the kitchen, arriving just as the cellar door burst open, just as the stranger decided to let go of the front of her mother's dress and push her backward.

Two radical problems with those scripted memories: the stranger still didn't turn to look at Emily, and what about the bat ... wasn't she the one holding the bat?

Several times in the next week Lauren picked up the phone to call Fern, but was never able to follow through. Oh, she could apologize—that was easy, but what then? It would only get them back to that same issue. She wasn't a fool—clearly Fern disapproved of her relationship with her husband, and as much as she loved her big sister, she couldn't allow her to interfere. After all, it wasn't up to her to object—it was Lauren's relationship, her marriage, her life.

Jonathan was gone for the morning on business, and Chelsea elected to go to the supermarket with Beatrice. Though she had never liked grocery shopping before, now with things quieted down for the summer, it was clearly a way for Chelsea to break the monotony of always being at home. and at this point Lauren was only grateful that she had Beatrice to dote on her.

Emily and she were alone, but the house and grounds being so big, it was easy to stay out of one another's way, almost forgetting there was someone in the house. So when the screams came from upstairs Lauren was startled; then recognizing it as Emily, she rushed upstairs. Her first thought was fire, but when she smelled no smoke, and the screams led to the bathroom, her fears intensified. Emily had tried to take her life once, had she tried again?

She rushed inside to find Emily in her underwear in a corner on the floor, her knees up, her arms hugging her legs, and her body shaking. Lauren looked to the sink, looking for signs of pills, razors, something, but there was nothing. She looked to the window, then back at Emily. "What's wrong?"

Finally she knelt down beside her. "Emily, whatever it is, you must tell me. I can't help you unless—" But that's as far as she got, that's when she spotted the fresh blood on Emily's panties.

Lauren sighed heavily, relieved as well as surprised: her period, Emily had gotten her period, and apparently it was for the first time.

She wasn't sure if it was the blood panicking the child or the trauma of the experience—either way, Lauren was stunned to see how frightened she was. Which made her feel stupid and irresponsible—she not only hadn't known that Emily hadn't begun to menstruate, but she hadn't even thought to ask.

She lightly placed her hands on her stepdaughter's shoulders, almost as though she were afraid too much pressure applied would frighten her more. "It's all right, Emily, please, you mustn't be afraid. What's happening is perfectly normal. Do you know about menstruation, about having your period?"

Emily shuddered. "The curse. A friend of mine at school died from it."

"From her period? No, that's impossible," she said, caught off guard by the ancient term of curse.

"Oh, yes, there were pools of her blood everywhere! She bled to death!"

"Not from her period, Emily."

"Yes! I said, she did!"

She started to bawl then, big wracking sobs that wouldn't stop, and that Lauren suspected had to do with her mother's blood as well. And when Lauren opened her arms, she went right into them, resting her head against Lauren's chest while she rocked her. Finally she stopped crying, and when looked up at her stepmother, she drew back. But Lauren took one of her hands.

"What was your friend's name, Emily?"

"Jessica. She was just nine. I kind of watched out for her. You know, kept the older kids off her back."

The older kids off her back? No, she didn't know, in fact, such a thing had never even occurred to her. She had thought of Bates as a respected clinic only, but now thinking about it, she realized it was, after all, a place where emotionally disturbed children lived, and acted out, and tried to get well. It couldn't have been easy to live there, to deal with so many different children, so many different problems. "How did Jessica die?" Lauren asked finally.

Emily took a deep breath, then swallowing hard said, "She slit her wrists."

Oh, dear God . . . She could feel tears in her eyes.

So she showed her how to put on a sanitary napkin, which led to some lessons in feminine hygiene, which ultimately led to talk about eggs and ovaries and the different parts of a woman's body and whatever else Lauren could remember from when her mother went through the story with her so many years before. Lauren now took notice how in the few short months since Emily had been home, she'd begun to develop, and it was important she understand the changes in her body and what they meant, not to be reliant on information gotten from the girls at Bates.

"You're a lovely young lady, Emily," Lauren said, slipping her hand from hers and fluffing the girl's dark hair. Though short, her hair had grown in some, and the style was pixieish and becoming. "And someday, you'll be a lovely woman."

Emily didn't say anything, and Lauren hadn't a clue as to what she was thinking, until she suddenly got up and went to the door. "I'm going outside," she said, and in the next instant, she was gone. Later, looking out the window, Lauren spotted her with her dog, Stew. She noticed Emily didn't wear those work boots anymore ... Had she never found that missing shoe?

Jonathan and Beatrice pulled into the driveway at pretty much the same time. Chelsea and Jonathan helped Beatrice with the bags, then he suggested a swim, which Chelsea leapt at. Chelsea ran upstairs to change into her swimsuit and Jonathan said, "Where's Emily, maybe I can convince her to come out and join us?"

"No, I don't think today," Lauren said as Beatrice took some items into the downstairs bathroom.

"Is there a problem?"

"No, not at all, on the contrary. Your daughter got her period. First time."

"Really?" He looked concerned, and maybe a little upset.

"Come now, it's nothing to be upset about."

"She's only a little girl."

"Not so little, that's what I've been trying to tell you. Your daughter is a young woman."

He nodded, still not too comfortable or pleased with the concept, as most fathers she supposed were seeing their little girls grow up. "Was she okay. I mean, was she scared?"

"Actually she was at first, but that had more to do with other things. We talked, and it was good. With respect to her period, she seems fine with it now."

He put his arms around her then, at least able to be pleased about that part. "See, what did I tell you? She's warming up to you, trusting you, relying on you, and you're there for her. I knew we'd be okay—if only people would leave us alone."

Who knew, Jonathan might be right again—she certainly hoped so. There were no halfways or maybes or could-bes with Jonathan—when he loved someone, he gave total faith and commitment. Despite all the times it looked so suspicious for Emily, he had never doubted her. Or even if he had, he simply did what was necessary to protect her—she couldn't help but admire that. Oh, Lauren wasn't trying to make it seem like all was suddenly perfect with their marriage, she knew better. There were issues still to be worked out . . .

But Jonathan gave a hundred percent, and he deserved to get at least that much in return. He might not have gotten it from Nancy, but he would from Lauren.

*   *   *

"Mr. Grant's fertile imagination would get him into some nasty trouble when he was a little fellow," Beatrice said as she gestured out the kitchen window, motioning to where Jonathan was clowning and miming for Chelsea who was giggling with glee.

"How so?" Lauren asked, looking over to them, smiling, then sitting back with her tea. She liked it when Beatrice was reminded of a story about Jonathan.

"Well, Mr. Grant loved to perform, to put on skits and shows, things of that kind. I often was his only audience. One day he took a stray male cat and dressed it in a bonnet and dress that he made up from some silky material he'd found and he put the animal in his performance. That day his mother walked in, and she was fit to be tied."

"Why, was he hurting the animal?"

"Not that I could see. But apparently Noreen Grant thought he was somehow demeaning the animal. As punishment, she took Jonathan up to her room and dressed him up in a similar fashion, even to the same girls' flowery bonnet. This makeshift dress had a slit for a tail, too—she had affixed a length of white fur to his underwear. He could not take the outfit off all day, and she warned the staff that when they called him, they were to say, 'Here, kitty kitty.' "

Lauren looked up, aghast.

"Oh, yes indeed, his mother could have chosen no punishment more humiliating. Even as a child, he was always aware of his masculinity, a trait deserving the highest esteem by both his mother and father. Feminine ways had no place in that household."

Lauren could hardly speak, what the mother had done was more than cruel; it was obscene. She wondered how Beatrice could simply have watched such inhumane treatment of a child and kept quiet, but Lauren supposed being in a position such as hers wasn't easy, often offering no choice if you valued your job. "That's a terrible story," Lauren finally managed to say.

"Noreen Grant viewed it as character-building."

"So tell me, how did her lowly tactics work? Did he rebel?"

"Well, not so you would notice."

"What does that mean?"

"Oh, he'd usually get back at her, but without her knowledge—he was good at subterfuge. This one time in particular though I shall never forget. You see, the Grant house was a big old structure near a lake; it was not uncommon for rats and mice to find their way into the cellar. And Wesley, the groundsman, would regularly set out poison to get rid of the vermin. Well, that day the boy took a little tin shaker from the pantry, went down to the basement, and scooped poison into it from one of the cardboard containers. He put the shaker in his pocket and brought it to the dining room, and before his mother arrived for dinner, her food was seasoned just right."

Lauren put down the teacup she was holding and looked at the woman with disbelief, but she could see by the firmness of Beatrice's jaw, she was telling the truth. "But, Beatrice, it was poison—"

"Yes, and his mother was quite ill that night, but she put it off to a stomach virus."

"He could have killed her."

"Well, I doubt he thought of it in that way. Remember he was bright, ingenious, and reliable, not the sort of young man to make that kind of grave error. What he wanted was to make her violently ill, and that's what he did."

Lauren could have sat there till doomsday trying to understand how a rational adult could have stood by and let an eight-year-old do such a potentially dangerous, life-threatening act, but it wouldn't have helped. Apparently, no disaster resulted from the act, if only by the grace of God. But the entire story upset her, she found it chilling, and wished Beatrice hadn't told it.

The day before Lauren had felt like she and Emily connected—but if headway was to be made, she had to jump in and take advantage of the moment. So that's why during her morning walk, she directed herself to a spot where Emily was sitting with the dog.

When she got there, she said, "Can I sit?"

Emily nodded and Lauren parked herself nearby on a rock, facing her. She decided to cut to the chase and take her chances. "Remember when you gave me permission to search your room?" Emily still only looked at her. "Well, I did it. Not at the time, though, more recently." She took a deep breath, nervous about what Emily's reaction would be. "And I found the jewelry, Emily. Your mother's jewelry."

"I didn't want it," she said, sounding as though she were upset that she had it.

"Then why did you take it?" When there was no response, she went on. "I recognized the pieces from your father describing them to me once. But please, don't misunderstand, I'm not trying to judge you for taking them ... I can understand you wanting to have your mother's things, in fact, I can't imagine who else should have them. Of course the police should have been told."

She was met with more silence, and Emily's eyes closed as though she were focusing inward. Lauren's thoughts went to Nancy's affair, and though she had promised Carla she wouldn't tell anyone about it, Emily already knew—she was sure of it. And chances were she was dealing with it or not dealing with it, alone. Wouldn't it be better to at least have some adult input? "Emily, I know about your mother and Gordon," she said finally.

Emily looked up, surprised. "How?"

"Carla. She asked that I not tell anyone, but of course, you already knew. And it made sense to me once I did know, I mean, why you would be angry at Willie Campbell. I imagine he said mean things about your mother."

Emily hung her head now, her expression impossible to read, and Lauren went on, deciding in that moment that for Emily's benefit she would put a few words in for Nancy's defense. "You know, darling, sometimes someone we love and trust does something we consider wrong. But the thing is, that person might have a reason, a good reason, but one we don't understand. But maybe in time we'll understand better. So I guess what I'm saying is, if we love a person, we should be careful not to make snap judgments."

Emily brought her eyes up, and suddenly they were Jonathan's eyes, so dark they seemed to burrow right into her—a shiver began at the base of her neck and rolled down her back. "I only took the jewelry because Daddy made me."

Lauren drew in her breath. "You're lying, Emily. And I don't understand why. I'm not angry about the jewelry—honest. I just thought if we could get it out—"

But Emily had already jumped up, and without any further explanation rushed off with the dog at her heels. Lauren picked up a branch lying on the ground and snapped it. *What was she, a masochist, why did she have to go and bring that up now?*

Chapter Seventeen

"I thought you would have called by now," was how Carla greeted Lauren when she took the phone from Beatrice. It had been three weeks since their last talk, since Carla turned down Jonathan's invitation to the pool party.

"I've been busy," she said. "Besides, the phone rings both ways, you could have called me."

"Well, now, that's funny, and here I was thinking that's what I was doing."

"I guess you are," Lauren said, thinking their conversation sounded juvenile—second-grade level—at least from her end. "How have you been, Carla?" she asked finally, deciding to put a stop to it. "I've missed you."

"Really?"

"Yes, really," she said, thinking how much she missed dropping by at Carla's, their visits, their phone calls. "Well, I imagine you're up-to-date on the news. By that I mean the arrest of Jay Philips for Gordon Cummings's murder?"

"Oh, sure, and what a relief it was. Actually to everyone in town. I figure he killed Nancy, too. I know they weren't able to prove it back when it happened, but with the connection between Gordon and Nancy, well, it seems too much of a coincidence."

"I agree. Can I ask a question?" she said, getting to something she'd been wondering.

"Sure, go ahead."

"What's the scoop with Nancy and her family? Her parents and siblings ... did they get along? It dawned on me not long ago that since Emily's been home, they haven't once tried to get in touch with her. Not a call, not even a measly postcard. Since I take in the mail, I would have seen."

"Well, the relationship wasn't all that great, I suppose. Actually I think it was good at one time—at least Nancy always talked as though she had a perfectly normal, happy childhood. But I think what it was is her family and Jonathan didn't hit it off all that well. They were worlds apart, of course, her folks being farm people, real simple folk. And Jonathan—well, apart from living in a small town, he comes from a far more sophisticated life-style."

"But still, Emily is their grandchild, their niece."

"I can't answer that, Lauren, maybe they feel as though they'd be butting in at this point. Particularly if they're aware that Jonathan has remarried and has a new family. Remember, I felt pretty much the same myself, I suppose it's natural." A slight pause, then she changed the subject. "Lauren, come on over here with the kids. And before you jump right in to say no, I want to propose a compromise—it's something I've been thinking about. Well, the upshot is, if you come over to my place today, I promise to visit with you there—that is if you still want me. Differences with Jonathan and bolted gates aside."

Lauren realized she had not really had a desire to go out these past few weeks, getting lazy and content to say put, but now, suddenly, she was eager to go. Jonathan might not like it, but he'd have to live with it—after all, Philips was locked up, and that was his main focus in them not leaving the grounds. Besides which Jonathan was out inspecting a bridge and wouldn't make it back for lunch.

She didn't expect him back until three-thirty. So if she went now, she could still have a leisurely visit and be back with the girls in time for Jonathan, in no way edging into their time together. Now all obstacles out of the way, she decided, why not?

She looked at the clock in the kitchen—it was nearly noon. Then said, "Now I don't suppose that offer includes lunch for three?"

"Sure, yeah, of course! I would have asked, but I figured you'd be with Jonathan."

"No, actually it works out fine. He sort of stood me up today. Of course, I'm used to taking a nap at about two . . . so if I start to fall asleep on you."

"Not to worry, I'll roll you into the hammock. Oh, this is great," Carla went on excitedly, "we'll have a picnic out back. Francine will be absolutely spastic."

First she found Chelsea who was sitting in the sandbox carrying on a conversation with one of the latest dolls Jonathan had brought home. Though she seemed agreeable to go, she had immediate second thoughts. Apparently Beatrice and she had made a date to make tollhouse cookies after lunch.

"I'm sure she'll be willing to change it to another time. Now, quick, go wash."

Emily looked at her curiously when she called her over and told her, clearly surprised that she was willing to buck the powers. And thinking of it that way, Lauren suddenly wasn't so sure that's what she wanted to do. But the decision was made—she had told Carla, and she wasn't going to back out now.

Beatrice had apparently come into the kitchen while Lauren was outdoors with the children, because when Lauren returned to get her purse and freshen up, the housekeeper was nearly done preparing lunch: sandwiches for the girls, and for Lauren fresh vegetables surrounding a mound of turkey salad.

"Oh, I'm sorry, Beatrice, I should have told you, we're going out for lunch."

"But Mr. Grant didn't mention—"

"No, he wasn't aware himself. In fact, I just decided."

"I think it's not wise. Besides I've already made this."

"Beatrice, please. Save it for tomorrow."

"No, my dear, I simply cannot do that—Mr. Grant would not approve."

Now her patience had reached its limits; Lauren took a deep breath. "I won't discuss this further, Beatrice." And she supposed the woman deserved some credit—she managed to contain herself when they drove off, at least not attempting the same stunt as before. Had she, Lauren was prepared to run her down.

Carla grilled on her hibachi out back near the run-down picnic table: fried chicken in spicy barbecue sauce, served with half sours and the best potato salad Lauren had ever eaten. "Carla, this is to die for. If it gives me heartburn, it'll have been worth it."

They finished lunch at about one-thirty, and she felt wonderfully relaxed just sitting there, chatting with Carla, with none of the amenities, and without the protection of the fences in the distance. She forgot how good normal could feel, or perhaps it didn't feel so good until you missed it. Either way, she didn't want to go into it with Carla—she would never understand . . . she wasn't so sure she did herself. The kids had gone off to the bird sanctuary, and Carla asked how they were doing as she opened a Coke can.

"Actually not bad. Chelsea is wild about the pool, and she seems to get a kick out of helping

Beatrice with the household chores—she's always at her heels, that is, when she hasn't managed to drag Jonathan out to play. With Emily, it's different, she's nowhere as happy, she still seems to be working things out, but it seems we've made a connection. She got her period not long ago, well, we talked a bit ... no trumpets blaring yet, she still tends to keep to herself, but slowly we're getting there."

"That's great."

"Actually the one she's attached to most is the dog, Stew. My one brilliant idea." She stood up and pulled her shirt tight around her. "And in case you haven't noticed, I'm starting to show. Not a lot, mind you, but Jonathan likes it."

"He would," Carla said, then concerned that her comment would be somehow misconstrued, she covered her hide. "Now what I mean is, some fellows like their women pregnant. It's true ... don't look at me that way. They think it's sexy."

Lauren sat back down on the picnic bench, laughing. "It's hard to imagine the fascination, but be sure to remind me of that in a few more months when I'll surely be testing the theory." Then her thoughts moving along, she said, "Carla, if I wanted to get in touch with Nancy's folks, how would I?"

Carla put down her Coke, clearly surprised. "Are you saying you want to?"

"I was thinking about it, and well, could it hurt? If you're right about them feeling awkward because of Jonathan's remarriage, I'd like to personally assure them I'd welcome their contact with Emily. It would be a good thing for her, maybe even better than therapy. After all, they are Emily's family."

Carla nodded approvingly. "Well, Nancy's maiden name was Renscilier." She spelled it out for her, and Lauren wrote it on the back of a napkin. "Now, I don't know the father's first name, but they have a chicken farm in Windham, New Hampshire, which according to Nancy is a one-horse town. Probably the only Renscilier around so you shouldn't have trouble finding them." Lauren folded the napkin and slipped it in the zipper compartment of her purse, and had just set her purse on the ground when she heard Carla's "Uh-oh."

She looked up, and noting her expression, she followed to where she was looking—the bird sanctuary: Jonathan, who had parked his car behind Lauren's in the driveway, was now standing at the door of the little wire and wood enclosure, gesturing to Emily and Chelsea to come outside and get to the car.

"What in the world—" Lauren began as she got up and started toward him. Carla came along. "I'm right here, Jonathan," she called out, waving her hand. "It's all right."

But he ignored her while Emily and Chelsea, following his stern direction, marched in front of him. Rushing, Lauren finally caught up to him at the edge of the driveway. But before she could begin to protest, he turned to her with narrowed eyes. "Look at you," he said. "You're out of breath."

"Well, if I hadn't been in such a rush to get down here—" She stopped, took a deep breath. "Jonathan, I don't appreciate this. The girls obviously are here because I brought them, and they're having a swell time. Do you realize how long it's been since we've been out?" She glanced at Carla whose arms were folded at her chest in a combative position, then to Jonathan. "Darling, please. Can we discuss this later?"

"Of course . . . at home."

She looked at the girls . . . "If you could let them stay now—"

But he wasn't listening to more, he was already directing the girls to the car. He opened the back-seat door, and they climbed inside. Chelsea looked out at Lauren, her eyes troubled and confused, while Emily stared down at her hands in her lap, unable to even look at her. Carla and Francine stood back a little, but were within hearing, when she said to Jonathan, "I didn't expect you home until three-thirty."

"I rushed my business so I could make it home earlier, concerned that you might get lonely. It seems I'm the fool here. You'll have to forgive me, if my being home early disappoints you," he said, opening the driver's door and getting in.

"I didn't say that, and I didn't mean—"

His voice lost some of its crispness when he nodded to Lauren's car. "Why don't you follow behind?"

Because she couldn't allow herself to be dragged away from Carla's like a misbehaving child, that's why. Couldn't he appreciate that much, couldn't he see how he was humiliating her?

Apparently not, because he looked at his watch and said, "It's after two, Lauren, and you've been up since nine." Exactly nine, she thought, thinking it peculiar that he would know such a thing when he left the house before she got up. Was she that predictable? "And seeing you now, it shows— you're hot and tired and stressed. I think a nap is in order about now, don't you?"

"I'm fine," she said, lying. Certainly she was hot, but not because of the weather, and stressed . . . but as a result of the circumstances. She took a deep breath—though he was treating her like a child, she was trying not to feel or act like one. Particularly not before the captivated audience. "I'm staying, Jonathan," she said finally.

Without another word, he looked into the rear-view mirror, then backed down the driveway— Chelsea was kneeling on the back seat, looking out the rear window at her as they drove off.

Carla sent Francine off to play, though she, too, was noticeably upset and confused at the abrupt and unexpected end to her friend's visit. Then with her arm draped over Lauren's shoulder, Carla walked her back to the picnic table and insisted she sit. "Don't you think it's time we talk about this?"

Lauren threw up her hands. "What's there to say? The problem is, he expected me home, Carla. Here he went and rushed through his business appointments just so he could be with me. I mean, how many husbands do you know who would do that?"

Carla sank down onto the bench across from her. "I can't believe I'm hearing this."

"Wait!" Lauren said, holding her hand up. "I know you don't understand, but don't say anything that will make it impossible for us to remain friends. Please, Carla." And gratefully she stopped. But again Lauren wanted for her to see some of the things she saw every day, things that were special about Jonathan. "He really is a wonderful man—kind and considerate, a superb father and husband. Carla, you can't imagine the way he spoils us. All we need do is ask him for something ... there's nothing he won't—"

But she stopped, her attempt worse than useless—though Carla wasn't refuting her words, she also wasn't making the least attempt to understand them. Lauren sighed, then reached for her purse and said, "I think I'd better go."

"But only a couple of minutes ago I heard you tell the man you were staying, and you sounded so sure. Couldn't you at least let him stew awhile?"

And then Lauren thought of Jonathan's intolerable silences, the last thing she wanted was to bring on one of those. "But the kids are with him," she said. "And though I'm sure they're fine, they'll be upset if I don't come along. I think it would be better."

Carla, now clearly incensed, didn't make any move to walk Lauren to her car. But she stood up. "Before you leave here, I just want to say I was wrong."

She wasn't referring to what had just taken place or her negative opinions of Jonathan, Lauren felt certain of that. But she went along nonetheless. "Oh, about what?"

"I once described you as a tough city girl—confident, sophisticated, in command of your life. You're none of those things. You're no different than Nancy."

It was one of those memories that had slammed Emily in the face the other day when she wasn't even looking; that's how it was when out of nowhere she had announced to Lauren that her father had made her take her mother's jewelry. And then she ran off, leaving Lauren sitting there, while thinking to herself she must have finally lost it, how could that possibly be when her father hadn't even been there?

That was still the number one question, one she'd been bending her mind ever since to answer. And while she hadn't been able to find an answer yet, she had uncovered in her brain an old stinking barrel of bad feelings connected to her father. Nothing she could put her finger on, give any real reason for ... but like how now, sitting in the back seat of the car, studying his cool, handsome profile as he drove them home, she could feel herself go cold.

What would he do to Lauren if she didn't follow along like he told her to? So what made her think he'd do anything? Her memory flashed to a time she had burst in on her mother in the bathroom as she was stepping out of the shower. Her mother who was always modest about her body, never undressing in front of Emily, quickly grabbed for a towel, but not before Emily spotted a bunch of black and blues across her backside and gasped. "What happened?"

"Oh, that, nothing, I fell, just a silly old accident," her mother said, her cheeks crimson as she quickly wrapped the towel around her. "You see, your father has a strong, captivating singing voice, I just can't seem to dance fast enough."

She was only about nine then, she hadn't understood ... but now she did.

Lauren drove home in a daze, not even remembering the route she took to get there. And when she arrived, Jonathan was standing in the living room waiting for her. Beatrice peeked in from the kitchen, then with a somber shaking of her head, she disappeared out of sight. Was she truly distraught over what was happening, or was she the one who called Jonathan home? This time Lauren was first to speak. "How could you do that to me?"

"Don't you think you have things a little turned

around here, I'm the one who came home to find you and the girls gone."

"Gone? My gosh, you say it as though we went on a trip. I simply went to Carla's, and then only for a few hours. I didn't expect you home so I saw no harm in it."

"No harm? Haven't we gone through enough that I don't need to have that statement once again thrown in my face? Have you forgotten the hell we went through with Emily? Her being nearly attacked only a couple of miles from our home? And have you forgotten what happened to our tenant?"

"You're not being reasonable about this. The man who did that has been found and locked up. So there's no reason for us to be so frightened." He turned away from her now, the flat of his hand going high against the molding of the archway to the dining room, and his face bowed. She slowly walked up to him, then lifted her hand to his shoulder. "Jonathan, what is it?"

He turned to her, then sighing, said, "He's out on bail."

"But no, it can't be. How? I thought Detective Kneeland said the bail was so high?"

"It was. But somehow he managed to get a hold of the money. He's been out since last week."

She could feel little pins and needles at her back hairline as she thought of him out there, loose again. It was so unfair, so ridiculous, so outrageous. "Why didn't you tell me?"

"Because the last thing I want is to worry you,

that's why. Don't you know I'd turn heaven and earth to make things right for you and the girls, but there're obstacles to deal with. What was the point of you worrying needlessly—as long as I knew for certain that you were abiding by my decisions."

Now she went to the sofa and sank down, feeling incredibly exhausted as Jonathan had predicted not that much earlier. Would this never be over? She looked up at her husband, thinking again of the humiliation he had put her through.

He walked toward her now, remorse in his face as he knelt beside her and took her in his arms. He called to Beatrice, and she came right in, as though she'd been waiting in the wings. "Yes, Mr. Grant?" she said, relief softening the creases in her face.

"Draw a bath for my wife please?" And as she started to go, he lifted Lauren's handbag and held it out. "And while you're at it, take this to our bedroom."

Jonathan insisted on taking Lauren upstairs to help her undress, then help her into the sunken tub—the hot water was heavily laced with lavender ... How nice, her favorite, she thought, seeming to have stepped back to view everything from a distance. She needed the distance to think ... or not to think, whichever felt more comfortable. He reached in his pocket and took out a vial, then removing the cap, he spilled a pill into his palm and handed it to her with water. She pulled herself back to reality, at least, enough to ask, "What is this?"

"Just something to help you get rid of tension."

But she had felt so good earlier at Carla's, she thought. Of course she hadn't been aware of all the dangers then. Ignorance is bliss, wasn't that what they say? She only wished Jonathan had handled it better by telling her earlier about Jay Philips being out on bail. But she didn't say that to him, not wanting to imply he wasn't trying his best, when she knew, of course, he was. He was so sensitive, so vulnerable . . . all to do with his horrid childhood, she was sure. And then she remembered about the pill and said, "But I'm pregnant, I can't—"

"I got it from the doctor the other day, not to be concerned. It's a perfectly harmless sedative. In fact, it's so mild, it's regularly used for children."

Why had he suddenly decided it was necessary to get it, she wondered, but didn't bother to ask. "I just feel uncomfortable taking a drug when I'm pregnant."

"Lauren, the bottom line is, anxiety will do more harm to the baby than this pill. I didn't make that up—I've read it a number of times in reliable medical journals. It's just a matter of taking the appropriate medication, not trying to prescribe for oneself. And Doc Stevens assured me of the safety of this himself. Do you understand what I'm saying?" She nodded, and his voice was gently scolding, "Well, don't you think it's about time you showed some faith in me?"

She took the pill, dropping it on her tongue, swallowing it down with the water. That's exactly what it was about—she needed to stop being so distrustful and suspicious and uptight. She needed to put herself in Jonathan's able hands. If not her husband's hands, then whose? There had been a perfectly sane and logical reason for what had happened at Carla's, and she knew damned well that Jonathan would never risk her or the baby's well-being.

Yes, if she knew nothing else, she knew that . . .

It was later in the bedroom, after he towel dried and powdered her, after he helped her into a nightie and folded down the sheets and bedcovers for her to nap and she was feeling wonderfully content and calm, that she shook her head and said, "Oh, my darling, it's hard to believe I was so angry at you."

He reached inside the thin gown, lightly caressing her breasts. "Again, my darling, it boils down to your trusting me to do the right thing for our family."

"But I do—"

"Do you? I hope so. Because there's dangers out there, Lauren. For you, our children, our unborn child . . . And if I can't count on you to exercise good, sound judgment, then I have no choice but to take stronger measures to insure your safety." With that he removed his hand from her breasts and reached over, lifting her purse from the night table and taking out her car keys, her gate and house entrance card. "I'm going to be holding these for a while. Okay, Lauren?"

"But it's not necessary. I mean, we've talked . . .

you've explained—" She started to sit up, but he placed his hand on her shoulder, gently stopping her.

"It's only a temporary measure," he said, dropping the items in his shirt pocket. "It's really about me, not you. Do you understand? I need to have a clear head when I'm working; I need to have trust in you, know you'll do the right thing. I love you and the girls so much, I couldn't live if something were to happen. So please, humor me, just allow me this peace of mind."

She didn't answer. She didn't know what to say, but it didn't matter because it didn't seem to require an answer. He brought the sheet up to cover her, kissed her, then stood up. When he got to the door, he turned around. "Earlier you mentioned how long it's been since you and the kids have gotten out, and you're right about that. I only wish you had said it sooner rather than keep your discontent secret and become defiant. Do we really want the kids exposed to that? Remember, Lauren, whatever you want, you need only ask . . ."

He smiled that slightly crooked smile she loved. "So I was thinking, how about next Saturday I take my girls to the fair?"

So what did it mean, she thought, lying there, now cool and comfortable, and free of that anxiety that was crushing her only an hour earlier. Did it mean she couldn't come and go as she pleased, that she was a prisoner in her own home? Oh, come now, wasn't she being a little melodramatic? It wasn't as though she couldn't walk out the door if she chose, or that Jonathan wouldn't drive her wherever she insisted to go. Had he ever refused her?

For that matter, the house security was hooked up to the police department—not exactly a prison setup. The question was, could she put up with his restrictions? Or sooner she should ask, did she no longer love this man who adored her, cherished her, who could make her hot with only a look?

When all he asked was that, until the danger let up, she and the girls remain within the grounds. Not such a big deal, was it? It wasn't all that hard, she had been doing it for weeks, hardly even noticing she was doing it, more like being stuck in a country club. And . . . the big and—it was only temporary.

Carla's hurting words comparing her to Nancy came to mind now, but she nudged them aside. It didn't matter what Carla thought, she couldn't let it matter. She was only trying to do the same thing that Fern was, run Lauren's life.

Two tears trickled from her eyes, down her cheeks to her ears . . . she didn't know where they came from or why they were even there, and was too tired to lift her hand to wipe them away. She thought about Emily's words from a few days earlier. *Daddy made me take the jewelry* . . . What a peculiar thing to say. Worse than peculiar, preposterous. It would have had to mean that Jonathan had been right in the house with Emily when Nancy was killed.

Chapter Eighteen

No unchaperoned outings, but phone calls and Western Union messages allowed, a voice in her head jeered the next day as she sat on the deck chair and took the napkin with Nancy's maiden name written on it from her purse. Was she losing it, would she soon be having two-way conversations with herself?

The strangest part was everything couldn't have seemed more normal and right. Jonathan had been sweet and loving and attentive to her at dinner the night before, even taking her for a walk under the stars later that evening. It was as though nothing bad had ever occurred. In fact, when he came to the bedroom that morning to kiss her good-bye before going on business, she had to actually fight the urge to hang on to him and not let him go.

And if Emily seemed quieter and more disturbed than usual, Chelsea was alive and talkative, going out of her way to engage her daddy and now Beatrice who she'd been following from room to room all morning, mimicking her every move. "Please tell me if she gets in the way," Lauren said.

But Beatrice shook her head, reaching down and running her strong fingers through Chelsea's blond curls. Yes, Beatrice had definitely taken a shine to Chelsea over the weeks, and vice versa. Surely it was a good thing for Chelsea, the woman was there for her when Lauren was feeling under the weather, unable to give her the attention she needed, something that happened too often these days. So then why should their friendship irritate her?

Now holding the wrinkled napkin in her hand, she realized Beatrice was coming toward her. "Can I take that for you?" she asked, but Lauren dropped it back into her purse and stood up. "No, I'm fine, it's just the sun getting to me. I think I'm going to go to the bedroom for a while and lie down."

"Are you sure—"

"Absolutely, I'm fine." Then directing her attention to Chelsea, "Darling, let me again go over the rules—no going near the pool unless Beatrice or Daddy or—"

But Beatrice cut in there. "You are not to worry. Don't you know, she's my little helper?"

The first thing Lauren did when she reached her bedroom was to pick up the telephone.

When Beatrice told Chelsea to switch on the communications system going into Mommy's bedroom, Chelsea wasn't at all surprised, it was all

part of running an efficient household, Beatrice
had taught her. Her mother wasn't allowed upstairs alone without being monitored. After all she
was pregnant and delicate and not at all sure of
herself these days. Chelsea could see that for
herself.

So when she'd sleep late or take a nap—those
times when Daddy wasn't there to watch her, he'd
leave orders to have her monitored. Because Beatrice had to be ready to rush upstairs if Mommy
needed her: for instance, when she'd wake and
need her crackers so she wouldn't upchuck, or
getting out of the bath.

But the use of the communications system was
one of Beatrice's household secrets, not the sort
of thing Chelsea should confide in her mother.
"Your mother is one of those ladies who likes to
pretend she can do it all herself," Beatrice told
her. "And that's perfectly fine, it's nice for her
pride. So if it's at all possible, we ought not to
wound that pride, what would be the point? However, Daddy's in charge of this house, and we
must abide by his rules."

Sometimes Beatrice would put Chelsea in
charge of the monitor while she was busy with
other chores, but this time when Beatrice looked
over and saw Mommy lift the telephone receiver
from her nightstand, she came over and turned
up the audio. And they couldn't have been standing there more than a few seconds when they became aware that someone was in the kitchen:

Chelsea and Beatrice looked up to see Emily, and she was watching them.

And without another warning. Emily spun around, rushing to the counter with arms stretched, grabbed at whatever was lined up there, and sent it sprawling to the floor: the toaster went crashing, the blender, the can opener, a couple of dishes, papers!

"Oh, dear me, she's gone crazy again!" Beatrice cried, running over to try to stop her. But Emily shoved her out of the way, going straight for Chelsea!

Lauren had called long distance information, and Carla was right, Martin Renscilier in Windham, New Hampshire, was not difficult to find. She called the number and when a woman came to the phone, Lauren introduced herself, only to be met with silence and astonishment and suspicion. But soon Barbara Renscilier, Nancy's mother, dropped her uneasiness, confiding that she had lost her husband from a heart attack only six months before.

The woman went on to ask a lot of questions about how Emily was doing and feeling, about her emotional condition, and Lauren tried to answer as accurately as possible. Finally she said, "maybe it would be better if I have Jonathan call you, he's naturally much more familiar with the doctor's reports and—"

"No, I don't want that."

"But it shouldn't be a problem."

"Does your husband know you've called me?"

"No. But he wouldn't mind. I mean, after all—"

"If you thought he wouldn't mind, why is it you didn't tell him?"

"I don't know, I just thought—"

"What you thought was that he wouldn't like it."

Lauren was beginning to feel uncomfortable at the sudden aggressiveness of this woman, making her feel as though she were being interrogated. "Look, Barbara, I don't know what you're getting at or why. I only called because I wanted you to know that you're welcome to see or contact Emily at any time. In fact, I think—"

"Never mind what you think, young lady ... What does your husband think?"

She paused for a moment, somewhat taken back—the woman had switched moods, this one not being nearly as pleasant. "He wouldn't try to stop you if that's what you mean."

"Oh, that's where you're wrong, dear. He mostly certainly would try to stop me. Or my children. For heaven's sake, he stopped us while Nancy was alive."

"Are you saying Jonathan personally stopped you from seeing your granddaughter?"

"Oh, no, nothing so honest or direct. He was foxy and well practiced at his control games. Whatever he thought got said through our daughter, and the hideous part was that she couldn't see it was all coming from his head, not hers. He drove such a wedge between us, she would barely speak to either me or her father, let alone let us see our grandchild. Yes, our daughter did all the talking, but he was standing back in the wings, pulling the strings."

This story wasn't all news to Lauren, but the dramatic spin she had put on her version made Nancy come across as though she were emotionally abused, and Jonathan, of course, as the villain, and it was making Lauren furious. "Look, that was back then, and I don't know what went on. But this is now, and Jonathan is nothing like what you're implying. He's a fine man, a good man."

"He's a sick man!"

Lauren took a deep breath; she was beginning to feel sick. And to make matters worse, she thought she was hearing loud voices coming from downstairs. Oh, dear, calling her had been a terrible mistake. She had opened up an old but still-infected wound; these were things she knew practically nothing about, things she had no business knowing about. And just as she was about to hang up, the woman began to sob. "He killed my daughter," she said.

"Stop it now, that's a lie! Okay, so you didn't get along with your son-in-law, maybe you hated him, but it's still no excuse to say such a terrible thing! God, how can you—"

"Because it's true!" she shouted over Lauren's protest. "Oh, I can't prove it—if I could, I would have headed to the nearest courthouse. You want to know what really killed my husband, young lady, what finally wore out a heart that should have been strong enough to go on for at least another decade?"

Lauren didn't want to hear it, but Barbara Renscilier was going to tell her anyway. "Not the grief of Nancy's death—oh, no, we had gone through that grief years back, having lost her when she said, 'I do' to Jonathan Grant. What really killed my dear husband was that unrelenting fear that hammered away inside him. Knowing that when his granddaughter got out of that rat's hole that bastard stuck her in, she would be forced to go back to live with him!"

Lauren dropped the receiver and wrapped her arms around herself. It was warm in the room, she had felt it when she came in earlier, yet she couldn't stop trembling.

Daddy had walked in right in the middle and it was a good thing because Emily had already whacked Chelsea in the mouth and though Beatrice was trying to drag Emily away, she was going for her again. And Daddy was angry.

While Beatrice had gone off to wet a cloth and get a spray from the medicine cabinet for her bleeding lip, Jonathan backed Emily up against the wall. "Your sister is five years younger than you and half your size. Why would you do that to her?"

Emily didn't answer, just gave him that mean face, the one she had down to a science, and Daddy turned toward Beatrice who had just come back to the kitchen and was washing Chelsea's lip with peroxide. "Where's Lauren?"

"In your bedroom, Mr. Grant," she said. "She wasn't disturbed by this at all."

He looked at the monitor that was now in the off position. "I'll discuss what's going on here later. In private. But for now, where's the dog?"

"Out back, I believe."

And that's when Emily really started to sweat— she was looking away as though she didn't care one way or another about the dog. But Chelsea knew better, and so did Daddy.

"I want the dog put in the cellar," he said. "Until further notice, it's to sleep, take its meals, and exercise there." Then turning back to Emily. "And I don't want you anywhere near that animal, not until you can learn how to behave, to treat people with care and respect. I've put up with enough of your bullying tactics, but enough is enough! I think it's about time you start acting like a lady."

"Like her?" she cried, gesturing to Chelsea.

"Yes, exactly like her!"

With that, Emily dashed up to her room, and Jonathan came over to Chelsea and knelt down. "Oh, gosh, Angel, that doesn't look so hot," he said, wincing as though it hurt him, too. "How does it feel?"

"It hurts bad."

"Beatrice, did you put antiseptic on it?"

"Oh, I surely did, Mr. Grant." Then with her hand gesturing upstairs toward where Emily had run, she said, "Would you like me to call my niece?"

He shook his head. "With all due respect to your niece, I've had my fill of psychologists. Look at the results here," he said, throwing up his arms. "I've got a daughter that's loud and rude and insolent. In fact, call and cancel Emily's sessions with her until further notice—it's time we had some discipline around here!"

Then Daddy turned to Chelsea and she swallowed down hard—she had never seen him so angry, and when he talked like that, it scared her. "Beatrice," he said, his mad face still not wholly gone. "I'm afraid we're going to have to use a stronger medicine on this little girl of mine." But before Chelsea could get out her objections, she could see his gleaming teeth and smile. He tossed her easily over his shoulders.

And he was off with her, out the back door with her as she laughed and held on tight to her amazing bucking bronco, no longer even feeling what had seemed to hurt so badly only minutes earlier. And she didn't feel a bit sorry for Emily either. Why should she? Emily had whacked her hard and for no good reason at all—Chelsea was only trying to be what Daddy wanted her to be, his perfect little girl. A position Emily had given up all on her own.

Lauren had been sitting on the bed in that position for about fifteen minutes before her body stopped trembling, before she finally snapped back to some semblance of normalcy. That terrible woman—if that was any indication of what Nancy's simple farm people were like, no wonder Nancy hadn't gotten along. Considering the way Barbara Renscilier felt about her son-in-law, it must have been an impossible situation.

The gall of her—actually accusing Jonathan of her daughter's murder! For God's sake, Jonathan had an alibi, wasn't the woman aware of that? Or was she but just didn't care? She apparently was the sort of person who made up her mind about things based on emotions, throwing facts to the winds.

Maybe it was all this thinking about family that made her suddenly long for Fern. She reached out to pick up the phone just as Jonathan opened the door, and she quickly brought back her hand. But he didn't miss the gesture. "It looks like my beautiful wife is awake. Have I interrupted something?"

"No, of course not," she said, shaking her head.

Well, in that case, do you suppose I could interest you in lunch. Just you and I."

"Out?" she asked, feeling immediately excited, hoping his answer would be yes.

And it was, of course. He nodded and said, "Wherever you say, my love."

She rushed off to her dressing room to change and fix her face, her hands still trembling from her earlier conversation, her motions as she tried to apply her makeup a little frantic. But she wanted to look extra nice for Jonathan. Meanwhile he headed downstairs to talk to Beatrice—apparently there had been some to-do between Emily and Chelsea, explaining the loud voices she had heard earlier. Jonathan would find out what happened, and handle it.

"What did Beatrice finally say about the girls?" she asked as the gate lifted and they drove through.

"Nothing to concern yourself about, it's all fixed."

"But I saw Stew being taken to the cellar." Lauren was downstairs when Beatrice was bringing him in from outside.

"A temporary punishment. Emily has got to learn how to act civil, let alone like a lady."

"Then it got physical?"

He glanced at her. "Why are you doing this?"

"What?"

"Going on about the children's fight when I already said everything was fine?"

She shook her head, then shrugged. "No reason, just curious." She looked out the window, still feeling a slight trembling in her chest. "So where're we going?"

"I told you, it's your choice."

"I can't make up my mind. Please, you decide, Jonathan." He studied her, his eyes narrowing some. "What?" she asked, beginning to feel self-conscious.

He shook his head, his eyes went back to the road. "Let's go to Rogers," he said. His choice sounded fine to her—the food at Rogers was good, but it's main charm was the terrace overlooking the lake. She sat back, preparing herself for the twenty-five-minute drive—that's why she was surprised when he pulled into a coffee shop parking lot not five minutes onto Route 91.

"I thought we were going to Rogers—"

"We are," he said, opening the glove compartment, pulling out a packaged Handi Wipe, and handing it to her. "But first let's get rid of about half of that makeup."

"What're you talking about?"

Shaking his head with good humor, he folded down the visor mirror on the passenger side so she could look at herself. "You mind telling me what you had in mind when you put on all that gunk? Were you thinking of picking up a guy?"

She looked at him, a little surprised to hear that kind of teasing remark from Jonathan, then studied her reflection—in trying so hard to look good for her man, the result had ricocheted, her makeup had been applied with a too heavy hand. She flipped the visor up and said, "Okay, you win. I'll fix it once we get to Rogers."

He sighed, then moved back his bucket seat, as though he were preparing for a long sit. "Do you really think I'm going to let you step inside Rogers or any place looking like that? That I would let men see you like that?"

"Like what?"

"Like a slut, Lauren."

She felt like he had punched her in the stomach—she took a big breath, shut her eyes, leaning her head back against the headrest. Was this going to deteriorate even further, turn into silence? Was he going to punish her by turning the car around and taking her home? Was she ready for either of those alternatives? A few minutes passed in silence, when finally she sat forward, brought down the mirror, and held out her hand. "Give me the Handi Wipe."

Jonathan got a table on the terrace, the one she liked best, ordering salmon for her—blackened the way she liked it. Jonathan was at his most charming, now, and it was wonderful to be with him. And it was all because she had been mature enough to give a little. There was a time when she mightn't have been able to back down like that ... a time before Jonathan. Really ... was it so terrible that she fixed her face before they got to the restaurant? The issue was the makeup, and clearly she had put on too much.

Several times during their lunch she thought of the phone call to Nancy's mother, each time getting bogged down in the ugly accusations, and twice coming within inches of asking Jonathan about his alibi. But both times she stopped herself before speaking. Surely he'd insist to know what had brought on such a question ... what made her even think of Nancy's murder now. So if there was one single thing Barbara Renscilier might have been right about, it was why Lauren hadn't discussed calling her with Jonathan beforehand.

The truth was, she hadn't been sure what his reaction would be.

Jonathan had an alibi, she knew that. She knew it because he told her so. But he had told her so many other things as well, things that had turned out to be only shades of the truth. Was this one of them? But she would never have dared ask Detective Kneeland if the opportunity hadn't presented itself when he stopped over unexpectedly two days later. Beatrice and Chelsea had gone to drop off Jonathan's shirts at the cleaners, and she and Emily were the only ones home.

"Maybe I should have called first," he said, sitting in his car at the front gate.

"No, that's okay, not a problem," she said, this time finding herself delighted that he'd dropped by like this. One of the security pluses that came with a small town versus a big city, she thought, then realized how foolish she was being—hadn't Jonathan seen to it that the Grants were the last in town to need additional security? She released the front gate to let him through and by the time she got to the door, he was getting out of his car. "I didn't see your husband's Lexus," he commented as she let him inside the foyer.

"Do you need him? If so, I can give him a call."

"Naw, it's not necessary, you can tell him just as easy. it's good news so I thought I'd deliver it personally. Philips is back in jail, and I'm not beyond boasting it was me who got him there."

"Oh? How did you manage that?"

"A little ingenuity is all. I remembered he had a girlfriend over the New Jersey border, so I made it my business to follow him for the past few days. Last night I hit paydirt. You see, the conditions of his bail were quite precise, he wasn't to set foot out of state. So, the upshot was, Judge Nestor revoked bail."

Would this end Jonathan's concern? She was afraid to consider that it might not. "Oh, that's wonderful," she said. "What are the chances, he'll get out again?"

"None if I have anything to do with it. The way I view it, he's going to be convicted and put away for quite a spell. Meanwhile he's going nowhere. To be frank, I was surprised the judge had even set bail for him, though I suspect like the rest of us, he figured the kid didn't have money to get a bondsman."

"But he did. How?"

The detective ran a finger along his mustache, smoothing it, then shook his head, apparently mystified himself. "This guy Hutch, the guy who was about to perjure himself to give Philips the alibi, suddenly puts up money for his bail. The question being, where did a loser like Hutch get that kind of money?" He shrugged, taking hold of the doorknob. "But one mystery at a time."

"What about Nancy Grant? I mean, do you still wonder who might have done that?"

He looked at Lauren thoughtfully, then said, "I'll tell you something. Mrs. Grant—on the q-t. I thought it was Philips killed the woman back then and I still do. So don't think I've given up on that. I set out to do something, it may take a while, but sooner or later it gets done. I see it that with Jay Philips back behind bars, the whole town ought to be whistling 'Dixie'."

"It certainly does seem to me that the town owes you a debt," she said, stalling some, thinking how she would bring up the question of Jonathan's alibi.

He pressed his lips together, his words purposely humble. "Hey, that's my job. they don't owe me nothing, other than a paycheck at the end of the week."

She shook her head. "No, you're being modest, Detective. From what I can see you do the job better than most. Keep in mind, I lived in Manhattan most of my life, so I got an opportunity to see how badly city police operate. The fact that you even remembered Philips had a girlfriend in New Jersey is impressive."

"The truth is, I've got an outstanding memory when it comes to police work. I might have mentioned that before." Then chuckling, he said, "Of course, let the wife tell me to pick up more than three items at the market and forget it."

Kneeland opened his car door and stepped inside, but she followed after him. "Detective, I bet you have tons of information about Nancy's murder stored in your head?"

"Let me tell you a little something, Mrs. Grant," he said, smiling, "I interviewed no less than fifty people in that case, and if I had to sit now and list 'em out for you, I likely could." He put the key in the ignition.

She leaned down close to the window. "Really? What day did it happen?"

It took him only a few seconds. "Tuesday, twentieth of May, two years ago. A sunny day, not a cloud in the sky. Your little stepdaughter, Emily, called 911 at about twelve forty-five P.M."

"And where was my husband?"

"Pardon me?"

"You know, when it happened?" Okay, she had asked it . . . was he looking at her peculiarly, or was that only her imagination?

Apparently it was, because he said, "He was in Syracuse." And she did remember that Jonathan had said Syracuse when he first told her. She also remembered Jonathan saying, he hadn't known the guy before, he'd never done business with him before or since. "You know, I can't recall the fellow's name offhand, but I do recall his operation—Party Construction. Why do you ask?"

She felt the knot inside loosening . . . "No, no reason." Did she look like a liar, sound like a liar? Even if she did, what did it matter? Jonathan had an alibi.

Chapter Nineteen

Lauren met Jonathan at the door, eager to tell him the good news about Jay Philips, but he stopped her cold, giving her a bouquet of spring flowers with a string of pearls hidden in between the stems. "Oh, my gosh, they're lovely," she said, fishing them out and admiring their brilliance as she stayed put and let him fasten the latch. Finally after arranging the flowers in a vase on the coffee table, she followed him to the study where he was already sifting through the mail. She sat across from him. "Darling, will you listen to me now?"

He looked up. "When have I not listened?"

She smiled. "Jay Philips is back in jail."

And he listened calmly and quietly as she told him about his bail getting revoked. "Maybe Detective Kneeland is not so inept after all," she said, then, "Jonathan, listen, I was thinking of driving to the mall this afternoon. Would you mind, darling? I need maternity clothes, it seems everything I own is becoming tight."

He went back to the mail. "Hold it until a little later this afternoon, and I'll be free."

"But the idea was to go now—"

He glanced up from the letter he was reading, his eyes scolding. "Lauren, please, you're whining."

The accusation hit her like a slap, but she swallowed down the hurt. "I wasn't aware that I was. But if I am, I'm sorry. It's just that I've been thinking about going off shopping since I learned about the arrest. It's safe out there now, Jonathan, at least relatively safe. Will you look at me," she said, feeling almost giddy talking about it, "I'm like a kid, all excited at the prospect of going off somewhere—"

"And you shall go. I'm simply saying, I can't take you at this moment."

"No, but that's not what I mean. You don't have to—"

He tilted his face toward the ceiling, closing his eyes as though asking for divine guidance. Finally he looked at her. "I take you wherever you ask; I buy you beautiful and expensive gifts; I rush around all day to get things done so that I may have more moments to give to you. You want for nothing, yet I think if you could, you would steal the last breath from me and claim it as yours. Like a spoiled, pampered little child, you 'want' and 'demand,' yet are never satisfied. What is it, Lauren, can't you find it in yourself to be happy?"

"But I am happy," she said, and she was ... or would be. If only he could understand how she felt.

He stood up. "Are you? You could certainly

fool me. Other women would be ecstatic to have what you have. Am I wrong about that, Lauren? Because if I am, tell me." She shook her head, and he came over to her, stooped down, and took her hands in his hands. "Maybe it's my fault after all."

"What?"

His eyes seemed to smoke, burning into hers. "I think when you act like a child, I shall need to treat you like one. That's what you want, isn't it, why you test my patience?"

She began to gag, and he hurried her into the bathroom, holding her head as she vomited. By the time she finished, she was exhausted, and he took a cold cloth and washed her, then helped her upstairs and put her to bed. And though it seemed like only minutes later when she heard Jonathan calling, "Lauren," she saw from the bedside clock that ninety minutes had elapsed.

She began to sit up, to go to the monitored area of the bedroom to talk to him, but he said, "No, no, stay put. I have an appointment. It'll take me about an hour, but you're not to worry, Beatrice is home, taking care of everything. she's going to take Chelsea in the pool later. Tell me, darling, do you feel well enough to go shopping?"

She nodded, then it dawning on her that he couldn't seen her from the bed, she said, "Yes."

"Okay, good. Then as soon as I get back, we'll go. Would you like that?"

"Yes," she said. "I would."

"One small qualifier. I want you to stay in bed

until I return. Beatrice is now making lunch for you, she'll be up with it shortly. All right?" Lauren didn't say anything and he said finally, "Lauren, I want an answer here?"

"I don't understand, why. I can just as easily get up and come downstairs—"

"If you're going out with me, I want you rested."

"But I am."

A pause, a sigh, then, "What is it, your choice, do you want to go or don't you?"

And she cleared her throat. Yes, of course she wanted to go. Jonathan was saying he would take her shopping for new clothes and she wanted desperately to go. "All right," she said.

"Please be more specific."

"Yes, I'll stay in bed."

Another sigh she heard over the system, but this one was likely locked into a smile—she had pleased him. "I love you, Lauren," he said, his voice deeply charged with feeling.

But she didn't want to focus on love so she zoned in on the new maternity clothes she would get. So many lovely new styles since she had last been pregnant. Should she telephone Fern? Naw, it wasn't really necessary. They'd likely run into her at the mall . . . Her older sister was a real mall rat . . .

Though Lauren stopped every few minutes, looking high and low for Fern at the mall, Jonathan finally needing to take her by the hand so she wouldn't lag; big sister wasn't to be found.

Lauren couldn't understand it, darn it, couldn't Fern see Lauren needed her?

As Lauren lay in her husband's arms that long, sleepless night, her thoughts and feelings circled around as though they were on a conveyor belt, and she'd grab one, only to have it turn away before she got the chance to think it through. One moment loving Jonathan, feeling the warmth and joy of having him pressed against her, and sure she was a hopeless ingrate like he had suggested—always taking from him, always demanding more, never giving back. While the next instant, she feared him, and felt her insides shrink from him.

She thought of calling Fern many times, finally the last time making a pact with herself that no matter what the morning brought, she would call her sister. And so it was for only that reason that she did finally call, because the next morning she found herself clinging to Jonathan, missing him before he even left her, feeling jittery at the thought of being separated from him. But he spoke calmly, reassuring her he'd be back as soon as he could, and saying, "I want you to be happy, I want that more than anything in this world, Lauren."

And she was, how could she not be? Wasn't he giving her a hundred percent, focusing his entire existence on making her happy? "The whole thing is to not fight what you feel, do you understand?" he said, and though she wasn't sure she did, she said so, wanting to give him all the reassurance he needed. And as she watched out the window his car leaving the grounds, she realized she had no desire to leave the grounds unless Jonathan was with her.

She knew it was preposterous only because the realization made her start to cry.

Though she felt calm and together later when Beatrice left with Chelsea to get groceries and run errands, she decided to follow through with her pact. Dressed in a new maternity backless sundress Jonathan had picked out for her the night before and feeling particularly pretty and feminine wearing it, she came in from the deck and called Fern.

"Fern's out with a client. Lauren, is that you?"

"It is," she said, knowing, of course, it was Sarah Lincoln, the same girl Fern had since she first opened the real estate agency, the same girl she had always chatted amiably with whenever she called But now she had no desire to be friendly.

But Sarah pushed on anyway, "Well, hi," she said. "Where've you been?"

"Oh, around. I've been busy. You know how it is?"

A strained silence, then Sarah picked it up. "Look, if you want, I could try to reach her. I think I have—"

"No, don't bother, it's not that important. Just ask her to call when she gets a chance," Lauren said. Then she hung up and returned to the deck to look for Emily.

347

When she didn't spot her, she came back to the kitchen and turned on the communications system. She plugged in Emily's room, getting the monitored area and calling out, "Emily, you there?" No answer. "If you are, please answer."

But she heard or saw nothing—so she pressed what she thought was exit, and turned out to be the master bedroom. And she gasped when she saw the viewing area was not the original area she and Jonathan had chosen, but a larger area that took in the entire room, that took in their king-size bed. So that's how Beatrice knew when Lauren was getting up in the morning, when to bring those crackers to fight her nausea . . . She'd been watching her—and the thought of it made her angry. *Well, stupid, what did you think, the old lady was psychic? And was she watching with Jonathan's blessings? Of course she was, what ever happened in his house without Jonathan?*

She turned around suddenly and there was Emily, watching her, staring at her . . . waiting. Then with no malice in her voice, she said, "Not so smart, are you?"

Remembering she had been looking for her, Lauren asked, "Where have you been?"

"In the cellar."

Yes, of course, with the dog. She nodded. "Emily. Will you tell me again?"

"What?"

"About the jewelry you took from your mother."

"I took it because my father was standing over me, telling me to take it."

"But isn't that impossible, Emily? I mean, when the police came, the jewelry was gone from her body. And your father was off in Syracuse. He wasn't even there until—"

"I don't know how, I can't explain it," she said. "But I remember that!"

Emily ran outside, leaving Lauren standing there, thinking about it. She had to have been wrong, perhaps being so frightened that she imagined Jonathan telling her. Jonathan had an alibi, a good alibi. A man he'd never met before, had never even done business with, swore he was with him. Fern . . . yes, again she felt an overwhelming need for Fern. But instead she picked up the phone and dialed the 315 area code plus the number for Syracuse information. "Syracuse," she said. "Have you a number for Party Construction?"

As she was dialing, she realized she had no clue as to what to say to whoever answered. Were you with my husband on the day of his first wife's murder, and if so, when exactly did he leave you? What will he think? That she's insane, of course. Did it matter though what he thought? The man barely knew Jonathan . . . would he look him up now just to tell him Lauren had called him? Her jumbled thoughts stopped midstream as a receptionist answered, and she cleared her throat. "Uh, excuse me, but the owner . . . what's his name?"

A pause then, "His name is Elliot Sandrew. May I help you?"

"I need to talk to him."

"Who may I say is calling?"

"Lauren Grant."

"Just a moment," the voice said, apparently the name Grant not meaning anything to her.

The man's voice was gruff, and when she introduced herself and mentioned Jonathan, neither name rang a bell to him. "Do you want to tell me a little more?"

"Well, apparently you and he had done some land tests that day. This was back about two years ago, of course. You see, the reason I need to know—"

"Hold on, right there," he said. "I think I've got the problem nailed—you don't want me. I took over this company a few months ago; I bought it out."

"Oh, I see. Well, how can I reach the former owner?"

"You can't, not unless you're a mighty amazing woman."

"Pardon me."

"I don't mean to make light of it. The former owner was killed about . . . oh, let me see, nine, ten months ago. A freak on-site accident, they tell me—maybe you'd recognize the name: Jerry Reardon?"

Lauren felt as though her chest was on fire as she lowered the phone. Though she didn't know how the new piece fit, it had suddenly turned everything around, creating a whole new picture. But Jonathan's alibi was not a stranger at all like he'd told her, but a man who he had considered a close friend. She'd met Jerry only that one weekend that they stayed at his condo, getting along wonderfully well, and, of course, she was aware that he owned several businesses ... Apparently one of them ... was Party Construction.

And she wasn't sure how she got to her husband's study, only that she was there and she was looking through his desk drawers, taking out papers, scouring through them. Finding a key that fit the filing cabinet, she began to go through it, too. She had to uncover the lies. How could they have a marriage based on all these damned lies?

She wished Fern would call ...

Lie number one—uncovered in a folder labeled Noreen Grant. Jonathan's mother was still alive. After his father's death, Jonathan had gone in with—from the looks of the papers—a high-powered law firm and had her declared incompetent, then put her in a nursing home where his checks continue to be sent.

Uncovered in a file labeled Jay Philips was a list of dates and specific instances where he was stalking Emily. Jonathan wasn't simply aware that he was following her, according to what Lauren was seeing—and she read it over three times to be sure she was not misinterpreting it—since mid-March, since Emily arrived home, Philips had been on Jonathan's payroll. Along with that was an envelope containing half a dozen blue threads—threads from Philips's baseball cap? Also, a sizable sum of money had been mailed via his attorney to an out-of-town bondsman, to get Philips out on bail.

She wished Fern would call . . .

Uncovered in the bottom file drawer were two replicas of her birth control vials. Were they dummies, had she been taking placebos? Had Jonathan switched her pills so that she'd conceive?

In a file labeled Bates were several sizable canceled checks, made out to the Building Fund. Was it possible that Jonathan had been manipulating Emily's therapy?

And as ghastly as all else, it was when she saw the next file labeled Beatrice Barr that Lauren thought her heart had stopped: in it were records of monthly checks, amounts far more generous than those to his mother. And photographs of Beatrice . . . then looking to be in her twenties: dressed in frilly see-through nightgowns and dresses, surrounded by stuffed animals and toys . . . in provocative childlike poses, baring parts of her body. For little boy Jonathan?

Jonathan killed Nancy . . . Jonathan killed Gordon. And what about Jerry Reardon? Was it possible Jonathan had killed him, too? But why? Jerry was the one who gave him his alibi. More important, how could she have shared a bed with him all this time and not known?

Suddenly she looked up to see Emily in the

doorway. "Beatrice and Chelsea just came through the gate," she said.

Lauren stared at her—words were in her head, but she couldn't get them past her lips.

"Put the papers away!"

Lauren still stared until finally Emily came in and began to close files and shove them back into drawers—Lauren sat there, watching, unable to even help. And by the time the garage door opened bringing in Beatrice and Chelsea and the grocery bags, Emily was out of the room and Lauren was still at Jonathan's desk in his study.

Emily and Chelsea were out in the hallway, peeking in at her; how ironic, she thought, it was the first time she had ever seen them so close to one another. They both looked frightened. Of what, of her sitting there crying? Was that scaring them? Suddenly Jonathan appeared in the doorway and the children were quickly sent away, and she was grateful to him for that.

He came directly to her, taking out his handkerchief and drying her eyes, and she thought, how bizarre it was, she hadn't even known she was crying. "What is it?" he asked, looking around the room to find something amiss, but Emily apparently had done a good enough job. When Lauren didn't answer, he went on, his voice tender, his hand massaging the back of her neck. "Beatrice called and said you weren't feeling well," he said. She swallowed past the thickness in her throat, then nodded. No, she didn't feel well at all. How did Beatrice know that? "Would you like me to take you to bed, darling?"

Yes, that was what she wanted—Jonathan always seemed to know just what she wanted. She let him pick her up, and she circled her arms around his neck. Just then, the phone rang, and her insides snapped alive, making her want to race to get it, to see if it was Fern. But when Jonathan saw her concern, he said, "it's okay, Lauren, Beatrice will get it. You're too upset now to talk to anyone."

Again, he was right—for pity's sake, she couldn't even seem to get a word past her tongue, let alone race off to get the telephone. And could anyone blame her? She had only just found out that the housekeeper Beatrice had had some lewd, sick affair with her husband when he was only a child, and her husband was a pathological liar who manipulated and terrorized his family.

He was a murderer.

Oh, my dear God, somehow she had to get herself and the kids out of there.

Fern was gone most of the day with the client, but was thrilled when she arrived back at the office to hear Lauren had called. She had called twice in the last few weeks, but the housekeeper both times had said she refused to come to the phone. She then decided it would be better to wait until Lauren was ready.

And apparently that was now—but when the housekeeper answered this time and Fern asked to speak to Lauren, she got first silence, then the woman asked her to hold. But it wasn't Lauren who ultimately came to the phone, it was Jonathan. And if there was anyone she wasn't feeling kindly toward, it was her brother-in-law.

But she put those feelings aside when he said, "Listen, Fern, Lauren's not feeling too well."

"What is it?"

"The doctor was here, he gave her something to calm her."

"I don't understand, she's pregnant."

"Christ, Fern, do you wonder why people don't tell you anything? You jump all over them. Now are you going to shut up and listen, or do you want to do the talking?"

"Okay, I'm sorry, Jonathan. But as far as I know, pregnant women shouldn't take drugs."

"Well, if you mean is it an ideal situation, then you're right, it's not. But that's not what we're talking about here. The doctor felt a mild sedative was better than the anxiety she was suffering."

"What anxiety, what's happened?"

"Today she went into my study, sat down at my desk, and started bawling. For no apparent reason. Ask the kids, they saw, they were scared to death. Beatrice had to call me home, and if I hadn't seen it myself, I wouldn't have believed it."

"What was her reason?"

"I'm telling you, she had none. Lauren is scared, Fern."

"I don't understand, scared of what?"

"Just scared in general—stemming from the

murders ... Jay Philips stalking Emily, getting so close to hurting her."

"Of course. But he's locked up, isn't he?"

"Yes, but as far as her fears go, it's not that simple; she worries not only for herself and the girls, but for the safety of the baby. You've got to remember, we've got special hormones at work here. And she's taken a lot, more than most could manage. You're a smart girl, Fern; I thought for certain you'd recognize what was going on when you saw she didn't want to go anywhere."

A silence, then a deep sigh—no, maybe not so smart after all—here she thought Lauren's reclusiveness had somehow been Jonathan's doing. "It looks like I owe you an apology," she said finally. "I figured you were behind it."

"I simply didn't want to pressure her is all. There was no need to, if she wants to stay put until she feels more secure and confident, then it's not the end of the world. It's not like she hasn't been willing to go out in my company."

Though Fern didn't like hearing any of this, what he was saying made sense, at least temporarily until the baby arrived. Then, of course, if the fears didn't go away on their own, she'd need to see a therapist. Damn it, how had this happened, and, of all people, to Lauren, who prided herself on being self-sufficient? At least until she met Jonathan. Still Fern had to be grateful that Lauren had enough trust in Jonathan to be able to go off the grounds with him. "What can I do, Jonathan?"

"Just don't push her. Let her know that staying inside is fine ... whatever makes her happy. We want her to be comfortable with whatever she decides. That's what counts now—not only for her sake, but for the baby's."

"I want to see her."

"It's not a great idea."

"I want to see her."

"Okay, but you should know, it's against doctor's orders. Come over tonight, at about eight."

When Fern hung up the phone, she felt despondent, wondering why her sister had called that morning. Was she feeling scared then, had she wanted her big sister?

"I'm sorry, Jonathan, I'm going to have to take the girls and go home," she said, her tongue still having difficulty manipulating. Like she had drunk a fifth of bourbon ... she didn't even like bourbon. Besides, she would never—she was pregnant.

"Darling, you are home," Jonathan insisted, and looking around, she guessed he was right.

"Where are the girls?"

"They're fine. They don't understand all this, but they love you and want you to feel better. By the way, I spoke to Fern, and she's coming to see you later."

"She is? You're letting her?"

"What do you mean, Lauren, why wouldn't I let her? Did I ever not let your sister come here? Or for that matter, did you ever want to see her that I refused?"

Was that true? Put that way, she guessed it was. But what about everything else? What else did she mean? She wasn't exactly making sense to herself, she thought, but when Fern came, maybe she'd be able to cut through it for her. Right now, Lauren was too tired, too confused to think straight.

When Fern came, Jonathan bowed out, leaving the two sisters alone. Of course, that didn't mean he wasn't watching, Lauren thought, suddenly remembering the intercom and camera in the master bedroom. "Smile pretty, Sis, I think ... he's watching us. Listening, too," Lauren said.

"What do you mean?"

"You know, he's got to take care of me."

"Well, sure, of course. Why wouldn't he? He's your husband, he loves you."

"Then you're not angry at him anymore?"

Fern took her sister's hand and squeezed it. "No, of course I'm not. I'm not angry at either of you."

"Well maybe you don't know about me then," she said, lining her hand at the side of her mouth as though ready to tell a secret. "I only go off the grounds when he takes me."

Fern didn't seem at all surprised or horrified, nor did she act like it was a big deal. "Where do you go?" Fern asked.

"Out to eat," she said, thinking she might cry, but she didn't. "The mall."

"Good, that's fine. It could be worse, right?"

Hadn't she heard what she said, hadn't she realized the weirdness of it? She guessed not. Maybe it was only Lauren's interpretation of it that made it so weird. What would she say if she knew Jonathan killed Nancy? Would she say, "Well, it could be worse" or would she shake her head and think she was nuts? Either way, she didn't tell her—her tongue was too big and clumsy to keep lifting it. Better get a backhoe, a crane, an excavator . . . or whatever that thing was . . .

As soon as Lauren nodded off, Fern left the room, went downstairs to Jonathan's study where he was sitting there, looking morose. With respect to that drug Lauren was taking, she didn't understand—it was clearly too powerful. Jonathan was too smart and savvy for this, he knew better. "I don't like it," she said, sitting down.

And he looked up. "What does that mean?"

"It simply means, my sister is pregnant, and you've got her doped to the hilt—she couldn't stay awake, let alone make sense. What are you thinking?"

He sat back in his chair and sighed. "I knew I was a fool to let you see her like this. You know, Fern, the last thing she needs is to see you look at her as though she's gone mad. Look, do me a favor, Fern. You know how much I love your sister, trust me to do right by her."

"I don't like all this medication."

"And you think I do? She had to be brought down right away, she was hysterical. But by tomorrow, the medication will be cut significantly.

And then it'll be a matter of rest and quiet. Total rest, Fern, not these visits that you two are famous for."

"So what're you saying, you don't want me seeing her?"

"Fern, you're going to be pissed at me saying this, but if anyone can stress Lauren out, it's you." Though she started to argue, he raised his hand, stopping her. "Listen up a second before you go off on me. I simply mean that it's important to Lauren that she look capable and confident in her big sister's eyes, she's confided that to me herself. So if it's a big mystery as to why she hasn't talked to you about these fears, it's because she's ashamed, embarrassed that you see her so frightened."

Though she still wanted to argue, Jonathan might have hit upon something. As bad as Lauren felt when she had just seen her, as drugged as she was, hadn't she kept on insisting how awful she was, expecting what? That Fern would judge her, condemn her?

"Just give her a week free of needing to make good impressions, giving explanations and excuses. That's all I ask. Look, we both want the same thing, don't we?"

"By tomorrow the drugs will be cut?"

"Significantly, if not totally."

She nodded, then stood up. "I'll expect a daily report."

"You've got it."

She had asked him if there was anything she

could do to help, but they didn't need her help—they had Beatrice. Though the relationship between the housekeeper and Lauren had begun badly, it had begun to work. And thank goodness it had. The important thing was to get Lauren well ... damn it, why did this happen?

Chapter Twenty

She woke up terrified—the buffer no longer being there to protect her from the things she'd learned. She vaguely remembered Fern being there, but that seemed almost impossible—surely she would have been able to see what a mess she was, and not have left. The telephone—Lauren turned toward the bedside stand only to discover it had been removed, and Jonathan opened the door to the room. He was holding a tray with tea and Beatrice's wafers.

She looked at him, studied him as he placed the tray on the bedside table: the dark, brooding eyes, the cleft in his chin, the strong majestic features. He was the man she slept with, loved for all this time—her husband for heaven's sake, yet suddenly there was nothing about him that seemed familiar.

He got down beside her, resting on his elbow, watching as she picked up a cracker and bit into it. "I can't overlook what's happened here, Lauren," he said, and she immediately caught her breath—did he know she had gone through his papers? But apparently not, because he continued on in another vein. "You not only have your well-being to consider here, you have the baby's. Still you insist on bucking me every step—questioning my decisions or doing the opposite of what I say.

"You've put us through hell, Lauren—Emily's abduction, the fiasco with the party, I could go on but I won't." He lifted his hand to her face now and she jumped. "Easy, my darling," he said. "The purpose of me coming down on you is not to stress you further. Damn it, I love you, Lauren, I worship you . . . How the hell much do you think I can take?" It was gratefully a rhetorical question because she didn't have an answer. In any event, he went on. "What you need, my darling, is discipline. Since you refuse to do what is healthy and reasonable on your own, I'm going to temporarily limit your activities."

Limit her? What exactly did that mean? The cracker laid like dried paste in her mouth—while she had been listening, she'd forgotten to swallow. So she tried now, taking a sip of tea to loosen it, to swallow it without choking.

"Lauren?"

He was calling her, and she looked up at him. "Yes," she said, the word only a whisper.

But he heard her and seemed pleased that she was keeping up. "I don't want you to be frightened, there's no reason to be. This will simply be an exercise in love and commitment. You will put yourself in my hands, understanding, of course, that I would only do what is right for you. And once you learn this, once you can trust me so implicitly without fighting and whining and stressing, life will become all the good things you want it to be."

As she was trying to digest that, he advised her, "Temporarily there'll be no telephone calls." "I want you to stay up here in our bedroom and rest. No television, though if you'd like music on the radio, that's fine. If you need anything, darling, call on the intercom to Beatrice or me, I'll be in my study."

There had been a certain lightness in his voice at the end of the speech, so she dared to speak. "Jonathan, did you give me anything. I mean last night. Like alcohol, or maybe a drug?"

"Yes, a drug, nothing too strong, of course. It was necessary to settle your nerves."

"But I'm pregnant—"

He stood up, his features a mixture of anguish and disgust. "It was just that once, Lauren, and I will repeat, it was necessary to calm you. Besides this is what I mean, the way you whittle at me. I make a decision, and you question it immediately. No matter how much I give to you, how much patience I have, it seems never enough! Do you see it, do you see what you do?"

Her hands began to tremble, and seeing it, he sighed, lifted the cover off the foot of the bed, and spread it over her. Now his voice was lowered, kinder. "Do you see it, Lauren, tell me you see it."

She nodded, she swallowed. "Yes."

"Good. More often than not, the solution lies in recognizing the problem. Now, you mustn't advise me on what's good for you, just rely on your husband to know."

She said nothing, and he smiled. "Of course, that doesn't mean you can't ask for things. You know, you need only to ask. And if it's not harmful—"

"My sister, can I see my sister?"

"Your sister saw you already—last night, and she was disgusted and disappointed that you would do this to yourself and the baby. She's agreed it would be best not to come by again until I let her know you're ready for visitors."

"The children?"

He hesitated, considering it, then pursing his lips. "How about, we'll see, if you're a good girl. When Beatrice comes with your breakfast, she'll fix your hair and dress you. I'd like it very much if you'd cooperate with her. You might wonder about my choices initially, but again, trust me to know what looks good on you."

"But we picked out . . ." She shrugged. "Together. Just the other night."

"You're right, we did. But this is different, better. The things Beatrice brings will be custom-designed, how I'd like to see you dress more often. Do you have a problem with it?"

She shook her head, though she barely understood what he was talking about. He kissed her briefly and left, promising to be back soon. And though she tried to go over what he'd said to her, tried to come up with some plan of how to escape, she was feeling dizzy, and the ideas cruised by her, not letting her touch them.

This was simply a bizarre gimmick designed to bully her, she thought, when she woke forty-five minutes later, but better able to concentrate. Jonathan was a sophisticated and intelligent man, how long did he really think he could keep her prisoner? Besides which there was always Fern to contend with, her sister wasn't one to be put off, and Jonathan couldn't easily intimidate her ... Fern would come back as soon as she had a chance to think about it all, demand to see Lauren, and then what would he do? It took a few seconds for the proposition to take seed ...

What would he do, would he try to hurt her? And then like a ball of lead butting her brain, she reminded herself that Jonathan was a killer! She got up and rushed to her remote station—and when she went to turn the knob that Jonathan had always explained was connected to police headquarters, she found it locked. And that's when Beatrice walked in the bedroom ... no point in knocking, Lauren thought, seeing some bit of dark humor in that. Her privacy had never been anything but a sham from the beginning.

"Good morning, my dear," Beatrice said. "I've got a nice breakfast—"

"I'm not hungry," she said, the last thing she had on her mind was to eat.

Still the housekeeper was not put off, she carried

breakfast to the table, replacing the other tray with it. "You have a baby to think of. Besides, there's no point in acting spoiled. Your husband will see you get well despite yourself. Goodness, that man about jumps through hoops to take care of you. Why do you insist on behaving this way?"

"I said I'm not—" But Lauren stopped. She didn't want to appear uncooperative; it would serve her no purpose. "All right, I'll try." She picked for a few minutes at the food, then gesturing to the bathroom. "Am I allowed to go?"

"Are you allowed?" Beatrice chuckled. "Why of course you may go to the bathroom. Whatever are you thinking, my dear?"

To listen to Beatrice or Jonathan, she was the crazy one. Did Fern think that? And the girls, how about them? After seeing her yesterday, what else could they think? So if that was the consensus, wasn't it possible she was crazy?

As she headed to the toilet, she immediately spotted an envelope on the floor beside the tank. She looked around, wondering if there were cameras watching her. And though she saw nothing, she had seen nothing unusual over her bed either. So hoping she wasn't being watched, she bent down and lifted the envelope ... it was heavier than she expected. She opened it, and inside was the gold necklace Jonathan had given her ... accompanied by a note.

Okay, so you were right, I took the necklace and now that you likely don't want it, here it is back. You can always count on no-big-help Emily. By the way, the bathtub has a camera, so don't get in unless you're into giving shows.

I would help you if I could, but I don't know how. My shrink is off-limits these days, and telephones are scarce. The one Fern gave me for my birthday up and walked out of my bedroom yesterday, while Chelsea and I were in the dining room being filled in about your mental breakdown. Fancy that, huh? I bet it's doing time somewhere with my missing combat boot. But what do I know, I'm only a messed-up kid who just got her curse, but seeing you pull his study to pieces, I thought you never looked saner.

Whatever you do, Lauren, beware of the handsome prince charmer—I think he's crazy.

Lauren began to cry, beneath Emily's quirky way of expressing herself was a deadly serious message, the curiously put warning at the end taking Lauren's breath away. But there was a positive effect, too, it told her she wasn't the crazy one . . . and though she couldn't pick out the particular words anywhere in her stepdaughter's message, it seemed to be asking her to be strong.

But she was absolutely wrong about being no-big-help Emily . . . it was she who had put away the files and papers before Beatrice arrived home. If Jonathan thought that Lauren knew about him, what then? Would he have had to kill her?

"Is something wrong, Lauren?"

It was Beatrice, and Lauren folded the note up again and slipped it into one of her drawers. "No, nothing, just missing the children, I wish I could see them."

"You'll have to ask your husband about that. Meanwhile why don't you come out and eat a little more breakfast so I can get busy making you pretty. I wouldn't want to interfere, of course, but if you don't mind me suggesting ... If you're about to ask your hubby for a privilege, it certainly wouldn't hurt to look your best."

Yes, if Beatrice said so, she was likely right ... Lauren didn't know who Jonathan was, but surely she did. So she brushed her teeth, showered, put on underwear ... ready or not.

She remembered the acting she had done in college—hopefully she had gotten better.

But as prepared as she thought she was when she came out of the bathroom, she wasn't—the horror of it hitting her full face when she saw Beatrice lift the dress that she must have gotten when Lauren was showering and carefully remove it from the hanger.

A girl's dress, a style more appropriate for a ten-year-old.

"I know you're going to wonder where in the world I found this in your size," Beatrice gushed, apparently thrilled with the concept of playing dress-up. Though Lauren was too shocked to ask, she went on to explain. "You see, I'm quite a proficient seamstress—just give me a description of what you have in mind, and that's all I need. And of course your husband is a man who knows what he wants. Nancy was a good seamstress as well; he did most of the designing though.

"Once we get you over this emotional upheaval you're going through, I'll be happy to teach you to sew as well."

The dress was pink with a white bib and ties in back—full enough for the pregnant figure. But before she put it on, Beatrice insisted she take off her bra and panties: a camisole and lace panties would go much better. She stood in front of the bed while Beatrice put the hair she had been letting grow for months at Jonathan's request into a French braid. "Oh, my dear, you look so pretty," Beatrice said, rushing out in front of her, shaking her head, all but beaming as she looked over to the wooden clock on the fireplace mantel across from the bed.

Where the camera must be, Lauren thought.

Her cheeks were aflame, she felt humiliated and violated, but she brought her toe back and smiling into the camera, she curtsied. Which Beatrice thought was adorable and right in the spirit of things. And Lauren rushed off to the bathroom to be sick. But not having eaten much, what was there to throw up?

But she gagged ... and gagged again. And again.

Until Beatrice got nervous and notified Jonathan ... and he stood at Lauren's side, concerned and upset, his cool hand on her forehead, until her body was too tired to go on, and the spasms ended. Jonathan carried her to the bed, slipped off her dress, and covered her.

When he came back later, he pulled a straight chair up beside the bed, and when she opened her eyes, she found him sitting there quietly. And she seemed able to recognize parts of this man, the way he was looking at her. But then he turned and gestured to the dress, hanging over the upholstered chair, and a curtain dropped over whatever seemed familiar. "Please dress up for me, Lauren?"

She sat up ... suddenly fully awake. "I want to see the children," she said. "Not in here though. I don't want them to think I'm sick."

"They've already been told you're ill."

"Then you must tell them I'm feeling better. Because I am, Jonathan, really. I don't feel as stressed any longer, how could I with you taking such good care of me?"

He smiled at her, but somewhat skeptically, still not giving her a definitive answer. Instead he handed her the dress, and she took it into the bathroom. When she came out, he drew in his breath, and she stopped where she was. "No, come to me, my darling," he said. "You are magnificent."

She tried to clear her throat, she was having trouble swallowing. Oh, dear this was awful and sick and ugly. But she lifted one foot in front of the other, then sitting alongside him, with his one arm around her, she listened to him tell her how much he loved her and the girls. And even sitting a prisoner of his castle, she could actually feel the strength of his love, though only moments later other things wormed back into her head ... He had Emily followed to frighten her, to frighten Lauren, to keep them under his control. How could he have done so evil a thing? And then she had to remind herself still again—Jonathan was a murderer.

"Do you understand why I can't let you and the girls go out alone?" he asked at one point, after going on about the violence on the streets. "I've got to know my family is right here, safe and waiting for me when I come home. It's where I can best protect them. I'm not exaggerating, Lauren, look at some of the statistics, there are men out there, just waiting."

For a moment she found herself agreeing, after all, was he saying something untrue? Still, the danger to Nancy came from the inside, not the outside, she reminded herself.

And then he came to her, took her in his arms, and began to fondle and undress her, and if for the first time her insides began to shrink, she couldn't show it. She was married to the man, for heaven's sake, it wasn't like it was rape. . . . And if it was, did it matter? All that mattered was that she convince him ...

But somewhere in the playacting, she lost her way ... finding herself being swept so high and reaching a climax so furious and powerful, it left her weak. To his amazement, she turned from him and began to sob. "What is it, Lauren?" he said.

"It was good," she said, her voice barely audible.

And God help her, it was good, it was better than good, but the tears were not for that. For that, she despised him ... and even more, she despised herself.

But for Jonathan's end, he was pleased at her progress, and he arranged for her to visit the girls in the upstairs sitting room the next morning. Again, Beatrice produced another dress she had made, and helped Lauren on with it before fixing her hair. But the meeting was strained and awkward, both Lauren and Emily unsure of who was watching or listening. Though Chelsea was apprehensive at the start, likely remembering her mother's hysteria in her father's study just two days earlier, she came around, complimenting Lauren's new dress and braid, then telling about things Beatrice was teaching her.

It wasn't until Jonathan came to the door and told Lauren it was time to get back to bed that Lauren went and hugged Chelsea, then Emily, whispering to her stepdaughter, "If you're strong, it'll help me be strong. I'm going to try to get us out of here ... please watch out for Chelsea." Emily's not shrinking from Lauren's obvious show of affection seemed to surprise and delight Jonathan.

And he was right, too, she did need rest, just that brief walk to the sitting room and she was tired. A tiredness deep in her bones and so much more incapacitating than she'd ever felt while carrying Chelsea. Almost as though she were ...

She gasped at the thought. But it was impossible, totally, completely, utterly impossible. She would know if she were being drugged, wouldn't she?

"How's Lauren doing?" was how Fern greeted Jonathan when he picked up the line.

"Whatever happened to those common courtesies that used to be?" he teased in his usual charming fashion, which immediately picked up Fern's hopes.

"Am I to take your attitude as reflective of Lauren's condition?"

"She is doing better, Fern. I'm pleased and so is the doctor."

"Oh, that's wonderful! Can I talk to her?"

"Hey, I thought we had an agreement here?"

"We did, we do. But I'm not a fool, I wouldn't bring up anything negative—"

"We went through this, Fern, it's not you per se, it's Lauren's determination to please and impress—"

"Okay, okay," she said. "You win, Jonathan."

"Any messages?"

"Yes. Tell her I love her."

As soon as she put down the receiver, she broke

into tears ... and here she thought there were none left.

"Why're you watching me?" Chelsea said, looking up from her sandbox. She had noticed Emily hanging around more, but she didn't know why.

"I want to see what a real nerd looks like."

"What did my mother whisper to you yesterday?"

"I'll tell you if you take a walk with me."

Chelsea couldn't believe her ears—now, after all this time, she was making moves to be friendly? Well, it was too late, she didn't need her now. "You must be desperate without your dog to talk to."

"Yeah, I am."

"Well, you sure deserve the punishment. After all the rotten things you've done."

Chelsea began to walk along with her, strictly out of curiosity. When they had gotten a good distance, she stopped and with her hands on her hips said, "Okay, now tell me, what did my mother say?"

"She said to watch the nerd."

"Yeah, sure. Then she must be as sick as you."

"Maybe."

"She did look pretty though, didn't she?" Chelsea said.

"I suppose. My mother used to wear her hair in that kind of braid."

"So what is that supposed to mean, she owned the style?"

Emily didn't come back with any of her usual smart answers. Instead she looked out toward the road. "Don't you think it might be good to get out of here."

"I get out plenty ... with Beatrice. Besides, I like it here. Just because you don't like anything, doesn't mean—" But at that moment she heard her name called, and she turned to see Beatrice on the deck, calling her. "Uh-oh, got to go."

"Why?"

"Beatrice's going to teach me how to make a special no-bake strawberry cheesecake that Daddy dies for."

But just as she started off, Emily said, "You know I was thinking of opening that jewelry maker."

"Yeah, so?"

"Maybe you'd want to do it with me."

She thought about it a minute, then shook her head, she wasn't about to get bought off so easy these days. "Naw, I think I'm going to ask Daddy to buy me one of my own." With that, she took off, sure Emily was watching her go.

Though Chelsea was the one Emily was looking at, she had the picture of how Lauren looked earlier in her head. Her mother used to wear that same kind of braid. Because Daddy liked it. Her mother used to get scolded or punished by him, too ... when she did things he didn't like. And she supposed Lauren was now doing things Daddy didn't like—but at least he didn't know about her being in his files. Little things were starting to come back to Emily, but not the stranger's face.

No matter how many times she pleaded in her head, he wouldn't turn to look at her.

That night Lauren was feeling particularly desperate and claustrophobic, and when Jonathan came in, she had difficulty being cheery and agreeable, let alone convincing that she was serene and free of stress. Particularly when he asked her to pose for pictures.

"What kind of pictures?" she asked, then she remembered the pictures of Beatrice, and she thought of herself being pregnant. "No," she said, I can't."

"I'm going to insist."

"Then insist if you must," she replied. "But it won't help—I have no intention of posing."

His features went to stone as he approached her, and though she instinctively raised her hands thinking he might strike her, he scooped her into his arms instead. He carried her to the bed, laid her down across his lap, and lowered her panties to her knees, then like some sick ritualistic fancy, he began to wallop her, his hand coming down hard, stinging against her bare flesh.

And not until she had no more strength left to struggle did he finally stop and roll her gently onto the bed. She pressed her face into the mattress, her sobs muffled. Had it boosted his ego, or perhaps aroused him sexually? For her part, it had hurt and humiliated her . . . far beyond any humiliation she'd ever suffered. Okay, she would pose for his nasty little pictures, but on her terms.

She fell asleep right after, and woke the next morning, still feeling the hurt. She waited for him to get up and go to his own bathroom before opening her eyes and forcing herself up out of bed. She had to urinate; she had to vomit, and with her sore bottom was having difficulty maneuvering, but when she reached the bathroom, the pain became secondary: she spotted another one of Emily's envelopes ... this one was larger than the one before, something was in it.

She hadn't a clue as to how Emily snuck in without being found out, but however she was doing it was fine. Inside the envelope was half a roll of Ritz crackers. And the short and sweet and wonderfully helpful message that came with it was the explanation: *Watch out for those crummy little homemade Beatrice wafers: they make you feel good only to make you feel bad.*

She felt like she were caught in some nightmare. Not just the other night when she'd felt like she'd been zonked, but all that time being pregnant ... the six weeks or so since she'd been eating those damned wafers, all those times she'd complained of being tired, she was actually being drugged?

So when Beatrice came soon after with the wafers and tea, Lauren slipped them in her bedside stand while Beatrice busied herself fixing up the room, getting fresh linens for the bed: there was blood on the sheet Lauren hadn't even noticed earlier.

Once finished tidying the room, Beatrice had her turn to her side and raise her nightgown and if Lauren had any inclination to protest, she stifled it, considering her discomfort. While Beatrice washed and medicated the open cuts and bruises, she babbled on. "Why would you refuse to take pictures for your husband?"

Was there nothing Jonathan didn't tell her? Was that true, always, she wondered.

"After all, you're married; you're adults."

What about an adult and a little boy? Lauren thought, focusing on Jonathan and Beatrice years ago, but knew she couldn't say it.

"He loves you," Beatrice went on, "more so than any other woman he's ever known. And that is not easy for me to admit. There was a time long ago that I had some girlish fantasies—" She stopped and sighed. "But that was foolish, wasn't it? A fine, intelligent, handsome man like Mr. Grant doesn't up and fall in love with the house-keeper, does he? I'd say it's time you smarten up, dear. You ought to be grateful for his love and devotion; he doesn't give it out easily."

She thought she would scream during the sermon, but she didn't. And when it was over, she said, "But suppose it's too late for me, Beatrice?" Beatrice's fingers stopped applying the salve as she listened to Lauren deliver the rest. . . . "Well, now that I've had time to think about it and see how silly and prudish I was behaving, and with the man I love ... well, I think he might be so angry that he's stopped talking. Or else why wouldn't he have come up this morning?"

"And what are you saying, that there's reason for him to put his anger aside?"

And when Jonathan came up not too much later, he stood near the door waiting for her to speak—she was still lying on her side, she looked up at him. "I'm sorry, Jonathan," she said, trying her best to sound sincere. "I guess I'm just too used to being willful, fighting instead of trusting someone. And it's hard getting used to doing things I never even knew you wanted."

"Things you don't want—"

"No, it's not that. Really. I've just never thought about it. Now, suddenly, you hit me with all this, and I react instinctively. And I know that's wrong, too, I should not even think twice about it, just rely on you. I know you would never ask me to do something harmful."

He came to the bed, and got down next to her, gently touching her backside and wincing as though he were the one feeling the pain. "Does it hurt?" he asked, repentance now in his voice. And when she nodded, she saw tears lift into his dark eyes. "I didn't want to do it, Lauren, you may not believe it, but it's true. Please don't force me to do it again." He leaned over and kissed her belly, then moving to her arms, her shoulder, her neck.

He loves her, he loves her not, he loves her. . . .

She cleared her throat. "I need to talk to you, Jonathan."

And she could feel his warm breath on her neck as he answered, "Of course."

"I'm beginning to think something terrible is wrong with me."

"You've had an emotional collapse is all, Lauren. You're going to get better, I'm going to see to it."

"I'm afraid though; I'm afraid to be without you. Last night after you punished me and left me here alone, I was angry, but it gave me time to think, too. At one point I looked out the window to the gate, and was surprised to discover I had no desire to leave the grounds—at least, not without you. I think when you're with me is the only time I really feel safe."

"There's nothing wrong with that, Lauren. I don't know why you think there is."

"Well, it's just that I've gone through a lot of changes. I never used to feel this way. Who knows, maybe I've finally grown up. Don't they say a sure sign of it is when you no longer feel immortal?"

"They do."

She sat there in his arms a few moments, then said, "However, if you ask me, would I like a change of scenery, Jonathan, then I'd have to admit, the answer is yes. I would love to go on an outing, something like that with you and the children. Oh, I hate so much to be a pest when you are always doing so much for me and the girls, but please take us all on an outing." And when he didn't answer right away, she said, "Oh, please, Jonathan, please say yes."

He smiled. "Of course you know I'm a sucker for my girls."

"Then you will take us?" she all but shouted. Then she reached up, circling her arms around his neck. "It seems that I must learn to listen better."

"Why is that, my darling?"

"Because then you buy me gifts and say yes to whatever I ask, and it makes me feel so good, so full of joy and happiness and love. Oh, Jonathan, thank you!"

So when she went later into the bathroom to change into the first skimpy sundress he brought in, she was ecstatic about the prospect of getting out.

"I think it's better for you at this point to go someplace quiet and restful," Jonathan said as he got the camera stand set up. "The last thing you and the baby need is a lot of noise, compounded by a bunch of strangers in your face." And her heart paused ... no, the last thing she needed or wanted was solitude, but she had to be satisfied with whatever he was willing to dole out. "So perhaps a family picnic would be best. What about tomorrow night?"

"Oh, that's wonderful, darling. What about Grove Point?" she suggested, through the open door.

"No, that's out. They have a big playground, swimming until eight, too many people. I have a better idea, what about the duck pond at the fairgrounds?"

Damn it, leave it to Jonathan to come up with that. The duck pond was about a half mile from the other festivities ... no swimming facilities added to it being a weeknight, it was likely to be deserted. But if somehow they could make it to the main fairgrounds, down to where there were people. Lauren looked in the bathroom mirror, stuck a bright pink satin bow in her hair—a bonus for Jonathan—then taking a deep breath, stepped out into the camera.

Chapter Twenty-one

Lauren posed for Jonathan that afternoon, shedding one outfit for another, leaning this way and that, turning a smile or pout to fit his fantasy. But though he had a lock on her body, he no longer had one on her head—throughout the photo session she had charge of her feelings and was determined not to relinquish them. She kept her focus on the following evening—family night out.

The duck pond, a picnic spot with its own parking area, was separated from the main fairgrounds by forest with a winding tarred path going through it and abutting the animal shelters. While there was unlikely to be any picnickers on a weeknight, the fairgrounds would be something else . . . if she and the children could only get there. They had to reach people because people meant safety.

Not nearly as exhausted without the drugs in her system, she napped only once during the day. That night, however, she slept fitfully, being awakened by several nightmares, then a fierce electrical storm. Though she was extra careful trying not to disturb Jonathan, it was next to impossible—he was so attuned to her movements, he would jump up when she woke, immediately concerned. "The storm?" he asked her, knowing how she hated thunder and lightning, then folding his arms around her.

And when he was like that, so attentive and caring, she found herself wavering, wondering if it wasn't all just some bizarre error, some grave misjudgment she was in the process of making. But then she'd think of the monstrous things he'd done, and know if given the chance, he'd devour her.

And she would begin to tremble, which made him hold her even closer, determined to make her fears go, when all the while he was the one she was afraid of.

The next morning Jonathan brought up her tea and wafers. "Once your stomach settles, get dressed, then call me. I'll take you downstairs for breakfast."

She smiled, pleased to be making such progress. "I'm looking forward to tonight." But his reaction to her enthusiasm was a bit hesitant. "Jonathan, you promised. I was counting on it." He gestured toward the window—though the rain had stopped, it was cloudy and wet. "Well, so what?" she said. "Besides, it's early. Please, Jonathan, tell me I can go downstairs and make fried chicken and potato salad and all those bad things we like so much."

He was now getting a kick out of her excitement. "Go ahead, knock yourself out . . . I'll put up with dreary weather, but if it rains, it's postponed. Agreed?"

"Agreed," she said, wondering if anything in their marriage had ever been agreed upon. Oh, he definitely used the word a lot, and she like a fool had believed it. Once he left the bedroom, she flushed the wafers down the toilet, taking a couple of Ritz crackers from the package in her drawer and eating them. She noticed several more of Beatrice's outfits hanging in her closet, and after showering, she took the initiative and chose a red and white checkered dress with a scoop neck and a bow in the back. But before she put it on, she sat in front of the mirror and brushed and braided her hair.

Finally ready, she stood at the bedroom mirror, primping and posing for the invisible ever-present camera ... knowing Jonathan was watching and enjoying the show, but going along with the game, pretending she was alone. Finally, she went to the intercom and buzzed Jonathan in his study. "Come and get me, darling ... please. I'm ready." He responded immediately.

Emily was surprised to see her—Chelsea, too, but not particularly interested when Lauren announced they were going on a picnic that night at the duck pond.

"It's not very nice out," Chelsea said.

"Who cares?" Emily said, catching right on to Lauren's enthusiasm. "Can I take Stew?" she asked, looking at Lauren.

Lauren looked to Jonathan. "Please, darling, what will it hurt? I want this to be fun for all of us."

So that night, despite the weather never really clearing completely, Jonathan kept his promise. The four of them along with the dog headed to the fairgrounds for their picnic. And though Lauren had already suspected there would be no one there, when she saw she was right, she began to feel hopeless. Was she crazy or stupid? How on earth did she ever expect to get her and the children through the woods to the main fairgrounds without Jonathan stopping them?

It had been four days, and though Fern had promised Jonathan she'd stay away from her sister for a week, it was getting increasingly difficult. If Lauren was feeling better as Jonathan kept insisting, why didn't she call her?

Had Fern been so judgmental of Lauren, had she been so overbearing that her little sister felt compelled to hide her feelings from her? She had always thought that they had a good, solid, and supportive relationship ... Had she only been deceiving herself?

Though Lauren had never been the kind to dwell on her problems, when her first marriage split and she found herself suddenly a single, working mother, she hadn't tried to hide her anxiety. And at times, when Lauren had found it too much to handle, she had come right to Fern for help.

So why now was she so determined to hide what was going on with her?

She sat there a few minutes, thinking about Lauren, then fished in her purse for her car keys. Finding them, she checked her watch—it was nearly seven. Jonathan, Lauren, and the children would surely be done with dinner. According to her brother-in-law, he was at home full-time these days as his priority was to be there for Lauren if she needed him ... So when she picked up the telephone on her desk to call Jonathan and Beatrice answered, reporting that Jonathan was out on business, it didn't ring true. "When do you expect him back?"

"Later this evening."

"I see. In that case, why don't you let me talk to Chelsea."

"I'm afraid that's impossible. She's gone with him."

"On business?"

"Well ... maybe it wasn't all business. Mr. Grant doesn't give me an itinerary."

A long pause, then, "Who's with Lauren?"

"Well, I am, of course."

"Beatrice, will you be kind enough to put her on the phone? I'd like to say hello. I'll only keep her a few moments."

"She's sleeping."

"So soon after dinner?"

"She's not feeling at all well."

"Oh? Then why isn't Jonathan with her?"

"Look, Miss Sandler, I've had enough of your

questions. Why don't you call back later this evening at which time you can question Mr. Grant personally."

"No," she said, beginning to feel uncomfortable, as though there were a shortage of fresh air in the office. "I'm coming over to see my sister," she said. "If she's sleeping, I'll look in on her, but I won't wake her. I simply want to see her."

"I'm afraid that's not possible. Mr. Grant left strict orders that she's not to have—"

"I'm coming, Beatrice."

"Don't bother. I won't let you through the gates," she said and hung up. Fern sat there, stunned, listening to an empty line but still hearing her words. The housekeeper wasn't going to let her into her own sister's house? Why did this scenario ring a bell? Then she remembered the time her sister had tried to go to the store and Beatrice had planted herself in front of her car to stop her.

The woman might have mile-long ties to Jonathan, but she had a nasty habit of exceeding her boundaries. Fern yanked out her desk drawers and began to go through them, dumping articles on her desk as she went along, until she finally came upon the key card Lauren had given her the day she moved into the house on Mountainview Road. She stood up now, taking her own car keys and purse.

Okay, Beatrice. Let's see if you can keep me out.

They ate the potato salad and chicken and rolls with butter, and fed the ducks and even played kick ball, and if anybody had been watching, they would surely have thought they were having a pleasurable family outing. Lauren's brain felt as though it had frozen up temporarily, waiting for someone else to jump out and start calling directions ... until it started to drizzle and Jonathan said, "Let's pack up." That was what finally woke Lauren to the realization that her chances were running out.

There was a large outhouse about fifty yards from the picnic area. "I've got to go to the bathroom," she said. "How about you girls?" Emily chimed in, saying she had to go, too, and put Stew on his leash to take him along.

"Can't you wait? We'll be home in fifteen minutes," Jonathan said, beginning to pack up the dishes and food.

"Sorry, darling, pregnant women don't know the word wait when it comes to this area," she said, then looked at Chelsea, indicating she should come along.

But she had her own ideas. "Uh-uh, I don't have to go ... I'll stay and help Daddy."

"Chelsea, please," she said, trying not to sound as desperate as she felt. The ball was rolling, albeit slowly, but she couldn't have it fall apart now. She looked at Jonathan for some backing, but that was useless—what did she expect him to do, insist?

"Lauren, if she doesn't have to go—"

"But she will have to—"

Fortunately she never had to finish the sentence

because Emily took over, handing the puppy's leash to Chelsea. "Come on, you walk him, then take care of him while I go pee."

Chelsea looked startled, apparently it was the first time Emily had let her anywhere near the dog. "What's wrong with you? Since when're you being so nice to me?"

"Don't get carried away, Goldilocks, I'm not being nice. It's just that I need someone to watch the dog."

Jonathan shook his head at the goings-on, seeming to find it all somewhat charming. "Why don't I get the things packed in the car and wait for my girls there. Now make it snappy."

"I think there's only one stall, Jonathan, so please have a little patience."

Fern had let herself in, driven down the long circular driveway, and parked in front of the door. Jonathan's car was not there, still not home apparently—Lauren's car and Beatrice's station wagon were. Instead of knocking, she used her card key and was through the entry and about to take the stairs when she felt something heavy smack her head. She couldn't talk or scream or even turn to see what had happened—she felt herself sink as though she'd stepped in quicksand.

The outhouse had a wash area and three toilet units, which Chelsea remarked on right away, not liking her daddy to be misled. Nonetheless she stood with Stew in the wash area at the door, looking outside. "He's just going to the car now," she said loud enough for Lauren to hear.

Chelsea looked at her, then at her mother who was coming forward—she could see something was going on, but she didn't know what. Not until her mother began to tell her. "Chelsea, you and Emily and I need to get to the fairgrounds. We're going to go through the woods to get there. Being very quiet—"

"If you want to go, why don't you just ask Daddy? He'll drive us."

"No. Daddy mustn't know about this," Lauren said. "Something is terribly wrong with him," she said, the explanation sounding like idiocy even to her ears. The child had just had a wonderful picnic with a man she adored and who adored her, and here was Lauren trying to tell her that he was crazy. "I can't explain it further, Chelsea, not now."

"Not ever," she said. "I want to stay with Daddy. That's what he'd want me to do."

"Please, just trust me." She went to take her daughter's hand, but Chelsea yanked it back as though she'd been burned.

Instantly Emily jumped in between them. With one hand she grabbed Chelsea by her shirtfront, and the other she clasped over her mouth, then backed her up hard against the wall. Chelsea looked to her mother for help, but Lauren wasn't giving any, so she looked up at Emily. "You'd better listen to what she's saying," Emily said.

"Because if you don't, he'll kill her. Like he did my mother!"

And though Emily had always known the truth, her saying the words was what finally tore apart the curtain in her head. For the first time since that terrible day, it all came flooding back.

The stranger was pushing her mother . . . She fell backward, her arms and legs spread, her mouth open, her eyes terrified. Oh, please, oh, shit, no, she had never in her life seen anyone so scared! And it was then that the stranger became aware of someone in back of him.

And Daddy turned to see her.

She couldn't talk, she couldn't scream. She just stared at him.

"Why aren't you in school?" he asked her, but she didn't answer.

He took the bat from her with one hand and with the other reached out and took her hand, pulling her along with him down the stairs to where her mother was sprawled on the cement. Emily looked away, scared to see, but he took her face in his hands, forcing her to look, saying it was the right thing to do: Mommy's head was twisted at a weird angle, making it look like the body on her didn't belong. "Take off her jewelry," he said.

And she shook her head, trying to back away from him. But he pushed her down onto her knees. "It's all things I gave to her, Emily, beautiful things that I want you to have. She didn't deserve them, any of them. She was a tramp, Emily, a filthy lying slut who went out and got herself knocked up with another man's baby. You know all about that, don't you?"

She tried to swallow then, but it was like she had forgotten how. Someone had told Daddy all about it ... maybe Willie Campbell. No, probably Beatrice. Mommy always said that she hid out and snooped and squealed things to Daddy.

So she took off her mother's rings and necklace, then Daddy handed her the bat ...

As Emily shook off the dreadful memory, she realized she had let go of Chelsea. Tears were streaming down her face and Chelsea just stood there and gaped at her. Lauren looked like she was about ready to cry herself, but she didn't. Instead, she came up to her, put her hands on her shoulders, and said, "We don't have time for this. not now, Emily. Do you understand?"

She did.

"I need you to be strong ... to help me be strong."

Then Lauren turned to Chelsea, who was still standing there, looking a little freaked herself, and said, "I don't give a damn what Daddy wants, this time we're doing it my way."

The banging and bumping hurt her head, making her teeth shake as though they were coming loose, but it was finally what brought Fern back to consciousness. She became aware of being dragged down a flight of stairs, a rope secured at her ankles, around her wrists, then a door slamming behind her. She opened her eyes—the surroundings were blurry at first, but even as they cleared, it was unfamiliar. Finally she realized she was in the furnace room.

Oh, dear God, this woman must be crazy. What is going on in this house?

They began to run just as they heard Jonathan's car horn a second time—Chelsea holding Lauren's hand and Emily holding the puppy's leash. They hadn't gone far into the woods when they heard the horn beep again. Then it was about two or three minutes later that Lauren and the girls heard his voice calling out to them.

"Lauren, come back here, right now!" Then the stern voice disappeared and the hurt and confused voice took over. "Darling, I love you, please don't do this." She could feel her heart twist ... She paused, but only for an instant, then—biting into her bottom lip so hard that she drew blood—moved the girls along. And as they rushed on, the skies broke loose in torrential rains—thunder, lightning, the works.

Chelsea began to cry, hanging on to Lauren's skirt and barely able to see what was in front of them. They slipped on wet leaves, trying to avoid the sharp branches slapping against their faces, cutting their skin. Lauren could only pray they were traveling parallel to the path. And still over the downpour, they could hear threads of Jonathan's voice in the distance, calling to them.

Finally they reached the fairgrounds, which not surprisingly were deserted. The rain had let up, falling back to a drizzle, and they stopped for a few moments to listen. Jonathan was no longer calling, nor did Lauren hear any sounds of his approach. With another spurt, they rushed past the various animal shelters, heading toward the amusements, where Lauren had a memory of there being a pay phone.

Now with cold, stiff fingers she took out change from her purse, deposited it, and called Fern. First at the real estate office, then at home, but there was no answer. Finally she called Carla. She dialed her number and when her friend finally picked up, she began to bawl. "Oh, Carla, thank God."

"Lauren, is that you?"

She took a few shaky breaths, pushing herself to talk. Jonathan could be coming out of the woods at any moment, and though the park was gigantic, she didn't want to take any chances. "Yes, it's me. I'm with the girls ... at the fairgrounds. I've run away from Jonathan, it's a long story. Can you come get us?"

"Give me ten minutes. In the parking lot."

Fern had pushed herself to her knees, then little by little maneuvered herself to the furnace. Her hands pressed a sharp edge, and she began to run the rope back and forth. It had taken about twenty minutes, but it finally broke free.

She unknotted her feet and stood up, feeling a little off kilter but pumped up with adrenaline.

Now what? she thought, her mind starting to race. Now to find her sister.

But first she had to call the police.

Soaked and cold and exhausted, they sat huddled together on a ledge about seventy-five yards from the parking lot, leery about getting too close, but watching and waiting impatiently for Carla. Lauren hadn't stopped checking her watch—and only eight minutes had passed when Carla's trusty old green station wagon pulled into the lot and stopped. Lauren sighed in relief, then stood up, an arm around each of the girls, gathering them to her. "Let's go," she said, her voice teary. "It's over."

They headed to the car, Stew on the leash following, and Lauren's thoughts going to Jonathan—his cries of anguish back in the woods. She would have to send someone for him. Once they got to Carla's, she would call the police ... and then of course she would have to tell them everything she knew. But she would get him help.

A good defense, a good psychiatrist.

But only a dozen or two steps along, and her thoughts were cut—her heart seized. Suddenly there was Jonathan's black Lexus racing in from the entrance, toward Carla's station wagon. They all tried to call to her, scream to her, wave their arms, but she didn't know what they were trying to say—not until the roar of his engine got her attention.

But by then it was too late—she had jumped

out of her car, and when she turned, she was standing there unprotected, with not even a hope of escape. Jonathan didn't stop, he plowed into her, her body lifting high into the air, then falling.

Emily and Chelsea started to cry and moan and bob their heads—Lauren was paralyzed as she watched the Lexus finally come to a stop and the doors open as though he were telling them to get in and come home.

As soon as Fern reached the kitchen, she headed for the phone, and just as she lifted the receiver the housekeeper reappeared. Though it seemed as though it had been a hundred years since she'd last engaged in a physical contest, she didn't have a choice—Beatrice was coming toward her. She was smaller than Fern, but leaner, harder, in better shape—she rammed right into her, wrestling her to the floor.

But Lauren was at stake . . . in a maniacal fury, Fern raised her arms, groping for something, anything . . . Discovering the bun in back of Beatrice's head, she pulled at it, releasing brown-gray hair so long it came down and touched Fern's face. With both hands Fern grabbed bunches of hair near the scalp, ripping them out, tossing them to the floor. And while the woman was temporarily stunned by pain and surprise, Fern managed to push her off. She climbed on top of her, gripped her by her ears, and, with a force she didn't know she had, drove the woman's head into the floor.

She did it again ... and again—until she broke
her fury. By then Beatrice wasn't moving.

Panting, she got off and raced upstairs to the
master bedroom—Lauren wasn't there. She
shouted out names, but no one was there. The
telephone on the nightstand was missing, the one
in the hallway was missing, too ... She ran downstairs to the kitchen, so out of breath she thought
she might pass out. But before she could do that,
she had to call the police.

Lauren kept her eyes pinned to the black
Lexus, now with the headlights on, while she
pushed the girls back toward the fairgrounds. She
saw Jonathan get out of the car—slowly, taking
his time, like he had all the time in the world.
She urged the girls quickly around the side of a
building, out of his line of sight.

The first place Lauren thought to go to hide
was one of the enclosed animal shelters, but it
was a bad choice—the moment Lauren opened
one of the doors, Stew began to bark, and the
animals inside began to howl and squeal. They
backed off, racing instead to the game pavilion.
When they got there, they lifted one of the green
tarpaulins covering a concession and ducked inside from the back.

They got onto the floor, holding tight to each
other ... There were hundreds of display and
game and food booths at the fair, Lauren was
thinking, and it was already getting dark. Could

they evade him until morning, until people arrived?

But suddenly the tarpaulin was yanked free and with a swish tossed to the ground. A dead, bloodied lamb fell onto the counter with a thud. The girls and she screamed in unison—and there was Jonathan standing outside the booth, smiling down at them. "He comes bearing gifts."

The dog began to whimper. Lauren swallowed hard—she couldn't run, she couldn't talk, she could only listen to his voice as he went on. "Look around, Lauren, isn't this the place you picked me up?"

Picked him up? She remembered the shooting gallery where they met, was that what he meant? The booths looked alike to her. It was impossible to tell, but he seemed to think this was the exact one. "I knew you were a slut back then, but I thought I could do something with you. But you're hopeless, aren't you?"

Lauren somehow managed to get up, though as she was doing so, an unfamiliar pain dug into her abdomen, making her wince. Was it the baby? She took hold of the kids by their wet shirts and pulled them up with her, and they all started to back out of the booth. Jonathan stood there, arms folded at his chest, watching them as though they were toys whose batteries would soon run dry.

"Run," she whispered to the kids once they were outside, but just as they were about to, Emily stopped—the dog's leash had fallen from her hands. "Stew!" she shouted as the puppy started back into the booth.

Jonathan leapt over the counter, grabbed up the leash, and held the puppy out toward them. "Here, Princess," he said to Emily. "Come get your dog."

Lauren held Emily back, but while her effort was concentrated there, Chelsea wiggled away and rushed to her daddy to get the dog. Lauren reached out to pull her back, but Jonathan already had her tightly by the hand.

"Please, let her go," Lauren said, as another pain, this one so strong it stopped her cold, rammed through her. She turned to Emily. "Run, get out of here!" she said, but Emily stayed.

"Okay, the game's all over, girls," Jonathan said, holding out his other arm for Lauren and Emily. "Come home to Daddy to get your punishments."

Though it seemed like hours, it could have been only minutes later that Lauren found herself sitting on the ground, tied to a tree, the girls inside a game booth, watching out the back entrance as Jonathan directed. "The baby, something is wrong with the baby," she said to Jonathan, hoping concern for the baby would bring back his sanity.

But it didn't—it just gave him a place to begin. "The baby?" he said, looking at the girls and shaking his head. "Suddenly she is worried about the baby."

Another pain drove through her ... yes, she was losing the baby.

He went over to the booth now and stretched his arms for Chelsea. She shrank back to stand beside Emily, but now he insisted sternly, and she let him lift her out, then set her on the ground. They both walked toward Lauren. "Your mother has done terrible things, Chelsea, acted in a way not befitting a mother or wife or even a woman. Do you understand what I'm saying?"

Lauren would die, the baby would die, but what about the girls? Oh, please, God, she could not bear to think of the girls left alone with him.

Chelsea started to sob then, and he shook her gently. "Come on, Angel, you must always answer Daddy when he asks a question. Now do you understand?"

She gulped and nodded. "I think."

"Good girl," he said. "Yes, she's gone ahead and endangered the baby, to say nothing of my two girls. And why? Because she can't bear to act like a good woman. She's a whore!"

She could feel the blood trickling down her legs ...

Frightened by Jonathan's pronouncement, Chelsea jumped, then held her arms tight around herself, trembling. Jonathan turned to Emily. "You know what I'm talking about, right, Princess?" Emily said nothing and he turned to Chelsea, sitting on the ground at his feet. He took out a knife that had been slid into his pants and crouched down next to the child. "We're going to have to punish Mommy. And we're going to do it together."

Behind them, though the pain, Lauren could see Emily climb up and take something down from the game concession shelf.

Chelsea shook her head. "No, I don't want to," she sobbed. "Oh, please, Daddy, don't make me."

Lauren could see Emily coming from the back of the booth, sneaking slowly toward Jonathan whose back was to her, and holding something big and long. Oh, dear God. . . .

As Emily advanced on her father, another scene kept intruding on her mind, confusing her, driving her on.

"Don't be frightened, Princess, your mother is already dead. This is just a way of saying you love me and stand by me in doing what I had to do. You know she was wrong, don't you?"

"Yes, but I don't want to hit her with the bat, please don't make me do it."

"Do you love Daddy?"

She nodded. "Yes, but—"

"And I love you, Princess. Who else will be here for you when you need protecting?"

"Don't be scared, Angel," Jonathan was telling Chelsea now. "I'll put the knife in first, then it'll be your turn to do it. Like partners."

"It'll hurt, Daddy. No!"

Jonathan ran his fingers through Chelsea's curls, and Emily moved forward.

"Yes, but only for a bit. Then poof, it's all over.

If Daddy says Mommy's got to be punished, then that's how it is. You've got to trust Daddy to do the right thing. But you see, Angel, it's not so bad after all. I'll be here, watching out for you, just like I always do."

The knife was only inches from Lauren when Emily pulled her arms back and took the swing, the wood meeting her father's head, cracking it—he slumped over, then fell to the ground. Emily sank down to her knees right where she was, dropping the bat, and Chelsea, bawling now, rushed over to her, burying her face in her shirt. There was no longer a baby. Lauren had aborted. Just before she slipped unconscious, she could hear cars in the distance, see flashing lights. . . . Help was on its way.

Epilogue

"Everything is going to be all right. Listen to Daddy and swallow the pills, Princess ..."

Princess, Master, run a little faster. Tick tock, tick tock, the mouse ran up the clock ... a clock's as big as a fist, and a fist in time's worth nine. He stood over her with the pills in his open fist.

"Or else they'll figure out you were the one who killed Mommy. Is that what you want?"

Did she kill Mommy? she remembered the bat in her hand and hitting her ... No, she didn't want that, she didn't want them to find out she had hit her with the bat.

"Daddy's only trying to protect you from going to jail ... So don't fight me on this."

So she opened her mouth and he handed her the water glass. But the minute the pills dropped onto her tongue, she started to spit them out. This time he wouldn't let her. He held her jaw and dumped the rest of the pills onto her tongue, then clamped her mouth and nose shut, closing off her air. Her arms shot out in panic, trying to fight him ... and finally all she could do was swallow.

She went into a coughing spasm and slipped, hitting her head. The room began to spin and her head got heavy, dragging her under. "No, please, I don't want to die, I don't want to die, please, Daddy don't make me die!"

"I don't want to die!"

She was crying, beating her fists, fighting to keep her mind from drowning, and then her eyes flew open and Lauren was there, holding her.

There were a lot of those dreams. As soon as Nancy's murder became clear to Emily, all kinds of other memories came pouring forth, mostly hearing or seeing her mother being abused. But it was this memory of her father forcing her to swallow those pills and her terror of dying that was most disturbing.

It was many months later, at spring break when Lauren, Chelsea and Stew saw Emily off at the train station.

"I don't want to go," she said.

"It's only for a week, darling."

"But why do I have to?"

"Because it's your family."

Emily knelt and patted the dog. "I want to stay here," she said.

The trip had been planned for weeks in advance, with the encouragement of Emily's new psychiatrist. "Emily, your mother loved you a lot, these are her people, which means they're your people, too. They only want the chance to know

Nancy's daughter and love her. Besides, a chicken farm in New Hampshire sounds like fun to me."

"You're my mother, Lauren."

She could feel herself get teary—she leaned over and kissed her. "I know. I'm the other one, the lousy cook."

Once they saw Emily off, Chelsea—upset that she couldn't go to the farm with her big sister—finagled a stop for a pizza and two video rentals to take home. Home was a simple but comfortable six-room house in Nyack, less than forty-five minutes from Fern, whom they saw regularly, and ten minutes from Lauren's job producing news for WKAB, a small local television station.

Jonathan didn't die, but Lauren had filed for divorce, asking for custody of Emily, and he didn't object. Jay Philips was released from jail, the police no longer believing him responsible for Gordon Cummings's murder. Though they suspected Jonathan, and certainly believed he later tried to frame his employee Philips with the threads from his cap, there was only circumstantial evidence linking him to the murder.

Claiming Emily's testimony about her mother's death was too unreliable, and having no case for Gordon's or Jerry Reardon's murder, Jonathan's attorneys convinced the prosecutor to let Jonathan cop a plea in Carla's case—manslaughter, which came with a twenty-year sentence. He got another twenty years for his attempt on Lauren's life, but the sentences would run concurrently.

Only twenty years in all for what he had done. Not nearly enough : . . . yet when it came to Carla, wasn't Lauren to blame, too? If only she had been thinking more clearly, she would have called the police to come for them, not a friend.

When Lauren made the trip to the prison to see Jonathan about Emily, she bumped into Beatrice just leaving—though they hadn't exchanged a word, Lauren knew through Fern that the woman was back living with her niece, Dr. Greenly. Lauren didn't bother mentioning Beatrice to Jonathan, but she did ask him point blank about Jerry Reardon. Jonathan had killed Nancy because of her affair, finding out that the baby she was about to have might not be his; he had killed Gordon because he was fooling around with Emily's memories, perhaps trying to get at the truth, and he had killed Carla because she was about to drive off with his family.

"But why kill Jerry?" Lauren asked. "He lied for you, he gave you an alibi."

He smiled, that same smile that had charmed her that first day they met. "Aren't you a bit confused, Lauren? I was never accused of killing him."

"But we know just the same, don't we?"

It wasn't until she started to leave that he said, "Remember the weekend we spent with Jerry?" She nodded. Yes, she remembered it perfectly. "He liked you."

They did get along well. "So?"

"I mean he sincerely liked you, Lauren. So

much so that he was determined that you not become Mrs. Jonathan Grant, wife number two, as he put it. Not that his determination would ever have been a match against mine."

She drew in her breath. "He threatened to retract his statement . . . your alibi, that's why you killed him, isn't it?"

"There you go again, thinking the worst. Don't you know me better than that? Do you really think I'd intentionally hurt anyone, let alone kill? What happened to Carla was an unfortunate accident—you had me so crazed running off in that storm with the children, I couldn't think or see straight. The court believed it, Lauren, why can't you?" He put his face close to the bars now, and though he couldn't touch her, she could smell him, she could imagine his touch and she shrank back. "Don't you get it yet, my darling?" he whispered. "It's time to put the gloves down and celebrate it. I love you . . . you and the girls belong to me, and nothing you do will ever change that."

She ran out of the prison in a panic, and not until she had driven fifteen or twenty miles did she begin to breathe easier. She thought about Jerry now, the effort he'd made for her that had cost him his life. And she thought of the others who had expressed doubt or dropped hints about Jonathan, trying to let her know something was wrong—Carla, her sister, even she had seen what should have been danger signals. But she refused to pay attention. She relinquished her mind, her whole self to Jonathan, just for the asking.

Still she has trouble believing she did it, but apparently it is something women do with far more frequency than she did imagined—a phenomenon Lauren was learning more about in a women's support group she had joined. And though she couldn't imagine falling victim to such a thing again, she did have two precious daughters to raise and she wanted to arm them with qualities such as confidence and independence and self-respect to go along with a healthy wariness of any man who would ask that they surrender them.

INTRIGUING THRILLERS!